A FLAG OF TRUCE

A John Pearce Adventure

A FLAG OF TRUCE

DAVID DONACHIE

McBooks
Press

Essex, Connecticut

McBooks Press

An imprint of Globe Pequot, the trade division of
The Rowman & Littlefield Publishing Group, Inc.
4501 Forbes Blvd., Ste. 200
Lanham, MD 20706
www.rowman.com

Distributed by NATIONAL BOOK NETWORK

British Library Cataloguing in Publication Information available

Library of Congress Cataloging-in-Publication Data

ISBN 978-1-4930-6628-5 (paperback)
ISBN 978-1-4930-6165-5 (e-book)

∞™ The paper used in this publication meets the minimum requirements
of American National Standard for Information Sciences—Permanence of
Paper for Printed Library Materials, ANSI/NISO Z39.48-1992.

DAVID DONACHIE was born in Edinburgh in 1944. He has always had an abiding interest in British naval history of the eighteenth and nineteenth centuries, as well as the clandestine services during WWII. He has 51 published novels to his credit. David lives in Deal, the historic English seaport on the border of the English Channel and the North Sea.

To Jack & Beryl Denny

Such staunch friends – one an oasis of calm;
the other, active, erudite, kindness itself,
with a gift for creating
well-intentioned mayhem.

Chapter One

John Pearce, standing on the quarterdeck of HMS *Weazel*, could see the faint outline of Mont Faron, rising over two thousand feet behind the port of Toulon, but it was, despite the best efforts of Neame, the ship's master, coming no closer. A *tramontane*, howling down from the Alps into the Gulf of Lions, meant it was impossible to make any headway going north-north-east, and that was before it had acted upon the sea to turn this part of the Mediterranean into a maelstrom of wind-whipped water. The oilskins he was wearing were supposed to keep him dry, but every time a wave broke over the bows, sending back a cascade of furious white spume, it seemed at least a gallon found its way into those gaps between skin and garment, so that his clothes beneath were as wet as if he had been clad in them alone, and some of the salt had soaked the bandage on his arm, where a musket ball had grazed it, making the wound sting like the devil.

His presence on the deck was purely for show; John Pearce might be a lieutenant in King George's Navy, and in temporary command of the ship, but he knew he was not fit to be in charge of a vessel in this kind of weather. He lacked the necessary experience, having come by his rank through a royal command rather than the years of experience normally required to pass for his position. But given such a hearty blow, and the fact that there was some slight risk to the ship, he felt it necessary to adopt the position a proper captain would occupy; on deck, getting soaked, looking keenly ahead through salt-encrusted eyes, giving an impression of magisterial calm and an utter confidence that was totally at odds with his true feelings.

Occasionally, as also befitted his station, he would glance over to see how his consort, under the command of the young midshipman, Mr Harbin, was faring. The *Mariette*, captured after a hot action in a Corsican bay, was ploughing into the seas with as little effect as his own vessel, and the sight of her rearing and bucking, the tip of her bowsprit hitting wave after wave, the surge of the water from each coursing along her decks, was a mirror image of what was happening beneath his own widely spread feet. From her side a steady jet of water was blown asunder as the men below worked the pumps to discharge that which no amount of tarpaulins stretched tight across hatches could keep out. Likewise, the close-reefed topsails mirrored that above his head, with just a scrap of sail showing on both main and jib to allow the ship to hold itself into the gale.

'It be a bugger this wind,' yelled Neame, his mouth pressed close to the gap between the foul weather hat and John Pearce's ear. 'Can last for days, can a *tramontane,* and at its worst many a ship has foundered.'

The temptation to respond with an ironic, 'Thank you for that,' died on Pearce's lips. Neame he had to trust, he being the best man aboard to keep him and his crew from perdition, the man who could get them safely to the snug anchorage below that ring of mountains he saw ahead, one that Neame had informed him was impervious to the wind they were facing, and only at risk from a really heavy *levanter.*

Levanter, Mistral, Sirocco, Tramontane. These had, only months before, been words of mystery to John Pearce, north, south, east and west winds that – and he struggled from time to time to remember which was which – had come to dominate his thinking, when he was not concerned with the possibility of taking the vessel, a command he had inherited along with their recent capture, into battle. Above his head there was a man lashed to the mainmast cap, swaying through an arc of some thirty feet, eyes peeled on the disturbed horizon for any sign of an enemy vessel.

Safety lay ahead with the British fleet laying in the roadstead off Toulon. Lord Hood, the C-in-C, had taken over the town and harbour, as well as the French fleet, with the active connivance of the majority of the citizenry and leading elements of the French Navy – but that did not mean here, in the offing, some unknown enemy might not lurk, a frigate perhaps keeping watch, for there were known to be several enemy warships that had been at sea when Toulon surrendered. Seeing two vessels of a much lighter draught, one of them with the British ensign flying above a tricolour, evidence of a taken prize, they could perhaps risk an opportunity to make an easy capture.

'All hands to wear ship,' shouted Neame, his trumpet aimed at the sodden companionway that led below. It was an unenthusiastic crew that tumbled up onto the deck, but they went to their stations without orders, as Neame yelled once more in his commanding officer's ear. 'I feel an easing, sir.'

Pearce was startled and surprised, but he nodded in what he considered the required fashion; if Neame had detected something he had signally failed to interpret, he was not about to argue with him. Yet was he right, was the screaming note, as the wind whistled through the rigging, just a little less oppressive? His mind had wandered, his concentration slipped, and Pearce silently cursed himself for it; he had been thinking of what lay ahead – of the revenge he would take on Ralph Barclay, a man he considered a bitter enemy – rather than what was happening here and now. A lack of concentration was something which no end of people had told him could be fatal, the sea being an unforgiving element for a mind not focused.

'Lord Hood wishes HMS *Brilliant* to be kept in the inner harbour, Captain Barclay, that is all I can tell you.'

Vice Admiral Sir William Hotham helped himself to a slice of melon from the plate before him, a handkerchief at the ready to catch the juice which escaped from the corner of his mouth, the whole act of eating such a ripe piece of fruit made more risky by the way HMS *Britannia*, despite her twin anchors and the protection of the mountains which cut off the worst of the wind, was pitching and rolling on a heavy sea. Ralph Barclay, in hearing what had just been said, was incensed but it would never do to show any dissent to a man on whom he depended for so much.

'I am obliged to ask, sir, what purpose can a frigate serve in such a situation?'

'We cannot...' Hotham paused and wiped his

lips. 'We cannot get one of our own capital ships into the inner harbour, it would smack to our recently acquired allies of distrust.'

'Well-placed distrust, sir, if I may say.'

Hotham nodded and forked another piece of melon, which he held away from him as he answered. 'I agree. The French are our allies only in so long as it suits their purpose. A swing in the wind of their damned revolution and we will be fighting them again.'

'It would have been best, sir, to have seized every one of their ships, never mind that they raised the royal standard.'

It had been a shrewd ploy by Baron d'Imbert, the most active senior officer of the French fleet, once negotiations to take over the port had been concluded, to raise the royal standard, the Bourbon *fleur de lys*, thus claiming to be fighting the Revolution, supporting the true, if displaced, government of France.

Hotham frowned and waved his fruit on the end of his fork. 'I fear Lord Hood's promise to hold them in trust for a Bourbon Restoration places us in restraint. We cannot seize vessels that we acknowledge are the property of others.'

'Perhaps,' Ralph Barclay essayed, in a voice lacking certainty, 'Lord Hood allowed sentiment to cloud his judgement.'

Ralph Barclay considered the care he was

exercising well placed. Hotham and Hood did not get on, in fact they saw eye to eye on practically nothing, but that did not mean that a mere frigate captain could damn one admiral in the presence of another, men of such rank being a fickle and touchy bunch.

Hotham shook his head slowly, in that way which denoted a lack of firm opinion. 'It can only be that, for it is certainly not in the interests of the Navy or our country. Yet it may be that he has seen his error, not admitted it you understand, but seen it, and he had decided to take some necessary precautions.' The melon disappeared, which necessitated a pause while it was consumed. 'We have, in HMS *Brilliant*, the only armed vessel in a position to dominate the Ministry of Marine, the French Arsenal, and the better sections of the town. The wealthy citizens of the *Quartier* St Roch will not wish to see their properties demolished by cannon fire, which may do more to cement their loyalties to us than the armies besieging the port. Likewise, any sign of plotting in the French naval headquarters and we can reduce it to rubble.'

Ralph Barclay paid great attention to what had just been said, dissecting it for any sign of censure; his frigate was in that inner harbour because it had been captured prior to arrival of the main fleet, though Hotham had defended him stoutly for that in the face of a senior officer who felt that the captain of HMS *Brilliant* had acted in a rash manner. Then of course there was the other matter.

'Does this have anything to do, sir, with those base allegations made against me by that upstart Pearce?'

Another piece of melon made it to Hotham's mouth, and it was with a rather moist tone that Hotham replied. 'I see you do not grace him with his rank.'

'Given that both he and his rank are an abomination, I cannot bring myself to do so, even if it was awarded at the King's pleasure. And the fact Lord Hood saw fit to trust him with an important mission when it came to taking over the port beggars belief.'

The wipe with the handkerchief that followed was swift and irate; Hotham had somehow been reminded of his own position as second-in-command to a man who made it plain he had scant regards for his abilities, who had not bothered to keep him fully informed of his negotiations with the French Navy and the citizenry of Toulon, or that he had sent a French speaking emissary ashore. Indeed, at the height of those talks, a lowly creature like John Pearce, Hood's representative, had been more au fait with things than he had himself.

'Lord Hood may have other reasons for the orders I have just relayed regarding your ship, but as you know, Captain Barclay, he does not always grace me with the inner workings of his mind.'

'I am forced to enquire, sir, has he pronounced on this ridiculous notion of my facing a court martial?'

The silence that followed played hard on Ralph Barclay's nerves. Could Hotham be toying with him; the man was famous for taking his time in making any statement, even slower in decision, which made risible his nickname of 'Hotspur'. Also, there was the worry about the balance of their relationship. Hotham had been in receipt of certain favours from the man before him, and, in return, had given an assurance – though nothing was ever openly stated – that in future he would see Captain Ralph Barclay, given his previous patron was dead, as a supporter of his flag and position.

Such a thing was very necessary to both men; no admiral could count himself a success without a number of officers committed to his flag. In turn, the admiral would see to it that those men were rewarded with opportunities or commands. As a C-in-C, that was relatively easy, as a subordinate admiral it was much harder. Lord Hood held all the cards in this command when it came to advancement; officers like Elphinstone, Nelson and Linzee, clients of Hood, had already been favoured. Hotham would get enough scraps to hand to his client officers to keep him from open complaint, but nothing substantial would come his way as long as Hood held the whip hand.

'My enquiry on that score, at our last meeting,

was tentative, Barclay, but I fear that Hood is inclined to accede to Pearce's demand.'

The lie that followed, and the calm way in which it was expressed, took some effort, but it came out well enough. 'Then I shall just have to face it, sir, with a clear conscience. What can I possibly have to be concerned about? But I fear the strain on poor Mrs Barclay…'

Hotham spoke quickly for once, interrupting. 'Damn me, Barclay, I did not ask after your wife. Remiss of me. How is the good lady?'

'Toiling away at the hospital, sir, saint that she is.'

'Saint indeed,' replied Hotham, though the wistful look in his eye had nothing to do with sainthood. Emily Barclay was a beauty twenty years her husband's junior; there was not an officer in the fleet, of any rank or age, who did not harbour thoughts regarding her, not that anyone would do or say anything that could be construed as dalliance. Codes of behaviour were strict in that regard.

'Do pass on my compliments,' said Hotham, 'and assure her that I will speak again with Lord Hood on the matter.'

Neame was right, the wind had eased although it was still dead foul in its reduced state, but at least both sloops could tack and wear, making slow but discernable progress towards the southern coast of

France. A couple of miles offshore there came, carried on that wind, the first dull thuds of gunfire, land-based cannon fire echoing off the hills, which denoted an artillery duel going on inland.

'The rabble has obviously arrived, sir,' called Neame, oilskin hat now off, showing soaking wet grey hair above a ruddy, weather-beaten but healthy complexion.

Pearce had likewise removed his hat, and opened the top of his coat to remove his dripping comforter. 'Don't underestimate that rabble, Mr Neame. At Jemmapes and Valmy the same sort or revolutionary mass sent packing the cream of Europe's armies.'

Hard to recall how he had been in Paris when he heard news of those two famous victories for the citizen armies of France, and he could not now remember if he had been pleased or upset, still a partisan of the French Revolution, or already, like his father, prey to doubts. What he did recollect was the way the failing spirit of the Revolution had been lifted by the news, giving the people of France a feeling that they were on a worthy crusade to free the continent from tyranny, and vaguely he felt certain he had shared in that. Euphoria had not lasted; the September Massacres and the beheading of King Louis had soured any feelings of support. Now, following on from the manner of his father's death, he saw the Revolution as a deadly disease that must be contained and eventually defeated, though not with a restoration of monarchy.

'Beats me how they did it, sir,' Neame said, bringing him sharply back to the present. 'Happen they'd had a stiffening of good old British redcoats; it would have been John Crapaud on the run, not the Duke of Brunswick.'

'The world turned upside down, Mr Neame.'

The older man looked less than pleased at that remark, which was a reminder of the tune played by those British redcoats who had surrendered to the Americans at Yorktown. But Pearce had not meant it that way; for him, these last four years since the Revolution of '89 had been a world turned upside down, so much overturned and turned again and again that he was here on this deck in the middle of the Mediterranean, pretending to be a naval officer.

'I think I shall take the con, Mr Neame.'

The doubt was fleeting, as the master responded, and he had a good look at the diminishing sea state before he did so. 'As you wish, sir.'

The speaking trumpet was handed over, and he yelled though it, 'All hands on deck.' Pearce was pleased with the speed his voice engendered. Once more the crew came tumbling up from below and ran to their stations, as Pearce, knowing that Neame was watching him like a hawk, picked his moment, when HMS *Weazel* began to sink into a trough, easing the pressure of the wind on the hull and upperworks.

'Let fly the sheets.' The men on the falls, who had taken the strain, began to ease those as the marlin spikes were pulled from their holes. On the larboard side the other party of seamen were hauling hard on a yard that was under pressure from the wind, but haul they did, until the leading edge to starboard passed the eye. So had the bows and, as the ship rose on the swell, the wind hitting them aided the movement, the appropriate command was issued.

'Quartermaster, bring us round on to the larboard tack.'

Beside him the wheel was swung, not without effort, the rudder biting into the sea and, now aided by the still potent *tramontane*, completing the travel of the bowsprit from well left of Mont Faron, across the head of the Grand Rade of Toulon, until it was shaping for the eastern limit of the mountains that backed the port.

'Sheet home,' came the command, and the falls of both sides were lashed off with the yards braced right round, holding in place the sails that would inch the ship forward.

'Neatly done, sir,' said Neame.

Looking over he saw that Midshipman Harbin had performed the same manoeuvre and was still on a parallel course. The youngster would be watching his consort's deck with a keen eye;

whatever *Weazel* did, he would do likewise, until ordered otherwise.

'I think it has eased enough for the cook to get his coppers lit, Mr Neame.'

'It has, sir.'

'Do we need to signal Mr Harbin?'

'He will issue like orders as soon as he sees the smoke from our galley chimney.'

'I don't know about you, Mr Neame, but I would much appreciate some warm food and dry clothing and since we are near to port we might indulge ourselves, if you and our purser will join me for dinner, by finishing off the last of that Hermitage I fetched aboard. A pity such a heavy sea does not permit us to ask Mr Harbin yonder to join us.'

'Poor lad,' said Neame, without conviction.

'HMS *Weazel* has made her number, sir,' said the midshipman sent from the quarterdeck of HMS *Victory* with the message, 'and she has in her possession a prize.'

'Has she, by God!' exclaimed Admiral Lord Hood, his heavy grey eyebrows shooting up and his prominent nose following. 'If he has, then I think that Captain Benton has disobeyed his quite specific orders.'

'That is the other thing, sir. The Officer of the Watch made it my duty to tell you that her own ensign is upside down.'

'Benton dead, then?'

'He fears so, sir, though he had no knowledge of who is in command.'

'Signal to HMS *Weazel*. Captain to repair aboard immediately.'

'Sir.'

The lookout on HMS *Victory* was not the only one to see that prize, and the sight of their own navy's flag flying above that of the enemy, and a signal that a Master and Commander was dead, probably killed in action, set any number of hearts racing. It had every lieutenant in the fleet who was not ashore and unaware looking to their seniority and their relationship to Lord Hood. There was nothing callous about this; it was the way of things. War brought death as well as the chance of glory, and advancement in King George's Navy, unless an officer had impeccable connections, generally came through one or the other. Of course they would mourn for a dead comrade, that was only fitting, but his demise meant promotion for someone to fill his place, and that would ripple down through the fleet, affecting dozens of officers who would move up a place.

It caused as much excitement below decks on the seventy-four gun warship, HMS *Leander*, as the news filtered down, yet there was anxiety too. The fact that the captain was dead did not mean that others had been spared the same fate. Common seamen went on deck as little as possible, especially in a strong clothes-tugging wind that chilled even on a September day, so it was rare to see such figures as Michael O'Hagan, Charlie Taverner, Rufus Dommet and old leathery-faced Latimer leaning over the rail peering at the incoming vessels. If John Pearce had known his friends were so arrayed he would have abandoned his dinner, as well as his Hermitage wine, and gone on deck to wave, but he did not do so until the message came that the 'flag' had made his number and he was summoned aboard.

'A bad idea, sir,' said an even ruddier-faced Neame, 'to appear before Lord Hood with too much drink in your belly.'

John Pearce smiled as he rose to gather his despatches and put on his best, and dry, uniform coat. 'I take that as a hint, Mr Neame, that you and Mr Ottershaw should finish that bottle, around which neck you have your horny sailor's hand.'

The purser, Ottershaw, slurred slightly in response. 'Would not want it to go to waste, your honour, it being such a pretty drop, not the least troubled, it seems to me, by being shaken all about afore the cork was drawn.'

'You do not think to keep a drop for young Harbin?'

'It might not hold its true flavour,' Neame insisted.

'Be my guest, both of you. I shall treat Harbin to a capital dinner, if a besieged Toulon will run to such a thing.'

'Rufus,' said Michael O'Hagan, 'clamber up them there shrouds and see what's what.'

'Why me?' demanded Rufus.

'Sure, did I not say please, boyo, what with you being the lightest and most nimble?'

The words might be polite, even close to jocular, but the tone was less so, and Rufus Dommet, faced with the muscular bulk of his Irish messmate, was quick to move. With HMS *Victory* laying inshore of the anchored 74, they saw John Pearce come on deck, hat in hand, as both of the smaller warships sailed slowly by. The cheer that greeted him was spontaneous, and not to be outdone, all the ships within the roadstead took it up. Pearce looked over to the rail of HMS *Leander* and, sighting the agitated figures, waved to his companions. The world turned upside down, right enough, he thought. Three of those on that deck were the men with whom he had been pressed into the Navy, the men he had sworn to get free.

'Belay that damned noise.'

'Get down, Rufus, quick,' hissed Charlie Taverner, himself letting go of the hammock nettings and dropping back onto the deck. Michael O'Hagan did likewise, while Latimer, much older, his lined face a mask of worry, had to ease himself down.

'What in the name of the Lord Almighty do you think you are about?'

'We's cheering in the taking of a prize, sir,' said Rufus, too innocent to know that saying nothing was best when dealing with Lieutenant Taberly.

'Silence, damn you,' Taberly yelled, before turning round and shouting at a midshipman who had been part of the watch. 'You, sir, how can you stand to witness such behaviour?'

He eased himself up onto the hammock nettings and looked out to see John Pearce in plain view, and it took only seconds for Taberly to realise that the swine was actually in command of both vessels, the despatch case in his hand finishing off the image. On the other ships they were still cheering, which made his blood boil; that a charlatan like Pearce, with whom he had exchanged words already, should receive such accolades was intolerable. Very well, those aboard this ship he had dared to name as his friends would pay.

'You, sir,' he yelled at the midshipman again, 'are a disgrace to your coat. You cannot control the men.'

'With respect, sir, they are not on watch.'

'Not on watch, sir? They are not fit to be on watch, just as they are not trusted to be sent ashore without they would run, but they are fit to be punished, sir. Take their names and let us see them at defaulters tomorrow, then, with luck, they will taste at the grating. Let us see, sir, how keen they are to cheer then.'

John Pearce was still looking at the side of the ship, wondering why his companions in misfortune had disappeared so quickly, but that thought had to be put aside as Neame, slightly drunk but still competent, let fly the sheets, and rudder hard down, brought the ship in a wide sweep, to rest under the bulk of HMS *Victory*. He then ordered the boat lowered that would take his acting captain aboard the flagship.

Chapter Two

Standing on the quarterdeck of HMS *Victory*, waiting to be summoned below, Pearce looked inland to the shore and beyond, the sound of continuous cannon fire louder now. There was fighting going on around Ollioules, at the head of a valley which provided the western gateway by which the port and town could be invested. There was another to the east, narrower and more difficult but it was Mont Faron and its companion hills, studded with forts, now being reinforced by hastily built redoubts, which provided the main defence to landward. Below the ring of hills lay the town, an old and jumbled mass of narrow alleys around the outer harbour, more up to date past the Vauban-designed fortifications, a star-shaped, moated bastion. Beyond that lay the newest buildings, which had housed the hub of a formidable part of what had been the Marine

Royal, the Arsenal and the Fleet Commander's headquarters.

Toulon had fallen, first to revolutionary fervour, and secondly, to fear. Again his mind went back to Paris, to the certainty of that place two years before, after the Battle of Valmy, the centre and driving force of all that had happened in France. No doubt existed in most Gallic minds regarding the rightness of the '89 Revolution; the destruction of the Bastille had been an event waiting to happen in a bankrupt nation stuck in an outmoded monarchical system that saw the rich prosper while the poor starved. That it had been humbled was now seen as inevitable, though Pearce suspected few were so certain of the outcome at the time. What had happened since created enclaves like Toulon, where the citizens saw the strictures and actions of radical Parisian-based politicians in a less acquiescent way.

In the capital, factions fought for control, and sought to outdo each other in the purity of their revolutionary ideals, using the mob to ratchet up the tone of revolution. Yet even at the epicentre many a mind was sceptical of the direction in which events were moving. Worse, it had become impossible to object; to do so risked at best incarceration – the fate of his own father, who had spoken out against excess – at worst the guillotine, the ultimate fate from which his son had been

unable to rescue him. In the countryside the actions
of politicians constantly driven on by the excessive
demands of a Paris mob were viewed with alarm;
worse still, the penalties deemed necessary to keep
the Revolution alive. Having got rid of a
monarchical tyranny, the majority of Frenchmen,
especially those of some education or property,
were not keen to see the power of the Paris radicals
extended to replace it.

Lyon, the second city of France, was in full-scale
revolt and there were rumours of a priest-led war
going on in the Vendée. Marseilles too had risen,
and had tried to act in concert with Toulon; they
had even invited Lord Hood and his fleet to take
over the protection of the city, but he had deemed it
indefensible. The great port had fallen only weeks
before, and the exactions of revolutionary revenge
had begun as soon as it was captured: rape; murder,
both judicial and spontaneous; robbery and arson;
all the trials that since time immemorial had been
the fate of a city under sack. Toulon, fearing a
similar fate, had asked for protection and Hood,
because of its topography easier to defend, had
obliged and the task now was to hold the place.
Pearce, before he left on his cruise, had heard both
opinions advanced: that Toulon was impregnable,
as well as the opposite; it could not be held without
an army the defenders did not have. He had no idea
who was right and who was wrong, lacking, as he

did, the knowledge to make a judgement.

'Lieutenant Pearce.'

He turned round to face Capitaine de Vaiseau, le baron d'Imbert, an English-speaking French officer he had come to know well in the period leading up to the British take-over. Pearce had been Hood's emissary in the delicate negotiations, a reluctant one certainly, but left little choice, being in need of the admiral's support in his dispute with Ralph Barclay. The French captain had been instrumental in bringing about the surrender of town, forts and fleet. No man could claim more than he, given that his superior, Rear Admiral Trogoff, had vacillated mightily, avoiding decisions with a cunning that, had it been applied at sea and in battle, would have been hailed as genius.

'I hear I am to congratulate you,' said d'Imbert, his weary eyes sad, hardly surprising; he was a French officer and HMS *Weazel* had taken a French ship.

'Good fortune, sir, rather than competence, and not without loss.'

'Ah yes. Your captain…'

Pearce did not want to talk about Benton, the man he had been obliged to replace, who had died right in front of him. He might have been a drunk for most of the voyage, and damned rude with it, but he had shown real pluck in the decision to disobey his orders, which were to merely reconnoitre the Corsican anchorages and stay away from trouble. Had he lived he would have come aboard instead of John Pearce, no doubt in anticipation of a fitting reward for his bravery and application. As it was Benton was in a canvas sack at the bottom of the Mediterranean, with a cannonball at his feet, food, eventually, for the crabs.

'How are relations with Admiral Hood, sir?'

D'Imbert produced a wan smile. 'They are those of a junior officer, Lieutenant.' Seeing that Pearce did not comprehend, he added, 'Rear Admiral Trogoff has seen it as his duty to take the task of dealing with your admiral upon himself.'

There was a terrible temptation to say, 'He has a damned cheek.' Trogoff had done everything he could to avoid making a decision regarding the state of matters in the town, had failed utterly to control his junior admiral, a dyed-in-the-wool revolutionary called St Julien, and managed to absent himself when finally it came time to act. Indeed he had even stated his intention to escape via Italy with a view to joining the royal *émigrés* and the anti-French coalition armies under the late King Louis' brother, le comte d'Artois, at Coblenz, only failing to do so because there was a rag-tag French army on the Italian border blocking his way.

'Naturally,' d'Imbert added, 'when he needs my

advice and my ability to translate, as he does on a day like today, I am summoned.'

'So I surmise today we have a difficulty?'

'You will recall our problem with the sailors who supported St Julien.'

'I suspect from your tone they are still a problem.'

'They are. Most of them were recruited from the Atlantic ports, so they were never truly content to be in the Mediterranean, far from home, long before the matters came to a head here. Now our admirals are trying to decide what to do with them. We cannot just kick them out. Five thousand strong they would only swell the ranks of the besieging force, nor can we keep them here, either locked up or on parole, since they would then present an internal danger.'

'The people of Toulon?'

The French captain shook his head. 'Not every Toulonnais citizen is in agreement with our rapprochement with you. Combine them with those sailors and they represent too much of a threat in a place so feverish with rumour and dissent.'

'I seem to recall there were officers too.'

'I think, Pearce,' d'Imbert said, smiling properly for the first time, 'what you actually recall is my saying to Lord Hood there were none, that the men were leaderless.'

'You no doubt saw that as a necessary deceit.'

'You are more understanding than your admiral, who mentions my dissimulation frequently, and never without a black look to accompany his strictures.' From below came the sound of stamping marine boots, and d'Imbert began to move. 'I must hurry, or my admiral will depart without me, so far have I fallen from grace.'

'Then I suspect, sir,' said Pearce, with real feeling, 'that the sight of you reminds him of his own failures of duty.'

'Lieutenant Pearce, Lieutenant Pearce.'

The blue-coated youngster, a mere child in clothing too big for his slight frame, crying out his name, emerged from a companionway looking worried. The expression deepened considerably when the object of his search identified himself.

'Sir, you were supposed to wait outside the admiral's quarters on the maindeck.'

HMS *Victory* was a ship at anchor, wallowing in some of its own filth, and with some seven hundred men aboard her crammed into her lower decks, it was not pleasant in terms of odours, even on the maindeck. But that was not the reason he was standing on the quarterdeck: Pearce would not say that the courtesy normally extended to a visiting officer aboard a flagship, that of the use of the wardroom and perhaps a glass of some refreshment, had not been offered, as it had when he had come aboard before. He was slightly upset that it should be so, but in no position to do anything about it, and damned sure he was not about to beg.

'I like fresh air.'

'The admiral secretary is in a rare passion.'

'Well,' snapped Pearce, who had crossed swords with the supercilious sod before. 'A bit of passion might do him good. It might warm his blood enough to ensure he is still living.'

'You must hurry, sir,' moaned the midshipman, 'for my sake, if not your own.'

Much as he would have liked to dawdle, if for no other reason than to annoy, he had no choice but to follow at the boy's brisk pace. The crabbed look on the face of Hood's secretary was compensation. Normally a languid and superior sort, he looked quite put out as he followed Pearce into the great cabin, where sat Hood and the slightly more corpulent figure of Rear Admiral Hyde Parker, who held the position of Captain of the Fleet.

'Pass your despatches and logs to my secretary, Mr Pearce,' said Hood. This he did, and the secretary departed with them as the admiral added, 'I will have a verbal report on what was plainly a piece of downright and calculated insubordination.'

Pearce explained about the situation of the *Mariette,* and the apparently defenceless position in which they had found her. 'Captain Benton saw it as too good an opportunity to pass up, sir.'

In the face of a sceptical superior, Pearce went on to describe the action, praising, as he had in his despatch, the actions of the crew of HMS *Weazel*, and in particular the bravery of young Midshipman Harbin, as well as the tactical appreciation of the master, Mr Neame. He made no mention of his own wound; by now he was hardly conscious of it himself, and it was gratifying to observe, as he spoke, the look of outright hostility fade in Hood's craggy countenance, to the point where he looked quite satisfied.

'And, sir, might I point out that before deciding to act, Captain Benton asked me what he thought you, faced with a similar problem, would have done.'

'And what did you tell him, Pearce?' demanded Hyde Parker.

'If I may say, sir, that I have never been comfortable with flattery, I feel I will have provided an answer.'

'Well,' said a clearly mollified Hood, 'what is done is done, and I am told she is a fine vessel.'

'She is totally deficient in powder and shot, sir.'

Hood laughed, the first time Pearce had seen him do so with anything approaching real heartiness. 'Then we will fill her up from the Toulon Arsenal, Pearce, but not until my own master has had a look over her to assess her value.'

'The crew will be anxious to know if you will buy her in, sir.'

The humour evaporated as quickly as it had surfaced. 'I daresay, Pearce, just as I daresay that in their addled brains they have already spent the money she will fetch. But I must tread with care. I cannot say anything until Admiral Trogoff agrees that she is a prize, and not part of the Fleet which he commands.'

'On the other matter, the one we discussed when I first came aboard.'

'Remind me,' Hood replied, but he had a look that told Pearce he knew very well the subject mentioned.

'Captain Barclay's illegal impressments in London, sir. I was a victim and so were several men now serving, against their will, aboard HMS *Leander*. Barclay has broken every rule in creation and I demand that he faces punishment for it.'

Hood's face was suddenly suffused with angry blood. 'Demand, sir! You will not demand in my cabin.'

Hyde Parker interjected, speaking in a more measured tone. 'What Lord Hood is saying, Lieutenant Pearce, is that the matter is under consideration...'

'Which it was before I went aboard HMS *Weazel* two weeks past.'

Hood barked again. 'Damn you, sir, do not interrupt your superior.'

'If I feel the laws of England are being ignored then I have a duty to...'

Hood's voice this time, as he cut across that of John Pearce, was loud enough to be heard through three feet of planking. 'Don't you dare prate on to me about the laws of England, sir, not with your parentage. I was a member of the government that proscribed your father for his blatant sedition. Do not forget that he, and no doubt you, had so little regard for the laws of England that you were obliged to flee to France to avoid them.'

Said like that, there was not much Pearce could put forward in defence. His father, after the fall of the Bastille, had gone from being a peripatetic radical speaker who could be safely ignored to a much sought-after orator and pamphleteer in a country where many a subject of King George saw the events across the Channel as a bright new dawn. Known as the Edinburgh Ranter, Adam Pearce was perceived as a man of much sense and wisdom by those people who sought some of the same change in Britain. His attacks on the monarchy and the ministers who served the king had relied on logic and irony to show the absurdity of both, his message one that sought universal suffrage for both sexes, an end to the great landed fortunes, a fairer distribution of the wealth of the nation and the termination of royal dominion. He was not alone in this; there were others preaching the same message, one which alarmed those in power.

Excess in France, or the constant application of it, had moved opinion away from support for the revolutionaries. Edmund Burke had fulminated in speech and print against the mayhem and disorder of Paris and every event seemed to make nervous a population that saw Britannia as a more stable country than France. When opinion had shifted enough, the government decided it could move against the likes of Adam Pearce, one of his more fulminating pamphlets providing the excuse to imprison both him and his son. On release, made through the intercession of like-minded but respected members of various Corresponding Societies, old Adam had not diluted his message; he had, in a written pamphlet, demanded the removal of King George and his heirs. Those were the words that forced him to flee to Paris, to be originally hailed as a friend. That had not been sustained; people in power in Paris had no more time for a man who questioned their right to rule than Hanoverian Kings.

Refusing to be browbeaten, Pearce replied, 'I think, sir, if you examine the laws of England you will find that it was you and your colleagues who ignored them, not I, or my father.'

'Parker,' Hood spat, 'am I to be obliged to

dispute in my own cabin with a mere lieutenant?'

'I agree, sir, it is hardly fitting.'

'My case,' Pearce demanded.

'Will be dealt with, sir. Now please oblige us and leave.'

'Am I to go back to my ship?'

'Damn you, sir, she is not your ship. Shift your dunnage out of HMS *Weazel* this instant, so that I can find someone fit to command her.'

'Report ashore to Captain Elphinstone,' said Parker, 'who is overseeing the defence of the port. I am sure he can find a use for you.'

'Is there anything I can tell the crew of HMS *Weazel?*'

'No, Lieutenant Pearce, there is not.'

The temptation to stay and continue the dispute was strong, but Pearce knew if he did so he would not aid his own argument, just as he knew that in baiting Hood about legality he had not done his case any favours. Outside he walked towards the entry port, cursing himself, only to be intercepted by the flagship's premier, Mr Ingolby.

'Lieutenant Pearce, I have come to apologise to you.'

'Sir?'

'I was ashore, as was every other lieutenant, on an inspection of the French capital ships. That the Officer of the Watch, nor the master or the surgeon for that matter, failed to offer you the use of the wardroom is a disgrace, and you with a fine capture under your belt. I ask that you join me now.'

Still angry with himself, and not wishing to have to recount the recent action in the taking of the *Mariette*, which he would surely be obliged to do, Pearce declined. 'I have much to see to, Mr Ingolby, and I am ordered ashore, in any case, so I must shift my possessions. But should my duty permit, I would happily accept an invitation for some future date.'

'The wardroom of *Victory* will have you as guest to dinner, sir, you have my word on it. There is nothing like a table and a circulating decanter to add spice to the story of an action.'

'That young firebrand,' said Lord Hood, in a tone of regret rather than continued anger, 'will get himself shot on the quarterdeck one day.'

'I must say he has a genius for trouble,' Parker replied. 'Yet we must admit he also has a claim.'

'I can send him home, can I not?'

'You can send him to India if you so desire, but I have a feeling that will not rid you of him. He has a family history of tenacity. We must hope Captain Elphinstone will keep him occupied.'

'Maybe one of Carteaux's cannon balls will take off his crown.' Hood shook his own head. 'I don't mean that, Parker, you know I don't. If anything, apart from his damned attitude, I quite admire the fellow.' The old admiral's voice became somewhat wistful. 'And do you know he has seen nothing but action since he was received aboard *Brilliant*. I know of officers in this very fleet who have served for decades and not so much as seen a shot fired in anger, yet that young pest, wherever he goes, seems to get into a fight.'

'Captain Barclay?' asked Parker.

Hood drummed his fingers on the highly polished table he used as a desk. Only he was privy to all the facts that laid constraints upon that which he could do. Pearce had brought from England a personal letter from the First Lord of the Treasury and the King's First Minister, William Pitt, which laid upon Hood certain limitations. He had no time for William Hotham as a second-in-command or as a person, and they were on either side of the political divide at home, but with a war to fight, Pitt was looking for allies in some of his erstwhile political opponents. Hotham was close to the Duke of Portland, who might lead a breakaway Whig faction and give valuable support to the government. He had had from Pitt strict instructions not to upset the sod, which would have mattered little in this particular case if Hotham had not taken it upon himself to become Barclay's sponsor. Give Pearce his court martial for Barclay's illegal impressments – and he did not doubt the man had a case to answer – and that would alienate Hotham.

'We allowed Hotspur to send Pearce away on his cruise, did we not, Parker?'

A stickler for the correct form of words, Parker replied. 'We allowed him to despatch Benton, who was his protégé, on what was seen as an essential mission. It was he who sent Pearce along as his Premier, an elevation that makes no sense unless you count the notion that Hotham is determined to protect Barclay.'

'Can you see the way my mind is working, Parker?'

That was part of Parker's job, as Captain of the Fleet, to be an experienced and trusted sounding board for his commanding admiral. The other part was to oversee the fleet at sea, to keep the vessels on station and to receive and act upon the daily reports sent in by each ship's captain regarding the state of their ships and stores. Known as a man of sound and patient judgement he was not fool enough to reply. He had a shrewd idea what Hood was about to propose and he wanted no part of the responsibility for an act which might well rebound badly and harm his own career. It was all right for Hood; at seventy years of age, after a lifetime of service as well as participation in several successful battles during the American Revolutionary War, he was reasonably impervious to censure and this was probably his swan-song command. Parker had prospects ahead of him, of command to come and perhaps battles and glory to win and he was not about to jeopardise them.

'You don't reply,' said Hood, seeking to hide his amusement; he knew very well what Parker was about. 'You do not see that the problem really resides with my second-in-command. Barclay is attached to his flag, not mine, and I would not have the swine if he applied, so let Hotham deal with it. If he saves Barclay's hide, then he can preen himself, if he does not, then I cannot be blamed. Damn me, Parker, I'm beginning to wonder if I spent too much of my recent time in the company of politicians.'

'I think, sir,' Parker replied smoothly, and well aware that in the area of politics Hood was capable of looking after himself, 'in regard to Admiral Hotham, that is a proposition which could only come from you.'

Chapter Three

Being rowed ashore, Pearce could still feel the lump in his throat, a sensation which had come with the farewells attendant on leaving HMS *Weazel*. Mr Neame and Ottershaw had been loud in their regrets that he was departing, but that might be because the quality of the wine would diminish; the crew muted through either indifference or the notion that to show any sort of feeling would cause embarrassment. He left the likes of the gunner without regret; he was a man who saw his cannon as pets rather than instruments of war, and hated to see them, or his precious store of powder, in use. Freckle-faced Harbin had proved the hardest when it came to a parting; a youth with an abundance of enthusiasm and courage, he was also prey to a like amount of sentiment, and his tears at the news had nearly done for Pearce. But in reality, what saddened him most was the loss of independence. It

might have come about by accident but he had been
in command of a ship for several days, and he had
thoroughly enjoyed the experience, even, in
recollection, the storm through which they had
sailed. How different was the King's Navy when
you had freedom from oversight and the privacy of
a captain's cabin!

He would have liked to go aboard HMS *Leander*
and seek out his friends, to assure them that he was
still hot on the task of getting them freed, but that
bastard Taberly had made it plain he would bar him
from setting foot on his deck, so he decided instead
to visit the hospital on the St Mandrier peninsula,
where he had no doubt HMS *Brilliant*'s surgeon,
Heinrich Lutyens, would still be plying his trade;
Captain Elphinstone, whoever he was, could wait
awhile. He was thinking on that when he heard the
coxswain order the oarsmen to ship their sticks,
and looking for the reason he saw a senior officer's
barge racing across the bow, with the stoic and rigid
figure of Admiral Hood in the thwarts.

William Hotham did not enjoy many conferences
with his commanding officer, and certainly Hood
had never visited him aboard HMS *Britannia*. He
was, on the rare occasions he was consulted, more
likely to be summoned, so when he was informed of
the approach of Hood's barge all his hackles rose in
suspicion, a feeling not diminished by the greeting

the older man gave him as, in his best bib and tucker, with much piping and a solid stamp from the few marines left on the ship, he welcomed his superior aboard at the entry port.

'By damn, sir, you have a fine-looking vessel here, always liked her trim. Not been aboard her since I was Commissioner at Portsmouth. Rodney had his flag in her then, of course.'

'Quite,' Hotham replied, wondering at the mention of that admiral. It was no secret that Hood and the late Admiral Sir George Brydges Rodney had disliked each other intensely, and disputed the proper way of thinking and fighting so furiously that it was not a name to bring forth in his presence.

'Thought it about time I paid you a visit, sir. Can't have you forever getting yourself soaked to come aboard *Victory*. Too much of that and you'll be as much of a martyr to the ague as I.'

Having referred to that illness, Hood strode briskly down the short line of the remaining marines, nodded his approval, offered his greetings to the other ship's officers, then made his way aft. Hotham was a man known to like his belly, so it was no surprise to find a fine spread of sweetmeats and fruit in his cabin, plus a very passable decanter of claret hastily poured by his steward. Insincere courtesies exchanged, and hunger assuaged, Hood came to the first of his points, the problem of the five thousand French republican sailors and what needed to be done with them.

'We must get them out of the place, I take it you agree?' The nod was slow to come, but come it did. 'I have had words with Trogoff and proposed that we strip out a quartet of sea-worthy seventy-fours, all the cannon barring a couple of eight-pounders for signalling, fill them full of those damned seamen, and get them out of here.'

'To where?'

'It will have to be the Atlantic ports. Can't land them anywhere in the Med or they'll cease to be sailors and become soldiers. D'Imbert tells me they won't even think of Genoa, and I doubt the locals there would take kindly to having that number dumped on them. They were conscripted from Lorient, Rochefort and Brest anyway. He also says they were a damned nuisance long before we arrived, much tainted by being over-indulged with the disease of rebellion. There will only be a brace of officers per ship, but they have warrants as well, so sailing them should be simple.'

Hotham fiddled with a walnut and the instrument with which he would crack it. 'You would be handing the French Navy a set of capital ships. All they have to do is refit them with cannon, powder and shot, and from the Bay of Biscay they can go anywhere, even come back here.'

'Parker and I have discussed this at length, and it

is a dammed nuisance, but I can see no other way. But it must be done with the active participation of each one of the fleet admirals. I need you to agree, and in writing.'

'You do not see that as interfering with your prerogatives?'

'I do believe Byng had prerogatives, Admiral, and a lot of good it did him.'

Hotham nodded slowly at the mention of that name. Admiral Byng had been shot on his own quarterdeck for what was seen as a dereliction of his duty in not supporting the besieged British outpost of Fort St Phillip on Minorca against the Spanish in the Seven Years War, the result being the loss of both the fort and the island. Most of his fellow sailors had seen the execution for what it was, a political act by a vengeful government, aided by spiteful inferior officers keen to exculpate themselves from what was seen as a naval disgrace. It had, however, a huge impact; even the sage Voltaire had commented on it from Switzerland, terming it an action *pour encourager les autres*. He was right; the others were encouraged. Now, no flag officer would lightly take a decision that might threaten the same fate. Hood's junior admiral never answered any enquiry quickly – he was known for it – and he did not do so now. He messily cracked a walnut and nibbled at a piece of it first, no doubt weighing up the consequences. If he was looking for alternatives, Hood knew there were none; the only other option was to keep them here.

'I am, of course, at your service.'

'Obliged, sir. I have one other vexing problem, Hotham, and I need your advice. It is this Barclay business.' Hotham raised his eyebrows, as though offended, though Hood would have been at a loss to know if it was the subject that alarmed him or the abrupt way it had been introduced. Since he once more failed to respond, Hood continued. 'That too is a damned nuisance and I am at a loss to know how to handle it.'

'You are aware, I am sure, that this Pearce fellow has threatened to call Captain Barclay out.'

'Has he, by damn? He will not call a man out in my command. Has he not been told it is strictly forbidden for naval officers to duel by royal statute?'

Another piece of walnut had to be nibbled before Hotham spoke again. 'He has, but I fear any strictures of yours might be ignored, sir. He is not much given to obeying orders, even royal ones, hardly surprising given that he is not truly an officer.'

Hood had to bite his tongue then. Benton had been, like Barclay, Hotham's protégé, and he had failed in the respect of strict obedience to orders. It would have been nice to put Hotham in his place, to force him to defend the late Benton, but that would not serve.

'I intend to be candid with you, sir.'

The raised eyebrows in Hotham's smooth and well-fed face looked like disbelief. 'That is something I can only welcome, milord.'

'Ralph Barclay is not a man for whom I have much in the way of affection.'

'While I,' Hotham replied, with rare force, 'find him an excellent officer.'

'Oh, I don't doubt he is brave and runs a good, tight ship. It is the personal line I speak of. You know I saw him hours before this wretched business is supposed to have taken place.'

'Indeed I do, sir.'

'So you know I warned him about taking any actions which would be detrimental to the good of the service. It was a quite specific caution to be careful where he pressed, if he intended to do so.'

'I seem to recall being present when the matter was first broached in your cabin.'

And I, Hood thought, recall only too well how you stood up for the swine on both the loss of his ship to the enemy, and his impressment of the men Pearce wanted freed, making plain you would go to some lengths to protect him.

'Captain Barclay was short on his complement, was he not?' Hotham added.

'What captain sails to war with a full

complement, Hotham, eh? It is the fate of us all.'

'Can I offer you a walnut, sir?' said Hotham, proffering the nut bowl.

As Hood declined Hotham was thinking about what had just been said. Barclay had indeed sought men to man his frigate, short-handed to the tune of a quarter of her full crew, and when he had done so it was in the certain knowledge that Hood, at the time the senior sea officer at the Admiralty, had at his disposal several hundred proper sailors lodged at the Tower of London. But the man was angling for the Channel fleet, which would allow him not only to hold that command but to keep his political office at the Admiralty. The king wanted the Channel for his favourite admiral, Black Dick Howe; Hood could have the Mediterranean. Determined not to give in to the monarch without a fight, Hood was damned if he was going to release any drafts of seamen until he knew which fleet he would get. Whichever, no vessel in his command would be short on his complement when they sailed.

'You know that Pearce wants a court martial,' said Hood.

'And do you intend to oblige him?'

'Admiral Hotham, I cannot see, if he continues to press the matter, how I can refuse.'

Being slow of response did not mean that William Hotham was not a deep thinker; indeed it was that quality which defined him. He was wondering, having been through something very similar before, if Hood was looking for the same solution, namely to off-load the problem onto him. He prided himself on his ability to extrapolate from a given set of circumstances and to see the possible lines of consequence. Also, he knew where he stood in the scheme of things at home. Hood did not want to distress him, quite unaware that by his attitude up till now he had more than done so, a fact which had gone home in every letter Hotham had written to people of his own political persuasion.

But did he want what was being offered, and would Hood use it against him to show that he was prepared to protect someone like Ralph Barclay, even if it was clear he was possibly in the wrong? What was vexing was the fact that he needed to protect him; all of those captains who looked to him for advancement knew he had taken Barclay under his wing. They had dined at the Hotham table and seen for themselves the connection, no doubt more interested in the way it reflected on their own standing than on the mere fact of it being so. If he let Barclay down he would be diminished in their eyes, and that was an unwelcome thought.

For a quick-witted and decisive creature like Samuel Hood, watching Hotham's dawdling mental process was torture. He knew that silence was best, and it was as if his whole body was itching as impatience took over. 'I was wondering if you could see any way out of this dilemma.'

'I think, Lord Hood, you wish for me to continue to handle this problem.'

'I wish for your opinion, sir,' Hood lied.

Ten agonising seconds elapsed before Hotham gave it. 'I will make no secret of my feelings, sir. That a poltroon like Pearce can traduce the reputation of a brave and competent officer fills me with rage. Yet, he cannot, as you have admitted, be denied his court martial. So, let it be, and let us work as hard as we may to prove that the accusation against Captain Barclay is false.'

'Then,' Hood said, trying to hide his relief, 'I leave the matter in your capable hands. You may set the date and choose the officers to sit in judgement on the case. When you have your verdict, I will, of course, confirm whatever the court decides.'

John Pearce had not expected to run into Emily Barclay at the hospital, and in doing so now, there was that same frisson of awkwardness which had attended their last encounter, though he tried to cover that with a warm smile. She was dressed in a white pinafore, her hair pinned back under a mob cap, yet was still strikingly good looking; the young face fresh, the unpowdered cheeks rosy, and her eyes alight with appeal. Pearce experienced the same feeling he had when he had first clapped eyes on her on the deck of HMS *Brilliant*, when coming aboard as a pressed man. Then his smile vanished as he recalled the blow from her husband such attention had earned him.

'Mrs Barclay,' he said, with a slight bow that covered his frown.

She gave a minimal curtsy, thinking that the presence of this man disturbed her, for it raised not only memories of a serious marital dispute, but thoughts regarding her husband that she had been able to bury these last few weeks, thoughts that her spouse was not as upright and honest as he should be. It was difficult to know what to say.

'Lieutenant Pearce. Would I be permitted to ask after your arm?'

Lutyens had been seeing to that wound on the last occasion they met; it would be bravado to mention the other one. 'Quite mended, madam, and entirely free from any putrescence. I take it, by your attire, you are assisting Mr Lutyens?'

The slight laugh made Pearce's extremities tingle. On that cold wet day off Sheerness, with the River Thames grey and miserable at his back, he had found it easy to imagine paying court to such a pretty creature, and it was just as effortless to rekindle that here and now.

'I fear I may often be more of a hindrance to our good surgeon than a help.'

'Nonsense!' That sharp rebuke came not from

John Pearce but from Heinrich Lutyens, standing in the doorway, his eyebrows well aloft, his long nose also raised in his fish-like face. 'You raise the spirits of the men, Mrs Barclay, and that does more for their condition than any ministrations of mine. Do not think I do not see their faces cloud as I approach.'

Both John Pearce and Emily Barclay had an awkward moment then; every patient treated by Lutyens had a similar experience, generally a painful one. He was not cack-handed exactly, just distracted and indifferent, having often stated that the physical aspects of medicine held little of interest to him. His patients could not agree, and he always gave them cause to feel their opinion.

'John Pearce, you are returned.'

'And in one piece.'

Lutyens indicated the sea outside the windows, now bright blue and less disturbed. 'One of my patients, an ambulant fellow, pointed out the approach of your ship. I am given to understand that, according to your flags, you have suffered both a tragic loss and victory over our enemies.'

'The first ill-fortune, the second the opposite, of which I am the beneficiary.'

'We will take coffee together, and you may tell me all. Mrs Barclay, will you join us?'

She blushed bright red, nailing her reply as an excuse. 'I fear I cannot. I am expected, indeed I would be surprised if the boat my husband sends for me is not waiting at this very moment.'

As if to emphasise that she began to untie the knot at the rear of her pinafore. Lutyens, with a look of passive acceptance for an obvious untruth, just nodded. Being the surgeon of her husband's frigate, a man who had witnessed the confrontation of John Pearce and Ralph Barclay and who had also heard of the words exchanged at their last meeting, he knew only too well why she had declined. Both sets of male eyes followed her as she scurried out of the room, and had they been honest with each other, they might have admitted to similar thoughts.

'Poor creature,' said Lutyens softly.

'Why so?' asked Pearce.

The surgeon half smiled. 'That is for me to know and you to ponder. Now let us have that pot of coffee and your tale. A battle did you have?' Pearce nodded. 'Then I am particularly interested in your impression of the behaviour of the crew. I wish to compare it with my own recent experiences.'

John Pearce decided to keep quiet about the ball that had grazed his arm to Lutyens as well; given his method of treatment, it was less painful that way.

It was an hour before the boat arrived to take Emily Barclay back to HMS *Brilliant*, an hour in which she had fretted that she might again meet with John Pearce, an hour in which she knew it was an

encounter she would have to keep secret from her
husband. It was therefore truly unfortunate that
one of the two people rowing her boat was a fresh-
faced youth with a half-broken voice called Martin
Dent, doubly so that Pearce came into sight,
walking the shore with Lutyens in deep
conversation, as the boat made its landfall. The cry
of the name filled the air, and spotting not only
Martin but several other familiar faces, Pearce
walked down to the small jetty to which the boat
had been tied up.

'Well, Martin, you are still whole?'

'But too stupid to address you proper,' said the
man next to him, a bosun's mate called Costello.
'If'n the captain was here he'd flay him.'

'I heard you was wearing a blue coat these days,'
said Martin. 'Though the how is a mystery.'

The sight of Emily Barclay had done it, and
Martin Dent had the same effect; it took him back
to what had happened at the beginning of the year.
Here, greeting him like a long-lost brother was a
youngster who had at one time tried to kill him, and
who, he had no doubt, had been the cause of the
death of another. In the dress of a marine drummer,
Martin had been one of the party who had taken up
him and the others, men who became his friends of
necessity, from that Thameside tavern, the Pelican.
Even on a warm day, in bright sunlight, surrounded
by blue sea and the smell of burnt earth and sweet

flowers, he could imagine himself back in that smoke-filled tavern. The faces of those with whom he had sought to evade the press-gang swam before his eyes, especially Abel Scrivens, Martin Dent's victim. Then there was Ben Walker, the sixth member of his original mess, who had been washed overboard from HMS *Brilliant* in an encounter with a Barbary pirate ship; he would be alive today without his being pressed. Yet Martin had changed, had seen the error of his ways, had even apologised, and that was the fellow he addressed now.

'I fear, Martin, in public, you will have to touch your forelock if you spy me, but do not ever do so when no other officer is present, or I will be the one to flay you.'

'Should you have a ship, Pearce, it would be good to serve under you.'

'Do not, Martin, pin any hopes on that, and don't be so sure that service under me will be so pleasant.'

'You won't use the cat, Pearce. You was one of us.'

'Excuse me, Lieutenant.'

Pearce stood aside to let Emily pass, then proffered his hand to help her down into the boat, something she could hardly refuse. The tingle that ran up his arm was as strange as it was noticeable, and he wondered if, under a wide straw sun-hat hiding her face, she had experienced the same.

There was no way of knowing; she kept her face turned away, even when, in a moment of inspiration, he asked Cortello if he could cadge a lift across to the other side of the bay. The favour granted and his sea-chest aboard, the youngster, all bright eyes and excitability, managed to embarrass Pearce, intrigue Emily Barclay and bore the already aching arses off his fellow sailors, who had heard the tale a dozen times before, as he recounted how he and his old mate had once taken a whole merchant ship from under the noses of John Crapaud.

'I think you are forgetting, Martin,' Pearce said eventually, in an attempt to shut him up, 'that there were others present.'

'They don't signify to my mind, especially that toad Burns.'

'My nephew?' said Emily, surprised. 'Why do you call him a toad?'

Martin Dent would have loved to have told her he was worse; he was a cowardly rat and even then he did not know the mention of the name to John Pearce was inclined to make his blood boil. Toby Burns was a deceitful little bastard who had abandoned him to a second impressment within sight of the south coast of England. Much as he would have liked to say so, he could no more condemn the little swine with his aunt in earshot than could Martin Dent, who was obliged to emit an unconvincing apology.

'Slip of the tongue, mam. Term of affection really.'

'Shall we drop you off at the end of the mole, Lieutenant?' asked Emily.

The voice had a tremor which had Pearce wondering at the reason. While his mind alighted on the possibility of attraction, hers was centred on the truth. For whatever reason, if her husband saw this officer in his ship's boat, he would have a seizure.

'Obliged,' said Pearce, as he scrambled ashore, taking a slippery green ladder up the wall of the mole, his dunnage following. 'Perhaps we may meet again.'

For the first time he heard her being sharp. 'I fear it is unlikely, Lieutenant Pearce.'

'Take care, Martin.'

'You too, Pearce.'

The frigate, fully repaired from the battle in which she had been forced to strike her colours, lay in the inner harbour and her husband had moved them both back on board as soon as he could, happier, as he insisted, to pace his own planking than stay on in the tower in which they had been incarcerated as prisoners. He saw the boat approach and hurried down the gangplank to the quayside so he could assist his wife in climbing the ladder from boat to shore. Even after nearly a year of marriage, each time he saw Emily he still felt the need to pinch himself at his good fortune, which was not a thing he had enjoyed much favour from in his life. Deep down, he knew that for his wife, duty was part of their nuptials, an entailed property that would have seen her parents and the rest of her family displaced from if he had enforced his rights. But she was still a wonder to Ralph Barclay; beautiful, mainly dutiful, barring the odd squabble, and a positive asset in his dealing with his fellow officers. Not greeted by the habitual warm smile, he was taken aback at the pursed lips and unfocused look on his wife's face as she steadied herself on the quay.

'My dear, you look peaked. I do hope Lutyens has not been working you too hard.'

Emily was still thinking about the events of the morning; of the sudden appearance of John Pearce, and the unpleasant thoughts regarding her husband's honesty in the days immediately before Lord Hood took over the port. Then there was the tale told by Martin Dent in the rowboat, of the taking of that merchant vessel from a Breton port, which differed substantially from that which had been told to her right after the action by her nephew, Toby Burns. And why had Martin Dent called him a toad?

'We shall have a capital dinner to cheer you up, Mrs Barclay,' her husband said, in a hearty voice designed to lift her spirits. 'And I have invited young Burns to join us. You two may talk family to your hearts' content.'

That the thought had the opposite effect to that intended was made obvious by the deep frown which swept across Emily Barclay's face.

Chapter Four

Elphinstone's headquarters were at the citadel, the
main bastion inside the Vauban defences, the well-
ordered and designed buildings around it standing
in stark contrast to the confusion that reigned
outside the walls. It seemed he was responsible for
the defence of the eastern sector and parties of
marines and sailors lay about, each seeking shade
from the sun, looking listless and disengaged, this
while officers, both French and British, scuttled
about, seemingly to no purpose, if you discounted
that each seemed to carry in their hands written
orders of some kind.

Once inside the citadel, Pearce was hard put to
find anyone who could tell him why he was here
and what he was required to do, though he did find
that the officers had set up a mess, and being
provisioned by the French it was well stocked with
both food and wine. So, in the absence of orders he

made up for what he had missed by treating himself to a good dinner. It was when he came to bedding down, a need that took him right into the heart of the headquarters, that he ran into the first real problem.

'Go back to your ship, sir, like everyone else,' said a weary-looking civilian clerk.

'I do not have a ship.'

The clerk looked at him as if he had said he lacked a mother. 'If you have no ship, sir, I am at a loss to know how you got here.'

'I was relieved of my duties aboard HMS *Weazel* this morning.'

'HMS *Weazel*, sir. Did I hear you right when you said Weazel?'

The voice was strong, definitely Scottish, if of the refined sort, and when he turned Pearce knew, just by the man's presence, that he was important. The grey hair was curled and fine, the eyes were penetrating in a face that probably wore, most often, a disapproving scowl, though it was more a look of deep curiosity now. He also had, on his blue coat, the twin epaulettes of a Post Captain of three years' seniority.

'I did, sir. I had the honour to command her in the recent action off Corsica, after the unfortunate death...'

The interruption was sharp. 'Of that drunken oaf, Benton.'

'He was brave as well, sir,' Pearce snapped, 'and it does not become any fellow officer, of whatever rank, to speak ill of him now he's been killed.'

'You would not, you insolent pup, be trying to put me in ma place?' The smile on the man's face was at odds with the words; he was clearly amused by the notion. 'You will be Adam Pearce's boy? Hood spoke of you.'

'I am, sir, and proud of it!'

'My, that's a sharp rejoinder, laddie. There's no need to be ashamed of your bloodline, even if the man named was a damned menace.' Seeing Pearce begin to well up in defence, the Post Captain carried on quickly. 'But I'll no damn a fellow for his antecedents, man. If I did, an Elphinstone would have to stab half the population of Scotland on sight, since we have been at odds with every one of them at some time in the last few hundred years. So, boy, I will treat you as one of my ain, till you show me I am amiss.'

Not sure how to respond, Pearce said. 'I was enquiring about a berth, being now without a ship.'

'Och, we will soon sort that out, laddie, will we not Myers?'

Elphinstone was looking past Pearce to the now flustered clerk, who stammered his reply. 'We can board him on a local family, sir, but not at such short notice without we cause upset.'

'Then make sure it is a good one. Tonight,

Pearce, you can rest your heid here in the citadel.
Happen tomorrow we will find you something to
do.'

'Thank you, sir.'

'Have you dined?'

'Yes, sir, and most handsomely.'

'Then you can sit with me as I take my dinner
and tell me all about your wee skirmish.'

It was only when they had moved from wine to
brandy, a very fine brew from the Armagnac region,
that they left the subject of the Navy, captains over-
indulging in drink and battles, to move on to the
subject of Adam Pearce.

'I met him long before you were born, when he
was a young and I a stripling of a midshipman,' said
Elphinstone. 'Edinburgh is a small place in the
social sense, and he was a bright man making his
way. I think it was Boswell who introduced us but
it could have been the father of Malthus, the dour
fiscal philosopher, who was visiting Scotland.'

'And how, sir, did you find him?'

'I told you, laddie, a damned nuisance with his
ravings, but an amusing one. Much more so than
those who still hankered after that Popish fool of a
Stuart.' Seeing Pearce raise an eyebrow, Elphinstone
added, 'Don't imagine their dreams died in '45,
laddie. They see their erstwhile king as a romantic
hero, instead of what he really was, a wine-sodden

fop with nothing in his gonads but water.'

'At least I think my father would have agreed with you there.'

'For the very reason that he hated monarchs, laddie, Stuart or any other, which borders on blasphemy. He was a contentious man when his humour failed and I often wonder if it was just disputation or principle that was his abiding animation.'

'Let me assure you, sir, that it was principle.'

An aide entered and placed before Elphinstone a sheaf of reports, which he began to read, leaving Pearce nursing his glass in silence. In a haze of slight inebriation, brought on by wine and Armagnac, Pearce could recall his father in his prime – a fast-walking busy man, not the broken invalid he had last set eyes on – the fire in the eyes, the passion in the voice as he harangued crowds all over the land, seeking to bring them to a realisation of their plight as exploited labour. This took place while son John plied the crowd and tried to collect enough in his hat to pay for a decent night's lodging and a good dinner. Sometimes they got an invite to the nearest great house; odd how they had often been on the receiving end of hospitality from the very people his father condemned, rich men on big estates, who seemed happy to have under their roof, and to dispute with, a radical orator who wanted to burn their mansions over their heads, as well as give their land to their tenants. At other times Adam and John Pearce had been obliged to sleep in the open, or, if it was too cold, in a barn or a byre.

Yet it had been a happy time in the main, when as a boy should, he believed what his father advocated and trusted whatever he said had to be true. Occasionally they settled for a short period and he was forced to attend school, there to defend those parental ideas with fist and feet, teeth and elbow, this taking place out of the sight of masters who, when they were sober enough to wield the birch, saw that as the way to drum knowledge into young heads.

'Army of Italy!' barked Elphinstone.

That dragged Pearce out of a reverie in which the many hardships he had suffered, the Fleet prison included, seemed to be overborne by the good times; sunlit days, fishing, or tickling trout in sparkling streams, abundant apples on trees, with one eye out for a bailiff, eating heartily in Post House Inns amongst folk travelling from one place to another, all with a tale to tell to an eager young ear, at other times striding out along country roads to shouted greetings from those toiling to get in the harvest, occasionally sharing a pail of beer, and a memory of a parent who cared mightily to make sure his son was educated by patient instruction, giving him a smattering of Greek, Latin, of counting and grammar, plus his own interpretation of history.

'Damned fool name for a rabble.'

'Sir?'

'That mob of bare-arsed villains, who hold us in from the east, who favour themselves with this grandiloquent soubriquet. The Army of Italy be damned and if the man commanding them is a general I am a regimental goat. If they have ten pairs of boots between them I would be amazed, but it seems they are stirring, laddie, which is not good news.'

Captain Elphinstone dropped his voice, not to a whisper exactly but low enough to avoid being overheard, as though the French were listening in the walls. 'We wanted them supine, which they have been, thank God, since they hauled their bare feet from the Po Valley. Containing Carteaux to the west is task enough with what we have. If Lapoype...'

Seeing John Pearce's confusion, he quietly enlightened him.

'Their general, most likely a sergeant afore the upheavals, and a timid scunner at that. He has sat on his arse doing nothing, which suited us just fine.' He picked up one of the reports. 'But this tells me he is stirring to make an assault on the L'Artigues and Fort Faron.'

'Will he succeed?'

'Never, laddie, but any assault draws troops from the west for the defence, and no doubt we will lose

men we can ill afford to drive him back.'
Elphinstone looked at the report in his hand again,
and when he had re-read it, he waved it at Pearce.
'This does not tell me near enough. I need a man to
go to Fort Faron and give me a clear picture, and if
necessary take some action to contain him. That
you will do in the morning. I will have you roused
out an hour before dawn.'

Suddenly Pearce was a little more sober. 'With
respect, sir, I do not feel qualified to give you what
you need. I have no knowledge of military tactics.'

'Laddie,' Elphinstone said emphatically. 'You are
a Scot and a proven fighter, as well as the holder of
a King's commission and the son of a born
troublemaker. That, sir, will dae me.'

Neither the taste in Pearce's mouth, nor the fur on
his tongue, was in any way eliminated by the
hurried breakfast of bread, a fruit compote, and
coffee, consumed long before first light. Taking
from his kit all that he would need, he found
Elphinstone's clerk had written orders for him,
which meant that his master had stayed up long
after Pearce had staggered off to bed. Outside the
citadel stood a file of soldiers from the 11th
Regiment of Foot and a group of sailors he was to
take up to the position. The soldiers were under the
command of a weary-looking lieutenant called
Dilnot, to whom he would have happily

surrendered command, but a naval lieutenant out-ranked a red-coated one, and the fellow showed no sign of seeking to dispute his rights.

'Arsenal first,' said Pearce, having read his orders. 'We are to haul some cannon up those hills.'

The expression on the faces of the sailors was indicative enough of the undesirability of that task. Toulon sat in a bowl of mountainous terrain and anything going out to the defences, barring the road to Marseilles, meant going up a steep incline. Oxen, he was quietly informed by Robertshaw, the coxswain in charge of the sailors, could only do so much; manpower had to be employed, and he managed to make it plain that his tars would not take it kindly if the bullocks, soldiers drafted to serve in a marine capacity by the exigencies of war, thought they could just march alongside toiling seamen.

At the Arsenal, by the French fleet's gun wharf, the dockyard mateys, none of whom spoke a word of English, aided by his party, loaded nine-pounder cannon, weighing near two tons, and their separate trunnions, onto heavy-duty ox-drawn wagons, as well as the shot and powder that would serve them. Two cable-length pieces of rope were added as well, along with some lighter hemp, a couple of double blocks and some chain.

'Lieutenant, I wish your men to divest themselves of their weapons, equipment and red coats.' Dilnot looked at him with raised eyebrows, forcing him to continue. 'It will be quicker for us if we all work to get the guns into position. I have no desire to be on the roadway in too much of the midday sun.'

'Water,' said Dilnot.

'What?'

'The town is well supplied with clean drinking water. Might I suggest, sir, that the provision of that will make matters easier, especially when the sun is at full strength. That and some biscuit. As for midday, I doubt we will reach our destination before it is the naval time for dinner.'

'Make it so, Mr Dilnot,' Pearce replied, adding, as the redcoat turned to issue orders, 'and thank you for bringing to my attention something I should have thought of myself.'

'Sir.'

'Would it be possible to dispense with that too, Mr Dilnot? It is a courtesy only.'

That brought forth a smile. 'Happily, Mr Pearce.'

'Should you perceive any other errors of mine, please feel free to point them out. A naval officer ashore cannot surely be as knowledgeable as a soldier.' Pearce then indicated two of the largest and most muscular soldiers. 'We want two levers in their hands, long ones, to use as rear brakes. I fear the oxen will need regular rest, too.'

'And the men, Mr Pearce, let us not forget the men.'

* * *

It was a bedraggled bunch that finally made it to the redoubt facing the so-called Army of Italy. The oxen had found the *pavé* streets of Toulon hard enough, but they soon ran out, and it became a struggle on rutted tracks that had dried hard throughout the summer months, tracks that would become quagmires at the first serious downpour. Pearce had occasion to be thankful for both Dilnot, who marshalled his men well, and the coxswain from HMS *Swiftsure*. Robertshaw knew what to do without detailed instructions and frequent halts were required so that the sailors could rig lines with the stouter cable that helped the oxen on the steeper parts of the ascent, the two men at the rear also aiding that when they halted by anchoring the wheels.

By the time they were halfway to the top, Pearce had removed his heavy blue coat and asked Dilnot if he wished to do the same with his red one, so that they became, even if their shirts were linen rather than flannel, indistinguishable from their men. And taking Dilnot's point, Pearce made sure that everyone drank copiously, though the sailors were very vocal regarding the lack of the small beer to which they were accustomed, and adamant that it should have been replaced by wine.

Pearce, nursing the dull ache of a hangover, was quite brusque. 'I will tell you, and I have walked further and in hotter weather than this, that fresh water is best. Now belay your moaning, and rig the lines for the next section of track.'

Finally they created the rise and got onto flattish ground, their speed much more satisfying as they approached the rear entry port to the redoubt. The fellow who greeted them, another naval lieutenant, had no idea, with their coats off, that he was addressing officers of any service. He began to berate the entire party for what he saw as their slow pace and general appearance. Pearce, that dull ache of a hangover adding to his irritation, positively yelled at him, demanding the date of his commission, which was considerably longer than his own. So he lied, added four years to the date of his elevation, declined to give his name and left the poor fellow mumbling apologies for his presumption.

While the ox-wagons were laagered, Pearce and Dilnot, now properly dressed, had both produced telescopes to run their eyes over the French positions. Even Pearce could tell they, somewhat higher than their redoubt and over a mile away, were out of effective range of the cannon they had brought up, as well as the ordnance already in place, but he could not tell much more, except there was a mass of activity.

'They are making fascines,' Dilnot said, 'and ladders.'

'Indeed,' Pearce replied, wondering how he could

see in a mass of moving bodies what they were up to.

'So they are definitely preparing an assault. It will be bloody and I doubt, if this position is properly manned, they will succeed.'

'How long have you been a soldier, Mr Dilnot?'

'I am a forced marine now, Mr Pearce. I have been a soldier most of my life and I would dearly like to return to that occupation.'

Pearce did not want to get into a dispute about the status of army men obliged to switch their service; he had other concerns. 'Captain Elphinstone has asked me to make an appreciation of the situation, and I candidly admit to being at a loss to know what to tell him.'

The glass stayed at Dilnot's eye, but the response was good humoured. 'Then, sir, you are the only officer I have ever met of any service who admits to ignorance.'

'What do you observe?'

Dilnot did not answer for a full minute, simply sweeping his telescope slowly back and forth, but Pearce knew he was thinking and he appreciated the care the man was taking before replying.

'Left to make their preparations the French will attack at a time of their own choosing. Bad weather is not unknown in these parts and we are slipping towards October. If they carry out their assault on a wet and windy night, the rain will make the cannon difficult to load and fire, while the wind will go a great way to covering the sound of their approach. So it will require a substantial body of men to be placed here to be sure of holding them.'

'Without knowing for how long?' asked Pearce.

'If you are a self-confessed novice, sir, you have at least seen what they are about. The only men that can hold this position will have to be drawn off from those facing General Carteaux. Their absence presents him with an opportunity to push forward his own positions to increase the threat to the anchorage.'

'Is there an alternative?'

'Mr Pearce, in war there is always an alternative.'

Dilnot was sweeping his small telescope around the surrounding landscape again. 'Might I borrow your naval glass, Mr Pearce, it is more powerful than mine.' That to his eye, Dilnot kept talking. 'The best way to avoid having to move troops to here is to disrupt whatever preparations they are making over yonder.'

'How?'

'Cause casualties. Break up their piles of ladders, set fire to their fascines, which will be tinder dry, perhaps even blow to hell the general's tent.'

'Cannon fire?' When Dilnot nodded, Pearce added. 'At this range.'

'What if we could get closer?'

'Can we?'

Dilnot pointed to a rocky outcrop, halfway to the French position, slightly below the level of the enemy encampment. 'If we could get a pair of these nine-pounders out there, then we could give them a warm time.'

Pearce was looking at the terrain in between, boulder-strewn scrub with the odd stunted tree bent over by the wind. 'Judging by the job we had getting the guns up here, I cannot see that would be easy.'

'Easy, no, Mr Pearce,' the redcoat replied eagerly, 'but possible. A bold stroke.'

The army man was excited, obvious even if he was trying to cover it up, which had Pearce wondering at his enthusiasm for his bold stroke. But he had to surmise there was a chance of advancement in the military for something outstanding. Even if they did buy their commissions, a hike in rank could be achieved by success.

'I fear, Mr Dilnot, that you must tell me, for I would not dare to give an opinion.'

That came quickly. 'We would need two cannon on lighter carts, with trunnions, beams and pulleys to make a hoist, a path cleared just wide enough to make possible their passage and teams of sailors to get them onto the carts and to pull them, once used, back into our lines. The trunnions we can leave.'

'They will not sit still and let our cannon destroy their encampment.'

'No.'

'I may have little military knowledge, but I do know, Mr Dilnot, that losing guns is a cardinal sin. That is a transgression I have no notion to commit and whatever was achieved would surely be only temporary.'

'I do believe, Mr Pearce, Lord Hood anticipates that we will be reinforced.'

'Indeed?'

Dilnot was genuinely surprised at that display of ignorance. 'Have you not heard, sir? There are Austrian and Neapolitan troops on the way, and a request has been sent for the Gibraltar garrison, who are sitting idle when the Dons are our allies. And there may well be a draft from England. What we gain by delaying their assault could be immeasurable. Let me explain.'

'Please do so.'

Pearce had to return to the citadel to advise Captain Elphinstone, so he had Dilnot make plain his ideas, execute a drawing of the ground, write down the possible outcomes and work out the times needed to execute his bold stroke, one he insisted was better than sitting waiting to be attacked. Back at the fort, Pearce was waiting, as the Post Captain rode up on a stout, short pony, that had his legs near touching the ground.

'It might be inelegant, Pearce,' he shouted, 'but

by God it is better than walking round the defences.' Elphinstone dismounted, rubbing his backside, which was clearly a source of pain and discomfort. 'So, what is the position, as you see it at the Faron redoubt?'

'I consulted with an army officer, sir,' Elphinstone nodded in approval, 'and he has suggested the following course of action.'

Pearce outlined what was really Dilnot's plan, but he not attending, it left him with no alternative to mention as often as possible that he had been in receipt of military advice.

'Yes, yes, laddie,' Elphinstone barked, when he said it for a tenth time. 'Get to the point.'

He did so, aware of, and ashamed that it was beginning to sound as though he had formulated these ideas himself. 'The first task, sir, is to go out after dark and clear a route. The primary part of the evacuation, getting the guns out over the defences, will not be a problem, but we will need a stout body of men on the last part to haul the guns back in. If we succeed, it will give the French pause and may even disrupt their plans to the point where they abandon any idea of an assault.'

Elphinstone slapped him on the back. 'There! I knew you were a warrior, Pearce, most Scots are. It is in the blood, and it's a damned good job we have stopped being so disputatious with each other.'

'Do you know of a Lieutenant Dilnot, sir?' said Pearce, wishing to shift the praise.

The response was surprising. 'That poltroon. Don't mention his name to me ever, Pearce. The man is a damned coward, proved in battle. He failed at Oullioles and got killed a good man called Douglas, a fellow Scot as you will discern by the name. Should you come across him do what any decent officer would do. Snub him!'

Pearce was too dumfounded to respond, as Elphinstone went back to his small pony and stiffly remounted. 'I need to go aboard *Victory* and report to Lord Hood. Give my clerk what you need in writing. I assume you will begin the clearing straightaway, as we are without a moon.'

'Of course, sir,' said Pearce, who had only just realised that there would be, on this night, nothing more than a sliver of moon. Dilnot had, no doubt, calculated on that too.

Chapter Five

Pearce went out with the marine party in a borrowed greatcoat, relying on starlight to see his way, which led to many a stumble and under-the-breath cursing. Dilnot had thrown out a screen of armed skirmishers well ahead, with orders not to fire their muskets unless absolutely necessary, to protect those clearing a path from being disturbed. At the same time the party of sailors, under their competent coxswain, were laying out a pair of cables fetched from the arsenal and rigging blocks to stakes that a unit of sappers had sunk into the ground behind the ramparts to the redoubt; running the guns up the slope to that defence work, no doubt being pursued by the French, was not an option. The night was warm, with wind enough to rustle what foliage existed on such a barren landscape, with the odd clink of metal touching something solid freezing everyone in case it was the enemy patrolling prior to an attack, looking for a prisoner who could tell them the nature and numbers of the defence.

'Prosser,' hissed Dilnot to his sergeant, a small Londoner. 'We want some brushwood cut to lay on the passage, otherwise the clearances we have made will look too obvious once the sun is up. And don't just roll any rocks and boulders to the side. Move them a distance.'

The sound of hacking seemed like the knell of doom, so loud was it and that was when Dilnot's other ruse came into play. He carried a shaded lantern, and when he opened it to show a light to his rear torches began to wave and move about, only enough to light the area right in front of the rampart, and loud shouting filled the air, the idea that if all French eyes were on the redoubt, they would not be simultaneously looking into the darkened hollow ground that lay between the positions. They worked their way forward to the base of the outcrop, and here the ground began to rise, not by much, but enough to imagine the task of hauling a cannon up there to be a telling one.

'It has to be human muscle, Mr Pearce, we cannot risk an animal, but with good fortune we will have the whole night to accomplish it, and if we can get the cannon rigged on some reasonably level ground, I reckon we can make their encampment a place too warm for comfort.'

The party worked on until Dilnot, carefully unshading to take a look at his fob watch, called a halt. Having done that he went right to the edge of the small plateau on which he intended to site the guns and stared hard at the fires of the French encampment.

'You know, Mr Pearce, it would be a fine thing to open up before they *reveille*. Damn me, we could catch them in their smalls.'

'If I am not mistaken, sir, it is time we retired.'

'True. You go ahead, while I call in my skirmishers.'

They were all back behind the rampart walls as the sky turned grey, that soon followed by a red ball of sun rising behind the French camp, which led to an anxious period of waiting, till it rose enough to cease blinding those looking east, and showed that it would take a sharp eye to find the line of the track they had made during the night.

'Breakfast I think, Mr Pearce, then I fancy that you, like me, will welcome some rest.'

Dilnot stood his men down, and they immediately made up beds under the ox-wagons, shaded from the sunlight. Within minutes the first sound of snoring emerged, and that soon turned into a cacophony. Pearce, finishing a bowl of coffee, reckoned they had managed a good night's work, and he had to admire the way Dilnot had handled things, yet he was dying to ask what had caused

Elphinstone's outburst, while knowing that was an impossibility.

'I am curious, sir, what tempted you to become a sailor?' Dilnot asked

This had Pearce wondering if the man could read his mind, it being a perfect foil to deflect any questioning of him. To open up or dissemble? He decided on the latter; what Dilnot did not know would not hurt him, while finding he was in the presence of a military novice might affect his actions.

'Shall I say, sir, that I had little choice.'

'Choice,' said Dilnot wistfully. 'Few in this world have that.'

'You?

'My father was a soldier before me, Mr Pearce, and reckoned the army the best career a man could aspire to, so I was chosen for the profession. He would turn in his grave to see me acting as a marine.'

'Is it so arduous a burden?'

'Only at times.' There was a strange glint in his eye as he added, 'At others, like now, I would not wish to be elsewhere.'

'As you say, Mr Dilnot, time to sleep I think.'

'I must find a spot away from that racket my men are making.'

'Do you not have a billet in town?'

'I do, and so do my men, but it seems bizarre to

march all the way down to the Old Town, only to
have to march all the way back up again tonight.'

'Our party of seamen will do it.'

'Your party of seamen are not carrying sixty
pounds of kit, sir.'

A steady stream of supplies arrived as they slept,
all the things Pearce, advised by Dilnot, had
informed Elphinstone were necessary. A couple of
light carts, a dozen baulks of twelve-foot timbers,
some capstan bars, more blocks and pulleys, plus,
as the sun dipped into the west, a strong party of
tars who would be needed for what was hoped
would be the final act. Dilnot had his men lined up
and was, with his sergeant, checking their muskets,
ensuring they had the requisite amount of powder
and shot and that their bayonets, which tended to
get used for every job under the sun, had not been
blunted. The sound of trudging boots had Pearce
turn round, to observe a dusty midshipman
approaching, and seeing he had been spotted, the
lad grinned.

'Mr Pearce, sir. I have been sent to assist.'

'Mr Harbin, I am glad to see you.'

'And I you, sir.'

'Mr Dilnot, allow me to name Midshipman
Harbin who recently sailed with me. If he is to go
out with us tonight, I beg you ensure you keep an
eye on him, otherwise he will be attacking the
French command tent single-handed.'

Harbin blushed through ten thousand freckles as Dilnot greeted him. 'Mr Pearce, we need lifting frames erected with pulleys to raise both the cannon and their trunnions onto the carts. Of necessity they will have to be lifted over the rampart and their wheels replaced in open ground. It would be an asset if we could make that a single manoeuvre.'

When Pearce said he was glad to see Harbin it was not just from affection. The boy was not only enthusiastic and brave, he was intelligent and knowledgeable in areas where his superior would struggle, perfect for the task now in hand. Pearce listened carefully as Harbin outlined how he would carry out the manoeuvre, the right size of lifting frames, their location, a set of ropes and pulleys that would take the cannon over the rampart to a lower frame that would sit right on the level of the carts once that had been established.

'So, you see, sir, it will slide very neatly onto a bed of straw.'

'Excellent, Mr Harbin. I can leave you to get that rigged. The coxswain, Robertshaw and I, will see to the carts.'

A set of fascines were placed upright outside the rampart to create a screen behind which, with torches, the men could work, not perfect enough to entirely cut them off from view but enough to cause confusion as to their purpose at a distance. The wheels of the smaller carts had been knocked off the axles, and as soon as the light faded the body of each of the two were lifted over the rampart, the wheels put back in place once they were on the outside and the necessary tools, powder, shot and flintlocks loaded on; long, thick metal spikes, water for both men and *matériel*, levers to move the aim of the guns, spades to dig and a tub of unlit slowmatch to ensure that if the flints malfunctioned, the cannon could still be fired.

Harbin was as good as his word; if there was anything the Navy was good at it was shifting two-ton weights as though they were feathers. Using double blocks, the cannon were lifted clear of the ox-wagons that had fetched them up the hill, then slung onto a thick cable that sloped towards the cushioned bed of the carts. The trunnions followed quickly, and the gun crews who would fire these pieces took up the ropes with which they would haul, this as Dilnot sent his men out to form a defensive line in front of the party.

'Mr Harbin,' called Pearce, seeing something that had been missed, 'two more cables to the rear of the carts. If we have to beat a hasty retreat we will not have time to turn them round.'

'Our friends over yonder must wonder what we are about,' said Dilnot. 'If they come out in numbers to find out we will be in trouble.'

'Worth the risk, Mr Dilnot?'

'No doubt about it, Mr Pearce.'

'Right, you behind the parapet, take the strain. Quench the torches and drop those fascines.'

The creak of the wheels, which had been greased, still sounded too loud for comfort as the carts were eased down the slope into the hollow ground. Once there those cables were detached and left for later, as the seamen took up the strain on the front, leaning on capstan bars that had been lashed to the steering frame that controlled the front axle, a better method of forward movement over uneven ground than pulling. Dilnot bullocks walked fifty paces ahead, bayonets fixed, ten feet apart, the officer and his sergeant behind them to keep them dressed in the right line.

Several times a wheel dropped into a depression. These were impossible to see in the low light of the stars, plus a sliver of new moon, and the carts needed to be levered out, in one case hauled backwards and manoeuvred round the obstacle. It took three hours to get to the foot of the incline leading to the proposed position and at that point Pearce called to Dilnot to say every hand, his skirmishers included, would be needed to get up the slope, which was accomplished by a heave, moving it forward a few inches, with men again placed behind the rear wheels to jam in levers that would prevent the carts slipping backwards. Now a couple of inches would have seemed like a mile as the gun transports, in all weighing near three tons each, were eased up and up, until finally the front wheels crested the plateau and pushing became easier.

There was not a man, officer, seaman or marine who was not sweating buckets at the exertions, but there was no time to rest. Harbin had a frame and pulleys to rig, the trunnions coming off first, they being wheeled because they could be moved on their own, if not with ease, at least with effort. They were rolled into shallow forward-facing pits, freshly dug, designed to absorb some of the recoil and each cart was rolled over the top so that the cannon could be lifted straight in the air. The cart was then removed and the weapon lowered into position. Having twice carried out that manoeuvre, the next task was to rig the lines that would also act to control the recoil, though the stakes that would be needed to hold them would have to wait till near dawn; that was the last task to be carried out.

Powder and shot were unloaded and set in place, the cannon tompions removed and the barrels swabbed before loading. Flints had been fitted and the slowmatch lit out of sight, to fizzle in the dark bringing with it the smell of burning saltpetre, and ahead of them, still flickering in the dark, were the dying campfires of their enemy.

'A grey goose at a quarter mile, Mr Dilnot.' There was just enough light to see his quizzical expression, as Pearce added, 'It's is a naval term, sir.'

'I only ask, are we wholly ready?'

'We are, barring the stakes. Mr Harbin.'

The midshipman stepped forward to kneel down, a long metal spike in his hand, this copied by four other tars. Above them stood the strongest of the seamen's party, each having in his hands a sledgehammer of formidable weight. There was no way to do this quietly, so on the command those hammers swung and the clang, as they hit the head of the spike, reverberated around the hillsides, each blow so close it was impossible to tell what was real and what was echo. The looped restraints had been prepared in advance, and as each spike was sunk to as much depth as was required, those lines were attached and tightened.

'All done, sir,' said Harbin.

'Then, young sir, I would suggest it is time to let our friends yonder know we are here.'

'Gun captains,' Harbin called.

Both men nodded at Harbin's order, then admonished everyone to stand clear. This was no shipboard firing with trunnions rigged to be brought up short on thick cable restraints or a well-fashioned redoubt with properly sited artillery. No one had any idea what the cannon would do once fired. The gun captains themselves stood several yards back, holding the long lines that went to the flintlocks. Dilnot stood with his small telescope, Pearce with his larger instrument, their eyes fixed to observe the fall of shot, as both gun captains hauled hard. The flints fired the powder in the touch hole, which set off the charge in the barrel and a long orange tongue of flame shot from the muzzle as a nine-pounder cannonball was sent flying towards the French camp.

The cannon shot backwards, the wheels in soft ground, the rear of the trunnions running on to hard packed earth, the barrels threatening to rise enough to tip backwards until they were brought to a halt by the ropes, but it was obvious as each whole ensemble dropped back to the ground it was not exactly in the same place from which it had been fired.

'We shall have to aim every time, lads,' shouted Pearce, trying and failing to see where the balls had landed. What he did see was the utter confusion of an encampment rudely awakened. They had pickets out to ensure they did not fall to a sudden ground assault, but clearly they had not anticipated this.

'I would say, Mr Pearce,' shouted Dilnot, 'that rate of fire will count for more than accuracy.'

Pearce was not listening. He was watching the French gunners, shirts flapping in the breeze, rush to their own cannon, and he was aware that this was something he had not thought of, perhaps forgivable given his lack of knowledge. What was surprising was that Dilnot had failed to foresee it either.

'You will also see, Mr Dilnot, if you look left, that we are about to be in receipt of return fire.'

'Then it will be warm, sir,' Dilnot replied in what sounded like a happy tone. 'Very warm.'

Pearce was content to let the gun captains re-set their cannon, but it was going to be a worryingly slow rate of fire, all the while thinking he could not agree with Dilnot. If their purpose here was to disrupt French preparations then the cannon fire must be concentrated on achieving that. At least the sun had edged up behind a bank of cloud on the horizon, providing a clear sight of where the balls landed from their second salvo. They would not get off another without being paid back in kind.

'Do we need to aim one cannon left?' Pearce asked, as the first of the defensive battery opened fire. It was obvious, from fixed and prepared positions, they would be able to lay down more accurate fire, obvious that their outcrop, without the same kind of protective revetments as the French enjoyed, was dangerously exposed.

'We have but a small window, Mr Pearce. Let us concentrate on what we can achieve.'

Odd that Pearce felt more vulnerable on this plateau than he did on the deck of a ship where at least there were bulwarks, more so as the first French ball ploughed into the face of the outcrop and sent up a huge plume of earth. It pleased him that his naval gun crews seemed impervious; they carried on as though no fire was coming their way, even when a ball hit the very edge and ballooned up to fly over their heads. Their salvo in reply sent two balls ploughing through the rows of tents in the centre of the encampment, causing mayhem as half-dressed men and officers ran in all directions, in truth, a mistake, since there was no telling which way the next cannonball would go. And now the counter-battery fire was steady, yet if it was that, it was unlucky, for though much earth was moved, not one ball came close enough to their position to render it untenable.

'Infantry forming up,' shouted Dilnot.

Following his pointed finger, Pearce saw a mob of soldiers being hurried into formation, with swords flashing and waving, some he suspected being used on the confused men. Both gun captains tried to hit them before they had any kind of proper shape, and one ball, falling short, bounced off a protruding rocky outcrop to shoot on, sending dozens of bits of stone flying to leave a clear line of bodies, some recumbent, others writhing, through the now-disordered ranks, while what had been chipped off the rock took several men not yet in line. The next salvo achieved what they had been trying to do since the outset; it hit the pile of scaling ladders that lay in the open, and reduced most of them to matchwood, sending splinters of the kind more common aboard ship to inflict gaping wounds on those who were close enough to suffer.

With several more balls erupting around their position, Pearce suspected that it was only a matter of time before luck shifted from them to the French gunners. Dilnot stood at the very edge of the plateau, seemingly impervious to the idea of death, his glass still trained on the enemy formation, as they formed up in column before their own earthworks. Looking at the distance they would have to cover, and the distance back to their own redoubt, in daylight, from the only place that a man could make a proper judgement, Pearce realised that what looked like a possibility from their own redoubt looked like madness from here. Getting these guns away was a nice idea but probably an impossible one. There was a reluctance to take charge; he knew little of warfare compared to Dilnot, but his gut feeling was such that he felt he had to.

'Mr Dilnot, I would suggest it is time to deploy your men away from the guns. They will be safer in a place to cover us and slow the enemy when we retire. I trust you will know what to do once you are in the hollow.'

Dilnot's voice had an agitated tone as he responded. 'You intend to withdraw, Mr Pearce?'

'I do. We have done that for which we came, and to stay here is to invite annihilation. I fear I must make that an order.'

There was a pause, then Dilnot said. 'My men can give you time, sir, with their muskets.'

There was something about Dilnot's expression. Not disappointment, but a look in the eye that told Pearce he might welcome death, as long as it came with a dash of glory, and Elphinstone's words about the man being 'a damned proven coward' came back to him. Was that what Dilnot was about, trying to lay the ghost of a reputation and not really caring a damn whom he took with him in the process?

'Please do as I ask, Mr Dilnot, though I will, in my report, acknowledge your reluctance to accept such a command.'

That seemed to mollify the man and he issued crisp orders to withdraw, following his men as they scurried down the slope in single file. The next order from Pearce was one he had to give, even if he did not want to. He could not risk the men he had led out here any more than he could risk Dilnot's soldiers. The ball that went over his head with a whoosh of displaced air, and by so little a margin he was sure he could feel its heat, was all he needed to be convinced.

'Gun captains, load with canister and double charges, depress your elevation, then you too retire from the point of danger behind the screen of the bullocks. Mr Harbin, you and I will take over the lanyards.'

'Sir.'

'Robertshaw, I want the men with sledgehammers standing by and two more of those metal spikes.'

That got a touch of the forelock and an, 'Aye, aye, sir.'

'And get everything on to those carts and set them alight.'

Pearce got himself and Harbin as far away from the guns as he could, which was just as well because the French finally got the range and powder charge right and a ball took one of them on the muzzle, sending it flying with a ringing sound and cracking the cast-iron casing of the barrel.

'Mr Harbin, you are now redundant, sir. Get back.'

Pearce was watching the column of soldiers advance. It was an untidy formation, no doubt made more so by the uneven ground. A glance behind him showed the carts beginning to burn, Harbin disobeying his orders and holding a spike, looking like a dwarf beside the man with the sledgehammer, and in the hollow his sailors were running for dear life. Dilnot's men were strung out in a line, muskets at the ready, waiting for him.

His judgement of range was pure guesswork. He might have discussed ballistics with HMS *Weazel*'s miser of a gunner, but he was still an ignoramus in that department, so as the column reached the halfway point between his position and their own, he pulled the lanyard more in hope than in anger. The cannon actually jumped clear of the ground as the double charge went off, spewing hundreds of metal balls in the direction of the French troops and the damage it did was immense. The man in charge of the assault, a fellow with his hat on his sword and a tricolour sash round the waist of his black coat, took the eye of the salvo, hit with so many balls that he was tossed about like a rag doll. The effect behind him was equally telling, as men fell, were blown back, or dropped to the side.

'Harbin,' Pearce said as calmly as he could. 'The spike.'

The boy rushed forward to a cannon now on his side, the crouched giant with him, and calmly placed the point in the touch hole, this as another French ball ploughed up the earth no more than a dozen feet distant. The clang of the two blows was an unspoken signal to Dilnot, who though his enemies were at long range for musketry, opened up to let them know that the action was ongoing. Rushing past the blazing carts, and remembering they still had on them barrels of powder, Pearce cursed himself for forgetting that too. If they went off now, he, Harbin and the hammer-wielding sailor would be blown to perdition.

The powder had the good grace to wait until they were clear, finally exploding in a deafening roar when they retired behind the men of the 11th Foot, who were firing, reloading, moving back ten paces and firing again, as the remnant of that column came on to contest the ground, they too stopping to deliver volleys of musketry, and since the range was closing, those musket balls were whizzing past their ears.

'Mr Dilnot, undignified as it may appear, I think it is time to run.'

'After you, sir,'

Pearce nodded and obliged; it was only when he had gone twenty yards and he glanced back that he saw Dilnot had not moved. His men were running like the sailors, but the army lieutenant stood with his pistol in his hand, which he discharged as soon as he thought the range close enough. Then he took out his sword and waited. The shouts Pearce aimed at him may have been heard, but they were ignored, and he had to flee himself or face the oncoming horde of bayonets. It was afterwards that he heard how Dilnot had charged those same weapons, his sword waving, until he fell on their sharp points, gaining for himself what he obviously intended from the outset, a hero's death.

'Well, I canna say I am sorry, laddie,' Elphinstone said as he read Pearce's report. 'The man had disgraced himself, and now he is redeemed by his action.'

'His foolish action, sir.'

'Don't go traducing military glory, Pearce. It's what we all live for.'

'Dilnot died for it.'

'He saved his name.'

'Is his name that important?'

Elphinstone leant forward to emphasise his words. 'It obviously was to him and when his family hear how he died they will be proud of him and that is something. Better I think than being snubbed in the mess by his fellow officers refusing to talk to him.'

Realising he was wasting his time, Pearce said, 'I'm sorry we lost the guns, sir.'

'Who cares about them!' Elphinstone barked happily. 'They were French, laddie. The mair of them we lose the better.'

Chapter Six

Sitting in the thwarts of her morning transportation, Emily Barclay kept looking intently at Martin Dent as he worked the oars, dying to question him about his terming her nephew a toad, continually forced to look quickly away if he lifted his head. His quick excuses had done nothing to divert her curiosity; she might be a captain's wife with the station and honour that carried, but she was not yet nineteen years of age, and childhood jibes were not so distant that she could not recall their meaning. Toad was in no way a jocular, genial term; it was an appellation designed to wound and to call into question a person's character. She had in her time, though she would blush to admit it now, used the expression herself.

Emily had brought up the subject of that action in Brittany at dinner the day before, much to the chagrin of her husband, who hated to be reminded that he had lost the vessel in the first place, humbugged by a clever adversary, even less that, in an attempt to regain the *Lady Harrington* he had personally failed, suffering many casualties. Indeed, he had been close to despair, looking for ways to explain to authority, first of all how he had lost a ship from the convoy he was tasked to escort, and secondly why, in the face of standing orders not to do so, he had abandoned the rest of his charges to try and remedy the situation. Toby, sensing his captain's discomfort, sought to change the subject: his aunt insisted he tell his tale.

She had heard the story before, of course. Toby had regaled her with it right after the event; the landing in the wrong place that had seen the cutter wrecked and the commanding lieutenant drowned, the way her nephew had taken charge and formulated a bold plan to get the remnants of his party back to HMS *Brilliant*. How, outnumbered and out-gunned, he and the brave men he had led retook the merchant ship from under the noses of her French captors. Given that he must have told the tale many times since, it should have come out well rehearsed, which made surprising the stumbling explanation he now offered, until she realised it was the added presence of his captain which was causing the boy to falter, and it had nothing to do with uncomfortable recollection.

The look she saw was one of scepticism, as

though her husband knew what he was hearing was not the truth, while the interjections he made to clear up the odd point engendered in the youngster an air of deep discomfort, making him wriggle inside his clothing as though his entire skin itched. Instead of clearing up any doubts, her enquiry had only served to increase them, which left her with an even stronger desire to find out the truth. She could not ask Martin Dent for an explanation; that was impossible given their differing stations. It was well into the morning, when sharing a cup of coffee with Lutyens, a person so close they were now on first-name terms, that she posed to him the question.

'I cannot fathom why you are asking me, Emily. The merest hint of recollection will remind you that I was not present. Both you and I were treating the wounded from the other boats.'

'It is just that, having heard Martin Dent tell the tale, and having had my nephew reprise his version, I seem to see so many discrepancies as to make me wonder at who is being truthful.'

'Battles, according to those I have questioned, are confusing affairs. After our ship was taken, I embarked on a quest to find out the truth of the action and I have to say that not one account agreed with another.'

Emily Barclay waved an impatient hand. 'It is not just the action itself of which I speak, but of that which happened before. According to Martin, once they found themselves stranded ashore, John Pearce was the prime mover in organising them. In his telling, Pearce formulated the plan to retake the *Lady Harrington* and oversaw the execution, yet if you hear my nephew Toby's account, all the decisions, however much he seems to wish to be modest, were made by him. Certainly my husband treated him as a hero when he came back aboard. If he did not think him so, he surely would not have given him the task of taking that very same vessel back to England?'

A surgeon on board a King's ship heard much that was not vouchsafed to commissioned officers, and that was doubly so in the case of someone like Lutyens, originally termed by the crew 'a right Nosy Parker'. Forever eavesdropping on the crew's conversations, or watching men at their duties – never without one of his little notebooks to hand – he observed more than most. At first he had engendered much distrust, but the men soon found that nothing he saw or heard went to the ears of authority, so slowly they had begun to trust him, and with that trust, as he treated the cuts, abrasions and the occasional broken bone which were a daily part of shipboard life, there came a degree of disclosure.

To begin with, the mess that termed themselves the Pelicans had not been popular with the crew; pressed seamen rarely were, but their very collective defensiveness had singled them out for disdain. The first crack had been made by the Irishman, O'Hagan, fighting and beating the ship's bully-boy fair and square, the next when Ralph Barclay had overstepped the mark to punish John Pearce for merely admiring his wife. She had shown her displeasure at her husband's actions and the crew had done so too, in a way that left the captain of the frigate no way of even acknowledging their act of defiance.

From that, the Pelicans gained a degree of acceptance, and to have brought out a ship so recently captured, when Ralph Barclay's own attempt to do the same had so signally failed, could only enhance that regard, so many were sorry to see them go, bound for England and freedom. After their departure the surgeon, treating the sailor Dysart for his broken arm and a head wound, was regaled with the true story of what happened in the estuary of the River Trieux by someone who had witnessed it, which differed substantially from what had been claimed by Emily's nephew, and seemingly accepted as truth by his captain.

Toby Burns was seen by the crew as a useless little turd long before that action; nervous of authority as well as any notion of making a decision, the type that would see a man flogged rather than own up to an error, so it had come as no surprise to the crew of HMS *Brilliant* that he had demonstrated precisely those qualities when he found himself stranded on the French shore, nominally, because of his midshipman rank, the man in charge. Given a chance to prove himself as a naval officer he had failed abysmally, displaying craven cowardice rather than leadership, a vacuum that John Pearce had more than adequately filled.

Many members of the crew suspected Ralph Barclay must know more of the truth than he had ever let slip, and if he did, it rendered inexplicable his subsequent actions. Not one of the tars, much as they disliked the man, thought their captain a fool; he must, despite the boy's fairy tales, be able to see him as clearly as any common seaman. They did know he had been given cause to hate John Pearce and speculation suggested he had taken the opportunity to rid himself of a man he saw as a pest, one he might not be able to tame, as well as one around whom discontent could fester. Toby Burns must have been given command of the *Lady Harrington* because he was a nephew by marriage, not for any competence or lies about personal bravery. Or did Ralph Barclay want rid of him too?

But there was one certain fact; having listened to all these truths and theories in confidence, that was something that had to be respected. 'My dear Emily, I cannot see why you are troubling yourself with something which happened months ago.'

Now it was her turn to avoid disclosure; not even

to someone she saw as a close friend would she say that, on the truth might hinge her attitude to her husband and her marriage. It might also impact on the way she saw a blood relative, for if, indeed, Toby Burns was a toad, then she might have no choice but to treat him as such.

'I am a woman, Heinrich.'

'Explanation enough, my dear Emily,' cried Lutyens happily, determined to change the subject. 'Now do you think we can do a round of our patients.'

'As you requested, sir,' said Ralph Barclay, 'the copies of my muster books since I weighed from Sheerness.'

Copies they had to be; every three months the logs and books of a serving vessel were sent off to the Admiralty and the Navy Board to be perused by penny-pinching clerks, men who earned more in a wage than serving officers. It was a wise captain who kept duplicates of everything, for when disputes arose about stores consumed or condemned, ropes and spars used, even the quantity of nails employed in repairs, which they did with depressing regularity, an officer needed the protection of his own accounts to argue his corner.

'Good,' said Hotham. 'Now please be so good as to sit with my second-secretary and identify those on the list you see as both knowledgeable and reliable.'

As yet unaware of what Hotham had in mind, he could do nothing but comply, and as he went through the crew of HMS *Brilliant,* he put a small mark against those who had any knowledge of the impressment which had taken place at the Pelican, and another if he felt he could call on them for support. When pressing, a captain tended to use men who were able to obey orders, however unpleasant, and he was aided by the fact that he had, thanks to Admiral Hotham, at Lisbon, managed a complete change of junior officers. Midshipman Farmiloe was a worry; he would not see where his true interests lay if questioned, so he put a tick against his name. Toby Burns? The boy had not been present, but he was so deep in his uncle's debt he would answer as he was instructed.

Devenow, a huge, beetle-browed bully who was a follower of his, would say whatever he could to help his captain. Kemp, the rat-faced creature whom he knew hated Pearce, also got a double mark and he put a question mark against one of the men he had taken aboard that night, though not from the Pelican, a slippery fellow called Gherson, whom, he had been told, was not at all a friend to those he messed with. Having completed his task, he went back to face Hotham, who had a quick glance at the book.

'It is enough, I fancy, though I see here the name of one of your original lieutenants, Henry Digby.'

'I lost him at Lisbon, sir, if you recall.'

Hotham looked at him from under questioning eyebrows, but he did not point out that Barclay had lost his two other lieutenants in that action off Brittany, one dead, the other so badly wounded he had been shipped to a shore hospital.

'But he is here in Toulon. I put him into HMS *Weazel*, then shipped him out before Benton sailed for Corsica to do work ashore.'

Barclay's smile was one of gratitude; Hotham had sent Pearce off in that ship to deflect his demands and he hoped he was looking to do the same again; the longer the matter could be delayed the less likelihood, in a service which scattered its personnel continuously, there would be to have the number of witnesses required in one place.

'I daresay you are wondering, Barclay, what I have in mind?'

'All I know, sir, is that whatever you intend, I will trust you to have a care for my reputation.'

That piece of sycophancy was accepted by Hotham as his due and now it was his turn to smile. 'I doubt I need to remind you of the case of Captain Bligh.'

'No, sir.'

'Or of Midshipman Thomas Hayward.'

The connection was obvious. Hayward, one of the *Bounty* mutineers forcibly fetched back from Hawaii, had faced a court martial, but he had powerful support from his uncle, Admiral Palsey, and he had the ear of the Admiralty and some influence at court. There was little doubt the boy was guilty, and indeed he had been found so by the court, only to be pardoned by the king. It was generally acknowledged that had Bligh been present to give evidence it would have been so damning that Hayward would have hanged. So the powers that be made sure Captain Bligh was at sea when the court martial took place, which allowed Hayward to escape his well-deserved fate, one faced by a trio of the ship's lower ratings.

'With Captain Benton gone,' added Hotham, 'I have a mind to see Mr Digby promoted into the command of that French capture. He was after all the Premier of HMS *Weazel*, albeit not aboard when she was taken.'

'With respect, sir, his commission is not one of long standing. Will that not put out of joint several more deserving officers, not least some on your own flagship?'

'You are right to point that out, Barclay, but I had in mind a temporary command on a particular service, the reason being that more experienced officers are required here at Toulon for the defence of the port. Since the duty is a tedious one, and there may well be hot action here, I think those officers you mentioned will be well satisfied with my decision. And, if we man that vessel from HMS

Brilliant, plus the waifs and strays from *Leander*, she will have complement enough to do what is required.'

'You are certain, sir, Lord Hood intends to buy her in?'

Hotham's face clouded at the interruption. 'Lord Hood will do so if I request that he do so. And I shall!'

'Forgive me, sir, in my enthusiasm...' He left the sentence unfinished, because what Hotham intended was plain, merely adding, 'Thank you, sir.'

'Brilliant!' shouted the coxswain to the quarterdeck of HMS *Leander*, identifying the captain of that vessel wished to come aboard. Having seen Ralph Barclay's barge approach, Taberly, Officer of the Watch, had called for the half-dozen marines still aboard, and every available midshipman, to make their way to the entry port to greet him. The ship's captain was informed, but he would not stir for an officer of less seniority than himself. Indeed the captain rarely stirred ever, content to leave his officers to run the ship and only come out at the sight of an enemy warship, problems, or defaulters. He was a man more concerned with his rare butterfly collection, and it was, in fact, unusual to find him aboard off a shore with so many species that were not native to England.

'Sir,' said Taberly, lifting his hat.

The visitor did likewise, aiming it at the unseen quarterdeck of the ship and the flag on the mizzen. 'Captain Barclay.'

'Welcome aboard, sir. The captain has been informed of your visit, and I am sure would be happy to receive you in his cabin.'

That was a lie; Barclay would be received, but with reluctance.

'My compliments to the captain, but would you please explain to him I am here on a particular task, on the instructions of Admiral Hotham. He has requested that I fetch some men out of your ship, so that he can have them interviewed. I must return to the flagship with all despatch.'

'Of course, sir. Their names.'

That got Taberly a small piece of paper, and when he saw the four names he was far from pleased. 'I have to inform you, sir, three of these men are due a flogging, two dozen at the grating for insubordinate behaviour.'

'It will have to wait, Mr Taberly, for Admiral Hotham will not. Please be so good as to fetch them to me.'

There was no option but to comply, and one of the mids was sent off on the duty, leaving Taberly and Barclay together. 'It seems you have found them troublesome?'

'It does not do to be so on this ship,' Taberly barked, then realising he was talking to a superior officer he softened his tone. 'The fellow Gherson is a very useful man, sir, and no trouble at all. I would say he would rise to a better rating if he applied himself and given that he can read and write with a clear and elegant hand, and has too a head for figures, it would be no surprise to see him as an assistant to a purser one day.'

'Indeed.' Barclay, reminding himself of Gherson's aversion to Pearce, took Taberly's arm and led him far enough away from the rest of the welcoming party to avoid his low question being overheard. 'Would you say he was reliable?'

Cornelius Gherson had done Taberly many favours, and by identifying O'Hagan as a pugilist of great ability, just after they had weighed from Spithead, he had helped enliven what was slated to be a dull voyage, as well as filling the Taberly purse. Being the only one aware of the Irishman's prowess, he had cleaned out his fellow officers when they had arranged a bout with another known champion. Gherson collected a fair amount in winnings too, to add to the guineas which a grateful Taberly had paid to him. Such detail, of necessity, being illegal under the Articles of War, must remain secret, but the lieutenant knew nevertheless how to answer Barclay's question.

'He is, sir, a man who knows where his duty lies in regard to discipline.'

Deciphering that was no trouble at all; it was authority-speak for a man who would not take the part of his shipmates against those set over him.

The four men, three rubbing red-raw wrists, sore from wearing irons, emerged from below, and it was clear from the distance the trio of defaulters kept from the blond-haired fourth, that they were not friendly. Ralph Barclay examined them with some interest, although he had seen them all before. The curly-haired, square-faced Irishman, O'Hagan, was too big, too much a creature of muscle, to require real scrutiny. Which was Taverner and which Dommet he could not tell, one fair of hair, with a tricorn tipped back on his head in an insolent fashion, which went with his truculent expression, and the other a pallid-faced youngster of slim build and a passive eye. What they all had in common was the shock on their faces as they recognised their old captain.

'Aboard my barge,' he ordered, noticing the slight hesitation, which had him looking hard at O'Hagan, who would doubtless be the leader of those in trouble. 'I believe you are due two dozen. If you don't want that doubled, you will move instantly.'

Michael O'Hagan recognised the expression on Ralph Barclay's face, a scowl that made real his threat. The crew of *Brilliant* had said he was a hard-horse captain, a bit free with the cat, though they had known worse. To Michael O'Hagan he was a downright bastard. The four men lowered themselves into the barge and crowded into the bow, and, after another exchange of compliments, Barclay joined them, sitting in the thwarts and glaring forward. Soon his main attention shifted to Gherson, who had an absurdly handsome face, almost girlish given his petulant expression. A man who would inform on his shipmates, who could read and write in a clear hand, and knew his numbers, might be useful.

John Pearce came to HMS *Britannia* unaware of why he had been summoned, and going below to tell Hotham's secretary that he was on board, he ran straight into Henry Digby. It was amusing to see, in a place of little natural light, his old divisional officer did not react until he spoke.

'Lieutenant Digby, I am pleased to see you.'

Digby leant forward. 'Do I know you, sir?'

'You do indeed,' said Pearce, lifting his hat. 'Have we not served together?'

Digby lifted his hat too, but his eyebrows seemed to go higher. 'It cannot be you, Pearce?'

'It is.' Digby's eyes took in his coat, his breeches, even his shoes, the whole so plainly the garb of a fellow lieutenant. 'I feel it would be in order to explain.'

'Move your arse, lads. Admiral's got a quill scratcher waiting.'

The loud voice made Pearce glance round, and Digby looked over his shoulder for the same reason, to see their old shipmates, three Pelicans and that swine Gherson, being shepherded to another part of the admiral's quarters.

'Michael,' Pearce shouted.

The Irishman turned, grinned, and shrugged his shoulders. Rufus waved, Charlie Taverner gave him a queer look, and Gherson glowered as they were ushered through a small, glass-paned door. The rasping voice made them attend to the other man approaching; Digby tipped his hat, Pearce fingered his sword.

'Mr Digby,' said Ralph Barclay.

'Sir,' Digby replied, 'it seems I am to be subject to no end of surprises today.'

'I will not address the person you are with.'

'You will address me one day, Barclay, over any weapon you choose.'

Digby was shocked at the way Pearce addressed their one-time captain, still confused that someone he had last seen as a common seaman was now of the same rank as he, as well as wondering what it all portended, but at that moment he was called into the Admiral's day cabin. Barclay followed, leaving Pearce standing alone, unable to decide whether he was happy or fuming.

He went to the door through which the four seamen had been ushered, and looked into the small glass panes to see Hotham's under-secretary with quill, and a candle to light his papers, taking notes on the other side. Impulse made him open the door, which earned him a furious look from the scribe.

'Do you mind, sir. I am taking depositions from these men pending the forthcoming court martial of Captain Barclay.'

'Sorry,' Pearce replied, immediately shutting the door.

So he was going to get Barclay in the dock! That thought pleased him mightily, and, much as he wanted to put a sword or a ball though him, John Pearce decided that the ruin of him must come first. Only when he had been shredded of his naval dignity would he challenge Barclay to the duel in which he would pay for the insults he had heaped on him.

'Mr Digby, you are to take command of the vessel captured by HMS *Weazel,* now renamed HMS *Faron,* your duty to escort four French seventy-fours, and some five thousand seamen, to the Atlantic ports from whence they came. They are a bunch of revolutionary vermin, who will not accept orders from their commander. You are to have no consort with them or their officers, your duty is merely to see them into their home ports and return here with all despatch. You will be seconded by Lieutenant Pearce and your crew will be made up with drafts from HMS *Brilliant* and HMS *Leander*. You will, of necessity, be short-handed, given that we need here every man who can be spared, but since I anticipate no action that will not be a burden. In fact, it may make sure you are not tempted to go prize-hunting.'

Digby had seen a great deal of Hotham; he had for a short time, before being shifted to serve under the now dead Benton, been one of the eight lieutenants on this very ship, though given the superior attitude of his fellow officers, not least the Premier, it had been a far from happy experience.

'I must point out, Mr Digby, that this is a temporary appointment. You will know from your own date of commission that you lack the seniority for such a position, yet Captain Barclay here has told me you are a competent officer.'

Digby had to nod his thanks to Ralph Barclay, but he wondered at the words. He had the impression that he was not much liked by the captain of HMS *Brilliant*, as well as the knowledge that the feeling was mutual, something he had been obliged to disguise on seeing him again.

'It will, of course,' Barclay said smoothly, 'enhance your record. After all, having through circumstance served as my Premier, such a commission as this can do you no harm.'

Why did he not believe him? And how the hell could John Pearce, who from the earlier showing was a mortal enemy of this man, be an officer fit to serve under him. It did not smell good and the temptation to exercise his right to decline the commission was strong; he felt he was being set up for a fall. Yet if he did decline, he would look in vain for advancement elsewhere. The word would spread, and being as lowly as he was in rank, he could think of no gloss he could put on such a rebuff to Hotham that would make it sound like a correct response.

'Please proceed aboard the prize, Mr Digby. My secretary has your commission on his desk, as well as your orders. Check your water and wood, and indent the Toulon Arsenal for stores, powder and shot and any cordage and canvas you require. Captain Barclay will send over your crew at once. I want you prepared to weigh within twenty-four hours.'

'Sir.'

'And Mr Digby, on your way out, please ask Lieutenant Pearce to come in.'

Chapter Seven

'You must understand, Pearce, that if I am going to sanction a court martial on an officer of the standing of Captain Barclay it has to be properly prepared and that will take time.'

Pearce, sitting opposite Hotham, was wondering where the man in question had gone. Barclay had entered the cabin with Digby, but he had not exited and there was no sign of him being present now, but then there was more than one door to the spacious area occupied by an admiral. He had come in with Hotham's secretary on his heels, and that fellow was now taking notes.

'Are you attending to what I am saying, sir,' Hotham barked. Pearce said sorry before he felt it to be feeble; apologising to anyone who claimed authority always made him feel that way. 'Good. As I was saying, Captain Barclay is an officer who is highly regarded in many quarters, and that of which you are accusing him could put a serious blight on his career. I cannot see busy officers of the required rank rushing to sit in judgement on him, and I do not look forward to putting pressure on them to attend.'

'I was rather hoping, sir, that since pressing men who are not seamen is illegal under the law of the land, it might lead to a criminal prosecution in front of a judge of the King's Bench.'

'You are showing an unbecoming degree of bile, sir.'

That made John Pearce sit forward and raise his voice. 'I was, sir, taken by force from a location that made his actions doubly illegal, in short, the Liberties of the Savoy.'

Hotham's face took on a look of pure distaste. 'I will not ask what you were doing in such a disreputable place, Mr Pearce.'

'Which only confirms to me, sir, that you know of it, know that no bailiff is allowed within its boundaries, and certainly no naval officer intent on seeking men. The whole area is protected by ancient statute. Might I add that not only were myself and more than a dozen others taken from there, but we were then subject to a treatment that could only be called, at the very least, common assault.'

'I must say,' the secretary cut in, having seen Hotham close to an explosion, 'you seem very knowledgeable on the law.'

'Having been hounded by the so-called law for a fair degree of my life, sir, that is essential. If I may continue…'

Hotham slammed his hand on the table. 'Enough. My secretary will take your deposition in writing, the same as is being done to those you claim are your companions, but we are not here for that, we are here to discuss your next commission.'

'Whatever it is, I will probably decline it.'

'Then, sir, I must tell you that your companions in your claimed misfortune will be returned to HMS *Leander*, forthwith, where, I am informed, they are due to face punishment.'

'What kind of punishment?'

Hotham looked at Pearce as if he was a fool, and in truth it was a dammed silly remark. There were options on punishment, but the way the admiral had said it, it could only be a flogging. He suppressed the temptation to enquire the nature of the offence; it made little difference to those who would suffer.

'However, should you accept to serve under Lieutenant Digby aboard the prize taken by HMS *Weazel*, now HMS *Faron*, I will release them into your charge to serve aboard that vessel for the duration of the commission.'

The wording of that was interesting; Hotham could not bring himself to say, as he no doubt would to any other officer, that Pearce, as the officer in command, had taken the prize. Yet it was the truth; he had only been part of it, knowledge of which lessened what was no doubt intended as a slight. As to the options he had, they were zero; he could not abandon his friends to an unknown number of strokes from the cat or deny them the chance to get away from the harsh regime they were presently under.

'And the duty, sir?'

'I do not think it is my place to inform you of that. I would not dream of interfering with the prerogatives of a Master and Commander. Ask Mr Digby.'

'And the date for the court martial?'

'Yet to be decided, but not before your return, which I anticipate will be not more than one calendar month.' Pearce looked at the scribbling secretary to ensure he was writing that down, and Hotham added, 'By that time, matters should have settled here in Toulon and officers can be spared from other duties to see to the matter. Now go with my secretary and make a deposition, which the person who volunteers to defend Captain Barclay can read.'

'You are Gherson, are you not?'

The man was standing well away from the three others with whom he had been fetched aboard, and he looked, Ralph Barclay thought, angry enough to spit. The reason was simple, though Ralph Barclay had no knowledge of it; he had not been taken out of the Pelican like the others, he had been fetched out of a roaring River Thames, having been chucked off London Bridge by a pair of ruffians hired to pay him back for his sins, both carnal and fiscal. The City Alderman who had engaged those brutes had been his employer; the man's wife, a much younger creature, often left alone while her husband was out on his pleasures or his duties, had succumbed to the Gherson charm and become his lover. She had also opened her household account to him, and when that was added to the money which he stole in his capacity as the Alderman's bookkeeper, young Gherson had enjoyed a comfortable existence, dressing well and eating and drinking his fill.

It had ended that night, as, stripped of everything but his shirt, he had hit the freezing water of the Thames, which was like a tidal race as it came through the arches of the bridge, sure he was going to drown. That he had landed right by a naval cutter was pure chance, and with men of strength aboard they had hauled him in and fetched him aboard their frigate. In telling his tale to the clerk the quartet had just left, he had been informed that his case against the man before him was specious; his impressment, as a body saved from certain death by being fished out of the river, was legal.

'Answer me, fellow.' The soft voice, so unusual, made Gherson look up at his old captain. There was no affection in the look of either man, but there was curiosity. 'I spoke with Mr Taberly when I came to fetch you. He tells me you write with a clear hand and you know your numbers.'

'What if I do?' Gherson demanded, clearly suspecting a trap.

Ralph Barclay had to hold himself back from cuffing the insolent sod; he would not take that kind of tone from any rating. 'Tell me, Gherson, what is your opinion of John Pearce?'

'Why do you want to know?'

'Sir!'

Gherson lost his arrogance and seemed to shrink, touching his forelock with an expression of abject alarm. The man questioning him was an officer with years of experience, so he immediately put him down as a physical coward, which, oddly, acted for, not against him.

'Pearce thinks he's God's gift.' He indicated the other three men, standing well away and looking at the exchange with deep interest and Gherson's voice rose so they could hear. 'Which might work for those fools yonder, but it don't for me. Pearce is now't but mutton dressed as lamb, and he was that before he donned that blue coat.'

Ralph Barclay saw the man O'Hagan clench his fists and he knew, if he had not been present

Gherson would have paid for that outburst. He kept his voice deliberately low as he responded.

'Then you are in for a hard time, man. As of today, you will be under his command.'

'Never! I'll run rather than suffer that.'

Ralph Barclay laughed. 'To where. Into the arms of the Revolution perhaps?'

'Somewhere, anywhere.'

'I have to say that I feel sorry for you, Gherson, so I am going to make you an offer. I sailed from England without a clerk to keep my papers in order.' He was not prepared to admit it had been brought on by penury; he put down a relative's name and pocketed the money a clerk would have been due as a captain's servant. 'So I have a position free for a fellow with the right abilities. If you agree, I will have you transferred back to HMS *Brilliant*, and give you the position I have just mentioned. It will be temporary, but if you apply yourself with diligence, it can be yours permanently. At least you will not have to sail under Pearce.'

Gherson, whose eyes had widened as Ralph Barclay spoke, positively grovelled, trying to take his hand to kiss it. 'Belay that man. Pick up your dunnage and go to the entry port. My barge is standing off. Call it in and get aboard.'

'Your honour.'

'One more thing, Gherson. I expect, that when I

face the court martial being forced on the admiral by Pearce, you will bear witness to the truth?'

'Happily, captain, happily.'

'Might I ask who has taken on the task of defending Barclay?'

Hotham's secretary corrected him immediately. 'Captain Barclay, and the answer is no one yet, though I anticipate there will be many who will put themselves forward.'

'Am I free to go?'

The secretary lifted up the several pages of writing which was Pearce's written evidence and made a show of looking at it. He then proffered a quill and the last sheet to be signed, which John Pearce did with a flourish. A languid hand indicated that he should depart and as he came out on to the maindeck, he saw Barclay ending his conversation with Gherson, saw the treacherous sod pick up the small ditty bag that contained his possessions and head for the entry port, giving Michael O'Hagan a wide berth. Looking back, Gherson saw Pearce as well, and the gloating look on his face made Pearce wonder what the bastard was up to now. Barclay had turned and re-entered the door from which he had no doubt exited, leaving Pearce to walk over to his friends.

'Michael, Rufus, Charlie.' As their hands moved to touch their foreheads he barked, 'Don't you dare.'

'Sure,' said Michael, grinning, 'it's only for show, John-boy.'

'Are we free?' asked Charlie.

'Not free, no, at least not yet.' That made Charlie frown; he was always the most vocal of their plight, and the one inclined to remind Pearce of his previous failures to get them free. 'But you are to have the misfortune of serving under me, and I am about to serve under our old lieutenant, Mr Digby.'

O'Hagan's face lit up, all his teeth were visible. 'Holy Mother of God, John, after what we have had, it sounds like free to me.'

'Then pick up your bags. I must go to the Officer of the Watch and request a boat.'

'Will we be free, John?' asked Rufus.

'If it can be done, we four will do it. There is going to be a court martial on Barclay when we return, so the sooner we get moving the sooner that might be. Now come along.'

They were all grinning as they responded. 'Aye, aye, sir.'

Looking at the up-to-date muster book, Ralph Barclay was seeking those men it would be best to send into the prize. Sykes, his bosun, he would like to have sent, but the movement of a ship's standing officers, Bosun, Gunner, Carpenter and Purser, was not within his powers, and the man would hardly volunteer to go into a ship half the size of his present warrant. Still, he could ask. For the rest it would be the standing officers' assistants who would get the nod, though he had a care to keep with him those who he thought he could call as witnesses in his defence.

At another table, Gherson was examining the rest of the ship's books, which told of what stores HMS *Brilliant* carried, had a record of what she had consumed in a list of articles that ran into the hundreds. Having raided the Toulon Arsenal, the ship was well found in everything, and Gherson was looking for those gaps where he could purloin a bit, something to set aside which he could sell should the occasion arise. He would need the connivance of the correct members of the crew; only the gunner had access to powder, a valuable commodity, likewise the carpenter with timber and tools. The purser would have his own peccadilloes, so there it was a case of finding out what he was up to and hoping that a little would fall his way. Canvas, cordage and lifting tackle was an impossibility: Sykes, the bosun, was too honest.

The man who had employed him thought he had the measure of Gherson; he knew he would try to cheat him, all clerks did, just like the servants at home in Frome. But for a man who had needed to be careful of his purse before taking up this command, indeed one who had had the tipstaff banging their staff of office on his door, it took a canny soul to bamboozle him. Let Gherson try, that would at least bear some testimony to his competence – but he would be brought up with a round turn, and told, in no uncertain terms, that the proceeds from anything purloined must be shared, and must be done in a way no admiralty clerk could spot.

The knock on the door admitted Midshipman Farmiloe, gangly and fair, and somewhat in terror of his commanding officer.

'Mr Farmiloe, we have orders to remain at this berth, which will be the death of an enthusiast like yourself. I have therefore agreed that you should have a temporary shift to HMS *Faron*. It's that French prize you saw come in. Mr Digby commands her and she is off on a cruise. Much more suitable than languishing here, what?'

If Ralph Barclay had not been so cheerful, Farmiloe would have accepted with the grace that was clearly expected, but smiling good news was not his captain's habit, so his response was mumbled.

'I want you to sort out the following men. Gherson, take note of these names. Costello, Dysart, Dent, both the Kempshalls, Dorling, Lanky Smith...' The names were reeled off, with Farmiloe wondering how Gherson had got to be where he was. Mind, he was a useless bugger on deck from what the midshipman could recall, so he was probably better off here. 'Tell them to get their dunnage together and be prepared to shift.'

Ralph Barclay stared at the deck before him, and sifted through troubled thoughts. His bosun was a real problem, since he could be called to give evidence. 'Send Mr Sykes to me, if you please.'

Toby Burns knocked and entered. 'Mrs Barclay approaching, sir.'

'See your aunt aboard, Mr Burns. I am busy.'

Cornelius Gherson was looking hard at a set of figures, but he was not really reading them now. He had forgotten the captain's delicious wife, and the thoughts he was harbouring as he recalled her would have seen him chucked overboard. She was very young compared to her husband. He never even considered that such actions had got him into trouble before; that had been someone else's fault, not his. This was, quite possibly, going to be a bit of better good fortune than he had at first surmised. When she entered the cabin, and made what was memory dull by the reality of her presence, he felt his blood race.

'Don't stare, Gherson, it lacks manners.'

Barclay's rebuke had him looking at his books again, but an introduction had him on his feet.

'My dear, allow me to name Cornelius Gherson. I have engaged him to be my clerk.'

'I know your face, Mr Gherson,' said Emily.

He nearly blurted out that he knew hers, but he forced himself into an obsequious nod.

'He was one of my Sheerness volunteers, my dear, and damn me...' Seeing the look that minor blasphemy brought to his wife's face he looked contrite, yet thinking it was a burden to be with sailors one minute and a wife of strict manners the next. 'Anyway, I had no idea he was accomplished in the clerkish line, but now I do.'

'Is this to be his place of work, husband?'

Please, thought Gherson, unaware of why the question had been posed. It was because of Ralph Barclay's sailor-servant, Shenton, who had been with him for years of bachelorhood and had not taken kindly to his master having his wife aboard. He was, to Emily Barclay, a nuisance, never knocking when he should and, in his own subtle way, letting it be known that he saw her as an interloper. Another person with unrestricted access to this cabin was not to be welcomed.

'No, my dear. We will find him a crib in which he can work.'

Another knock and Sykes entered. 'You sent for me, sir.'

There was a terrible temptation to scowl at the man. Sykes was competent but lacked the necessary fire, being a bit soft on the hands, and Ralph Barclay had had to rebuke him more than once for what he saw as Sykes mollycoddling them, which always produced a look of injury. But it would not do; he had to look gracious. A quick explanation followed, in the same vein as that given to Farmiloe, with the captain unaware that by now everyone on the ship knew what was afoot.

'I just wonder if the experience will be better than sitting here, Sykes, when we are fully rigged and only the odd bit of grease or tar needed to keep us shipshape. I can tell you we will not weigh until Toulon is either secured or abandoned, and I know that Mr Digby could use a capable man.'

The alacrity with which the offer was accepted quite offended the giver; the man might have at least have pondered, but then he did not know how much Sykes disliked him, nor had his mind moved at the same speed. The bosun could go on a detached duty, but his place aboard the frigate was secure. No one but Lord Hood could take it from him, and even if he did Sykes could appeal above the C-in-C's head to the Navy Board.

'Very decent of you, sir, and I thank you for your consideration.'

There was a terrible temptation to do the same to *Brilliant*'s master, who was a useless timid sod, but that would be a step too far. 'Right, Sykes, ask Mr Glaister to join me; we must work out some revised watch lists.'

'And, Mr Digby, I have to inform you that I lack the knowledge to do the task for which I have been selected.'

Digby had listened with increasing disbelief as Pearce had outlined his adventures of the last six months, since he had seen him go over the side of HMS *Brilliant* off the Brittany coast, already having seen action. To be pressed once was bad enough, to be pressed twice was hellish, yet there was also a strand of envy mixed up with wonder at the amount of conflict Pearce had seen. It was the stuff of a junior officer's dreams. The man, despite his insistence on naming other people as responsible for what success he had enjoyed, seemed touched by some divine providence in the article of opportunity. To help in the capture of a French 74, which might have sunk a British 50, was fantastic.

'Might I suggest that you seek the appointment of another officer.'

That was tempting; to have as his second-in-command someone of so little experience was bound to place an extra burden on him, and it was not as if Pearce wanted it. What he asked next was what killed the notion.

'I would of course want O'Hagan, Taverner and Dommet released into my care.'

Digby was quite brusque; Pearce ashore and close to Barclay with that trio to aid him was too risky to be considered. The man might not be beyond secret murder, and where would that leave him!

'I must decline both requests, Mr Pearce. We

have been given a duty to perform and it is up to us to execute that to the best of our ability. Now you will cease to be so unconstructive and help me to work out how we are going to fill the various offices that must be occupied. Not one of the men Captain Barclay proposes to send us, apart from Mr Sykes and Costello, has a true rating over able seaman, and we are still short of a master and probably another midshipman.

'Then can I suggest, sir, you request that they should come from HMS *Weazel*. Mr Neame, you must know, is an excellent master, and Harbin I rate very highly.' Digby was nodding slowly, while Pearce was thinking that with those two aboard some of his inexperience could be disguised. 'Oh, and my Pelicans have requested that we ask for a couple of hands from *Leander*. Their names are Latimer and Blubber Booth. Both good men who can hand, reef and steer.'

'I will see what I can do, but we must show some haste, for there is much to be taken aboard in terms of stores. We have to be ready to weigh by this time tomorrow.'

Chapter Eight

Coming aboard the newly commissioned HMS *Faron*, Lieutenant Digby was greeted by the boy who had brought her in, Midshipman Harbin, who was immediately asked if he was prepared to stay aboard. It was telling that he hesitated, pointing out that his ship was HMS *Weazel*, and only assented when he heard from where the recommendation had come, and that the same fellow who made it would be joining them. Farmiloe came aboard with the draft from Ralph Barclay, and though he seemed a personable enough lad, the mention of that same officer produced a dramatically different result; the notion of Lieutenant John Pearce sharing the same deck did not please him at all.

'Mr Sykes, at your service, sir, and right glad to see you again. Captain Barclay has agreed that I may serve on your ship on this commission, if that is acceptable to you.'

'Acceptable, Mr Sykes, it is damned handsome,' Digby replied, not willing to say what he really thought, that it was damned odd.

'It is only because he has orders to keep our ship in the inner harbour with enough men to man the guns, a floating battery so to speak. Admiral Hood intends to keep Johnny Crapaud honest. Any sign of backsliding and it's a cannonball through the winders.'

Digby raised an eyebrow, not at the notion, which was sound, but at the easy way that Sykes talked of it; surely such a thing should be in the nature of a secret. Mind, he had never ceased to be surprised at the way sailors found out things that should not be vouchsafed to them. Keeping a secret aboard a ship was something generally held to be well nigh impossible unless the captain was so close-mouthed he told no one of any action he contemplated.

'Then you will know, Mr Sykes, of our intended duty.'

The bull-necked bosun grinned, reminding Digby that, with the exception of his dealings with Ralph Barclay, the man had a habit of general good cheer. 'Whole port and fleet knows that by now, your honour.'

'Then the whole fleet will also know how much time we have to complete our stores. Best get to work, Mr Sykes, and I suggest you start by inspecting how we are fixed in the article of canvas and cordage.'

Sykes gave instructions to the men with whom he had come aboard, and Digby greeted each one he could remember by name as they passed him, pleased that they seemed content to be coming aboard his ship, then immediately concerned that the reason could be that they might see him as soft.

'Mr Farmiloe, I have here a list of stores compiled after ship's capture. Please be so good as to go below and ensure it is accurate.' Farmiloe looked at the sheet, and pointed out that it was dated not more than a week past, to which Digby replied, 'Time enough for tempted fingers to diminish it substantially. I need to know precisely what to request from the storehouse ashore, and I would not dare start off short.'

'Mr Pearce approaching, sir,' called Harbin.

'Very good, Mr Harbin. See to Mr Farmiloe, tell him where to stow his dunnage, and then report back to me.'

Digby was suddenly aware that the approach of Pearce, with the three other Pelicans in the thwarts, had taken everyone's attention; in fact no one was doing anything. In a voice that was heard in half the ships in the anchorage he yelled at them to 'get a move on', and was pleased by the response, forced to turn away to hide his smile. Men were rushing to their duty; he might be remembered a considerate soul, but he was not going to be thought lenient.

'Sure that's a fair old roar, John-boy,' said Michael O'Hagan, 'are you sure it was Digby?'

The men on the oars, all from Hotham's flagship, looked at each other to register their surprise, not for the first time, that a common seaman should address an officer so.

'That, Michael, is the voice of one in command, and if you think it loud, wait till you hear me. I think you will be surprised.'

O'Hagan laughed out loud. 'Jesus, never. Did I not tell you once that you were made for a blue coat?'

'And I saw you as a positive tyrant,' added Charlie Taverner, with just a trace in his voice that the remark was not wholly tongue in cheek.

Pearce knew he had a problem with these three, probably he would have a problem with the crew he was about to face, because they knew him more as one of their own than as an officer. He had been gnawing on how to deal with it, and come to the conclusion that it would find its own level, for he could not behave in any other way than his conscience dictated. If any act of his caused offence, so be it, but now was as good a time as any to lay down a marker.

'I have learnt, my friends, a ship must run smooth, that there is no place for laxity, for the sea will surely take you if you do not treat it with respect, and so will an enemy. I hope you too have absorbed this lesson.'

'I don't know what you mean,' said young Rufus.

Charlie's voice had no humour now. 'It means, Rufus, that when John Pearce shouts shit, the likes of us jump on the shovel.'

'Stow it, Charlie,' Michael responded, as the boat came alongside. He was already following Pearce through the gangway, when he added, 'John-boy will not become a Barclay just because he has the dress, but obey him we must, if he asks us to.'

'It'll be hard, Michael.'

'I do not recall it so. I seem to remember we was happy to follow his lead when we were last in real trouble.'

The reference to Brittany made Charlie Taverner shut up.

'That'll be a damn rum vessel an' no error,' said the man coxing the *Britannia*'s boat, as they pulled clear. 'Paddy's Market by the sound of it. Ain't never heard the like, disputing with an officer like that. Navy's goin' to the dogs.'

'Mr Pearce,' said Digby, responding to the raised hat. 'I welcome you aboard, though I have a feeling it should be the other way round.'

Pearce did not want to think of that, nor of Digby occupying quarters the like of which had so recently been his own. 'I hope you recall our old shipmates, sir?'

'That I do, Mr Pearce, and I welcome you aboard also. I have sent in a request to the flagship to be allowed to warp into the mole to take on stores, so we will need the boats manned as soon as that is given. Please be so good as to tell Mr Sykes this will be his next task after he has checked the sail lockers and the cable tier.'

'Aye, aye, sir.'

As they made for the companionway, Digby called Pearce back to him, and said quietly, 'I know, sir, you have an attachment to these fellows that exceeds the bounds of normal duty, and while I respect it, I cannot allow it to interfere with the running of the ship.'

'I know of the problem, sir, as I know that it is one with which I will have to deal.'

'Let me say with some sincerity, it would not please me if that problem were to become mine.'

It was a sight easier to load stores from the mole than from boats or floating hoys, though there was no other way to bring aboard water, which was being pumped by hose from the seaward side, each barrel assembled from staves by the cooper, then sealed as much as was possible when full. It was damp work, but since the day was warm it was also pleasant, better than just hauling on ropes to hoist in beef and pork from the carts on the shore, so the men shifting the water barrels were rotated with others so that the tasks were shared out evenly. Digby did not drive the men with harsh words, but encouraged them with orders dressed as requests, and both Pearce and Robert Sykes took their cue from him. They carried the same weight as barked commands, but were not resented.

Ralph Barclay was on his poop, a glass to his eye, watching the progress of the work, unsure if he should be pleased or resentful that it seemed to be going smoothly. Occasionally he could see Pearce and on more than one occasion the man was laughing, either at some remark he had made, or a response he had received from the men of whom he was in charge.

'Unbecoming, damned unbecoming.'

'Sir?' Barclay turned to see Midshipman Toby Burns beside him, small, his face a mass of adolescent spots, his eyes full of what could only be trepidation. 'You sent for me, sir.'

The glass went back to Barclay's eye. 'So I did. I wish you to proceed to yonder ship, the French capture, and ask Mr Digby if he would care to dine with Mrs Barclay and I tonight. And Burns, I wish you to make a point of issuing that invitation in the hearing of that blackguard, Pearce.'

'With respect, sir, could I decline the duty and send another.'

'What!'

Inside a uniform coat still too big for him, though

less so than when he had first donned it, Toby Burns was trembling at the prospect; it was too easy to recall the silence that had allowed Pearce and his friends to be pressed for a second time, when a word from him could have saved them. The cold threats John Pearce has issued at their last encounter, to pay him back for his duplicity, were potent enough to terrify him.

'With respect, sir...'

'Damn your respect, sir. Give me one good reason why I should accede to such a foolish request?'

The quiver in the boy's voice was unmistakable. 'On our last encounter, sir, in strict obedience to your orders should the *Lady Harrington* meet a King's ship in soundings, I fear I made an enemy of Pearce by making no attempt to interfere with his being pressed again. Had I done so I am sure he and his companions would have retained their liberty, and I have no doubt that should the opportunity present itself he will seek to exact revenge for my actions.'

'If you obeyed me, Mr Burns, you have nought to fear.'

Bollocks, the boy thought, blushing at the mere notion that this uncle by marriage might discern his silent disagreement. Ralph Barclay had made it plain when he sent the *Lady Harrington* away that such an encounter was very possible, and also that it was one which would please him. But he had not been within sight of the coast of England, had not seen the look in Pearce's eye at being so close to freedom and having it taken away by another King's officer, had not heard the way the words had been delivered, promising deadly retribution to a youngster whose life he had saved. And it was not just Pearce who felt betrayed by him, but that huge Irishman, O'Hagan.

'Lieutenant Pearce...'

Ralph Barclay interrupted the boy again. 'Please do not grace him with that rank in my presence, Mr Burns.'

'I was about to say, sir, that the fellow has no knowledge of my return to HMS *Brilliant,* and if I could keep it so, I would be grateful.'

Saying that, Burns had reminded Ralph Barclay of why he had got shot of the little bugger in the first place, it being too good an opportunity to miss. Quite apart from being useless, and, from what he had heard about the action in the Trieux Estuary, more than a touch shy, he was Emily's nephew, and that complicated the relationship between them; he could not as easily chastise her cousin as he could another mid, and the boy was a whimperer. God, the little sod looked as though he could burst into tears right now!

'Very well, Mr Burns. Go and ask Shenton to deliver my message.'

'I am grateful, sir, so grateful.'

'Get on with it, boy,' snapped Ralph Barclay, once more training his telescope on the toiling figures both on Digby's deck and on the mole.

Burns rushed into the cabin, for Shenton was not in his pantry, to find his aunt sitting there at her embroidery. What was it about the look she gave him that was so different, not the kindly smile he had come to expect?

'I have been sent to find Shenton, Aunt Emily.'

She was now looking intently at her stitching. 'I believe you will find him with the cook.'

'Thank you,' Burns called as he rushed out.

Emily lifted her head then and looked at the open skylight no more than a few feet above her head, through which she had heard every word of the exchange between her husband and her nephew. What orders had the former given that had left Toby in terror of John Pearce; again, what was so different from her perception of what had taken place, as against the reality? The sharp stab of the needle into her finger was almost deliberate, and as she sucked on the blood it produced, tasting the salt, her thoughts were more uncomfortable than any puncture of the skin.

'I fear I must decline Captain Barclay's kind offer, Shenton. Admiral Hotham has requested that we be ready to weigh tomorrow and I dare not disobey such a command. Do however convey my gratitude

to the captain and his wife and say should my duty
permit on another occasion, I would be happy to
accept.'

Daft sod, thought Shenton, who knew his master
better than anyone, having served with him through
good times and bad since he was first made post.
Shenton prided himself on knowing how his
captain's mind worked. He had issued the invitation
to Digby, but his look had been fixed on Pearce, so
the upstart should not mistake the message; the
invite did not extend to him. As for Digby, would
he guess at Ralph Barclay's ploy? The newly
promoted Master and Commander was never
expected to accept; it was only a way to send an
insult to John Pearce.

'My compliments to your master,' said Digby,
'but we must get back to our task.'

They were still working after the sun went down,
lanterns hoisted into the rigging, dinner taken for
officers and men almost in between assignments,
not resented by the lower ranks for being a shared
experience, until, near ten of the clock, Henry
Digby could pronounce himself satisfied as he
looked over his untidy decks. He was, with the
exception of that, ready for sea.

'The decks,' Pearce asked, knowing it was his
duty to do so, for they were in an unholy state.

Digby replied in a voice loud enough to be heard
from taffrail to bowsprit. 'Can wait till the

morning, Mr Pearce, and I think an extra tot of rum for the men would be in order.'

'I fear it will have to be brandy, sir,' Pearce said. 'This is, after all, in the article of spirituous liquor, a French ship.'

'Brandy it is then, Mr Pearce, but do not ever say such a thing again. This is a King's ship, an English King's ship.'

'With respect, sir, I think our vessel is British.'

'Well said,' came a voice from nearby, which Pearce recognised as that of another Scot, Dysart.

Digby frowned at the remark, then actually laughed. 'Well, will a couple of prickly Jocks take a French drink with me?'

'Most happily, sir.'

Digby added quietly. 'Pearce, remind me to indent the fleet store ship for some rum tomorrow. Should the crew become fractious, brandy will not serve. It's bad enough having wine instead of beer.'

It was typical of the King's Navy, or at least of the senior officers who ran it, to insist on haste where none was necessary. Digby had worked his new crew hard, yet when they warped out into the anchorage and began to put the decks in order, no instructions came to do anything. Mr Neame had come aboard at first light, and as soon as the ship was away from the mole he declared it so far down on the stern as to be close to dangerous, which involved a great deal of shifting of the stores already stowed. This took place while the master and the captain stood off in a boat examining the change in trim, while Pearce had the unenviable task of telling everyone what to do.

Not that it mattered; they found that the ships they were designated to escort had not yet been even cleared of their cannon, powder and shot. It was in musing on that fact, once the captain and master were back on board, which caused Pearce to call into question what their ship could do if any one of the French seventy-fours decided the course they were supposed to steer could be changed.

'You have a point there, Pearce,' Digby replied. 'If we cannot coerce them our only reason for being along is to ensure they are not impeded, which is, I suspect the way the admiral's mind is working. We need the means to invoke a degree of fear as well.'

'A couple of carronades would serve, sir. Since they are to have nothing but signal guns, we would have the ability to come right up to pistol shot and put a ball in their hull.'

'I have to confess, Mr Pearce, to never having seen a carronade in action, and only on the odd occasion one loaded in dumb show.'

That was a telling admission and an admirable one. 'Then let me tell you, sir, I have, and they are a fearsome weapon. The scantlings of even a 74-gun ship-of-the-line will not stand sustained fire from that weight of shot at close range.'

'I shall put a request in to the admiral. If he agrees they must come from a ship which at present has them aboard. It is not a cannon we would find in the Toulon Arsenal, given the French don't have them. Mr Harbin, fetch me the senior gunner and the acting carpenter. If we can get a pair, I need to know where we can site them.'

Watching the exchange, when the two acting warrants engaged in the discussion, Pearce could see Digby almost caressing the ship, and insisting on a clear opinion from his inferiors, evidence that he had already formed an almost physical bond of the kind he had already observed in other vessels. It was in the nature of sailors to love their ships, and to talk of them in familiar terms, not surprising in such a superstitious setting, and also one that if it failed to float left little to look forward to but drowning.

'He seems a good man, John-boy,' whispered Michael O'Hagan, who had come alongside.

'I think he is nothing like Barclay, Michael.'

'Holy mother of God, I hope there is only one of that stripe.'

'Sadly, my friend, I doubt there is, and you know as well as I do, because we have been told, there are worse.'

'Then we will be well out of it.'

'We will.'

'Charlie and Rufus want to know when that might be?'

'Not you?'

O'Hagan grinned. 'Me too.'

'When we return here, there will be a court martial on Barclay, and I have no doubt it will find our case as proven. The evidence is overwhelmingly in our favour. You will then be within your rights to demand transport back to England.'

'And you?'

'I will come with you, of course.'

'I wonder, John-boy. I have watched you this last day and it seems to me you are happy in what you are doing.'

Pearce was guarded; Michael was touching on thoughts he had harboured himself. So much had happened since his sudden, unwarranted elevation. The packet that had brought him from Portsmouth to Gibraltar had been commanded by the sterling Captain McGann, who insisted that a naval career was not a bad one for a man who had no idea for any other. After Corsica, with Benton dead, he had sat in the main cabin as a captain, and enjoyed the feeling of being in command of men who looked up to him, not least freckle-faced Harbin. But the crew, buoyed with the success of the recent action, had shown a marked degree of respect for his office, and that too had been pleasant.

'I will make the best of what I have, while I have

it.' Discomfited by the point Michael was making, he called to the other midshipman aboard. 'Mr Farmiloe, if you please.'

'Sir,' said the mid, his face far from happy.

Though he had worked as hard as any other to load the ship, he had done his best not to get close to Pearce or any of the others he had helped to press from the Pelican Tavern. He knew, from being aboard *Brilliant*, just how much they resented what had happened to them, but what he had just heard was a command; he had no choice but to respond. It was worrying that Pearce had called to him while standing next to the big Irish bruiser. In his young mind, all sorts of threats manifested themselves in the few seconds he took to cross the deck.

'Mr Farmiloe, I know you were a member of the party who pressed O'Hagan and I from the Pelican Tavern.'

'I was obeying Captain Barclay's orders, sir.'

'I was just about to say, and I think I can speak for the others, that we are aware of that. We hold no resentment to you personally. Am I right, Michael?'

'Sure, he's only a strip of a lad, John-boy.'

Farmiloe tried and failed to hide his surprise at that familiarity, yet it registered one salient fact; that these men were still a close-knit group, and one he would do well to be careful with.

'So, Mr Farmiloe,' Pearce continued, 'you have

no need to be evasive. We are to serve together and if I have learnt anything in the limited time I have been afloat, it is best to be civil rather than fractious.'

'Thank you, sir.'

'So, you can sleep easy in your berth.'

Farmiloe touched his hat and went back to his precious position.

'Well said, John-boy, and necessary.'

'Tell the others to treat him with respect, Michael. It will sound better coming from you.'

'This court martial, when is it to be?'

'When we return here. They cannot have it without we are present and the fact has been taken down in the presence of Admiral Hotham's secretary. So, instead of sitting around fretting, I am happy to go on what is set to be an uneventful cruise.'

'Flag signalling, sir,' shouted Harbin. 'Captain to repair aboard.'

'Orders at last,' said Digby, minutes later, as he went over the side.

Chapter Nine

'Here we are in the midst of a damned siege, and what does our French ally propose, a costume ball.'

'Captain Barclay, I must remind you of the lack of politeness in your language.'

He reacted as a husband sick of being pulled up, which he was, both figuratively and physically, for he had to cease pacing to respond. 'Surely, madam, it does not signify in the privacy of our own quarters?'

Emily spoke firmly, but was careful in her tone, trying not to sound shrewish. 'It is a habit, sir, and one that will spill out in polite society. I will not, of course, refer to my own feelings on the matter.'

Humbugged, thought Ralph Barclay, for in the face of that invocation there was nought to do but apologise, though it was a mumbled one he felt retained a little of his dignity. There was resentment too, and another occasion to wonder if his notion of bringing her to sea with him had been wise. That it had saved expense seemed less of a pressing reason now he had some prize money coming both from what happened off Brittany and the recapture of a merchant ship he had effected on the way to Toulon. Even so, it took no great exercise of memory to recall how strapped he had been on taking up this command. Already in debt, he had had to incur more to show even a half-decent fist of the requirements that went with his rank.

What really offended him was the change in his young wife. Both at home in Somerset, and on coming aboard, she had been meekness itself, deferring to him in all things as was right and proper in a marriage. Yet that had not lasted and he could date her first act of defiance to the day he had punished Pearce, and it had not been private rebellion, but a very public one. What he did not know was how Emily saw the same events; saw that her much older husband craved her good opinion, and from such a discovery she had found the means to make more even their relationship. He was even less aware of the thoughts which had intruded to trouble Emily recently, and given the depth of concern that such musings engendered it was her intention that he should never know.

'You are scowling, husband,' she said. 'I do hope that I am not the cause.'

'Of course not,' he lied. 'I was thinking sitting here

in the inner harbour is a da…a tedious duty. I think I must ask the admiral for something more active.'

It was an inadvertent thought, yet there nevertheless; Emily would welcome such a thing and to cover her embarrassment she said quickly, 'If there is to be a costume ball, we must look to what we have in the way of attire.'

'My inclination is to decline to attend, sir. I fear, at a ball and in drink, some idiot will say something and I will be obliged to react.'

'You cannot hide away, Pearce,' insisted Digby. 'You must face those who would condescend to you and force them into acknowledgement.'

'They resent my rank, and for all I know my person.'

'Then you must remind them that you are commissioned by the king, and if they would like it, you are quite prepared to write to His Majesty and list their objections. That should shut them up.'

Wondering at Digby's persistence, Pearce was gifted with a revelation. His commanding officer did not want to go on his own; he too felt he would be badly treated by other officers, especially lieutenants with longer commissions than his own. 'If you wish me to hold your hand, sir…'

'Hold my hand,' Digby barked, so fulsomely that Pearce knew he was right. 'I need no one to do that, sir!'

'We must take Harbin and Farmiloe along with us. It will do them good to experience polite society.'

Digby laughed. 'God knows what it will do for polite society to be exposed to that pair.'

It might be called a costume ball, but for most naval officers that extended no further than a small face mask. Lord Hood and Admiral Sir William Hotham eschewed even that, and seemd to be quite embarrassed at the way Rear Admiral de Trogoff had got himself up as a Roman Emperor. In all, the French officers took the matter of dress more seriously, while the other trait they exhibited was a certain abstemiousness when it came to food and drink. The British officers and mids were never far from a punch bowl or a platter, and Pearce, watching the behaviour of both, was amused at the quite obvious difference in national habits.

'Drink up, Pearce,' said a red-faced and sweating Digby, his voice raised over the nearby music. 'You are supposed to be here to enjoy yourself.'

Tempted to reply that guzzling was not a prerequisite of pleasure, Pearce decided it would be inappropriate, sank what he had in his cup, and was persuaded to take a refill. But having done so he detached himself from Digby and his ilk, and as he made his way amongst the French officers, all dressed in some form of costume, he regretted not having done likewise. The whiff of Paris was again strong, surrounded as he was by people speaking French, as well as the behaviour and the dress. For all the fervour of the Revolution, it had to be noted, as a nation, these people took their entertainment seriously. While never having experienced Parisian life before the year '91, he guessed that such masques and balls had changed little from monarchical times. With his fellow officers, the object seemed to be to get drunk; with the French, it was dalliance, each lady present surrounded by suitors, most respectful, some deadly serious in their attempts at seduction.

'Lieutenant Pearce, you look to be in some kind of study.'

Captain d'Imbert was wearing a very florid and feathered hat of the seventeenth-century period, and a tabard over breeches and boots that had on it a large blue cross, the blade at his side kept short for decoration. He could hardly be said to look martial, given his age and shape, but he did look striking.

'I was just observing, Monsieur le baron, the differing natures of our two nations. I fear my fellows lack the refinement of your own.'

'It is as well that you did not see the place prior to our conjoining. We had as many of that type in our navy, which was hard to swallow, but then, the British Navy is open to all, whereas under the

Bourbons, commissions were really the preserve of the well connected.'

'Yet there were stout fighters and good sailors amongst them.'

'I believe you are to escort those who refuse to serve back to their ports.'

· 'I am.'

'Then observe them well, Lieutenant Pearce, and might I also say, watch them closely.'

Pearce was looking across the room, to where Emily Barclay stood, barely visible, surrounded as she was by Frenchmen. That was another difference in temperament; no British officer would so openly display admiration in the presence of her husband. Their hosts suffered from no such constraints; if a woman was beautiful, and she was that in her milkmaid's outfit, then paying court to her was an obligation as well as a pleasure.

The slight disturbance behind her took his eye and he saw a bunch of midshipmen facing up to an equal number of French youths, who would mostly be the sons of the locals. Knowing how the mids thirsted for a fight wherever they were, and guessing that the Provençal character was equally contentious, he decided to intervene, so he made his way across the room, passing as he did so Emily Barclay and those paying court to her. That also allowed him to see Ralph Barclay, deep in conversation with Elphinstone, though his eyes were on his wife, and even in a mask, it was plain he was displeased.

'Mr Harbin, what's afoot here?'

Harbin was drunk, and a quick look at the others present showed them to be in a like state. Those they confronted were not, but since the mids were armed with their dirks, it was reasonable to suppose their opponents were likewise equipped. It would not do anything for Toulonnais/British relations if they fought each other; someone was almost certain to be seriously wounded.

'They insulted the king, sir.' Harbin slurred, 'said he could keep his head as it worn't worth the chopping off.'

'This was said to you in English?'

'No, sir,' said another midshipman, equally inebriated. 'Not one of the buggers speaks like a man should. It's all heathen tongue.'

'Might I remind you young man, it is their tongue, and if you do not understand it I am at a loss to know how you can say with such certainty that they insulted the king.'

Pearce was also wondering at the reaction, or lack of it, of his fellow officers. He could not have been the only one to see the possibility of a confrontation, yet they were so intent on drinking and eating that they seemed content to let it pass. He went over to the sullen-looking group of local youths and, addressing them in French, asked them what was amiss, holding up his hand, given they all seemed to want to speak at once, pointing to one of the tallest to extract an explanation. Garbled as it was, it was clearly a case of misinterpretation; they had not said what was supposed. Just as clearly, faced with a bunch of equally belligerent youths, their honour was at stake and they were not going to back down. Admonishing them to do nothing, Pearce went over to where Elphinstone stood, which forced Ralph Barclay to move away.

'Sir, I fear we may have an outbreak of violence.'

'You mean the shavers, laddie,' Elphinstone replied, indicating the knot of still agitated mids. When Pearce nodded, he just laughed. 'Happens aw the time, Pearce. You'll never stop young men strutting. The only way I have ever found is to pack them off to a whorehouse so they can work off their energy on a moll. There will be sair heids come the morn.'

'Then might I suggest, sir, that we relieve them of their dirks?'

Elphinstone was quite shocked at the idea. 'What, and leave them with no defence?'

Plainly he would get nowhere with a man like Elphinstone, so he went back and called to Farmiloe and Harbin. 'Both of you, if you get into trouble tonight, I will masthead you for a week, as well as stretch you and have you kiss the gunner's daughter every day for the same length of time.'

It was fortunate that some of the local adults had also seen what was brewing; they were shepherding their youth to the other side of the room, so that the promised trouble seemed to abate, so the clutch of mids went back to drinking. Crossing back to where he had set out, he inadvertently caught Emily Barclay's eye, and it was the devil in him that took him towards and not past her, displacing, with the effect of his arrival, the Frenchmen paying her court.

'Mrs Barclay,' he said, with a bow.

'Mr Pearce.'

He laughed. 'I am so pleased you talk to me as a civilian. I must say I am uncomfortable still at being addressed by my rank.'

'I find it hard to see you as other than the person I first observed.'

'I fear you saw me in some straits.'

Pearce had not intended to refer to her husband, but he had done so merely with those words, which brought a very bonny touch of rouge to her cheeks. He felt again the attraction he had experienced on first seeing her, that reinforced every time he had witnessed her forays on to the deck of HMS *Brilliant*.

'I fear it would do little good, sir, for me to apologise.'

'I cannot see what you have to say sorry for.'

'I sense a kindness in that response, which is

unwarranted. I fear I was the cause of my husband's displeasure.'

'Madam, I was the cause of my own misfortune. How could I observe you and not wish to engage you in conversation.'

The fan she was carrying waved violently. 'Sir, you are too bold.'

Pearce smiled. 'I think our French friends have been somewhat more so.'

Suddenly animated, she was lovelier than ever. 'They are, sir, to the point of rudeness. Some of the allusions they made were bordering on the obscene.'

The look of shock on her face was stunning, and had Pearce wishing they were somewhere else. The poor girl did not know that the *outré* compliments to which she had been subjected were normal in French society, and it was a habit he had absorbed when seeking to make advances to women in Paris. Since they were as prepared to accept them as he was to press them, he had, as a handsome, well-set youth, enjoyed great success, even acquiring in Amelie Labordiére a mistress of high social standing and great beauty. That was what Emily Barclay would have enjoyed had she been French; her husband, like Amelie's, would have acceded and got on with his own affairs, but provincial English life did not extend to such things. London, perhaps: out in the country, no.

'Their compliments were well intentioned, I do assure you.'

That fan was violent again. 'I cannot see it as so, sir.'

'It is the nature of the country.'

'Then I can see why, if they cannot control their tongues in polite conversation, they are so in thrall to Revolution.'

Pearce burst out laughing, loud enough to turn what few heads had not been surreptitiously observing the exchange between him and the wife of his known enemy. Lutyens appeared out of nowhere, and taking his arm, paid Emily a passing compliment and forcibly led him away.

'What are you trying to do, Pearce, alienate every fellow Briton in the room?'

'I cannot imagine what you mean.'

'Then you are a fool. How can you pay court to a fellow officer's wife and have any hope of gaining their respect?'

'You mistake my position, Heinrich. I neither need, not desire, their respect.'

'Yet you wish for their judgement. Who do you think will sit on the Board of Court Martial that examines your case against Barclay.' Seeing doubt in Pearce's eye, Lutyens continued with some feeling. 'Precisely. The very people who are in the room. What they think of you does matter to you and your friends, so do not commit the sin, a cardinal one in the eyes of those present, of openly admiring Emily.'

'Emily? I see you are familiar enough to name her so. Am I encroaching on your preserve?'

'I do not deny, Pearce, that I have harboured stimulating thoughts in that area; who could not with such a creature; but that is all they are and all they will remain. I recommend you do the same.'

'That will be a cruel fate. I cannot believe that old sod of a husband satisfies her as she should be. Emily Barclay needs a man between her thighs, not a doddering tyrant.'

In being so outspoken, Pearce realised that he was slightly affected by the drink he had consumed. Fortunately Lutyens was not offended, in fact responded with a thin smile.

'I suspect you are trying to shock me, Pearce, but you are wasting your time. Recall my profession.'

The sudden commotion from across the room took the attention of both, but only Pearce moved, glad to see that finally some of his fellow lieutenants did likewise. It was dangerous getting between the two sets of belligerents, with the midshipmen wielding their dirks and the locals with knifes of all shapes and sizes. There were a lot of theatrical threats with those weapons, but Pearce knew it was only a matter of moments before one was used, and seriously, so he buffeted around the ear the first midshipman he came across, then started to lay into the others, belabouring right and left and bellowing orders to belay. Harbin was on his knees, blood dripping from his head, Farmiloe standing above him, dirk out and pointed to protect the boy from further harm.

'What happened, Farmiloe?'

'A cut to the head, sir. One of those Frog swine sneaked up and slashed him.'

'Get him out of here. Mr Lutyens is over yonder. Move.'

To the sound of a rondo from the orchestra, lieutenants were wrestling drunken mids, trying to get them away from their opponents, while adults dressed in everything from togas to Red Indian headdress were struggling to do the same to the local boys. To Pearce, only one thing worked, a sound punch, and he laid into his side with gusto. Out of the corner of his eye he saw Elphinstone laughing so heartily he was having to hold his sides, clearly enjoying the spectacle, and when some peace had finally been restored he went over to remonstrate, which got him a rebuke.

'Have a care, laddie, you're not rank enough to take me to task.'

'I do think it could have been stopped, sir.'

'Then you show your ignorance, Pearce. I was a mid once, and I canna think of a ball or amusement that did not end up in a spat with someone. I have had fights from Lisbon to Calcutta, with one or two thrown in on the North American station before that war, and I have never served at home that a night in the taverns did not end in riot. Boys will be boys, and we canna expect them to stand up to roundshot and musket if they will no stand up for themselves at a bash like this. Now if I were you, I'd find some French fancy and ask her to dance.'

Pearce looked at the floor area set aside for dancing, not yet full, and the temptation to cross over and ask Emily Barclay to step out with him was strong. But her husband was close to her, and judging by the way he was leaning over and addressing her, he was not pleased.

'You have embarrassed me in front of every officer in the room, Mrs Barclay.'

'I have done no such thing,' Emily pleaded. 'Lieutenant Pearce approached me. What would you have me do, turn my back?'

'Just that, which would tell all here that you hold him in the same regard as I do. The man is an impostor, a damned revolutionary and don't you dare remonstrate with me for my language.'

'Keep your voice down, husband. You are making a spectacle of yourself.'

Barclay hissed at her. 'It is you who have made the spectacle!'

Emily lost her temper then, something she had never completely done with her husband, but she was not going to stand still to be publicly accused of unbecoming behaviour. 'I daresay you would like to punish me as you punished him, and with the same want of justice.'

'I punished him to protect your honour, madam.'

'Claptrap, sir. You punished him for your own pride. And tell me, sir, what instructions you gave to my nephew regarding Pearce and his companions when they sailed for England?'

'Instructions?'

'Yes, husband. I was in the cabin when you and Toby were conversing on the poop. What has that boy done, sir, on your orders, that makes him fear retribution from John Pearce?'

'That is naval business and none of your concern. I think now, also, that it is time we returned to the ship.'

'You return if you wish. I am staying awhile.'

'Madam, you must obey me, I am your husband.'

'Must I ask my nephew what it is he fears, and why?'

'I forbid that.'

'Then I can only assume it is because you dread what I might learn. Like the day you named someone in a King's blue coat a traitor, yet I ran into John Pearce in that very same-coloured coat at the hospital, before any other officer in the fleet came ashore. I have to surmise they were one and the same person.'

'Wrong,' Barclay replied with a defensiveness that damned him. 'It was a different fellow.'

'Was it? I fear you have allowed your hatred of the man to cloud not only your judgement but your self-esteem. And I, as your wife, will obey only a man who shows me the courtesy of being open and honest, which you, sir, plainly are not.'

Fan waving violently, Emily moved away from her husband, who, looking after her, noticed that nearly every eye in the room was on him. The argument had not gone unnoticed and it was galling that in the looks he was getting, a good proportion had a trace of being thrilled. He strode across to where Elphinstone was supping another cup of punch.

'Sir, I must tell you that I am ready to serve ashore as from this very moment.'

The Scotsman looked at him through bleary eyes that denoted his inebriation. 'Have a cup of punch, Barclay. Carteaux and Lapoype can wait till morn.'

Chapter Ten

They might have been termed as useless or dangerous, but there was no mistaking the desire of those five thousand French sailors to get out of Toulon and back home to their Atlantic ports. They worked with gusto to get out the ship's armament, no easy task since each cannon had to he hoisted out through its own gunport by a system of ropes, restraints and pulleys, in a complicity of knots that completely foxed John Pearce. Thankfully, his only task was an occasional one of necessary interpretation, and that was confined to the dozen officers, most of whom seemed a damn sight less Jacobin than he had been led to believe.

While the guns were being hauled out, another party was working on the capstan bars, to drag out of the lower reaches of the holds the nets full of round, chain and case shot, as well as the powder barrels from the gunner's store, with just enough of that commodity left for signalling. Out came muskets, pistols, pikes and boarding axes, cutlasses and knives, indeed anything that could be used as a weapon and he knew each man and his dunnage had been searched on coming aboard so not so much as a knife was going to be allowed.

The sail locker was stripped to the bare minimum thought to be required, with only jibs, courses and topsails left, no topgallants or kites, while every spare bit of timber from planking to spars had been removed, as well as the hundred items of standard stores every vessel carried. Every inch of space would be needed; with each vessel carrying over twice her normal complement, food had to be loaded that would keep them hale for the entire length of the voyage. Beef and pork in barrels, sacks of peas and biscuit, water and wine for a month, which was reckoned at the maximum. Hood had made it plain that no stores could be collected from Gibraltar; this outing was being paid for by the remains of the Bourbon Navy, not the Admiralty, for it was generally held throughout the fleet that his decision to gift the French Navy four sound ships would not be welcomed in London. That was trouble enough without added expense to the Navy Board.

Making his way aft when the work was complete, Pearce entered the main cabin, to find it crowded with the possessions of the officers, a knot of the dozen lieutenants working out from copious lists the way they would man their watches. In his hand, Pearce had a copy of the Admiralty signal book, which he passed over to the most senior, a small stocky fellow who had earlier introduced himself as Gerard Moreau, who would command the lead vessel, *Apollon*, explaining that when they needed to contact *Faron*, this was the book they must use.

'But, monsieur,' Moreau replied in French, with a slightly mystified air, 'none of us here speak English.'

'Then, monsieur, you will have to use that one most.'

Pearce opened the book at the signal that requested another ship to come alongside, adding. 'I doubt you will need much signalling anyway. Our course is to the Straits and, once through, to the Bay of Biscay.'

He also left a list of instructions; lanterns to be rigged and lit every night fore and aft, no boats to be launched without express permission, the speed of the whole to be dictated by Captain Digby, who in a lighter and better-equipped vessel should always have the legs of them. They must heave to if they encountered fog and use the signal guns to mark their position.

Moreau had a ready smile and a twinkle in his eyes as he responded. 'I think you mistake our purpose, monsieur. We have no plans to evade you, we merely wish to get home.'

'I fear, monsieur, that my seniors have little faith in your intentions.'

Moreau smiled. 'Perhaps we can convince you over a glass of wine?'

Pearce pulled a face. 'I am afraid, Lieutenant Moreau, that I, along with all of the men who will escort you, have strict orders not to mix.'

'Ah!' Moreau replied, throwing up his hands in a very Gallic way. 'They fear you will become Jacobins perhaps?'

'Perhaps,' Pearce replied.

Yet he smiled to ensure that Moreau knew such a notion was as absurd as the Frenchman supposed. Seeing that his attitude was creating ill-feeling – the others in the cabin were frowning seriously – he decided that his superiors could go hang. They saw things in a too black and white a fashion, always separating Frenchmen into virulent revolutionaries or the opposite. Pearce knew different: such Manichean simplicity did not exist; every shade of opinion existed. There would be, no doubt, aboard these four capital ships, some bloodthirsty radicals, but they would be few and unlikely to be much of an influence. In the main these were seamen wanting to return home, and that was a sentiment with which he could not disagree.

'One glass, monsieur, to be amicable.'

L'amitié required that to be several glasses, not one, and he got to know the names of the others who would command the vessels. Pasquale Garnier was the next senior lieutenant and he would command *Orion*. Hector Jacquelin, a less friendly fellow came next in line and would take charge of *Patriote*, the most junior, Forcet, having *Entreprenant*. The other eight lieutenants present would be the watch officers on each vessel, and they showed uncommon civility as they sorted out their needs, leaving Pearce thinking that they were employing a good method to achieve their ends. It was, on the whole, Jacquelin excepted, a very sociable atmosphere, one which was not appreciated when he went aboard his own ship to face Henry Digby.

'You are supposed to have nothing to do with them, Mr Pearce, and here you come back on my deck with the odour of their wine on your breath.'

'I took a glass to be friendly, sir, and I cannot find it in me to condemn them for their aim of getting home.'

'And what about their politics?' Digby demanded.

It was a sad reflection, Pearce thought, as he looked into the irritable face of his superior, that even one as intelligent as he seemed to be, could not get hold of the notion that Frenchmen were no different to Britons; they were just as fractious and

divided as any other race and that included his own.
Like Scotsmen; to put any two of that race into
private dispute was to garner three opinions.

'We are to go alongside one of the store ships,'
Digby growled. 'Lord Hood has sanctioned your
notion of us carrying carronades. Oh, and that
fellow, Lutyens, is to join us, since no French
surgeon would agree to serve such Jacobins. Once
we have those aboard, all we need is a wind.'

Shenton, at the door of his pantry, could hear the
conversation in the main cabin, and though he
wanted to intervene he was powerless to do so.
Toby Burns, dining with his aunt, was on the rack,
and much as he twisted and turned he was slowly
being roasted. The truth was coming out as she,
quietly but persistently, posed question after
question and they had moved on from the retaking
of the *Lady Harrington*, to what had happened
subsequently.

'I was told,' the boy said, head lowered, 'should
a King's ship seek to press Pearce and his
companions from the *Lady Harrington*, provided
they did not jeopardise the safety of the ship, I was
not to interfere, it being legal for the Navy to do
so.'

'And it was my husband's express order that you
should act as you did?' The positive reply was so
soft as to be almost inaudible. 'Then though I find

it hard to fathom, Toby, I cannot condemn you. It is too much that one as young as you should be given such a terrible amount of responsibility.'

That got a louder response. 'I felt the responsibility keenly, Aunt Emily.'

Which engendered a sharp rejoinder. 'Not keenly enough to decline to be treated as a hero.'

How distant that seemed to a now-crestfallen Toby Burns. If he had ever seriously harboured the thought that he had betrayed John Pearce it had quickly faded on his arrival back in England. With the war only weeks old, he had found himself feted as a typical chip off the old oak block of Albion. Never mind he was barely breeched, he was a tar to his toes, even at such a tender age capable of the prodigious deeds listed in Ralph Barclay's despatch, which credited him with the leadership of the whole enterprise in the Trieux Estuary.

In Deal, at the Three Kings Hotel on the beach, every person in the dining room had stood to applaud as he entered, and the owners would not hear of him paying for his provender. He had suffered an interview with the First Lord of the Admiralty and going home to Frome he had been hoisted on the shoulders of boys with whom he had done his schooling, friends they said they were, even if he could not remember it being so, carried through the streets to cheers, only to come to his own home and find it full of the leading citizens of

the town waiting to greet him and shake his hand.
And more than that, they demanded he tell his
story.

He had not wanted to come back to sea, having
found his first experience too harrowing for words;
the filth of a midshipman's berth, the foul language
and downright thievery that was seen as the norm,
that and the constant threat, which he never knew
to be real or joshing, that he would keep happy the
older boys if he cared to join them in some dark
place. Nor did being on deck suit him, given he was
not a commanding presence; quite the opposite, in
his ill-fitting clothes made for someone expected to
grow by the foot. He found his newly acquired
Uncle Ralph to be a harsh and unpleasant man, the
crew people of a type he had only ever hurried past
in a street, and his Aunt Emily, who he had looked
to for a softer touch, unwilling to cross her husband
to ease his predicament.

But he was a hero; how could he not want to get
back to that element which would provide him with
more opportunity to garner glory for himself and
England? Not even his mother, to whom he was
closest, seemed to see the doubt in his eyes when his
return to HMS *Brilliant* was broached, while his
father positively glowed, seeming to quite forget
that warships got into battles in which people on
board were maimed or killed in the most ghastly
fashion; he knew just how bad that could be, for the

sailors on his uncle's frigate had taken foul delight in telling him so. And then there was that affair for which he was being praised; while he accepted the accolades, Toby Burns knew the truth, knew that he had acted in a cowardly fashion from the moment he was thrown up on to the Breton shore till the act of retaking the merchantman was complete, and he was deeply fearful that faced with the prospect of death or injury, he would once more behave in a less than impressive fashion.

'I did my best to deflect the accolades, Aunt Emily, but I was overwhelmed by enthusiasm.'

I bet you were, you little shite, thought Shenton, who knew that it would not be the boy who would suffer for these revelations, but his captain, and he was right.

'Toby,' said Emily with a serious face. 'I shall not mention this again, and I would request that if you are asked to describe the conversation of this dinner yourself, you decline to do so. And I think you should draw a veil also over the exploit for which you are praised.'

That was a hard request with which to accede; on the voyage out in HMS *Victory* he had more than once been the guest of the wardroom, and on one occasion had even dined in the company of Lord Hood. In the mid's berth he had been treated with respect, the same on deck, and free from any duties, being a supernumerary, he had quite enjoyed the experience of being at sea in what was, in truth, a cruise. Even if deep down he knew it to be misplaced, to be treated as a hero was exceedingly pleasant.

'It would wound me to have to insist, Toby.'

'I will do as you say, Aunt Emily.'

'Thank you. And not a word of this conversation to Captain Barclay.'

'He'll hear it all right,' Shenton said softly to himself. 'Every bleedin' word.'

He then entered the cabin and asked, with a large and insincere smile. 'Is you ready for the cheese, Mrs Barclay?'

Emily nodded, then said, 'Please ask if a boat can be ready after dinner to take me over to Mr Lutyens.'

'Aye, aye, mam.'

'I will be back in a few weeks at most, Emily,' said Lutyens, aware that the news of his departure was not being well received.

'Then I will have no one to talk to for that time.'

'Your husband...'

'Is no longer much aboard,' Emily said quickly. 'He is ashore working on the defences around Fort Mulgrave, and when he returns it is only to snatch a quick meal and sleep.'

'If I read your tone aright, you have not repaired the breach that occurred at de Trogoff's ball?'

'No,' Emily replied, then, in a rush, added, 'Heinrich, can I confide in you?'

'I hope you feel you are safe to do so.'

The story came tumbling out, every detail, and as he had done before, he pretended no knowledge of the truth. As Emily talked of her nephew, Lutyens' mind went back to the original observations he had made and noted at the beginning of their voyage. He had watched Burns as he had everyone else: the boy was plainly not cut out for the life, always with a face either miserable or concerned, with no appearance of knowing what he was to do, or an ability to absorb his duties; quite certainly no capacity for bluff. Hardly surprising, then, he had acted the way he had. There was no condemnation from the surgeon; that was his purpose for being at sea, to find out how men, even boys, in the confines of a ship, exposed perhaps to harsh punishment, certainly to rough company, possible battle and death, would react. He had left a profitable practice and the prospects presented by a well-connected parent for this, and here was Emily Barclay, another object of observation, confiding her deepest worries to him. His hand itched to get it all down on paper, yet he also had to be pragmatic.

'I must advise you, Emily, that no man is perfect. Your husband is acting, by his own lights, in a proper manner, and harsh as it may seem to you...' He left the rest hanging in the air. 'You must, I think, find a way of healing this spat, for from what I have seen of Captain Barclay, I fear he is not equipped to do so.'

'I find it hard to forgive him.'

'No doubt, but forgive him is what you must do, because, if you do not, I fear that the rest of your married life will suffer.'

Emily either did not want to consider such a thing, or admit that it had occurred to her already. Instead she looked at his chests, the one with his clothes, the other with his potions, unctions and the tools of his trade. 'I see you are ready to depart.'

'I have no wish to hurry you, my dear, but I am expected aboard.'

'Mr Lutyens, I welcome you, and say, without a word of a lie, I am happy to see you once more.'

'Thank you, Mr Digby.' The surgeon turned to acknowledge John Pearce and behind him all the Brilliants who were aboard. Martin Dent, the cheekiest, made a dumb show of him scribbling. 'I believe you have instructions not to fraternise with the Frenchmen you are escorting.'

'That is so.'

'It is also impossible, sir. They do not have any medical men of their own, apart from one or two who may have served as mates to a surgeon, so if anything occurs, and on a voyage like this I suspect it must, I will have to go on board their vessels to treat them. And since I do not speak their language with anything approaching felicity, I fear Mr Pearce here will need to accompany me.'

'Let us get to sea Mr Lutyens, away from the prying eyes and ears of admirals. When needs must, we will do what is necessary.'

'Heinrich,' said Pearce, 'allow me to name to you the Master, Mr Neame, the fellow with the bandage you have already encountered.' Lutyens nodded to Harbin, who had his head swathed in white linen. 'Mr Harbin, see Mr Lutyens to his quarters.'

'Ahoy *Faron*.'

The shout had them looking over the side, to a boat which contained, apart from its oarsman, one old sailor with a face as lined as leather, and another substantial fellow who went by the name of Blubber. Pearce called over to them to welcome them aboard.

'Latimer, Booth, I bid you a hearty welcome. I must say I never thought Taberly or his captain would release you.'

'He was in a right old passion when he got his order an' no error,' said Latimer, as his feet touched the deck, this at the same time as his knuckle brushed his forehead. 'I o'erheard him say that he would dearly like to horsewhip you, your honour.'

''Thought he was goin' to do it to us,' added Blubber. 'Never seen the like.'

'Not that you'd have felt it, Blubber,' called Michael O'Hagan, 'you're too well padded.'

'Belay that,' shouted Pearce, aware that Digby was not pleased with the interjection, which smacked of ill-discipline. 'See these men below.'

'Have you taken note of the wind, Captain?' asked Neame, sniffing as though the breeze, which had shifted, had a smell.

'I have, Mr Neame. I think, gentlemen, we are in all respects ready for sea. Mr Pearce, please go aboard *Apollon* once more and speak to...what's the fellow's name again?'

'Lieutenant Moreau, sir.'

'I daresay he is in the nature of a Commodore now. Anyway, tell Monsieur Moreau to start warping his ships out of the inner roads.'

`Aye, aye, sir.' Pearce replied, before calling for a boat party.

They looked, with their gunports closed, like the real threatening article as they emerged into the outer roads, a quartet of seventy-fours being towed by their boats, the rowing men straining mightily to haul their bulk. Digby was aboard HMS *Victory* receiving last minute orders from Rear Admiral Hyde Parker.

'Stay inshore of them at all times, where practicable. Their departure cannot be a secret to the Jacobins, Digby, and we must expect General

Carteaux to be salivating at the prospect of taking them ashore as reinforcements.'

'I doubt they would be willing to serve, sir. Lieutenant Pearce assured me they are intent on only one thing, getting home.'

'And how, pray, does Lieutenant Pearce know this?' Parker demanded, his round face suffused with irritation.

Digby realised that he had dropped a brick, but he could see no way out of it. 'He was in charge of the vessels when they were stripping out their guns, sir. I believe he felt it necessary to describe to them our signals, and in that process he discerned that they are not looking for any other outcome than a swift journey to their home ports.'

'You will remind Pearce, as I will remind you, to stay away from these rascals, and that goes double for your crew. They carry with them a bacillus of disturbance which could affect the whole fleet.'

'Yes, sir.'

Parker dropped his voice, not wishing to be overheard. 'And if they show the slightest sign of waywardness, sink the sods, to my mind the best thing that could happen to them.'

'You will ignore that, Digby,' said Lord Hood, from the doorway to his sleeping cabin. 'Admiral Parker is merely teasing you. These men are like us, sailors. I cannot think of a circumstance in which we would watch fellow-seamen drown.'

'Sir.'

'It does however occur to me that you may find it more convenient, certainly to our cause, to let them go ashore in something other than a French naval port.'

Digby looked at Hood for a moment in silence, a gaze that was held with a quizzical expression on the old admiral's face. 'Do you wish to give me orders in that regard, Milord?'

The slow shake of the head spoke volumes; there would be nothing in writing, indeed no more said, and the only three people who knew what Hood was proposing were in this cabin, one of whom would soon be gone, the other being his right-hand man. He was being told what to do in a fashion that meant it was truly a secret, and in working that out he was also thinking that Lord Hood was a devious old sod.

'I wish you God-speed, Mr Digby,' Hood finally said. 'Proceed to sea at once and await your charges.'

HMS *Faron* led the way out into deep water, due south to begin with, to gain both sea room and remove any temptation to pass within even long sight of the positions of the besieging Jacobin forces. Digby was all activity, wishing to show his charges that the ship he commanded was nippy enough in stays to get quickly to any point of danger, the firing of the carronades in practice an added warning that should they transgress, he had the means to chastise them. Pearce was happy too; he might not have got his friends free, but they were with him now, away from the threat of arbitrary punishment; the sun was shining, the sea was smooth and life was good.

'Mr Pearce,' Digby called. 'The signal gun if you please, and prepare to hoist the orders to alter their heading to due east.'

Farmiloe hooked on the flags, Martin Dent and Dysart were there to hoist them, the gunner had loaded his brass signal gun with a blank charge, and as he fired off his puff of white smoke, Digby put down his helm, this as Mr Neame trimmed the required sails, and HMS *Faron* came round on her new course in a trice. Flags eventually flew from *Apollon* and the other seventy-fours began their turn, more sluggish certainly, but not without grace.

Across the intervening waters came the sound of cheering, for in making the change of course the five thousand men aboard those ships had no doubt now they were headed for the Straits of Gibraltar and home.

High up on Mount Faron, Ralph Barclay had a telescope to his eye, watching the enemy vessels depart. He kept them in view long after they were out of sight of those at sea level, this being something that, as a naval port, made Toulon so formidable. No fleet could approach without they would be spotted while well offshore. He had concerns, of course; his wife and the need to make peace with her, but overriding all that was the certain knowledge that John Pearce was on that newly captured sloop, and that was good riddance.

Chapter Eleven

'Captain Barclay,' said Admiral Sir William Hotham gravely, with only a glance at his secretary to ensure he was noting the words. 'It is my sad duty to inform you that I have no choice but to convene a court martial to study and adjudicate on the events described in a complaint made by Lieutenant John Pearce. Namely, in the month of February this year, you did illegally press men, not of the sea, out of a place from which you were forbidden by statute to do so.'

'Might I ask when this is to take place, sir?'

'I think, Captain Barclay, the sooner the better. It cannot be pleasant to have a cloud of suspicion hanging over you. Five fellow-captains of the requisite seniority have been alerted to attend upon my flag this coming Thursday, and it is to be hoped that the proceedings will take no more than one day.'

'I must then, sir, organise my defence.'

'I have appointed Lieutenant Pigot to handle that.'

'An excellent choice, sir, I am sure.'

Barclay barely knew Pigot, except by reputation; he was held to be a choleric fellow who took that trait to extremes in his capacity as premier of HMS *Theseus*. He was a man who saw the cat o' nine tails as the best means of maintaining discipline and Hotham was known to hold him in some regard; he always did with a strict disciplinarian. It was quite possible that Pigot would gain as much from defending Ralph Barclay as his principal would from being so defended.

'I will require both you and Lieutenant Pigot to make yourselves available on Wednesday night, when you must reside aboard HMS *Britannia* in preparation for the court martial. In this, naturally, you have my permission to sleep out of your ship. The court will be convened at ten in the morning. Is there anything you wish to put to me?'

'No, sir, I am entirely happy with whatever arrangements you propose.'

'Good, then please be so good as to return to your duties.'

If Ralph Barclay's wife seemed less than happy, at least she was talking to him, as he explained why her presence at the court martial would not be in her best interests.

'Surely, husband, you mean your best interests?'

'No, madam, I do not. I have often tried to point out to you that naval service is sometimes, of necessity, harsh. Things may be said that will trouble your conscience, which is in its very nature, given your sex, of a gentle disposition.'

'If it ever was, Captain Barclay, it is less so now. And might I remind you that my mother made it plain to me that a care for those less fortunate than ourselves was a duty we should never shun. I have, sad to say, held dying babies in my arms, expiring from want of nourishment. I have seen women pass over in the throws of childbirth, men mangled by accidents caused by being driven to unsafe work by uncaring masters and, as if that were not enough, I have assisted Mr Lutyens in treating wounded men on two very bloody occasions in the cockpit of this very ship.'

How could he put it? He did not want her there because he wished to allude to the character of John Pearce, to paint him as a rabble-rouser tainted not only by his parentage but by his two years of contact with the Revolution, in short to so blacken him that his complaint would be seen in the light of revenge. Emily knew that to be short of the truth, though her husband suspected there was more than a grain of veracity in what was, in any case, his opinion of the fellow. The nightmare he harboured was of his own wife standing in Hotham's cabin and denouncing such an accusation as false; she had embarrassed him before and might do so again.

'What would be your reaction, Mrs Barclay, if I said plainly, that I do not want you present...'

He never got a chance to add that she being there would not only distract him, but every member of the court, because Emily cut right across him. 'I would say, husband, that at least you were being honest!'

'I hope and pray that you think me so always.'

She could not reply; to do so would reveal just how much she knew, so it was dissimulation that had her saying, 'I think, sir, by your own lights, you see yourself as such.'

It was his turn to be sharp. 'I cannot imagine by which other light I am supposed to function?'

She could not look at him; Emily had given him a chance to plead his career, to say that even if he had been in the wrong by any objective, non-service analysis, he had acted as a naval officer should. It might not be clear-cut to a landsman, but it was a necessary to a sailor, and essential to a man commanding a ship of war. If that was hard to see as right, it was at least justification.

'I can see by your attitude you leave me no choice,' Barclay continued, knowing as he spoke that the payment for his words would be a lengthy period of retribution. 'I do not wish you to attend. There, I have said that which I sought to avoid.'

'Never fear, husband,' Emily replied, with biting irony. 'I know you have been forced into this by my unbecoming intransigence, that it is all MY fault.'

'I fear I must request the use of my cabin. I have people I need to interview, and my defending counsel, Lieutenant Pigot, is waiting on deck to aid me. If you wish I will arrange a boat to take you to the hospital.'

'I think you are forgetting, Captain Barclay, that Mr Lutyens is no longer there. If you provide me with an escort, I will go for a promenade around the town.'

'Shenton!'

'Sir,' the servant replied, trying to sound as if he was deep in his pantry rather than at the very door of his hutch.

'Fetch Devenow, at the double.'

'Double,' Shenton said bitterly to himself as he went out on deck, 'I ain't doubled this ten year past, damned cheek.'

He had not yet told Ralph Barclay of the way Burns had dished him; the time to do that was when there was some advantage to be gained, always a consideration with a master who could be mercurial, all sweetness one minute, and a damned tyrant the next. If he threatened to check the stock of his wine, for instance, that would be the time.

The Premier, Glaister, was on deck, fair haired, skeleton-faced, to Shenton another Sawny Jock leaching off English goodwill, to whom he passed on the message. Various shouts brought forth Devenow, the bully and brute, who had once been put in his place by Michael O'Hagan; he had soon reasserted his clout once that man had shifted his berth. Most of the crew were afraid of him, first for his fists and second for his attachment to Ralph Barclay. To Devenow, the captain was in the order of a secular saint and could do no wrong. When he appeared, to be given his instructions, the man in question wondered if he needed coaching, for he would be a witness for the defence. Then he decided it was unnecessary; Devenow would say what he was told to say. As soon as Emily, parasol in hand, departed, he called in Pigot, a beetle-browed man whose bushy black eyebrows almost touched above his nose. He had a saturnine complexion made more so by the broken flesh that denoted a heavy drinker, and a rasping voice that terrified the first person Ralph Barclay called in to his cabin.

'It matters not, Mr Burns, that you were not with your uncle on that occasion. It is most pressing that you say you were.'

'Mr Burns,' said Ralph Barclay, in an unctuous voice, 'or may I call you Toby, since we are related?'

'Of course, sir, honoured sir.'

'Let me explain to you what occurred.' He looked at Pigot, who nodded to continue. 'I openly admit that I went pressing men that night, but Toby, you will scarcely credit this, I gave the task of finding the right spot to Farmiloe, and though I hate to blacken the boy when he is not here, I fear he got his navigation of the river very wrong.'

'I daresay that it easily done, sir,' Burns replied, in a gap that left him in no doubt he was supposed to respond.

'The problem is, Burns,' said Pigot in his deep, rasping voice. 'Farmiloe ain't here, and it would never do for a Post Captain of the standing of your uncle to admit that he entrusted such a thing to a shaver, and did not check the bearings the lad was taking, without the perpetrator there to confess it first.'

'Now you, young Toby, thanks in part to me, but very much because of your own actions, are highly regarded.' The smile on Ralph Barclay's face made Toby Burns think of a story his mother used to tell him about wolves devouring little lads who were naughty. 'And if you was to admit to such an error, then it would be seen in a different light, would it not?'

There was no need to outline the alternative; that the truth of what happened in the Trieux Estuary would become common knowledge. In the increasingly warped mind of Toby Burns, he had begun to blame John Pearce for all his troubles. If that sod had not been along they could have surrendered as soon as they encountered French authority, which is what he had longed to do; no fighting, food and drink provided, certainly uncomfortable, but no more so than service in a damned frigate.

'You see, Toby,' his Uncle Ralph continued, 'Farmiloe landed me in hot water. I daresay the lad meant no harm, but instead of putting me ashore at Blackfriars by the bridge, he took me into the Liberties of the Savoy, which are not more than a few hundred paces apart.'

'I can see,' rasped Pigot, 'that you know nothing of this place?' A shake of the head had him continue. 'It is a refuge for thieves and vagabonds, a home to those running from their obligations, the only hope they have of avoiding Newgate or the Fleet. There is not an honest man within its boundaries, yet no tipstaff can go in there and bring them to book.'

'The old Savoy palace stood there,' Ralph Barclay added, 'the one-time home to the Duke of Lancaster, who was King Hal's uncle. You know who he is, I am sure.'

It was a relief to be able to answer a question without thinking. 'Agincourt, sir. Who could not know it?'

'Well, within the confines of that old palace is crown land. A click of Farmer George's fingers would change the status of the place, but our king is not one to pass on a prerogative, however unseemly it is.'

'That,' Pigot insisted, with a look that accused his principal of wandering, 'is where John Pearce and his ilk were skulking. Imagine that a person of that stripe, forced to hide from justice for crimes of which we know not what magnitude, has the effrontery to bring a case against a man of the standing of your uncle.'

'Now if I can establish that I thought we was by Blackfriars, then the case is one of error, not assignment.'

'And Pearce, sir?'

'Will find his case void,' growled Pigot. 'Not that your uncle is guaranteed to escape censure, mind, but if he is found at fault, it will be for his errors and not his actions.'

Toby Burns had in his mind's eye then an image of his Aunt Emily, and the plain disapproval she had shown at that confessional dinner, but right in front of him now was the only man who could make his life bearable – his wife plainly would not try. Loyalty was a matter of the best thing for self, and damn John Pearce, to whom he owed nothing. His voice, when he spoke, was tremulous he knew, but regardless of that, the meaning was clear.

'I can see, sir, that you would be embarrassed by a disclosure such as that which you have outlined, and nothing would distress me more than it should be so. I am sure, even the Good Lord would say to me, if he could speak directly, to look to where my duty lay.'

'Good boy, Toby,' said Ralph Barclay, patting him on the shoulder. 'And do rest assured that my good offices are, as they have been in the past, entirely at the disposal of your future naval career.'

'Will that be all, sir.'

'Aye, lad. Be so good as to send to me Gherson.'

'Sir,' said Midshipman Farmiloe, '*Apollon* has hoisted a signal, but I cannot make head nor tail of it.'

'Then,' Pearce replied, 'if you cannot, Mr Farmiloe, there is little point in referring it to me without you pass me the book.'

They leafed through the signal book together, but it made no sense in any language, so Pearce went to Digby and asked permission to close. That given, Neame altered course and sails to take them up, hand over fist, to the leading French vessel. It was quite telling that with the other three vessels in its wake, none had chosen to repeat Moreau's message. Coming up on her decorated stern, Pearce could see the French captain leaning over the taffrail, a speaking trumpet in his hand, and he called out as soon as he thought he could be heard.

'Monsieur, I request that you come aboard, and bring the surgeon with you.'

'You have someone needing medical attention?'

'I fear I have someone who is past that, monsieur, but I wish to establish why it is so.'

Pearce was aware of Henry Digby standing to his rear, and he turned to translate the request.

'Odd,' was the captain's response. 'If the fellow is dead, bury him.'

'It is most important, monsieur,' Moreau called out. 'I do not assume it to be natural.'

Pearce also translated that to a sceptical Digby. 'That means that someone has been done away with, Pearce. If they are going to be killing each other I don't see how we can intervene.'

'I doubt Captain Moreau would ask for assistance if it was not required.'

'Are you sure? The fellow might be a hysteric for all you know. Do not tell me you can form a judgement on his character from such a meagre acquaintance as a few shared glasses of wine.'

There was a temptation then to tell Henry Digby that he had a very well-developed sense of the worth of people, formed by having met so many in his life, and having to make snap judgements of their character. The kind to trust and the kind to avoid were ingrained in John Pearce, who had shared company with both the elevated and the dregs, finding honesty and chicanery were not a matter of a man's earthly worth or his social standing. He had, it was true, only briefly met

Gerard Moreau, but he trusted him and suspected, in better circumstances, they might well have become firm friends.

'Can I say, sir, that I feel we have a duty to support Captain Moreau if he asks us to. I have the impression he would not do so lightly.'

Digby shook his head slowly, but it was not denial so much as with wonder. 'I cannot put this in the log, Pearce. Lord Hood would flay me alive for downright disobedience.'

'The fact shall certainly never be brought out by me.'

'Very well, you may take a boat and Mr Lutyens and see what our Frenchman wants.'

Pearce had a moment of pure regret then; he had never been much good at slippery gangways, and now he was going to face two, one of which was on a capital ship. As for Lutyens, Pearce could easily imagine that he was an expert by comparison to the surgeon. Good support would be called for. That was when he also considered the notion of danger. He was unlikely to face any of that aboard Moreau's vessel, but he could not be certain.

'Costello, haul in the cutter if you please and fetch it alongside.' Looking round, he saw O'Hagan and went forward to address him quietly. 'Michael, arm yourself and come with me.'

'We got trouble, John-boy?'

'I've got to get off this tub and on to that one

over yonder, and that is trouble in itself, but when I go aboard I would like you at my back.'

'Consider it done.'

Lutyens had been called and was now on deck in a thick coat, with a small leather bag by his feet. 'Martin, Mr Lutyens' bag, and be so good as to help him into the boat.'

Martin Dent was not one to miss such an opportunity. 'Now come along, sir,' he said, taking Lutyens' arm as if he was old and infirm, 'an' you just lean on me an' we will get you to where you are to go.'

'Remind me, Martin Dent,' snapped Lutyens, 'that the next time I treat you it should be painful.'

'Can't get more so than it is now, your honour,' Martin replied, which had everyone in earshot laughing.

'What are you talking about, man?'

'Get on with it, Dent,' said Pearce, who half feared that Martin would tell him his ministrations were far from gentle, that the crew would avoid him for anything minor, preferring the pain they had to that they would receive. He was a good surgeon, but he was also a careless one.

The sloop was sailing along at the same speed as *Apollon*, and the green water that lay between them had a disturbed quality that made Pearce queasy: this was going to be no easy passage.

'Mr Pearce,' called Neame. 'With the captain's

permission I will head-reach *Apollon* afore we cast you off, which will give you a chance to cross the divide as she comes up on you.'

'Make it so, Mr Neame,' Digby called, and the orders were issued to reset some sails and haul on others to get them drawing better, which brought an immediate increase in the ship's speed. Within ten minutes they were ahead of the 74-gunner, and the crew of oarsmen were in the cutter, just waiting for their passengers. Behind him Pearce could hear Michael muttering a papist prayer.

'Michael, it is only a short excursion.'

'If it is that, John-boy, would you be after telling me why your face is as green as that water?'

'It was having you behind me with a cutlass,' Pearce joked, as Michael passed him and went through the gangway. Pearce followed, putting his first foot on one of the sopping wet battens that led down to the boat, his hands gripping the man-ropes with as much strength as he could muster. He had had the ignominy of dropping into a bobbing cutter before now, and he did not want a repetition. The cutter was rising and falling several feet and thankfully he timed his skip perfectly, to land where hands could keep him and his dignity upright. Lutyens made the excepted fist of his boarding, but he was eased down by two of the oarsmen climbing up, one hand and one foot on rope and batten, to aid him down.

'Cast off.'

'Haul away, lads,' shouted Costello, as the cutter
was pushed off from the side of the ship. The oars
bit hard, the men near standing to get purchase on
their primary stroke, but they were clear, and
cutting an angle that would bring *Apollon* up on
them, with Dysart, boat hook in hand, taking
charge of ensuring the lumbering ship-of-the-line
did not run them down.

Moreau had obviously surmised, or perhaps he
had watched and seen, that Lutyens was no sailor,
so he had rigged a chair on a whip from his yards
to heave the surgeon on board. Self-respect
demanded that Pearce could not take that route,
and so he began a long climb that was nothing short
of hair-raising as the French ship swung and dipped
on the swell. He came to deck level sweating and
stepped through to raise his hat, only realising as he
did so that Moreau had taken down the Bourbon
flag with which he had been supplied, and replaced
it with a tricolour stretched across the poop rail.
The grin was wide, the eyes positively dancing, as
the Frenchman said,

'You salute the true flag of France, Lieutenant
Pearce.'

'One day, sir, I must tell you why it is a standard
for which I have little respect.'

Michael O'Hagan came through the gangway
with a hissed exclamation of, 'God bless all here.'

They joined Lutyens before being led below to a very crowded and gloomy maindeck, the only light and air coming from the open gunports, with Moreau shouting for space to be cleared, which was obeyed with sullen resentment, leaving Pearce to wonder at the looks they were all getting, the Frenchman included.

'I don't rate our chances much, John-boy, if this lot think to take us.'

'Then take your cutlass out of your belt, Michael, and let them see the blade.'

'Christ in heaven,' Michael exclaimed, as the crowd parted to reveal a body hanging from a hook, which had at one time been used to house the implements for working the guns. The face was black, the tongue protruding and half bitten through, this while the feet were toe down on the deck above bent knees.

Lutyens look at the cadaver and said. 'I do hope I have not suffered that journey in a boat just to tell you this fellow is dead.'

'No, monsieur. We know he is dead. What we wonder is how.'

Once translated, Lutyens responded sharply. 'Is that not obvious? He hanged himself.'

Moreau looked from Lutyens to Pearce and back again, and the surgeon's words, when related to him, made him terse.

'I would wish you to tell me, monsieur, how a

man can hang himself when he is taller than the space between the deck and the beams above. I want you to tell me if this poor fellow has been murdered and, if that is the case, I would be curious to know if you have a view of how that can be done without the knowledge of over fourteen hundred men in a ship so crowded as this.'

Chapter Twelve

'I do not have aboard so much as a sword with which to defend myself,' said Moreau, once they were in his cabin, which consisted of what would have been his sleeping quarters and a quarter gallery privy had *Apollon* carried its normal complement. 'Your marines searched everything before we were allowed near these ships. All our weapons were confiscated.'

'I cannot see, monsieur, what I can do about that.'

'Lieutenant Pearce, I barely know you, yet I think you understand more about France as it is at the moment than most of your fellow officers.'

'I have witnessed at first hand, Captain, that your fellow countrymen are no strangers to excess.'

He held Moreau's gaze then, wondering if he could guess just what he had seen; mobs from the filthy Faubourgs of eastern Paris, spurred on by ranting

orators, who had, one year past, broken open the jails
and massacred the prisoners; of crowds bearing
torches that illuminated the bloody remains of the
newly beheaded stuck on pikes as they marched,
spitting venom, through the streets, promising the
same fate to anyone of property. He could tell him of
the crowded prisons where people died for want of
the basics of life, while those who survived faced a
tribunal that had only one verdict; the guillotine. That
he did not do so was due to one fact only; he had no
notion to mention his own father and thus recall and
need to explain a painful memory.

'I have to tell you, monsieur, that every shade of
opinion is present aboard this ship, and I am sure it
is the same on our consorts. Most of the sailors
think nothing of politics, wishing only for their own
hearths, but there are die-hard Jacobins stalking
these decks, and, worse yet, men who think even
such blood-obsessed creatures lacking enough fire
in pursuit of revolutionary purity.'

'What is going on, Pearce?' demanded Lutyens,
whose French was too poor to keep up with such a
flow of words.

'One moment, Mr Lutyens,' Pearce replied,
before turning back once more to Moreau. 'What is
it you want?'

'Enough arms to enforce discipline, weapons
with which to ensure that anyone advocating any
kind of cleansing of those they call traitors can be

taken and confined, and if they are guilty of murder, hanged as surely as that man was today.'

Pearce broke off to explain to Lutyens, which had the added advantage of allowing him to think. He knew he could not make such a decision himself – it was up to Digby – but was it worth his while to put the case for arming the French against the express orders of Hood?

'If you do not provide this, monsieur, there are many who will not see the Straits, never mind Biscay, and I may be one of them.'

'Who was the dead man?' asked Lutyens, a question Pearce passed on, thinking it was an enquiry he should have made himself.

'He was mate to the sailing master, and he had only one aim, one I fear he made too public. To get back to his home port of Nantes and join with his fellow Vendéens to fight against what he sees as the Godless swine in Paris. There are others, of the rank you English term as warrants, who harbour similar views.'

'Why not kill them all now?'

'They will wait, but I know not how long. Perhaps it will happen as soon as they sight the approaches to our home ports, perhaps it will be tomorrow.'

'What would you require?'

'Pistols, cutlasses, a stand of muskets, enough to arm a guard I will appoint to ensure discipline.'

'And you would suggest that Garnier and the other captains are gifted the same?'

'I would.'

'How can you know they face the same problems?'

Moreau just smiled then, a full grin that spoke volumes, and Pearce surmised that, despite strict instructions not to do so, those commanding the four French warships had met and colluded, probably by boat and at night. The request he was hearing was from them all, not just Moreau.

'I will have to put this to my captain, Mr Digby. Only he can decide on this.'

'Might I add, for his consideration, Lieutenant Pearce, that we are yet to pass out of the orbit of Marseilles. Should these ships fall into the wrong hands, that may serve for some of the diehards as a port to aim for.'

'I hope, Captain Moreau,' Pearce snapped, 'you have seen we have the means to prevent that.'

Moreau's smile was grim now. 'Four capital ships, one sloop, armed with the means to do what? Hole them on the waterline and we, with men on board who know only too well how to contain such a thing with plugs and frapping? I would say that try as you might, you will not stop all four from getting to Marseilles.'

'There is something you are not telling me, Captain.'

'Monsieur, there are things I cannot tell you.'

'I will put the case to Captain Digby, I can do no more, and I will add, it might aid your request if you were to take down that tricolour from the poop rail and re-hoist the Bourbon flag.'

'No!' Henry Digby looked really angry that the idea had even been broached, though Pearce had been careful not to say if he was in favour or against. 'They must look to persuasion. Gifting them arms is not something that can be done in secret. I can just imagine the Admiralty clerks, or Lord Hood's scribblers, asking me where all our muskets, cutlasses and pistols had gone.'

'There is that. I doubt, once given, sir, we would get them back again.'

'Precisely! I leave it to you to work out how to tell Captain Moreau.'

That made Pearce's stomach drop; both the sea and the wind had got up while he had been aboard *Apollon,* so the journey back to his own ship had been a wet and, to Pearce's mind, a precarious one. As the cutter rose, fell and swayed, Lutyens had closed his eyes and Michael O'Hagan had called for the intercession of every saint in the Catholic canon, yet he had to admit that the likes of Dysart, Costello and Martin Dent had shown no fear, which he put down to the natural fatalism of all sailors. What Digby was suggesting was no more than a return journey, for such a message could not be imparted through a speaking trumpet. Just then, after the most peremptory knock, Farmiloe burst in.

'Lead French ship is signalling again, sir, and this time it is clear the message is distress.'

Both Pearce and Digby were on deck in a flash, grabbing telescopes and raking them along the deck of *Apollon,* not missing the fact that the tricolour was now at the mizzen masthead. Farmiloe produced the signal book and confirmed that his interpretation was correct, just as the signal disappeared, to be replaced by the raising and dipping of another tricolour, only this time it was on the mainmast halyard. This had Pearce thinking about Moreau, and the feeling he had harboured that the Frenchman was holding something back.

'Mr Harbin, aloft with a glass and keep an eye out due north. Sir, can we ask Mr Neame where we are in relation to the port of Marseilles?'

That got him an odd look, but it only lasted a second before Digby nodded, and he showed his appreciation of the point by immediately ordering a change of course from sitting in the wake of the bigger vessels, to being inshore of them.

'What do you anticipate, Mr Pearce?'

'I think, sir, since our departure from Toulon was so talked about there must have been some kind of secret communication from within that place with elements of the besieging force. So, knowing that only one destination is possible, namely the Straits,

an attempt might be made to take these vessels and
the men they contain into Marseilles.'

'If that is the case they will know both the name
and the nature of the escort.'

'I think it would be wise to assume that, sir.'

'Mr Pearce, do you think that Captain Moreau
still has control of *Apollon*?'

'We will only know that, sir, if our charges
change course.'

'Sir,' shouted Farmiloe, 'I call your attention to
the other three vessels.'

They needed no telescope to observe that now, all
four vessels were raising and dipping tricolours.
Whatever had happened on *Apollon* was being
repeated on her three consorts.

'I think,' said Digby, in a calm voice, 'that we
have a serious problem here, Mr Pearce. Beat to
quarters and clear for action. Mr Neame, we have
the wind, take me in close to *Apollon,* I want to be
across her hawse to let her know, whoever has
taken charge of that vessel, what they face.'

HMS *Faron* was a hive of activity, as everything
not required was shipped to safety. The cutter and
the jolly boat were hauled in and loaded with the
livestock – chickens, sheep and the ship's goat; if
matters got serious they must be cut loose to drift.
All the paraphernalia of a ship sailing easy had to
be cleared from the deck, while below the gunner
was handing out flintlocks and his made-up

cartridges to the gun captains and powder
monkeys, this while on deck, the restraining tackles
on the cannon were cast off, the gunports opened,
the ship showing her teeth as the guns were run out.

'Deck there,' shouted Harbin. 'Due north. I see
boats approaching, sir, not warships, more like big
luggers being worked by sweeps and I think they
have been rigged with cannon in the bows.'

Digby shouted, but even doing that he sounded
calm. 'To the number of?'

'Four sir, and very low in the water, which will I
think be the guns and perhaps the number of crew
they are carrying.'

'A lot of men, Mr Pearce, and to the number of
four. I would hazard they intend to board their own
national vessels. Mr Harbin, I need to know the
calibre of those cannon as soon as you have a clear
enough sight of them.'

'Aye, aye, sir.'

Coming up hand over fist and passing, inshore of
each French ship in turn, the silence from them had
an eerie quality. Certainly there were men on the
quarterdeck conning the ship, but there were none
that Pearce could recognise when he went up the
shrouds to have a look. It was Latimer, with sharp
sight for his age, who drew attention to the flag
draped in the quarter gallery casements of *Apollon*.
Every other eye on all five vessels was looking
north.

'Wouldn't do, your honour, to make too much of lookin' at it.'

'A *fleur de lys* pennant,' Pearce said, as he swung his telescope in an arc that took in the whole French squadron. 'That, sir, has to be Moreau sending us a signal.'

'How can you be certain?' Pearce explained about the trick with the flags as he had gone aboard, which had Digby adding, 'If it is a signal, it is, I think, one only we can see.'

The quarter galleries were to the side of the main cabin and wardroom, necessary rooms and sleeping cabins for the ship's senior officers, captain on the maindeck, ranking lieutenants below. What was being waved in the casements of *Apollon* would not be visible over the stern, or from above.

'It is a pity they are occupying those, Pearce. I had half a mind to put a ball through those casements to remind them of the cost of rebellion.'

'If I may point to a dilemma, sir.'

Digby interrupted him with a bleak smile. 'I know, Mr Pearce. If we fire into any part of these vessels we may well maim or kill the innocent rather than the guilty.'

'What do you propose to do, sir?'

'Why, Mr Pearce, we must engage these vessels coming out from shore. Mr Neame, set us due north. I want to get within range of those fellows and sink them.'

'Aye, aye, sir.'

On a south-easterly wind HMS *Faron* swung onto her new course with ease, yards braced round to take the breeze on a good point of sailing.

'Twelve-pounders by the look of the armament, sir,' shouted Harbin.

'That is good, I feared something heavier.'

'Still formidable weapons,' advanced Pearce. 'Greater than our own, bar the carronades.'

'But low in the water, which will reduce their range,' Digby said, more to himself than to his second-in-command. 'Mr Pearce, I wish you to take charge of the larboard cannon with Mr Farmiloe. I shall call Mr Harbin down to assist me, but I need good eyes at the masthead.'

'Martin,' Pearce shouted, 'aloft and relieve Mr Harbin.'

'I want to fight them, sir.'

'Then spit at them from the masthead. Move!'

Martin was running up the shrouds in a flash, and as soon as he relieved Harbin of the telescope that youngster leapt for a backstay and slid down to the deck, reporting immediately to Digby.

'They have closed up, sir, to sweeps near touching, to increase the effect of their cannon.'

'Then, Mr Harbin, I think they have made a mistake.'

'How so, sir?'

'Go to your station, Mr Harbin, and you shall see, very shortly.'

John Pearce was watching Digby closely, impressed by his calm. He could remember going into action as the last officer standing and he knew his heart had beat hard enough to nearly burst out of his chest. Yet the man in charge now looked and sounded as though he had not a care in the world and if he had a plan he had yet to impart it, content as he was to merely observe the approaching enemy, now visible from the deck.

'These luggers seem to be better for fishing than fighting, and I doubt there is a naval officer aboard. If they are from Marseilles, the Jacobins will have removed the head of anyone competent when they took back the town. Raise your long guns to maximum elevation, and train them as far forward as is possible. I wish to show them the limits to which they might approach in safety. With luck they may turn tail.'

Digby ignored the audible groan that came from the gun crews; they wanted blood.

'And make sure the bow chasers are manned and loaded. Tell me when you are ready.'

Pearce tried to detect some impatience in that remark, but there was none. Digby waited until his gun captains had driven their elevation wedges in as far as they would go and levered the cannon round so the muzzles were near to touching the gunport sides, before ordering Neame to bear up, the ship turning on his command.

'One at a time, Mr Pearce, for the sake of our timbers.'

Pearce walked down the line of gun captains, each holding a lanyard which kept them several feet away from the cannon. He tapped each one on the shoulder and they pulled, immediately leaping back as the gun roared, sending forth a plume of orange flame surrounded by a blast of thick black smoke and a very visible ball arcing though the air. Each one of the six hit the sea well in front of the oncoming gunboats, sending up a plume of white water high into the air. By the time the last cannon was fired, the first was through the process of reloading, and within a minute Neame had them back on a closing course.

'They come on,' Digby said, before turning to address the crew. 'It seems, lads, we have a scrap on our hands. What say you to that?' They cheered as hard as their lungs would allow, and when that died away, Digby added. 'You know, if I heard that I would put up my helm and run for safety.'

The blast from the reply reached them before the balls that were fired, and *Faron* was treated to a show of plumed water herself, but a good cable's length ahead of her bowsprit: neither elevation or wind favoured the enemy.

'Thank you, my friend,' Digby said to himself,

'for gifting me your ultimate range.' Louder he called, 'Mr Neame, stand by to bring us round again, but this time hard on to the starboard tack. Mr Pearce, all cannon to remain at maximum elevation, but I want the second broadside to be double shotted. These fellows need to be surprised.'

'Will they not reply in kind, sir?'

'I hope so, Mr Pearce, for if they do the recoil will probably sink them.'

'Now there,' said leathery old Latimer to his best mate, Blubber Booth, 'is a Johnny that knows his game.'

'Reckon there's any coin in this, Lats?'

'Not a bean, Blubber, not a bean.'

Overhearing that, Pearce was made acutely aware of the fact that he did not know his game. Faced with the same dilemma as Digby he would not have been sure what to do, and he only had to look at his senior to feel that he did. Mind, he reassured himself, there was no guarantee that his captain was in the right, but he had the appearance of knowing and an air of confidence that every man in the crew could observe, so Pearce moved from his position amidships and went to talk to him. Quietly, so that no one else could hear him, he addressed his captain, only to be just as quietly admonished.

'You have left your station, Mr Pearce.'

'I am curious, sir, as to what you intend.'

'Intend? Why to sink those fellows ahead of us or persuade them to turn tail.'

'May I be allowed to enquire how?' Seeing Digby stiffen, he added, 'I ask only for the purposes of wishing to learn, sir, and I am not so far from my station that half a dozen paces will not get me back to it.'

Considering that took several seconds, but Digby obliged eventually. 'Whoever commands those boats appears to be a fool, Mr Pearce, or he is no sailor. You will observe he is coming on grouped.'

'And that is wrong?'

'Gunboats on sweeps may move as they wish and ignore the wind. Thus they should split up and stand off a square rigger like us and use their power of manoeuvre to split our defence, get close, aim guns for the waterline, and try to hole us, then haul off hard to reload. The last thing he should want is to face a row of cannon, firing off a steady deck, at such a tempting target as four grouped boats.'

'You've seen this before?'

'Heard about it, for it is a nightmare to ships on blockade. The man in command yonder thinks that his guns close grouped have more effect, when the opposite is the truth. I think, in about a minute, we may shock him out of his misplaced complacency.'

'If they split up, sir, would you not be obliged to select one to attack?'

Digby smiled, but did not look at his subordinate. 'I would.'

'And the fate of that boat?'

'Total destruction, very likely, in the process of allowing his consorts to strike.'

'So, perhaps, the man in command knows what to do, but has failed to get one of his subordinates to act as a sacrificial lamb?'

'Very possible, Mr Pearce, which tends to imply he might lead them but he does not command them, a direct result I would say of the revolutionary ideas. Now please be so good as to go back to your station.'

Pearce obliged, and within a minute Digby shouted. 'Mr Neame, stand by to bring us up into the wind. Mr Pearce, fire as you bear.'

'Deck there,' Martin Dent yelled. 'French seventy-fours have put up their helms to close with us.'

'That I anticipated, lads,' Digby called out, 'pay it no heed. Now, Mr Neame.'

The rudder swung hard, as the sheets were let fly and Faron swung round in her own length with the wind slowing and steadying her. This time it was left to the gun captains, each crouched to peer through their gunport straight along the length of their piece, calculating the point at which to haul on that lanyard, a few heartbeats before the gun actually sighted on the target. The timbers shook as each gun went off, and though they could not see it, below, Lutyens instruments were flung from his sea chests to the deck by the vibrations. It was obvious that the enemy had just been waiting for the sight of smoke and all four of their cannon spoke simultaneously. But Digby had the better plan; their balls fell short, close enough to soak the decks but not enough to do harm. The balls from *Faron,* firing from that slightly higher elevation landed right amongst them, smashing two, one on the bows, another on its starboard timbers.

The first to be struck shuddered in the water as if a great hand had stopped its progress, the second fell away as the weight of the shot, and a man steering who lost his grip, took its bow on into a third boat, forcing it to sheer off. Just then, the first of the double shotted balls landed amongst them, bringing on chaos as some of the sweeps disintegrated.

'Mr Neame,' Digby commanded, in that same calm voice, 'get me back on course to close. Mr Pearce, the carronade will, I think, shortly come into its own.'

The one remaining fighting vessel was not done, and now that the range was closing it sent a ball flying up through the scantlings to the deck of *Faron* which caused splinters to fly in a dozen directions, the screams proving that it had been telling. Digby ordered the two bow chasers to respond, nodding at the way Neame used the rudder to ensure that each in turn could take good aim. They did not strike wood or flesh, but the amount of seawater that soaked their enemies must have been off-putting. That was confirmed by a wild shot in response that went through the rigging without doing much more than split a couple of ropes. The range had closed, and was now down to musket shot.

'Mr Pearce, as soon as she bears.'

Pearce was behind the carronade himself, lanyard in hand, this being a weapon he had come to respect. The ball, thirty-two pounds, would wound a capital ship, even a hundred-gunner if fired at close enough range. What it would do to a flimsy vessel that was in reality a fishing smack of the Mediterranean kind did not bear thinking about. As it bore just to the right of the target he pulled. The cannon, on runners instead of rope restraints, shot backwards onto its stops. It did not hit the enemy, not being a weapon for accuracy but effect, yet the amount of water it shifted told that last lugger what it faced, and as soon as the water which had obscured the vessel fell back, they could see the man in command had ordered his helm put down, his sweeps brought in and his single sail in the act of being raised, leaving his companions either sinking or fighting to stay afloat.

'That, sir,' said Digby,' is the first wise thing
you've done this day. Mr Neame, put us about and
close with *Apollon*. It seems we may have to go
aboard and rescue this fellow Moreau. Mr Pearce,
make up a boarding party, muskets to clear a way,
cutlasses and pistols to follow. We will be going in
through the wardroom and we must risk the
innocents. Anyone who seeks to impede you is to be
killed on the spot.'

'Sir.'

As HMS *Faron* came about, Pearce could see the
quartet of French seventy-fours spread across the
ocean, still coming on, despite the fact that those
sent to take them were either foundering or fleeing.

'No mercy, Mr Pearce, we do not have time for
that, for I fear we may have to subdue each vessel
in turn if we show any leniency.'

'Do we arm them, sir.'

'No need now, Mr Pearce. The troublemakers
have revealed themselves. Once we get aboard and
have re-established proper command, we will put
them in irons and keep them below.'

Digby took charge of the one cannon he was
going to use himself, ordering Neame to bring the
ship under the stern of *Apollon*, which they sailed
past in utter silence, with not a head peering over
the hammock nettings to see what was promised.
They had no means to retaliate, or to avoid what
was coming, as Digby had *Faron* steered until she

lay under *Apollon*'s rudder. As soon as Neame backed the sails he pulled the lanyard and sent a single cannonball smashing up through the flimsy casement windows and on to blast what wardroom bulkheads had been rigged. The sound of smashing glass and shredded timber had hardly faded when Digby said, in the same voice, devoid of emotion, which he had used throughout. 'At your own convenience, Mr Pearce.'

The man he addressed did not feel calm; his heart was pounding and he did not know if it was from excitement or trepidation.

'Come on, lads,' Pearce shouted, his sword waving in his hand as he jumped up onto the bulwarks of his own ship, which brought him level with the destroyed wardroom casements. That sword had to be used like a cleaver to get the splintered wood and glass apart enough for him to clamber through. Expecting a fight, he was surprised to see no one on the other side, and so he fetched aboard his muskets. They debouched on to the crowded maindeck through shattered bulkheads, more crowded now than before by the way the crew was pressed back in fear.

'Take aim,' Pearce said, himself raising his pistol, feeling sorry for those to the front of the crowd, trying to shrink their bodies from what was obviously coming. Then he said, in French. 'If someone does not fetch me Captain Moreau, this instant, I will open fire.'

As a group of messengers rushed off, he shouted, 'And bring to me that damned tricolour from the mizzen.'

Chapter Thirteen

With order restored, and the most radical of the Toulon sailors confined in their respective cable tiers, the rest of the voyage was set to be peaceful. *Entreprenant, Patriote* and *Orion* had all surrendered without the need to board and the flags at the masthead were once more flower-patterned ensigns. They spoke with a couple of frigates heading to join the fleet, but it was an exchange through a speaking trumpet only; they were eager to get to the seat of action, and Digby feared to lose touch with his charges. He dreaded the notion of being out of sight if they came across a Spanish warship. The Dons knew the lines of every vessel in the French fleet and they might see those Bourbon ensigns as a bluff and begin firing without establishing that the ships of their enemy had passports issued by Lord Hood.

Such easy sailing left ample time for Digby and

John Pearce to get to know one another, and mutual respect, already established, quickly deepened, though that could not be said about their politics or their religion. Digby loved his king and his Anglican God; Pearce had an abhorrence of monarchy and, like his father, saw religion as a conspiracy to cheat the gullible, which meant that it was most often a subject avoided. Their first bout, over one dinner, on that, had been quite enough.

'Have you heard of Liebnitz, sir?' asked Pearce.

'Who?'

He liked Digby, but he could see that he was a typical parochial Englishman: for him any kind of sense ceased at Dover. It was not malice that had him discount influence from abroad, just an upbringing which had been confined first to a mile or two from his home, a Dorset tenanted farm, followed by poor schooling, a midshipman's berth and a naval wardroom. His views were formed by the invisible walls of the world into which he had been born and inhabited.

'He is a philosopher.'

'Not a breed, Pearce, for whom I have much time. They seem to exist to disturb men's minds.'

'I think this fellow you would like. He maintained that everything that happened was the work of God.'

'In which he was entirely correct.'

'Even wars, famine, catastrophe?'

'I know what you are about, Pearce, but you will not undermine my faith with such mutterings.'

'Nor those of Liebnitz. He insisted such things were all part of God's great plan for the world, a notion that Voltaire quite exploded.'

'That rascal!' Digby snapped. 'There is a man who should have had a mouth restraint fitted at birth.'

'You have read him?'

'Certainly not. I have no notion to make diseased my mind.'

'Then does the name Hume mean anything.'

'Another philosopher I gather. At least he was an Englishman.'

'He was actually a Scot. My father studied with him.'

'I suppose you will use him to sustain your nonsensical opinions?'

'I shall put it to you and see, in only one of his propositions. The notion that if there was a Supreme Being for people to believe in, there was no need to extend to that entity the gift of supreme competence. It might be that such a God created the world in the aforesaid six days, in itself a remarkable feat, but surely to populate it with a contentious crew like the human race was not a clever idea.'

'God does not need to be clever.'

'Would that be because he has us to be so on his behalf?'

Digby reared up at that, seeing quite clearly that Pearce was baiting him. To the senior, such a debate was unheard of; he could not know how often Pearce had engaged with others to raise the question of an all-seeing deity, which was only one tenth of the times he had heard his father engage in the same debate.

'The only thing that can be said for religion, sir, is that it makes some men charitable, yet it has served as a refuge for a whole raft of scoundrels. We are approaching Spanish territory, are we not? Home to the Inquisition, where a lack of belief, even a question of doctrine, will result in a horrible death.'

'Papists, Pearce, who are backward in their thinking.'

'And the Musselmen to the south of us, who have the Prophet?'

'Misguided, but at least we share a God.'

'Travellers from the East talk of other religions. Can they all be right?'

That was when Digby killed off the discussion. 'I know I am right, Pearce, and I do not appreciate your attempts to get me to think otherwise. And I must tell you, for you obviously do not know, it is a tradition in the service to leave ashore notions of religion and politics. Nothing is so likely to split a wardroom as those two subjects. The effect of disagreement is pernicious, and although we are but two commissioned officers of this ship, I would see the same rule apply. Also, I would point out, sir, that the very ships we are tasked to escort have been brought to their sorry pass by the very kind of questions you pose.'

Pearce was tempted then to recount some of his experiences, of people learned, rich and sometimes both who paid lip service only to their religion, so as to keep in place those over whom they held power. He had seen it in the great houses of his own nation, but more so in the salons of Paris, where the men who had brought about the end of absolute monarchy had also brought to book the excesses of the church. Yet no Englishman, who would condemn an Archbishop of France for his venery and his open flaunting of his mistresses, would even begin to think it odd that the incumbent of the See of Canterbury needed an income of twenty-five thousand pounds to carry out an office that, if the words of Jesus Christ were to be taken literally, should be based on humility and personal sacrifice.

'Another glass of wine, sir,' Pearce said, knowing that such a thing was best left unsaid.

'Another glass of wine, Captain Barclay?' said Lieutenant Pigot, filling his own cup as he did so. All around them HMS *Britannia* was creaking and groaning, the timbers working and occasionally issuing a crack as it rode the swell.

Ralph Barclay was wondering, given Pigot's consumption, if he would have a clear enough head for what was coming in the morning, but felt it would be unwise to say anything. It was galling to be in need of such a fellow, and he could not but wonder why Hotham held him in such esteem, if you took out of the equation his inclination to flog.

'I think I had best keep a clear head for the morrow, Mr Pigot.'

'I generally has a bit of a fuzz most mornings, sir, but I find it soon goes once I have o'erseen the cleaning of the decks. Nothing like the wielding of a starter on a bare back to get the head clear.'

'You do not leave such tasks to your junior lieutenants?'

'Never, sir. As Premier I bear responsibility, and if I am going to face the wrath of my captain for a poorly swabbed deck, then I am going to make sure he who troubles my life does more'n trouble his own.'

Thank God I only have one night with this fellow, Ralph Barclay thought.

Pigot was a difficult man with whom to make conversation, he having so few topics that interested him, and he did not seem to appreciate, as would every naval officer Ralph Barclay had ever encountered, being told of the actions of others. Any attempt to recount his encounters with enemy vessels met with a frown.

'You know, Mr Pigot, I think I may retire.'

Pigot picked up the bottle. 'Why this, sir, it is as yet half full.'

'I am sure you can see to that, Mr Pigot, but I lack your constitution in the article of drink.'

For the first time Ralph Barclay sensed this choleric-looking fellow was pleased; the man actually thought he had been in receipt of praise. The Premier of the flagship had given up his own sleeping quarters to the accused, letting it be known that he entirely approved of the actions of the captain of HMS *Brilliant*, the general air in the entire wardroom, and Ralph Barclay appreciated such support from men who understood the problems attendant on manning a ship of war. They were not milksops like Pearce, but proper seamen who knew their trade. Having disrobed, washed and said his prayers, he slipped into the swinging cot that would be his bed, but sleep would not come, even with the ship rocking and snubbing her anchors.

As in all such situations his mind flitted from memory to idea and back again, all the way to his life as a midshipman, which had been damned unpleasant, though not much worse than what had preceded it; a trader father who drank like Pigot and was free with his belt, a mother too much in terror of her husband to intervene; indeed a woman who many a morning bore the marks of a previous night's beating. Servants of no refinement whatever who spied on everything and gossiped, so the whole town knew if the Barclays were in hock to their fellow-tradesmen or flush when some local aristocrat finally paid a bill.

What was he going to do with that Burns boy? The lad was as near to useless as it was possible to be, yet he was a relative by marriage and that meant an obligation. Naturally that led on to thoughts of his wife, of their wedding, with he being able to recall with clarity the cold but clear day, the cheerful friends, added to the wonder he felt that such a beautiful creature had agreed to marry him. He managed to blot from these recollections the fact that Emily's family occupied a house that was entailed to him; that he could have, on his father's demise, slung them out. No, she had come to him not just because of a sense of duty but because she admired him.

But that admiration had been dented. It was galling that she refused to understand, annoying that she applied the mores of her sheltered upbringing to a service that was nothing like family life in rural Somerset. Sailors were not bucolic farm hands or local labourers, some were rascals of the worst kind, others men who, not in the least refined, when conflict looked imminent and the fleet expanded, left the merchant service for the better conditions on a ship of war; not pay, but regular food, fourteen inches of sleeping space and a berth full of mates all eager to talk of prize taking. But there were never enough of them, so pressed men were necessary to man the fleet. The nation was at war, and they must be willing to face death so that their county could triumph.

There was a brief reverie of Ralph Barclay chastising his wife as his father had done with his mother; a good seeing-to with a birch would bring her to heel, bring her back to the proper degree of respect due to her marital master, but it did not last; he knew he would struggle to administer such a punishment and on reflection he guessed it would have, on Emily, the reverse effect of that imagined. Yet brought to heel she must be, and when he did finally fall into a deep slumber, that was the last thought he had.

'Mr Glaister, I see that certain members of the crew are being shipped into a boat.'

'Good morning, Mrs Barclay,' the First Lieutenant said, raising his hat with his one good hand, the other being still in a sling from a wound taken when the ship was captured. Polite as that was it did not answer her enquiry, which forced her to repeat it.

'They are to attend on Captain Barclay's court martial, ma'am.'

Looking into the boat she could see Coyle, the

Master at Arms, a bosun's mate called Kemp, whom she found unpleasant, Devenow, her husband's new clerk, Gherson and her nephew.

'I am at a loss, Mr Glaister, to think what Mr Burns can bring to proceedings. From what I gather he was not present on the night in question.'

'Captain's order, Mrs Barclay. Not for me to query.'

The way the blue-eyed Highlander was looking at her, his sharp-boned face disapproving, it was as if he was telling her that she should think likewise, which was not an attitude that she was prepared to accept.

'Fortunately I have only the bounds of marriage to constrain me, Mr Glaister, not those of the service. With your permission, I will join them.'

Glaister stiffened. 'I have orders, Mrs Barclay, that you are not to leave the ship.'

'You do not have, sir, the authority to confine me.'

'Madam,' Glaister replied unhappily, 'I have the authority to deny you that boat.'

She was tempted to snap at him, but that would be futile; the man was only doing what he had been told. The seat of this problem lay with her husband, not Glaister. 'When you say not leave the ship, am I to take it that includes a stroll of some kind?'

'No, but the man Captain Barclay would allot the duty of escorting you is not going to be available. As you will see, Devenow is in the boat.'

The jolly boat was pulling away and looking over the side into the refuse-filled water of the inner harbour, Emily was struck by the fact that Toby Burns kept his face turned away from her, which, given he normally looked at her with sheep-like devotion or deep worry for some imagined transgression, was disquieting.

'I shall take a walk, Lieutenant Glaister, and I shall do so unescorted. I have found that Toulon is quite safe now that all those radical sailors have departed.'

The two sets of eyes locked, those of the Premier troubled, hers like flints. She knew she had placed him in a difficult, indeed impossible position. As a gentleman he could not bar her from what she intended, but it was clear he should. Ralph Barclay had been quite specific, telling Glaister that should she demand, she must be denied a boat. He had said nothing about terra firma. In truth, he should have offered her another escort, but that, in his captain's eyes, might smack of collusion. Upsetting his commanding officer was not a good idea if he wished for advancement.

'Very well, Mrs Barclay, but I abjure you to keep a weather eye open. Toulon may appear safe with a hulk like Devenow a few paces to your rear. It might not be quite so secure for a lady on her own.'

'Nonsense. I shall fetch my parasol.'

Emily went below and did just that, but she also dug out her pin money purse, not containing a great deal of coin, but surely enough for what was needed, a one-way trip in a wherry to HMS *Britannia*.

The accused and Pigot entered the great cabin just after those officers who were interested had taken what seats were available for an audience. Ralph Barclay was encouraged by the smiles and nods of support he received; he was at least among his peers.

Hotham's secretary, acting as recorder, called, 'All rise', an instruction which everyone present obeyed. A file of five post captains, all with twin epaulettes, entered, and stood behind the long table ranged before the footlockers that ran under the casements. The President of the Court took out his sword and laid it on the green baize cloth, then sat down, followed by his fellow judges and the rest of the people in the room. Ralph Barclay had no sooner made his seat than the mention of his name had him and Pigot up again.

'Allow me to introduce the officers who will hear this case. On my left Captain Luckner and Captain Breen, on my right Captain Fellows and Captain Laidlaw. I am Captain Foregham, and I act as president. I must ask you, Captain Barclay, to confirm your name and rank, and name to the court your trusted friend.'

Barclay obliged, and that was followed by a reading of the charges, which were in all respects a repetition of what Hotham had said to him when he announced this court.

'I now introduce to you and the court, Lieutenant Elijah Birdutt, who will put the case for the prosecution.'

'Good,' thought Barclay; he knew the man and he was well known for his blustering stupidity.

Birdutt stood, his bright red face and untidy grey hair evidence of the time he had spent in his rank; he had to be one of the oldest lieutenants in the King's Navy, which was a direct result of his inability to both execute his duties and impress those in command. He had been denied promotion for the very good reason that he was unworthy of elevation, only a degree of influence keeping him in employment.

'May it please the court, I have nothing but the charges to levy against the accused, those claiming testimony regarding the case having been taken away from Toulon by their duties.'

'Those are?' asked the President.

'Lieutenants Digby and Pearce, Midshipman Farmiloe, Bosun Robert Sykes, and seamen Dent, Dommet, O'Hagan and Taverner.'

'Do we have any depositions from those missing?'

'Unfortunately not, sir. It seems there was no

time to take such a thing prior to their hurried departure.' Ralph Barclay was looking at Hotham's secretary, writing in an elegant hand words he knew to be total lies. The man's sangfroid was admirable. 'There is however the verbal testimony made both to Admiral Lord Hood, his Captain of the Fleet, Rear Admiral Hyde Parker, and to Admiral Hotham on a separate occasion. I asked those officers to provide written statements of what transpired and with the courts permission I would like to read them out.'

'It would be best to hear their remarks from their own lips, while also allowing Lieutenant Pigot an opportunity to question them for the sake of clarity.'

'May it please the court,' Pigot said, looking at his client and sending blasts of stale wine breath into his face as he spoke. 'We are talking of officers engaged in the most onerous of tasks, men with great responsibilities. I can speak for Captain Barclay when I say he would not wish them taken away from their duties merely to confirm their written word.'

'Very well. Mr Birdutt, you may read each one in turn, before passing it to the court.'

'The accusations stem from one source only, sir, and that is Lieutenant John Pearce.'

'None of the others mentioned in the witness list have made complaint?'

'If they have, sir, it is not recorded.'

'Carry on.'

Birdutt read in a sonorous voice, as if it was he who was the admiral and not the man making the complaint. Some of Pearce's venom was obvious in each one, indeed Ralph Barclay could practically hear the sod's voice in Lord Hood's testimony. Parker was more circumspect, relating only the facts, while Hotham's told the court that he had needed, on more than one occasion, to remind Lieutenant Pearce of both his inferior rank, the virtues of the man he was traducing, and the fact that duelling between officers of His Majesty's Navy, rank being immaterial, was forbidden. Once Birdutt was finished, the President cleared the court so they could read these documents in peace. Pigot was asked to remain for the same reason, but sent out when the five captains fell to discussing the contents.

'It's a damn shame about not duelling, sir.' Ralph Barclay turned to face Taberly, who was smiling at him. 'Nothing would give me greater pleasure than to call out Pearce.'

'You're not alone, Mr Taberly.'

'Can I say, sir, that you have the support of every right thinking officer in the fleet.'

'Thank you, Mr Taberly. Allow me to name to you Lieutenant Pigot.'

As if to underline his name, Pigot burped as he

shook Taberly's hand, and he turned away from the
fetid smell as a voice called. 'Gentlemen, the court
will reconvene.'

'Mr Pigot, do you have any remarks to make
regarding what you have read?'

'No, sir.'

'Mr Birdutt, do you have any more evidence to
introduce?'

'No sir.'

'Then, Mr Pigot, you may proceed to your
defence.'

'Thank you, sir. I call Midshipman Burns.'

Toby Burns was terrified long before he came
through the door, and the sight of a row of blue-
coated captains, and that sword on the table, nearly
had his knees giving way. He was directed to stand
centre room and Pigot immediately asked him his
name, rank and ship.

'Now, Mr Burns, please recount to the court the
events, as you recall them, that took place in late
February of this year.'

Toby Burns opened his mouth, but nothing came
out, which had the President say, 'Take your time,
lad, all we are after is the truth, and I would remind
you that you are not here on trial.'

The truth was all the boy was thinking of; if I tell
them the truth I'm dished. Slowly he spoke, hesitant
and rasping from a very dry throat, and all the
while the recorder's quill scratched across the page,

seeming to him louder than his own voice. 'The need for hands...the boat upriver...his task to land them west of Blackfriars...any mistake was his, his uncle being too indulgent in taking the blame on himself.'

'You steered the boat to shore?' asked Pigot.

'I did.'

The slight commotion made him look round, really no more than people shifting in their seats, one standing to let Emily Barclay sit down. The sight sent Toby Burns stomach heading down to the floor.

Chapter Fourteen

Ralph Barclay had turned at the same, small commotion, but his reaction was one of very obvious fury, yet he could do or say nothing and he fought to compose his features; who knows, people might assume she was here to support his case. Her defiance was known only to him.

'Mr Burns, please tell the court what happened when you landed.'

He had to go on, there was no choice. If he blurted out now that his previous evidence was a lie, he would be in the dock as much as his uncle. It was a good thing he had been so thoroughly rehearsed, for that took over and it was in something of a daze that he answered.

'It was pitch black, sir, which gave us no clue as to our true location, and the tavern into which Captain Barclay sent his scouting party would not have known they were in the wrong place entirely, no more than we outside did, as we secured the exits.'

'There was violence, was there not?' one of the other captains enquired. 'The men taken did not surrender without offering resistance.'

'One or two, sir, but not all. I would say that a goodly number of the men recruited took it to be their fate. How could they not, living in such squalor?'

All five adjudicating captains, Lieutenant Birdutt, Pigot and Ralph Barclay adopted stony expressions at that statement, lest such a blatant piece of nonsense elicit the reaction it deserved; profound disbelief. Every one of those captains had pressed men in their time, and though they had also recruited volunteers, with bands, posters, bribes and downright falsehoods about untold wealth, they knew that it was not done in the hours of darkness, and in a place where men were taking their ease.

'I take it,' asked Pigot, 'since he has been so vehement in his denunciation, that Lieutenant Pearce was not of that number.'

'I could not say, sir. He was not at that time Lieutenant Pearce, he was just another volunteer, one face amongst many.'

As Pigot gave the judges a meaningful look, the sound of a slight cough from behind, which he guessed to be his Aunt Emily, made Toby Burns' skin crawl. He was also aware that he was sweating, conscious that a cabin too full of bodies was turning stuffy, and licking his upper lip he tasted salt.

'The men were taken into your boats,' Pigot continued, 'shipped down to Sheerness, where they were given the chance to volunteer for service to the Crown.'

'Yes, sir.'

'And did you see any evidence of dissention?'

He had seen them coming aboard that grey morning, some bearing cuts, others scars and bruises, rubbing wrists that had chaffed at their restraints, one or two weeping, many confused, others emitting looks of sheer defiance. He had not known it was Pearce when Ralph Barclay cuffed him hard round the ear; that he found out later.

'Sir, I can recall, just before I went to my berth, that there was a great deal of jollity.'

'Jollity?'

'Laughing, an exchange of teasing.'

'Thank you, Mr Burns. I am finished with this witness, sir.'

'Mr Birdutt?'

'No questions, sir.'

'Mr Burns,' said Pigot, 'you may step down.'

As Toby Burns went to sit to one side, Hotham's junior clerk was despatched to fetch the Master at Arms. Coyle, still suffering from a leg broken in a storm, came limping in using sticks, then, with some difficulty, knuckled his forehead and removed his cap. The ritual of identity and the Bible completed he was asked very much the same sort of questions as Toby Burns. For Coyle it was simple; if the captain was to be had up over pressing in the Liberties, then that could apply to all who were with him on the night and he was not ever going to lay himself open to such a charge. Coyle had been a soldier before becoming a Master at Arms, and every brush with authority all his life had led him to treat it with mistrust. He was honest enough to admit he could not recall who was steering the boat and he quite cleverly managed to avoid saying that Burns was not there. As to location, he had no idea; such things were left to those qualified to decide and he obeyed what orders he was given once on dry land.

Violence? Some, not much. Despair? There were a few that took that line, but they soon came round and were ready for the King's shilling once it had been explained to them the joys of shipboard life and the prospect of prize money.

'I would say, sir,' Coyle intoned, in response to Pigot's final enquiry, 'by the time they made the deck they were as content a bunch of prospective hands as it has ever been my good fortune to help recruit.'

Birdutt was again invited to cross-examine, but

replied that he could see no purpose in it, as Lieutenant Pigot had been so good as to pose any questions he, himself, might have thought of. Ralph Barclay heard an approving murmur go round the great cabin, with much nodding of heads, causing the President to rap his knuckles on the green baize to command silence and attention.

Kemp came next, and such was his rat-like snivelling appearance, Pigot got through his evidence quickly, really a repetition of Coyle's, for he created an impression that every word he uttered was a falsehood. But he had one valuable addition to the tale; at the time, he had been a bosun's mate, and had had charge of John Pearce once he had been entered.

'He changed his tune when work was called for, your honour. A shirker he was, alas hanging back from what was needed to be done, unlike the rest who was willing. I had to encourage him more'n once.'

'Changed his tune?' asked Birdutt, when Pigot handed him over.

'Aye, your honour. He was happy enough to take the King's shilling, but not happy to meet his end of the bargain, and I heard him trying like billy-o to get others to rise up and rebel.'

'In the depositions this court has already studied from our senior officers, it seems that Mr Pearce was insisting on freedom for others. This he would hardly do without their connivance.'

'I won't say they didn't waver, sir, I don't say that at all, for Pearce had a silver tongue. An' I daresay for a time one or two fell into his way of seein' things. But hot and cold they would be, with Pearce when he was in their ears, happier with their lot when they was left alone to think it out.'

'So would you say, Kemp, that Pearce, as a newly recruited volunteer, turned into a troublemaker?'

There was almost gratitude from Kemp for having the matter being put to him so succinctly, and he oozed insincerity in his positive response. Devenow said much the same as Kemp, though in an inarticulate mumble that made his evidence hard to understand, so he was quickly got rid of.

'Call Cornelius Gherson.'

He had dressed for the occasion. In his new role as Ralph Barclay's clerk, he was free to come and go from the ship as he pleased, once his duties were complete. Gone was the checked shirt and rolled-up ducks which he had worn aboard HMS *Leander*. He had money to spend from his gambling profits as well as his letter writing for the illiterate, and he was in a port were folk of quality, who had come to Toulon as refugees, were having to dispose of their goods and chattels at any price offered to survive. He now wore fine linen underneath a well-made coat, stout breeches, white silk stockings and shoes with real silver buckles. His hat already off as he

entered the cabin, he executed a proper bow to the
judges, sweeping that shiny tricorn across his chest,
and showing an excellent head of near white, blond
hair that had been expertly barbered. He looked so
much the gentleman that Ralph Barclay resolved to
examine his accounts as soon as he returned to his
ship.

'Mr Gherson, you were recruited on the same
night as the men named in Lieutenant Pearce's
complaint.'

'I was, sir.'

'A volunteer?' asked Pigot.

'No, sir, I came to the service through an
accident.'

'Explain to the court, please, what you mean by
that.'

The smile was engaging and designed to be, the
slight brush of the hand over his attractive features
used to denote both reluctance and modesty. 'I was
engaged in a prank, sir,' he replied, addressing the
President directly, 'showing off to a lady on London
Bridge, balancing on the parapet, when I lost my
footing.'

Emily recalled him that day at Sheerness, because
he had on nothing but a shirt to cover his
nakedness. She had never thought on it before, but
seeing he had been engaged in his new task, and
would be in regular contact with her husband, it
suddenly became a matter of interest to her to know

the true circumstances of his arrival. She had no doubt he was lying, and no doubt either that of all those who had gone before him, he was likely to be the most accomplished. She could imagine many a woman finding him handsome, for if he had fine features, somehow there was an air of corruption about them, as if he was in fact too gilded a youth. Paris instead of Hector.

'It could be said to be ill-fortune, yet I landed right by one of Captain Barclay's boats, and stout hands grasped me and hauled me in, saving my life, for I would have drowned for certain in such a strong current as that which races through the arches of London's bridges.'

'Quite,' Pigot said impatiently, his face conveying the fact that he thought Gherson to be over-embellishing.

'As I say,' Gherson continued, not the least bit put off by Pigot's attitude. 'I would not be here now. So I was taken aboard with the others, fed and clothed and asked if I would like to volunteer.'

'Which you did?'

'Not immediately, for I had a lot to leave behind. A lady for whom I harboured some affection, a position of some trust to an elderly but kind gentleman. In short, prospects.'

Pigot seemed to cut across him again. He knew, if no one else present did, that Gherson was indeed gilding it. 'What changed your mind.'

'Why, John Pearce.'

Pigot exhaled a great quantity of air as he barked. 'Pearce!' He then turned to the judges and gave them that same meaningful look he had been practising for days.

'Why yes, John Pearce had volunteered, and he said it would be a fine thing if I did so too. He was full of talk of adventure, of exotic climes, perhaps the South Seas, and the money to be made from taking enemy ships. He invited me to join his mess and showed me much warmth.'

One or two heads moved at that statement; with a handsome youth like this fellow, warmth could only mean one thing.

'So I found myself persuaded, and went with Pearce to the then First Lieutenant and signed my name.'

'You were not coerced.'

The handsome face clouded over, and his easy manner was replaced by an unpleasant pout. 'I have to tell you, sir, that the notion is alien to me. Coercion would only make me stubborn. I am biddable, but not one to be bullied into anything.'

'The court,' Pigot said gravely, 'may find it hard to accept that a man who has since made such a fuss was the instrument of your joining the service.'

'Which makes doubly galling what happened next.'

Pigot did not like to see Gherson pout with

displeasure. It made him look weak, yet there was no way to stop the fellow. 'And that was?'

'A complete *volte-face*.' Gherson paused, so that those present could admire that touch of French, an indication that he was as educated as he now looked. 'Within hours he was at me again to say that I had been forced to serve, that I had been taken from some riverside tavern by violence. Naturally, I refused to be so duplicitous, and we became, I have to tell you, mortal enemies from that moment on.'

'Did you observe Pearce seeking to persuade others to the course he had proposed to you?'

'I did, and it gives me no pleasure to say that he had the ear of several, turning them from happy tars into malcontents.'

'No further questions, sir,' Pigot said, with a very satisfied air.

Birdutt stood up, which surprised and displeased his opposite number; Pigot was sure he had got everything to be had out of Gherson.

'Mr Gherson, you are now, I believe, no longer a common seaman?'

Damn the man thought Ralph Barclay, what is he at? He looked to Pigot whose face was clouded with fury.

'No sir. Captain Barclay, once he found I was serving on HMS *Leander*, took it upon himself, knowing my skills, to appoint me as his clerk.'

'Can I ask you, Mr Gherson, how you came to be on *Leander*?'

'An unforeseeable set of circumstances. I was part of the prize crew that took a merchant vessel called the *Lady Harrington* back to England. We were come upon in soundings by another naval vessel, HMS *Griffin*, and since a goodly number of the original crew were still aboard, the captain of that vessel took the men from Captain Barclay's ship into his own, he being short-handed.'

'You were, in effect, pressed.'

'Pearce saw it as so, I did not.'

'Mr Gherson, I put it to you that you have not been entirely honest with the court.'

The babble that created had the President shouting 'Order.' Gherson looked confused; indeed there was a hint of fear in his countenance. Ralph Barclay sat stony-faced, while Pigot was looking at Birdutt as though he would like to kill him.

'I put it to you that, in fact, you succumbed to John Pearce's blandishments, that you became, like him, a malcontent, and that Captain Barclay despatched you back to England to get rid of you.'

'Sir, I...'

'The truth, Mr Gherson,' insisted Birdutt.

The restoration of his composure was quick, for Gherson had a brain quite capable of spinning out the consequences of his own words. Suddenly he looked crestfallen, and then he replied in a voice that was nothing like that which he had employed before, being soft and embarrassed.

'I am forced to admit, sir, that I fell for Pearce's line, that I forgot my duty to my king and my own signature. Captain Barclay, as you say, took a chance to get out of his ship everyone who had fallen for the notions that Pearce had planted in their minds. Though it was never stated, I think he did not want aboard any man who was not willing to serve.'

'Can I ask you, now you have admitted to your error, what was Pearce's motive?'

'I doubt he had one, sir, other than to cause trouble. He seemed to relish that above all other things. When we were pressed into the *Griffin* I was still under his spell, but his influence waned and I came to my senses. He is a weathervane, sir. I was one for a while, but I am no longer such now.'

'Yet, you will have heard he was elevated to his present rank by the express orders of King George. You were present at the engagement which so impressed His Majesty, were you not?' Gherson nodded, head down; this was not going where he wanted. 'Did he deserve such an unusual amount of distinction?'

Gherson suddenly looked up, his eyes bright. 'I think he has taken much credit due to others, sir. I was not alone in advising him of the course of action he subsequently employed. The captain of

HMS *Griffin* was *hors de combat,* collective decisions were taken for which Pearce subsequently took all the acclaim, took what was a joint action and made it his alone. So, sir, the answer is no. I do not believe he merits his elevation. The king, may God bless and preserve him, was duped.'

'No further questions, sir.'

Pigot called his final witness, the accused. Ralph Barclay had prepared a long and, he thought, convincing account of his actions, a testimony that would incline the court in his favour, but was aware that Emily was behind him, knew that she would hear every word. He could not tell his version of events with her eyes boring into his shoulder blades. So he squared those shoulders, and said,

'Sir, I am the captain of HMS *Brilliant.* I personally commanded the party that night we were out seeking volunteers. If some violence was used I was not aware of it, but such ignorance does not excuse me. My commission gives me many things, but it also gives me responsibility. You have heard from others their version of events and I feel I can add little but this. That whatever the court decides, it is on my shoulders the verdict should fall. With command goes the responsibility of a ship's captain and I will not shrink from that.'

Pigot, who had a whole sheaf of questions to ask, looked dumfounded. He barked his next words. 'Mr Birdutt.'

The old buffoon looked at Ralph Barclay with his wet eyes, and said. 'I see no further point in questions, sir, I feel the case has been fully examined and to interrogate Captain Barclay would only make more uncomfortable to him what must be an extremely unpleasant affair.'

'Very well,' said the President, 'you may make your closing arguments.'

When Birdutt did so, anyone listening would have been hard put to know if he was acting as prosecutor or defender, so gentle was his tone. Every charge was larded with caveats, each point he made qualified by doubts, so that when Pigot rose to make his address, the job had nearly been done for him.

'Sir, on the night in question, Captain Barclay entrusted a task to a young man, who was not up to it. Yet this is the same young fellow who, within a week, would act on the enemy shore in a way to shame the heroes of antiquity. In short, sir, what may seem over-confidence in the young man's abilities proved to be an underestimation of his qualities as a budding officer in the King's Navy, a blessing, given that more senior members of the crew were either lost or badly wounded.'

Toby Burns, now sitting at the side of the court with Coyle, Kemp, Devenow and Gherson, had the good grace to blush, though he kept his eye fixed hard on the five judges and away from his aunt.

'So,' Pigot continued, 'if Captain Barclay is guilty of anything it is of placing too much trust in one so young. In the dark, he could not know of the lad's errors of navigation, nor, since he did not himself enter the tavern called the Pelican, could he see if violence, which I am sure he expressly forbade, was being employed.'

The long pause was for effect.

'It has been attested, under oath, that every man taken from that place volunteered, and it was only after time aboard John Pearce wished to reconsider, in fact to renege on his own freely given commitment. You have heard how he tried to suborn other members of the crew to also break their oath, causing so much trouble that Captain Barclay determined to get rid of him by sending him home on the first available ship. Sirs, you are all naval officers. I ask you, are these the actions of a man who had pressed men who were unwilling? No. It is the action of an upright officer, who does not want aboard his vessel any man who does not truly want to serve his king and country.'

Pigot walked over to stand beside his client. 'Captain Barclay is guilty.' That got a gasp from those too stupid to see where it was leading. 'But he is not guilty of illegal impressment. He broke the bounds of the Liberties of the Savoy in error, not as we have pointed out, his own. What did he find there? Why, men willing to serve, creatures whose life, in such a place, must have been hell on earth. He indeed would have been seen by many as a saviour. Testimony is plentiful that by the time the ship's boats raised Sheerness, even those who had doubts were happy to accept the King's shilling. And then what? John Pearce, who you have heard most accurately described as a weathervane...'

He had to stop then. Emily Barclay, in standing, had noisily pushed back her chair. She glared at Pigot, then spun on her heel and marched out through a door opened for her by a servant. The President, who would have rigged the grating for any officer who had dared to do such a thing, could only offer a weak smile, seeming to be making an excuse for the gentler sex.

'A weathervane,' Pigot intoned, picking up where he had left off. 'I will not rehearse again his actions, the court knows them only too well. He claims heroic status, let him live with the knowledge, for he must know, of what he did and what part others played in his good fortune. Suffice to say that released from his bond by Captain Barclay, he could have no idea that another officer would come along and press him out of that merchant vessel. I ask the court to find Captain Barclay guilty, but of indulgence, kindness, understanding and honourable behaviour.'

Pigot stood rock still for half a minute, then sat down. The President thanked him and Lieutenant

Birdutt, then asked that the room be cleared so they could consider their verdict. Once outside, the Premier informed Barclay and both counsel that refreshments were awaiting them in the wardroom.

'Mr Burns,' said Ralph Barclay.

'Sir?'

'Back to the ship with you and the other witnesses. The boat may come back for me, and be so good as to ask Mr Glaister to command it personally.'

They drank well and ate better, for there was nothing more to do, and Birdutt, no longer obliged to even pretend to prosecute, was fulsome in his praise of Barclay's actions, and convinced the court would see it that way. They were called back within half an hour and faced their five judges, and as the President spoke, the eyes of the accused were on his sword, the point aimed at him, the sign of a guilty verdict.

'Captain Barclay, please rise. The court has considered carefully the evidence brought before it and we feel a sense of deep disquiet that an officer of your experience should allow such a gross error of judgement be permitted.'

God, thought Ralph Barclay, I'm done for.

'However, taking into consideration all the facts, we find that there was no malice in your actions, that you saw yourself as acting in the best interests of the service. It is the judgement of this court that you should face a reprimand, and that no further action should be contemplated. That is the verdict we will pass to the Commander-in-Chief for confirmation.'

'Might I enquire, sir,' asked Pigot, 'if you will see it as necessary to forward the case to a civil court?'

'We will not recommend such a course, but, of course, Lord Hood may see it differently. For now, Captain Barclay, you are free to return to your ship and resume your duties.'

Chapter Fifteen

The Rock of Gibraltar was a welcome sight to any sailor, regardless of the direction from which it was approached, it being one of those points on a sea journey that denotes progress. Yet it was doubly so for a ship of the King's Navy, being a beacon of the nation's achievements, an outpost of British power that bearded the Spanish Crown and made impossible any secret egress to the Atlantic Ocean by elements of the French Mediterranean fleet. Such a body of ships, combined with those based in the Atlantic ports, would, given the Royal Navy's commitments elsewhere, represent near parity of force, a threat to the shores of England that would be hard to contain.

Wrested from Spain in 1702, following the Treaty of Utrecht, Gibraltar was the subject of an annual demand by the Spanish court for it to be returned, and just as often that request was denied;

it was, quite simply, too valuable a strategic holding to be given up, quite apart from the fact that it had been taken by the effusion of much blood, and held through several sieges with a costly expenditure of that same commodity. There it stood, towering over the Straits, nine miles wide at the narrowest point, affording to anyone looking out from its pinnacle a good view of the African shore and the approaches from both west and east.

It was a pity that the south-easterly that had given them such swift passage to the Rock swung into the other direction, south-westerly, just a day before it was sighted. Digby, Pearce and Neame now found themselves on deck all the time, as *Faron* and her charges had to tack and wear towards their destination, working their way in a wind which carried with it fine sand, coating everything it touched.

'It is the prevailing wind this time of year, Mr Pearce, and it do make life hard for a ship seeking to get out into the Atlantic.'

Pearce was curious; he had come through the Straits on the way out, as easy as kiss my hand. 'How so?'

'Current's set dead against it, flows through strong from the west.'

'But surely, as with all currents, it sometimes reverses itself. Water must flow out of the Mediterranean as well as in.'

'You'se taken no account of evaporation, sir, of which there is a deal in these warm climes, and it is reckoned by those who study it that there is a deep water current going out, and it is only the surface current coming in. So to make the outward passage, you need a wind, and even then it ain't plain sailing, you wait and see.'

'And with the wind foul?'

'It's weather the southernmost point and get into Algeciras Bay, where we will lay till the wind changes in our favour.' Then Neame shouted, calling all hands to wear ship, before adding, in a normal voice. 'Could be stuck for weeks at this time of year and the bay is no joy, what with it being open to the south-westerly swell.'

Pearce looked out at their charges, the squadron of French seventy-fours, wondering what the folk on the Rock would make of the ships and their human cargo. That got him to thinking about being forced to lie up and wait for Neame's wind; they would have to do likewise and that could create problems. Gibraltar was one of the few places where the rules regarding sailors going ashore were relaxed, quite simply because there was nowhere for them to run. The Spanish guarding the border at La Linea, in a time of peace, would clap them in goal before returning them; no British tar could be allowed to create dissention when they so badly wanted the Rock back. In war, a more common circumstance between the two powers, the case did not arise. The only other option was a boat to the Musselman shore, where anyone deserting the King's Navy could exchange life between decks for a life of rowing a Barbary galley with a whip as encouragement.

'I don't suggest that the French sailors be allowed ashore, sir. Some of them would be bound to try the Spanish lines, but I wonder about the officers, if they give us their parole. It would, after all, be a courtesy I think they would extend to us.'

Digby toyed with his wine glass, keeping a firm grip on the stem to ensure that the contents stayed within the confines of the bowl, with the ship bucking about on a heavy sea. Pearce could see that he was possibly amenable to the idea, yet not wholly convinced.

'I foresee a problem of perception, Mr Pearce. We now know, because of contact, the men we have dealt with are not so different from ourselves.' What a difference eight days makes, Pearce thought; at the outset of their voyage the men aboard those ships had been die-hard Jacobins to a man. 'Yet this is not an opinion vouchsafed to those in command at Gibraltar. It may be they already know of Lord Hood's plan, given the number of vessels bearing despatches which pass through this station. In which case they will think of them as rabid dogs, to be shot on sight should they snarl. I doubt the Governor will take kindly to folk like that roaming his bailiwick.'

'You and I could disabuse them of that notion, sir.'

Digby produced one of those throat-clearing coughs which were used to cover his embarrassment. He did not want to say that any recommendation from the likes of John Pearce would, if his name was known, likely have precisely the opposite effect to that sought.

'I have been told by Mr Neame that Algeciras Bay is an uncomfortable anchorage on this wind.'

'I will ask, Mr Pearce, but I cannot say that I can guarantee acceptance. Strange things are said to happen to those stationed at the Rock, something to do I suppose with the constrained nature of the posting. I have noticed it induces in them a level of hatred of the enemy that is exceptional in its vehemence. And when we are at war with Spain...' Digby raised wonder-filled eyebrows to denote that the Rock's inhabitants, in those circumstances, became quite mad. 'Now, Mr Pearce, I think it is time you and I returned to your numbers.'

It was Pearce's turn to inwardly groan. Digby had undertaken to help him with his geometry and the like, Mr Neame his previous tutor being too busy on this wind, and he could not decline. Yet he knew very shortly he would answer some gently put enquiry like an idiot, and the feeling that induced would not be ameliorated by an understanding look in his captain's saddened eye.

'Do you have any money, Michael?'

'A bit, which I got from that bastard Taberly for doing his bidding with my fists.'

'Rufus?' the boy shook his head, and Charlie spoke before he was asked. 'Not a pot to piss in, Pearce.'

'Nor yet a window to throw it out of,' Pearce added, finishing the mantra that Charlie Taverner was so fond of. He reached into his coat for his purse. 'Then I shall provide.'

'My, Pearce,' exclaimed young Rufus, which had O'Hagan looking around to see, due to the lack of respect in that remark, they were not being overheard. 'You are well found.'

It was money that he had been given to go ashore when Toulon was still in French hands, an advance from Hood's secret funds. Since no one had asked for it to be returned, and he had used so little, he now considered it no more than his due for that hazardous excursion. He tipped them two guineas each, amused at the way Charlie seemed able to palm it and make it disappear, but then he had been a sharp before being pressed, a man who lived off the gullible who flocked to London to see the sights. Rufus jingled the coins in his hand, leaving Pearce to wonder if he had ever held so much money before; perhaps, as a bonded apprentice to a tight-purse master, he never had, and that was why he had run to the Liberties.

Michael O'Hagan just grinned; he would have seen such sums and more, being a highly rated man with a shovel in a world being everywhere dug up; canals, foundations, drainage channels and cellarage for new buildings, hewing for coal, and the hardest task of all, a sinker of wells and mine shafts. Michael had done them all: what he had never managed to do, as far as Pearce could tell, was to hang on to what he earned. He was a man to whom it came easy, so he was a person to see it go easy, as well. He worked to drink and he drank or charmed a wench with his earnings, though he was inclined to turn contentious under the influence. Pearce could recall him that first night they had met; drunk, a bellowing bull who had tried to knock his block off, which had him wonder if what he had just done was a good idea.

'Don't get into trouble, any of you.' Pearce insisted, articulating the concern. 'Remember I will be part of the authority forced to punish you if you do.'

'Sure, John-boy,' Michael said with a grin, 'would we be after embarrassing you?'

Peace returned the grin. 'I bet you can't wait, Michael.'

* * *

Moreau and his fellow commanders had been through these straits before, and they required no orders to make a good southing so as to round Punta Europa. Pearce got a good idea of what Neame meant just by how long it took all five ships to tack and wear through the narrows, before they could give themselves enough sea room to put up their helms and clear into Algeciras Bay. The town after which that was named lay across the harbour from the Rock, and even if there was peace, even if Spain was at this time an ally, there would be no traffic between the British and the Andalusians on mainland soil. The flags that flew on Gibraltar, which could be seen through a long glass from Algeciras, were like salt on an open wound.

'It's a damn good thing that the Dons are with us, Pearce,' said Digby. 'I think if they were not we would be unable to leave five thousand sailors in view of temptation. We would have to anchor them right inshore and put a guard ship with loaded cannon on their weather beam.'

'Boat's ready, your honour,' said Dysart, who was acting as Digby's coxswain.

'Mr Harbin to accompany me, Dysart.' Then he turned to Pearce. 'I will leave you to take young Farmiloe ashore, Pearce, after I have seen the admiral. It will give you a chance to get to know him better and perhaps lay some ghosts.'

That was the first time Digby had alluded to the

fact that Farmiloe had been part of the press gang that had taken him up. Had he been watching them; his Pelicans, himself and Farmiloe, and noted that even after he had been reassured the boy still maintained a distance? On the one occasion Digby had invited the two mids to dine, the still bandaged Harbin, once having consumed a glass or two, had been all volubility. Not Farmiloe; he had sipped quietly, spoken little and stopped if he saw that Pearce wanted to speak. If Digby had spotted the reserve, and discerned the reason without asking, he was showing an acute sense of atmosphere.

'I know,' Digby added, as Harbin ran to change into his best coat, 'that this is a short commission, yet I sense the ship to be reasonably content. I would, if possible, have it fully so.'

'I will do my very best, sir.'

'I know you will, Mr Pearce, for if I thought otherwise, I would not have presumed to mention it.'

'When can we give some shore time to the hands, sir?'

'When I have done my duty to the flag officer, and have his permission.' Seeing the implied question in Pearce's reaction he added, smiling, 'Never fear, he will not withhold it. The tavern keepers and whorehouse madams of the Gut would have his intestines if he denied them their customers.'

'Then I look forward to taking Mr Farmiloe ashore, and showing him the sights.'

'For the sake of the Lord, Pearce, don't get the lad poxed.'

'Sorry to keep you waiting, sir,' gasped Harbin, lifting his hat to show an ugly red scar.

'You are keeping an admiral waiting, boy, not me.'

The shock of Harbin's freckled face made Digby burst out laughing and he patted him on the back as an encouragement to make for the gangway. Watching them go, Pearce thought it was indeed a happy ship, and the man responsible had just gone down into the cutter.

'Disputes, sir, I fear disputes. I am plagued with them on this station, which I put down to the wind, which is not only constant, but can be hot like the hobs of hell one day, and like Arctic ice the next.'

'Admiral Hartley, I agree with you about guard boats for the crews. I merely ask that the French commissioned officers be allowed some freedom.'

'I would gift it them, man, but I can tell you that in an instant they would be atop the Rock at dawn, facing some bad-tempered bullock. You have no idea what service on Gib does for soldiers. They are a dammed nuisance in any case, but stationed here brings out their very worst traits. I swear the apes behave better.'

'If we were to provide escorts, sir.'

Hartley was a fat little fellow, a perfect officer for a shore appointment, and probably damned glad to have it, given the only other option was a yellow flag and enforced retirement. As a sea-going officer he had struggled to gain respect, yet he had interest, the kind of connections that kept him from mouldering in the country or shrinking and losing money at the baths and card tables of some spa. Right now, he was rubbing one of his several chins, and musing on what had been proposed.

'Do you have a commitment to get every one of these rogues to Biscay?'

The implication of that question was obvious; if one of them got speared or struck down by a musket ball, would Hartley suffer for it?

'Not as individuals, sir.'

'Officers with officers?'

'I think we could do even better than that, sir. An officer and a chosen party of hands as escorts should keep them from mischief.'

'Very well, Digby, but ration them their time ashore, and make sure if the wind shifts they are not lost in the arms of some trollop. I want then out of my command as soon as possible.'

Pearce came on deck as soon as Farmiloe informed him that *Faron*'s cutter had put off from the shore, so it was only idle curiosity that had him looking to

the west when he sighted the familiar rig of a ship
he knew well, the Postal Packet *Lorne,* and if that
was the case it was almost certain that her Ulster-
born captain, Mr McGann, was conning her at that
very moment. Such a sight lifted his spirits, not that
he was in any way down, but McGann was a man
he esteemed, a fine sailor loved by his family of a
crew, who had shown him a degree of kindness on
the way out from Portsmouth to the Mediterranean
that had made a task, which he saw as a duty, a
pleasure.

'Mr Farmiloe,' he said pointing due west. 'I am
terribly tempted to give that ship opening the bay a
gun.'

The youngster was slow to respond, as he always
was with Pearce, but finally curiosity got the better
of him and he looked at it through a glass. 'Why, sir,
it is naught but a Postal Packet by its ensign.'

'I know the captain and the crew, and they will
be ashore at the same time as you and I, so I can
look forward to making an introduction.' He
looked over his shoulder, to see the cutter closing,
and gave orders for the gangway to be opened, and
everyone to be ready to receive, with due ceremony,
the captain aboard.

'How went it, sir?' he asked of Digby, once their
salutes were complete.

'Well, Pearce, very well.'

'The admiral said yes?'

'With qualifications. The French must be escorted at all times, and I have said it will be officers and a party of hands, but best of all Pearce, he has granted me permission to sleep out of the ship. Is it a dangerous thing for a sailor to say, but I long for a night in a motionless cot.'

McGann was not hard to find. The run of taverns that made up the Gut were crowded with sailors from all the ships stuck for a westerly passage, plus the army, though the officers and ranks of the garrison tended to favour different venues, and the odd local, who were Spanish in the main, but prepared to deny that for profit. The captain of the *Lorne* was well on his way to being drunk, with that glassy-eyed look and hint of a sway that Pearce recognised. Yet the smile was the same drunk or sober, and when he saw Pearce his arms went out, thumping inadvertently another customer round the ear, and in a trice he had his much taller friend in a crushing embrace.

'Mr Pearce, sir, can I tell you how happy I am to see you, sir. What good fortune attends.'

Pearce looked over McGann's shoulder and greeted the members of his crew, all of whom had been kind to him, as McGann shouted for more drink, this while one of his men sought to pacify the man who had been clouted.

Having, with some effort, detached himself,

Pearce introduced his companions. 'May I name to you first, *Lieutenant de Vaisseau,* Gerard Moreau, who I regret to say, speaks no English.'

'*Pas de problem, mon ami,*' exclaimed McGann, taking and pumping Moreau's hand. '*Voulez-vous prendre un boire avec moi?*'

'*Mon plaisir, monsieur.*'

'This,' Pearce interrupted, albeit he was amused by McGann's less than perfect French, 'is Midshipman Farmiloe, like me of HMS *Faron.*'

'Young man!' exclaimed McGann, in a voice that carried and bounced off the smoke-blackened walls. 'You too will drink with me.'

'And...'

'Say no more, Mr Pearce, until you have a tankard in your hand.'

That did not take long, McGann being a well-known customer; *Lorne* ran the mails and official despatches between England and Gibraltar on a regular basis. The people who owned this tavern knew his shout and knew how to serve him. Everyone within close proximity was handed a drink, including the total stranger he had accidentally buffeted, which mollified the man more than the apologies of McGann's crew.

'You will recall me telling you about the men I was pressed with,' Pearce said, his voice raised to cover the din of drinking salutation. 'I am happy to say I have them here with me.'

'John Pearce, you have achieved your object.'

'Not quite, but I want you to meet my Pelicans.'

Each got a hearty shake. McGann, who was a short fellow, looked like a dwarf beside Michael, and though Pearce sought to explain what had actually happened as opposed to that which McGann supposed, he had a strong feeling not a word penetrated. He looked at Moreau, who was laughing, not at the little Ulsterman, but because of him.

'*Un homme très amusant, Monsieur Pearce, je pense.*'

Funny yes, thought Pearce, but he could be trouble also, having a fatal flaw when in drink of assuming that every woman he met was madly in love with him, a fact he would act upon even if their escort, or the husband, was standing right next to them. He was a gifted fellow at sea, and an absolute menace ashore, something Pearce had had occasion to witness and confirm, which had him wondering what the combination would be of that man drunk, as well as Michael O'Hagan. It did not bear thinking about.

McGann was in deep conversation with Moreau now, while Michael, Charlie and Rufus had been taken up by the crew of the *Lorne*, which left Pearce with a rather stiff Farmiloe.

'I wish I could persuade you to relax, young man. I have already told you I bear you no malice, yet I fear you do not quite believe me.'

'I do, sir.'

Right then, Pearce resolved to get the boy drunk; perhaps then, whatever fears he was harbouring would emerge. He had just put his tankard to his lips, after signalling to the innkeeper for a round of refills, when a loud and peremptory voice interrupted him.

'There, sir, you sir!'

Pearce turned slowly to look into the red and furious face of an army officer, using his elbows to make his way through the crowd. There was something about him that was familiar, but Pearce could not place why it should be so.

'I see by your countenance, sir, that you do not recall me?'

'I do not.' Pearce looked at the insignia, unsure of the rank.

The man's hand swung, and though Pearce ducked away it still caught him a glancing blow on the cheek and all he could hear was the voice shouting. 'Perhaps, sir, that will refresh your memory, you damned coward.'

Pearce moved fast, just ahead of Michael O'Hagan who looked set to flatten the soldier. For him to strike an officer would be tantamount to a capital crime, not that Michael would hesitate because of such reasoning. Instead Pearce's hand shot out, open-palmed, and caught the redcoat under the chin, sending him reeling back into the arms of a group of fellow soldiers who had obviously followed him across the room. Suddenly there were two groups, those not party to what was obviously going to be a brawl, moving away.

'You do not run this time, sir,' shouted his assailant. 'Perhaps you have learnt not to be shy since we last met.'

Pearce recognised him now. On his last visit to Gibraltar, in the company of Captain McGann, he had been obliged to strike this fellow. Not that the redcoat was entirely at fault: McGann had been making advances to his wife, a voluptuous-looking creature with an ample bosom, who really should not have been in a place of such low repute. In seeking to apologise on McGann's behalf he had been, himself, insulted, and the major's continued refusal to accept it as an error had sparked Pearce into an action he had later regretted; he had punched the sod. A general mêlée followed, involving the officers of the ship that was to take him to meet Lord Hood, but he had been hustled away. With orders to weigh, there was no time for the duel which was bound to follow.

'Well, sir, what do you say. I have administered a blow. Are you going to run again, or is your plan this time to set a bunch of ruffians on me? Do so if you dare, I have my friends to aid me, and when all is ended I will still demand satisfaction.'

Pearce was still restraining Michael, who, looking at the line of redcoat officers, hissed. 'Let me be, John-boy, I'll crease the lot of them.'

That was when McGann stepped in front of both Michael and Pearce. 'You, sir, I demand your name.'

'And who, sir, are you?'

'I am the author of this sorry affair, the man who, I am told, insulted your wife. It was to defend me that this fellow struck you a blow.'

His crew must have told him; inebriated as he had been there was no way McGann could have remembered. 'It matters not, the blow was struck. Satisfaction is required.'

'Several blows have been struck, sir,' McGann slurred, 'but I am responsible. If you wish for satisfaction you must take it from me.'

'Wait your turn, dwarf.'

McGann, more steady than Pearce thought him capable of, walked straight up to the major and slapped his cheek.

'I will not wait, sir, I will be first, and I ask you to name your weapon.'

'Pistols!' the major barked, then turned to another officer and named him as his second. Pearce saw, out of the corner of his eye, the crew of the *Lorne* nodding; was it relief?

'Mr Pearce will be mine.'

'Good. When I have seen to you he can be next. Until dawn tomorrow.'

'Fernando,' McGann shouted, as the major stomped away. 'Our tankards are empty.'

Chapter Sixteen

They had to be up before dawn and with Digby
sleeping ashore Pearce could leave the ship without
having to explain his destination. He had with him
the surgeon Lutyens, to see to the wounded, and a
sword he fully intended to use – as the man struck
he had the choice – because despite McGann's
protestations of the previous night, which he
repeated ad nauseam, that he had no worries about
this coming event, there was no way a man as
drunk as he had been could face up, at the crack of
dawn, to an opponent versed in the use of arms.
Pearce intended to force him to step aside and it
was therefore something of a shock to observe,
when they met on the dockside, that the captain of
the *Lorne* seemed to be in fine fettle.

'I never suffer from the effect of drink of a
mornin', John, which I put down to a fine Irish
constitution.'

Introduced to Lutyens, they fell to discussing the seat of the heavy drinker's problem, which was held to be the liver and gout afflicting the big toe, with the surgeon talking of the dissections he had performed on victims of everything from an excess of gin to the occasional cadaver fallen to the perils of over-indulgence in claret, his opinion that the former was ten times more insidious than the latter, owing to the low quality of the brew.

'Though I have to say, Captain, that the gin drinker is the article more often to be found on the cutting table for another reason, they being more likely to suffer a pauper's death than a man addicted to wine.'

'The heart, sir, you must have seen the heart?' demanded McGann, in an exercise in morbidity that Pearce found strange given where they were heading. 'In that I do very much envy you.'

'Sir, I have seen it in its working mode on more than one occasion, and it is, the first time you set eyes on it, the most amazing sight.'

'Tell me more.'

Given an audience Lutyens responded, and was soon explaining what he had seen of kidneys, muscles, genitals of both sexes, the route of bodily waste through the gut to the fundament, in such detail that Pearce dropped back to be out of earshot. He had not thought himself squeamish, but such a precise description of the human innards was

not to be borne before a man had consumed a
hearty breakfast. One cup of coffee was insufficient;
it had left his stomach to rumble, a necessary
condition, it being held inadvisable for a
participator to eat before a duel.

'Mr McGann seems in a jolly mood.'

'Same as ever, our capt'n,' replied the crewman
McGann had fetched along. 'He don't change
much, as you will have noted.'

'Indeed I have,' Pearce replied. McGann drank
little or nothing at sea, saving his immoderation for
the shore. He too had a happy ship, and like Henry
Digby he was the cause, with a care for his crew
that bordered on the fatherly; ever smiling, his
orders always soft and supplicant, not harsh. 'Yet I
fear for him this day.'

The man slapped his hand on the polished box he
carried, which had to contain a pair of pistols. 'I
should fear for the man he slapped.'

'That was surely unusual behaviour for the
captain. I observed him drunk on our last meeting,
but he showed no hint of a violent temperament.'

The sailor just smiled, and there was no time to
elicit any more information as, puffing from the
steep climb, they reached an open space near the
top of the Rock, chasing away the apes that
occupied the heights. Looking east they saw that
the sky was tinged with grey, and their ears told
them the military party was approaching on

horseback. Lutyens and McGann were still deep in conversation, and the sailor was rubbing one shoulder as though it was causing him some pain.

Courtesy is the absolute requirement of duelling; whatever the offence waiting to be settled, everyone has to behave like a gentleman. Thus, polite greetings were exchanged by those not the principles, and introductions carried out, and Pearce received with grace the invitation from Major Lipton's second that an apology be offered. This, despite Pearce's pleading, McGann flatly refused to accept.

'Then let me fight him first, with swords. I have trained with some of the finest fencing masters in Paris and if it smacks of showing away, I am good with a blade. I fancy that, soldier or no, I can best him in that department and if I can you will not have to contest your dispute with him at all.'

McGann looked up at him with a belligerent expression. 'If you are the John Pearce with whom I sailed not two months past, you would not be seeking to kill the fellow, regardless of his bellicosity.'

'Of course not. I would seek a satisfactory wound. One that satisfied his honour and my own.'

'And then what happens? This Lipton is stationed here, and I am a regular caller at the Rock, as my duty demands. I daresay he would wait till your wound healed and still demand that I meet him. Best then to get it over with now.'

'You are determined then?'

'I am.'

'Then I hope your opponent has the same attitude you ascribe to me.'

'Pearce, I bet you a breakfast that I will eat mine with my own hand, but yonder major will need to be spoon fed. Now please be so good as to ask if the fellow will examine my pistols, which if he has no objection, I would prefer to use.'

That had Pearce consulting with Lipton's second again. He looked at the army pistols, a rather scarred pair of ordinary weapons in a well-travelled box. McGann's were as different as chalk and cheese, a beautiful pair of Lobey's, with the fine inlay and beautiful craftsmanship for which the Dublin gunmaker was famous.

'If you wish for accuracy and balance, sir,' Lipton's second said, as he held one in his hand. 'I doubt ours would match the captain's.'

'Very well,' growled the major, removing his coat. 'One ball does as much damage as another.'

'Then Mr Pearce and I will load them.'

There was another officer along with the military party, in a heavy cloak which kept hidden his rank, and a low hat that did much to disguise his features, no name being given as he stepped forward and supervised the loading, this as a red sun hit the horizon.

'We will wait till it is full up, gentlemen,' he growled. 'I would not have it implied that anyone lacked advantage from a want of light.'

It only took minutes till the sun was a rising red/gold ball. With neither man facing the light they stood back to back in shirts and breeches only, this while Lutyens squatted by his medical case, taking out various articles and laying them out ready for use and working on some bandages for the expected wound. From under his cloak, the unknown officer produced a pistol of his own, primed and loaded, the reason for his person remaining anonymous emphasised in his next words.

'The rules you know, gentlemen. Ten paces then turn, as I count them out. Anyone seeking to best their opponent before that I will shoot. On ten you may turn and fire at your own convenience. Should no shot strike either party I will call upon you to agree a conclusion or invite you to load again.'

The fellow, who could be had up for murder if he carried out his threat to shoot, had the voice for the count, deep and sonorous, and being garbed like the Grim Reaper gave him authority. McGann and Lipton moved, pace by pace, away from each other in slow measured steps. On the count of ten Pearce wanted to close his eyes, and his hand was gripping the hilt of his sword so much it hurt. Both men spun, the major pushing one leg back to get proper balance, so as to aim properly. McGann did not bother with such refinements; he fired as soon as he saw his target, and Lipton spun away, taken at the top of his shooting arm, which was sent sideways, his weapon discharged in the process, the ball fired harmlessly into the ground.

'I think you will find, Pearce,' McGann called, 'the major will not be looking for satisfaction from you this day.'

Lutyens was already by the wounded soldier, easing him into a sitting position and tearing at his shirt to get at the wound, a probe already in his hand. Lipton's second was dosing his pallid principle with brandy, this before he put the leather strap the surgeon had handed him between his teeth. The way the wounded officer took the treatment was admirable; the man was no screaming milksop. He sat, looking over Lutyens shoulder as the surgeon probed with the lack of finesse for which he was known and winced only when he found the musket ball, ignoring the copious blood that flowed from the wound. The cloaked adjudicator stood over the scene and enquired as to whether his companion would be in need of a hospital.

'No,' Lutyens replied, finally extracting the ball with a log set of tweezers. He then produced what he liked to call his magic formula, a German preparation called Mellisengeist, and pouring that onto a linen pad, he set to staunching the flow of blood.

'Pearce, fetch me that bandage I have laid out, and the other I have already fashioned into a sling.' The sun was up, bright gold and high by the time he had bound the wound and got the major back onto his feet, the man unsteady but determined. 'He will have to walk down, he cannot ride.'

'That is our responsibility,' said his second. He looked over to where McGann stood, well away from the ministrations, and added, 'The matter is of course settled. Gentlemen, I thank you for your attendance, and you, Mr Lutyens, for the attention you have given to my superior.'

The fellow in the cloak and his second either side of him, they led Major Lipton from the field, he hunched over in pain, as Pearce said, 'You were well prepared, Heinrich, were you not? A sling already fashioned?'

Lutyens looked at Pearce and smiled, his thin hair blowing in the increasing breeze, his face alight with humour. 'Captain McGann told me to get it prepared. In fact he told me the exact spot in which he was going to wound the fellow, the arm he would need to wield his sword. He laughed when he told me how you underestimated him. It seems that the good captain is a marksman of some repute.'

* * *

It was a week before they got their wind, with nights spent ashore in the company of the French officers. The captains were four very different men. Garnier, of wiry build and pale complexion, was less given to good humour than Moreau, but he was a very pleasant fellow, a well-read man who could hold a decent conversation, who also confessed liking to paint a little when ashore. Jacquelin was taciturn and not happy to share wine and food with folk he still saw as the enemy, which made being in his company hard going. Forcet of the *Entreprenant* was a fool, and uncouth with it, a man who would never have achieved any commissioned rank in royal service, and he gave the impression, as he damned the Jacobins, that he was as like to damn what went before and still save some bile for what might follow. He ate as though tomorrow was bound for famine, drank like a fish and became both coarse and incomprehensible when drunk, singing raucous and filthy songs which denigrated British manhood, this as the crew from the *Faron* were obliged to row him back to his vessel.

'A dinna ken whit he was warbling aboot, your honour,' said Dysart, 'But ah can tell by the looks it wasna sweet talk.'

'I will not translate, Dysart,' Pearce replied. 'We may well have to transport the fellow again and I know you will look for an opportunity to drown him if you understand his sentiments.'

Coming alongside the ships, he was faced with the other, junior officers, none of whom had been allowed to go ashore on that night, but people with whom Pearce had shared bread and wine. Not that they had failed to enjoy some evening entertainment if they were stuck aboard; ever since they dropped anchor the four ships had been surrounded by boats, some from Gibraltar, others all the way from Algeciras, selling everything they could possibly want, including women. The guard boats provided by Admiral Hartley did nothing to interfere in this trade, but they did seek to count the numbers allowed close, so that no Frenchmen could run when the boats pulled for the shore.

Eventually the wind swung round, cannons were fired as signals and the shipping in the bay became a hive of activity as they prepared to get under way. Digby waited until a whole host of merchant vessels had cleared the anchorage before signalling himself, hauling HMS *Faron* over her anchor and leading the way out past the western arm of Algeciras Bay. It was necessary to hug the Spanish shore, the Atlantic current being strongest in mid-channel and weaker by the land, yet even with a wind they made slow progress, inching along. At one point the current won out marginally over the wind, which had the boats out hauling the ships along. It seemed a blessing that it sprung up again before they passed the clifftop town of Tarifa.

'Look there, Pearce, at that damned fortress.' It needed no real indication from Digby to see the stone towers, dominating as they did the inshore waters, the muzzles of cannon very obvious in the wall embrasures. 'I would not risk being this close in if we were fighting the Dons, I can tell you.'

'Means waiting for a good blow,' added Neame. 'This puff would never serve if we was at war.'

'And it's every man on deck,' Digby said, 'guns run out and nets rigged in case the Spaniards send out gunboats or a capital ship from the bay.'

'What happens if the wind shifts again, Mr Neame?'

'Then you put up your helm, Mr Pearce, and run back for the safety of the Rock, 'cause the next thing on your larboard beam is Cadiz, home port to half the Spanish fleet.'

Things improved as they weathered Cape Trafalgar, the current easing as it became less intense, and Neame was able to alter course to take the squadron out into the deep Atlantic. He wanted sea room, not a lee shore, in case the wind did shift again, and soon they were leaving land behind, rising and falling on the Atlantic rollers that beat upon the rocky shore over the stern.

'You know the Bay of Biscay, sir?' asked Neame over a dinner in Digby's cabin. Lutyens was again present, but his face went blank at the mention of anything nautical. 'A foul place in the main.'

'I sailed though it on the *Lorne* and though Captain McGann told me of the reputation of the bay, it was a mill pond on that occasion.'

'Pray for something similar, Pearce, for it is a bad time of year to be around this part of the ocean. The south-westerlies of the autumnal equinox can be vicious.'

'Is that not the wind we seek?'

'I was thinking of getting out of the bay, Mr Pearce, for getting in on this wind is easy.' Digby paused, then looked around the table in a way that commanded attention. 'I have waited till we cleared the Straits before bringing up the subject of our destination.'

'I had it as Rochefort followed by Lorient, sir,' said Neame. 'That is what I have marked out as our course.'

'Those are the official orders.'

Pearce interjected; he knew the tone of his captain's voice. 'Which you clearly do not regard as binding?'

'That's sharp, Pearce, since I have yet to give an opinion.'

'There would be little need to mention it if you intended to just comply, sir.'

'I say this in confidence. Lord Hood's last words to me were a hint, no more, that such ports might not be the best choice and the act of gifting the French Navy four seaworthy ships was not one to cheer him or to ease his mind.'

'There are few others that could take ships of that draught,' said Neame.

Digby leant forward. 'We have already mentioned the seasonal gales that afflict the Biscay shore. If we run into such weather on our way back to the Straits we will be lucky to make any progress, indeed we may have to run for deep water…'

'If we gets the chance, your honour,' Neame interrupted with a gloomy expression.

'Well put, Mr Neame. The whole bay is a lee shore at this time of year, with few places of shelter that do not represent an even greater risk. In strict obedience of my written instructions I am to see our charges weather the Ile d'Oléron, allow *Patriote* and *Entreprenant* to detach for Rochefort, and let the other pair set a course north for Lorient, it being left to me whether I continue to escort them.'

'What would you rather do, sir,' asked Pearce, 'or should I say what would Lord Hood have you do?'

'I have no precise instructions, so let us look at the choices. I take it you would agree that gifting the enemy a squadron of 74-gun ships-of-the-line is not a good idea.' Both men nodded. 'So, can we take them to another port that will render them unusable? Bordeaux has the depth of water and has the advantage it is not a naval station, therefore unlikely to have the armaments necessary to re-equip the enemy vessels.'

Neame looked disquieted. 'It is a long way upriver, sir, and the wind you speak of could keep us in the Gironde for weeks.' The master did not say that the French officers would be as reluctant to sail up to Bordeaux port for the same reason; they could be stuck there till spring.

'Which is why I have discarded the notion, likewise Nantes. I would point out to you then what I have just said about a lee shore. If that is a threat to us for sailing in too far, then it is even more of that to a ship anchored in unprotected waters. I propose therefore to lead our charges to anchor off La Rochelle.'

Pearce shrugged; he had heard of the place; no student of any history involving France could not know of it, given it was the last stronghold of the Protestant religion in the time of Cardinal Richelieu, and besieged because of it. But that was the limit of his knowledge.

'Mr Neame, please confirm my thinking. Could a seventy-four be warped into the La Rochelle harbour?'

'I'd have to consult my charts, sir, but I have a strong feeling it ain't been used for capital ships since the time of the fourteenth Louis and that has more to do with the depth of water under the keel than the layout of the harbour. seventy-fours would probably ground well before they reached. Given it is a port and its position, if it could be used it would be. It's more a slaver's home now, that and sugar of course, notwithstanding most of that fetches up in Nantes.'

'I think you are forgetting privateers, Mr Neame.'

'Them also, of course.'

'So if our charges were anchored there, at this time of year—'

'No French captain would think of such a thing, your honour, it would be asking for trouble.'

'Without the crews needed to get them clear?'

Lutyens eventually spoke up. 'Would someone explain to me what you are talking about?'

'With pleasure, Mr Lutyens,' Digby replied. 'We shall bypass Rochefort and the mouth of the Charente, and sail on to La Rochelle. There we will land the crews of all four vessels and hope for a rapid change in the weather, namely the onset of the autumn gales that plague the Biscay coast. Given warning of that we will immediately put to sea and leave the French ships in a situation where it is very possible, with nothing rigged to get to sea, they will be driven onto the shore and destroyed. We will therefore have completed our task and kept Lord Hood's commitment, having landed the French radicals on their own soil in their own part of the world, but we will not have gifted our enemies four sound vessels that only require their cannon to be replaced to become as formidable as they were originally. How does that strike you, Mr Lutyens?'

'As dishonest,' Lutyens replied with a sparkle in his eye. He waited till Digby looked aggrieved before adding, 'But very clever.'

Pearce cut in. 'I admit to not speaking from any knowledge, but is not the weather a fickle instrument on which to base a strategy? It could be some time before the elements oblige.'

Digby nodded. 'Then we will be in a bind, Mr Pearce, for I cannot believe our presence will go unnoticed. I would expect a warship, very possibly a frigate, to be sent from Rochefort to seek us out.'

'Which we cannot fight with any hope of success.'

Digby brightened, but there was a gallows quality to his humour. 'There is always hope, Lieutenant Pearce, whatever the odds.'

'I merely ask, sir, because a certain contingency has to be covered.'

'Namely,' Digby replied, 'that we have to weigh in haste, and the crews ashore immediately return to their ships, or at least enough of them to raise sail?'

'Is that not why we fetched along the carronades, sir?' said Pearce.

'The prospect of breaking a given commitment does not bother you, sir, I see.'

The glint in Digby's eye took the sting out of what could have been construed as base thinking, and Pearce realised what he had been about; the captain had reached the very same conclusion they were at now, but in having this discussion he had brought them all to a like assessment. Questioned later, he could rightly claim it was not his orders that made his inferiors act as they did, but their own inclinations.

'Let us say, sir, that I am thinking like our enemy would think.'

'I too have put myself in that position, Mr Pearce, and rest assured, when I state they shall not have those ships, I mean what I say. I'll burn them to the waterline before I give them over.'

The eyes had become like flints, a measure of Digby's determination. 'Not a word of this outside these cabin walls, and this discussion was never held. We need to get our Frenchmen aboard and oblige them to accede to our intentions.'

Chapter Seventeen

'I would remind you, madam, that we are at war, and that I have duties to perform that are consistent with my rank and obligations. I cannot do so if I am under a cloud of accusation from the likes of that scoundrel Pearce.'

Ralph Barclay was deliberately loud in his discourse; having decided to fight back he knew that he must force his wife into the kind of submission that, alone, would grant them the prospect of a happy future. The expectation of her behaviour continuing unchecked was not to be borne and he actually slapped the table as he added. 'What was done was necessary!'

Emily replied in a meek voice. 'But was it true, husband?'

'It was as true as it needed to be. Every officer who sat on that court has found himself at some time in the same boat as I. The nation needs sailors to man its ships, and if not enough come forward what are we to do? It is not a pleasant task, but it is a necessary one. If we are to be threatened every time someone feels aggrieved we might as well send the French an invite to invade England and march their rabble down Whitehall.'

For the first time since the subject had been broached, she looked up at him. 'I rather had the impression you took pleasure from it, pressing men to serve at sea, I mean.'

'My dear,' he insisted, 'I hate it, but Hood left me no choice. I asked him, indeed begged him for hands, which he had in abundance, sitting on their ar...backsides at the Tower. Did he put the needs of his country before everything? No he did not. He put his own requirements first. I could do no other than take that as an example. If you do not accept such an explanation, then seek the opinions of my fellow officers. You can try Admiral Hotham if you like, he has asked us to dine aboard *Britannia* tonight.'

Emily looked alarmed; the notion of a formal naval dinner was not a pleasant one. 'Could I not plead an indisposition?'

The table got another slap. 'No, madam, you cannot. Anyone with enough spirit to get from ship to shore by themselves in a bought wherry can hardly plead ill-health twenty-four hours later. And, while we are on the subject, I will not have you defy me again. You put Glaister in an impossible position and that also will never happen again. Do I make myself clear!'

'You do, husband, but now I wonder if it would have been better had I not sailed with you in the first place, better if I had stayed at home.'

'Mrs Barclay...'

Emily looked directly at him, which stopped him speaking, well aware of what was going on. He was her husband, she his wife. Socially, legally, and in the eyes of God she was bound to obey him, but that did not mean she was denied an opinion.

'I mean only that I have seen a side of you that would have remained hidden had I not come aboard this ship. And do not think I am unaware that we live in a less than perfect world, do not suppose that I assume that what pertains on land must of necessity be any easier at sea, but something being necessary does not, of itself, make it right.'

'I did not set out to disappoint you, madam.'

'I know that, Captain Barclay,' Emily replied, in a tone of voice that left him in no doubt that was precisely what he had done.

'Please be so good as to see that my best uniform is ready for this evening.'

Emily replied, 'Of course,' with the sure knowledge the task given was one normally performed by Shenton. Her husband was asserting his will in an area in which it would be churlish of her to decline.

Two people overheard the exchange. The closest, Shenton, was pleased by it; his job had just got easier and, who knows, he thought, the captain might send his bitch home. The second was seeing it in exactly the opposite light; a husband having trouble with his wife was, to Cornelius Gherson, like pitch perfect music.

'I wonder, Mrs Barclay, if I could work in the cabin, by the light from the casements. It is so much easier than seeking to keep accounts by candlelight and I have a great deal of catching up to do.'

Emily, in the act of writing home to her mother, was taken slightly unawares; Gherson had not knocked but entered unannounced. But then Shenton did that all the time while pretending he did not know how much it discomfited her.

'I fear my eyes are not as strong as they should be.'

The silence lasted only a few seconds, but it was enough for Emily to think that Gherson was being less than entirely honest. Not that she could swear to such a thing, only that his words were at odds with the cast of his features, as well as the look in his eye, which was direct enough to be unsettling. Fearing to speak, lest she convey her doubts as to his motives, she nodded and pointed her quill to the footlockers and the cushions she had embroidered with the ship's name, then went, very obviously, back to her writing.

It was hard to concentrate; the thread of her letter had been lost and it was impossible to ignore Gherson carefully laying out, then standing to study his ledgers on those cushions. Finally he went to the furthest point from her, where the bulkhead of the side cabin met the stern, and sat down, at an angle which had him almost directly facing the table at which she sat.

'Please, Mrs Barclay, do say if I am disturbing you in any way. It would trouble me greatly if it were so.'

Was that a strange choice of words? So ambiguous as to be beyond response. Emily came to the firm conclusion that she did not like the man. He had an oleaginous manner and an air of misplaced superiority. Added to that, she suspected his testimony at the court martial had been as tainted as all the others, which made him a willing liar. Fortunately, there was little prospect of her needing to have much contact with him.

Had she been able to see inside Cornelius Gherson's mind, she would have been less sanguine: to him, he had merely fired the opening salvo in a campaign of indeterminate duration. Seduction was an art at which he prided himself; he reckoned he could charm men out of the trees like birds, and women too, though they required a more delicate form of flattery. Tell a plain women she was beautiful, treat beauty in one who possessed it with indifference. As he scratched away with his quill, totting up the columns of figures for stores acquired and used, he allowed himself an occasional lift of the eye to look at Emily Barclay. How long would it take? That was an unknown but he knew the first bridge to be the hardest to cross; the idea that dalliance was possible. Once a woman had accepted the possibility of infidelity, the rest of the defence would crumble, slowly for sure, but inexorably. The pleasure it would bring to both parties could not be in doubt; how could an old goat like Ralph Barclay compete in the bedchamber with a young buck like him. Let her get used to his being present first, then he could move on to being familiar, then friendly, and finally a person to confide in.

That delicious train of thought was interrupted as Shenton barged in with his usual lack of regard for proper behaviour. Emily had long since given up chastising him, because he paid no attention, and the time was long past when saying anything to her husband would have seen his servant put in his place. But it was telling the way he stopped dead, looking from her to Gherson, separated by the width of the cabin and the table at which she was writing, clear on his face the notion that something was going on which should not be.

Odd, thought Emily, how that pleases me. And he is bound to tell my husband, which pleases me even more.

For Ralph Barclay the prospect of Hotham's dinner rose as the morning went by, anything was better than being out here trying to impede the progress of the French gunners as they tried to construct new battery positions. His was at Fort Mulgrave, a bastion thrown up and named after the military commander of the Toulon garrison. Right at this moment he was engaged in an artillery duel, against an opposite number who seemed willing to push his guns forward into extremely exposed positions, obviously content to take the casualties this caused. It was no joy to see approaching the redoubt that pint-sized pest, Horatio Nelson, fresh back from Naples.

'Nelson,' he said, deliberately concentrating on the use of his telescope to avoid direct eye contact.

'Captain Barclay, it is so very good to see you again.'

What is he about, Ralph Barclay thought; is he so dense that he cannot see I do not esteem him?

He would not admit to a tinge of jealousy; Nelson was not far above him in the captain's list, but he had been favoured by Lord Hood in a way that had been denied to him. It was all to do with

Rodney of course. Hood hated that name even if the bearer was dead, buried and almost forgotten except by those who had admired him and prospered by their association. He could not see Nelson without recalling he was a client of Hood, who had held the power of appointment at the outbreak of this war as the senior Naval Sea Lord on the Board of Admiralty. Lord Chatham, William Pitt's brother, who held the position of First Sea Lord, was an idle fool, often drunk, and never very active, which left Hood making all the important decisions. Nelson had got *Agamemnon*, a 64-gun ship-of-the-line; he had got the smallest class of frigate in the King's Navy.

That train of irritation was broken by a salvo from the nearest well-set French guns, a battery they had called Sablettes as it was near the sandy shoreline. It was obvious they were seeking to suppress any fire on another battery position even closer to the fort, which the French sappers were busy extending with anything that came to hand; broken wagons, baulks of timber of all shapes and sizes, plus mounds of freshly dug earth.

'He is a bold fellow,' Nelson said, shading his eyes as he looked out over the undulating landscape.

'He may be a dead fellow soon, Nelson.' With that Ralph Barclay gave orders for his naval gunners to train their cannon round on the men digging hard to raise that earthwork. 'I want that mound knocked down, lads, and damned quick.'

'No easy task, Captain Barclay,' Nelson responded, in that high-pitched voice which so irritated many of his fellow officers. 'Loose earth will do nought but absorb the balls and the range is too great for case shot to kill the sappers.'

Why has this poltroon come here to tell me the obvious? Does he suspect I do not know?

'What we really need is soldiers to go out and take the ground,' Barclay said. 'But we lack them, as you know. Every available man is employed.'

'There is a draft on the way from Naples, sir, a substantial one. Perhaps when they are here we can sally out and undo the efforts of whoever commands yonder.'

'I will believe that when I see the glint of their bayonets.'

Another ball from Sablettes bounced in front of Fort Mulgrave, before sinking in to the glacis built before it.

'Sir John Acton was most pressing in his commitment.'

Ralph Barclay finally looked down at Nelson, noting, not for the first time the absurdly youthful countenance, the lack of inches, and those eyes so blue they were like sapphires, before he checked himself for thinking such poetic drivel. The man mentioned, Acton, was a power in the Kingdom of the Two Scillies, close to the Queen, Maria Carolina and rumoured to be her lover. The real ruler, her husband, King Ferdinand, was apparently a slobbering idiot whose only interests were hunting and fornication, so the task of running the country was left to his wife. As a daughter of the formidable Empress Maria Theresa of Austria her bloodline promised competence, not that it was guaranteed; her sister, Marie Antoinette, who many blamed for undermining the French monarchy, was at this every moment incarcerated in a Paris dungeon.

Still, it was remarkable that an Englishman should have achieved such a post in a foreign government, but not as extraordinary as the kingdom is which he served. Naples was by rumour the loosest and most corrupt place in creation where every wife had a lover, every husband one or more mistresses, a place where dishonesty was the norm not the exception. How could it be otherwise with such a sovereign?

'You do not fear that Sir John Acton has gone native?'

That remark coincided with the next shot from the French, which had a bigger charge or a ball that better fitted the barrel from which it was fired. It cleared the rampart and hit an empty wagon sitting at the rear of the battery, rendering it to matchwood. Barclay gave orders for the guns, now ready and aimed, to commence their counter-battery fire, and suddenly the two captains were engulfed in clouds of acrid smoke as the breeze, which aided the enemy fire, blew back the residue of their own weapons into their faces.

'In what way, gone native?' Nelson asked, once the smoke had cleared, and he had removed with a handkerchief some of the bits of burnt powder that had stuck to his cheeks.

Barclay took time to reply, busy marking the fall of shot and ordering an increased elevation. 'In making promises, Captain Nelson, that he has no intention of meeting?'

'Sir William assures me he has not.'

'Hamilton?'

'Who else?'

'You met him?

'I did and a better representative of England's needs could scarce be found. The man is tireless in his pursuit of our nation's interests.'

'What about his trollop?

'Trollop?' Nelson looked shocked, which made him look even younger than normal. 'I do hope, Captain Barclay, you are not referring to his wife, the inestimable Lady Hamilton.'

There was great temptation then to ask if Nelson had fallen for the lady's charms. After all, if a woman who had whored in London could capture the heart and loins of an old and noble knight, a friend of King George when young and related to a

Duke, this soft Norfolk fool would be like putty in her hands.

Instead he said. 'You found her acceptable?'

'More than that, sir. She is in possession of accomplishments that are quite astounding, is fluent in Italian, German and French, aided by not only natural beauty but a charming and elegant disposition.'

His fellow captain was thinking he had been right; he had fallen for her, the ninny.

'Also,' Nelson went on, 'she has the ear of the Queen and is, if I may say so, as important in the affairs of the embassy as her husband. The alacrity with which the Court of Naples agreed to send troops to our aid has a great deal to do with her powers of persuasion.'

'Is it not amazing, Nelson,' said Ralph Barclay, looking right at him for once, 'the heights to which some people can rise, given they have little in the way of a decent background to recommend them.'

Horatio Nelson completely missed the irony, which was in part aimed at him. 'Ability, sir. We live in an age where it cannot be gainsaid. Let us not think that blood is the only measure of success in these times. I have nothing but a distant connection to the Orford earldom to qualify me for natural elevation, yet I believe I have a destiny to do great service for England.'

He had to look away then; there was such
certainty in those blue eyes. It was hard for Ralph
Barclay to deal with someone like Nelson, who left
himself so open to ridicule, though there was the
advantage that when it was employed, it did seem
to go right over his head. Conversation was again
killed by gunfire, and this time some of the
earthwork thrown up by the French was
displaced, and in such a way that there must have
been losses.

'I will take your word for it regarding Hamilton's
wife, sir, not having met the lady. But she is, by
reputation, very different.'

'I fear reputation is a poor way to judge a person,
Captain. It is often the malice of the less able that
forms it.' Sensitive always to a potential affront,
that remark got Nelson a sharp look, and that was
not aided when he said, 'I believe you are to be
congratulated on the result of your court. I am
sorry I missed it.'

The words 'I'm not,' were formed, but like so
much that had gone before, left unsaid. He had a
horrible vision of Nelson sitting as Court President,
and it was enough to make Ralph Barclay shudder.
His next words he issued with gusto, well aware of
their pomposity.

'We arrived at the truth, sir, and that is all that a
man can ask.'

'Well said, Captain Barclay, well said.'

Thank God our guns are more accurate than his perception, Ralph Barclay thought, or England would be in dire straits.

Emily Barclay was, that afternoon, no happier to find herself next to Nelson than Ralph Barclay had been by his company earlier. In the nature of things she was not seated next to her spouse; he had been placed within easy conversational distance of Rear Admiral Gardiner, Hood's third in line of command, which presented to Ralph Barclay a chance to make himself known to another senior officer who might have some input into his future prospects. To Emily, this Nelson was a sneak, who had told her husband how much she had enjoyed the Assembly Room dance in Sheerness, the very night the men from *Brilliant* had been out pressing seamen. And his voice was not one to endear, especially when he had taken several glasses of wine, which seemed to affect him greatly.

'I cannot tell you, Mrs Barclay, how the Court of Naples glitters. Sir William...' Seeing her confusion he added, 'Hamilton, our plenipotentiary there, he and his wife took me out to view the royal palace at Caserta, which has to be a wonder of the world, bigger than Versailles, which he has also seen.'

Emily was only half listening as Nelson told her of hundreds of rooms, of painted walls and ceilings with a sort of descriptive ineptitude that rendered them dull, of statuary and furniture in such abundance that she wondered if there was room for humans. Politeness forced her to respond, but it did not mean that she had to concur with his enthusiasm.

'I must say, Captain Nelson, it does all sound a trifle excessive.'

'Mrs Barclay, I confess to a love of that.'

'While I, sir, am proud to claim an admiration for the plain.'

'Then might I suggest that you avoid a looking glass.' As an attempt at flattery, or perhaps even dalliance, it was seriously inept, especially from a married man, and Nelson seemed to realise very quickly he had pushed the bounds of good taste, for he added quickly, 'You must be very pleased at the outcome of your husband's court.'

As soon as he said that, Emily engaged her neighbour to the right in earnest conversation.

'Gould, I have no ideas what I said to so upset her, but I can tell you Mrs Barclay hardly exchanged another word with me.'

They were walking on the quarterdeck of *Britannia*, taking some air while the other guests smoked their pipes and downed their port. Davidge Gould, who knew Nelson of old, and also knew of his clumsiness with members of the opposite sex, gave the only reply he could.

'I'm sure, sir, you are mistaken. I know the lady to be kindness herself and a joy in company.'

'You devil,' Nelson replied, with a twinkle in his eye. 'Do not think I cannot recall how you danced with her in Sheerness. I was not the only one to mark the enjoyment you took in each other's company.'

'It was, sir,' Gould protested, 'entirely innocent of any other interpretation but amusement.'

'You sailed with Barclay, did you not, Gould? How did you find him?'

'Irascible, sir, to begin with, and he did stretch his orders somewhat to take a prize.'

Nelson smiled. 'Can a man go to excess to gain a prize?'

'Convoy orders leave little room for interpretation, sir. Captain Barclay was out of sight of his charges, though I have to confess that I allowed myself to be persuaded he had not done so and wrote up my logs accordingly.'

'Gould,' Nelson laughed, slapping him on the back. 'I hope then one day you sail with me.'

'I am given to understand you are off on another cruise, sir?'

'I am, with Linzee. We are to look into Algiers and have words with the Dey about supplies and not interfering with our trade.'

'An impossible task.'

'Rumour has it there is a French warship there,

Gould, so there is a chance we will see some action.'

Ralph Barclay had left the dinner to relieve himself at the heads, Hotham being no lover of the obvious chamber pot, and in returning he could hardly avoid the two promenading officers.

'Barclay,' called Nelson. 'I was just telling Gould here I am off to Tangier under Commodore Linzee.'

'What!'

Gould was looking at Barclay, Nelson was not, and as the smaller man enthused regarding the possibilities of his cruise and a fight with a Frenchman, it was very obvious that, if he upset Emily Barclay at dinner, he had just done the same thing to her husband, who growled his response, which was only correct in word not tone, then stomped off.

'I think I must get to know Barclay better, Mr Gould. After all, he appears a fellow who will seek action, even if his orders constrain him, in short my kind of officer.'

How much has he had to drink, Gould wondered?

Chapter Eighteen

The captain of HMS *Faron* was quite emphatic,
which was important, given he was not speaking in
French and he wanted to convey that he was
serious. 'Captain Moreau, I have my orders and I
will obey them.' He then turned to Pearce and
requested that he translate.

What followed was, to Henry Digby,
incomprehensible, but there was no question it was
protest, and not just from Moreau. Jacquelin in
particular was incensed, but then he was the more
zealous when it came to the Revolution. Digby was
forced to continue over the babble.

'Please also be so good as to tell our friends that
I have the means to enforce those orders and I will
employ them.'

Pearce was not enjoying this; he could see the
need, in fact he shared with his captain the notion
that it was a first-rate idea, but while Digby was

issuing the unpleasant news, he, being the one understood, was taking the entire backwash. Moreau was glaring at him as if he had betrayed a friendship, while Garnier had a hangdog, sad expression that was just as wounding. The other two he cared little for, either their person or their opinion, but to fall in the estimation of the two aforementioned distressed him. Time spent in their company at Gibraltar had deepened their acquaintance.

'We will weather the Ile d'Oléron and out of close sight of any lookouts,' Digby went on. 'I will take station on your lee, and I will run out my guns. Any attempt by your vessels to bear up for the Charente Estuary will be met by force. Now, be so good as to return to your ships and hold your course for La Rochelle. Mr Pearce, in French if you please.'

That set off another bout of complaint, and Pearce got seriously annoyed with Digby, who could sit there with an air of complacent indifference while he had to listen to a litany of reasons why that port was unsuitable for anything other than a decent frigate. All the reasons they had discussed were aired by the French, yet they must have realised it was to no avail; disobey and they would have *Faron* on their quarter, ready once more to pour shot into their undefended stern, an act, which if sustained, would bring about serious casualties.

'You may also say, Mr Pearce, that now we have

cleared Gibraltar, I see no reason for the continued flying of their royal ensign. You may give them permission from me to re-hoist their tricolour pennants.'

A small measure to mollify them, it barely succeeded, only the stupid Forcet appearing to be openly pleased. Moreau saw it for what it was, a sop to his dented pride, but the Frenchman kept his most wounding remarks for his exit through the gangway, turning to Pearce, no engaging smile now, but a furrowed and angry brow.

'I know what you are seeking to achieve and it is dishonourable. If I had a single cannon, monsieur, I would decline to accept this demand and fight you.'

It was hyperbole, both men knew it, yet it was telling.

'What did he say, Mr Pearce?' asked Digby.

Pearce let his own frustration spill over then; after all his captain would be unaware of the exaggeration. 'I'm afraid, sir, he likened us to the more solid contents of a chamber pot.'

'Damned cheek.'

Sailing north past Corunna and Cape Ortega, the weather turned exceptionally mild, with two days of sunshine and soft westerly breezes that wafted the ships along at a steady pace, devoid of haste on a sea of long, slow, rolling waves. The early parts of the evening were warm too, and under a series of

glorious sunsets, which turned into the canopy of
the Milky Way as night fell, and before the clear sky
sucked out all the heat of the day, the crew would
gather after their duties were complete, to entertain
themselves with songs, ditties and music from
makeshift instruments; the carpenter was a dab
hand on his saw; Sykes had fashioned a penny
whistle and Digby had gifted another fellow a pair
of spoons with which to beat out a rhythm.

There had been few chances for the Pelicans to
foregather, though it was no secret aboard that
John Pearce had a connection to Michael, Rufus
and Charlie that transcended the bounds of his
rank, as well as a soft spot for Latimer and Blubber
Booth, and looking from the quarterdeck to the
bows, he itched to join them in their revels, a fact
which he thought he kept hidden, but was clear to
anyone who cared to look.

'I think the men should be encouraged, don't
you?' asked Digby, his perception once more acute.
'Perhaps if you were to ask them if they would like
lanterns, Mr Pearce, so that they may see better
when the sun finally goes.'

That he did, and the men were grateful enough to
invite the officers to join with them. Digby felt that
his own dignity permitted him to witness but not to
participate, and had a chair fetched for the purpose,
but he saw it as his duty to insist that his
midshipmen should learn the art of singing a song

in public and be taught the steps of the hornpipe.

'Then perhaps ashore, my lads, you may behave with a little more decorum, instead of forever trying to stab the locals.'

Both looked abashed at mention of their bout at Toulon, the scar of which, though fading, Harbin still bore. Lutyens brought out another chair, and one of his little notebooks, occasionally scribbling something while the activities went on.

'What is he about with that there pencil?' whispered Harbin. 'He's ever at it, I've seen him more'n once.'

'Nothing, Dick,' Farmiloe replied, in a similar low tone, 'he was the same aboard *Brilliant*. We all got used to it and now pay it no heed.'

'And Mr Pearce,' Digby called to his second, who was already amongst the crew, 'if you feel your nautical education would benefit from the experience I would say you too should participate in a hornpipe.'

If it had been anyone else, Pearce would have suspected an attempt to diminish him, but not Digby. 'I fear, sir, that the kind of dancing I learnt in the ballroom would scarcely answer on a ship's deck, and I doubt there is one aboard as fleet of foot as a lady to accompany me.'

'I'll be your partner, John-boy,' O'Hagan joked in his ear. 'And I show you a reel that will spin your toes.'

Pearce burst out laughing. 'What a pair we would make, Michael.'

Blubber Booth was on his feet, and as the bent saw sang, the whistle piped and the spoons paced a soft rattle, he began to dance, arms folded across his chest, showing a surprising lightness of feet for a man of his size. Latimer then sang a fisherman's song, in a voice that had more gravel than musicality, that followed by Dysart reciting a warlike Scottish poem by the Lord of Stair, which he had learnt off by heart. That it damned every Englishman born or yet to be conceived was taken in good part by the rest. Harbin hornpiped with little grace but Farmiloe, a taller, more elegant creature, took his instruction well, as Pearce said to the Pelicans, who were all sitting close to him now.

'There are times, friends, when this we have been forced into has its moments of true pleasure.'

This is how it seemed to Pearce now; a calm sea with an air of camaraderie and no feeling of hierarchy, which brought back a fond recollection of the time he had occupied the captain's cabin of HMS *Weazel*.

'We have had few, Pearce,' said Charlie Taverner, though in a rare show of graciousness he added, 'though I will not dispute with you that this is pleasant.'

'Do you still hanker for the Liberties, Charlie?'

That made Charlie pensive; his life in those

crowded Thameside streets had not been pleasant; a cramped space in which to sleep, shared with three others, work some days, but few, and always for an employer who would dispute the due wage. For food, it was often a scavenge rather than a buy, evenings spent in taverns like the Pelican, usually without the means to purchase a wet, and certainly never the coin to tease a wench, or just sitting watching the filth of the River Thames float by for want of the means to do anything different. The night they had met, Charlie had dunned John Pearce out of the means to buy drinks with an ease that was habitual, but he could not go a few streets to the hunting grounds where, before he was forced to hide from the law, he had made his way. The Strand and the narrow streets and open market of Covent Garden were barred to him by the existence of a warrant for his arrest.

'I hanker for the right to go where I please, John.'

'I don't recall you had that, Charlie,' said Michael.

'For sure, you had better, for you had that. Come and go as you please it was, for you. Why you ever came to our part of the world, when you could have gone anywhere for your amusement, I'll never know.'

Michael gave Charlie a gentle poke in the chest. 'There was a certain apple-cheeked wench called Rosie you might recall.'

'I recall you buffed more'n her cheeks,' Charlie replied, with some asperity, for plump Rosie had been a bone of contention between them – Michael could afford to treat her with his daily earnings, Charlie, far better off in the article of looks and wit, could not – and that jealousy had been slow to fade, if indeed it ever had.

'I take it,' asked Pearce, 'the ladies of Spain saw to your needs on the Rock?'

That had both men grinning and nudging, though Rufus looked embarrassed, and the mention of that set the men closest to singing the song, which was so well known it was taken up by everyone. Rufus piped up as the last verse faded. 'I never took to the Liberties.'

'Just as you never took to being bonded,' Pearce insisted.

'I wish I had never left home. There was much there to enjoy. I used to like to attend the Goose Fair when I was a lad.'

'What do you mean when, shaver,' Charlie scoffed. 'You still are.'

Rufus would not be put off, going on to describe in enticing detail the stalls, the conjurors, acrobats, dancers and singers of the annual pre-Christmas fair. There was a wistful air to it, for it bespoke of a life that preceded his being a bonded apprentice to a harsh employer in the leather trade. Yet he had the others salivating with him at his talk of hot meat pies filled with beef or lamb, spit roasting pork, sweetmeats served by comely wenches, fresh-brewed special ales so strong they had everyone cavorting by darkness.

'I will go to that one day,' said Michael, 'for both the ale and the comely wenches.'

'Then have a care,' Rufus replied gravely. 'The watchmen carry stout clubs and will clout anyone causing trouble.'

'Me?' Cause trouble. Never in life. Sure, I'm as placid in drink as a Wicklow cow.'

That made them laugh, and wondering at the joke it was soon shared, so that insults of a joshing kind were soon flying around the deck. Michael, called upon, did an Irish reel that made up in sheer brio for what it lacked in polish, and Charlie did a few tricks, such as taking a coin from behind another sailor's ear, having put it in his mouth, a mock argument breaking out when he tried to pocket the object he had been given for the act.

Night fell and the sky became a mass of twinkling stars so closely packed that they seemed like a sheet drawn across the black. From across the water, under the lanterns rigged by the Frenchmen, came the sound of mass singing. Clearly they had no notion to be outdone by their escort, and even although it was that revolutionary anthem *Ca Ira,* it was hard to imagine at this moment that the two nations were at war.

'Mr Pearce, if you care to join me in my cabin, we may partake of some toasted cheese and a glass of wine.'

What seemed like an innocent invitation, soon turned out to be something else. Pearce knew as they ate and drank that Digby was building himself up to something, and when it came it was as unpleasant an idea as Pearce could imagine.

'The problem is, we need someone to go ashore with a flag of truce, and tell whoever is in control of La Rochelle of our mission, and get them to accept their sailors.'

'Do you, sir, know the meaning of the French expression *Déjà vu?*'

'Of course,' Digby replied, with just a trace of asperity.

'Then you will know that I was so charged with the same task by Lord Hood at Toulon.'

'Were you? I was not aware.'

'And I would point out that I nearly forfeited my life in trying to comply with his instructions.'

'You will be under a white flag.'

'You know, sir, because I have told you, I have some experience of the politics of revolution and I also have some hope that you understand this simple fact. The normal rules of chivalrous exchange do not always apply when dealing with such people. They see themselves as fighting the forces of reaction with a conviction that borders on the religious and anything that can be done to defeat that force is seen as legitimate.'

'They might not respect a truce flag!'

Obviously, to Digby, the notion was outrageous. To John Pearce he was again showing that parochial Achilles heel that he had noted before. To someone raised like his captain the idea that anyone would do such a thing was incomprehensible; war had rules and they must be observed. The only problem was, if he was wrong, he would not face the consequences.

'Is there any other way that we can communicate with them?'

'If there is, Mr Pearce, I am dammed if I can see it. Even if we had the means to signal such a complicated message they could scarce read it, and I cannot see anyone putting a boat off to bespeak us when we give the appearance of being five fully operational warships.'

'They might,' Pearce replied, clutching at the only available straw.

'We cannot wait for them, for we must employ haste, and that for all the reasons we have already discussed. If we linger, Mr Pearce, and the weather turns, it might be us that is slung on shore and drowned in the process, and that takes no cognisance of us getting into a battle with a superior force.'

'What if they refuse to accept them, sir?'

'Then tell them they have the choice of doing so or watching them drown. That will concentrate their thinking.'

Pearce felt the air go out of his lungs at the same time as any resistance he had collapsed. Digby could not comprehend, did not know any more than Pearce, who was in charge in La Rochelle. It was beyond his understanding that the representatives of the people who ran the Revolution, those who had retaken Marseilles and were bent on recapturing Lyons, were perfectly capable of watching five thousand men drown for the sake of their militant purity.

'Then you'd best get the Yeoman of the Sheets to cut me out a couple of squares of thin bleached canvas.'

'Good man.'

The approach was not straightforward, given they had to weather the Ile d'Oleron, really a long low-lying island more sandbar than rock, which jutted out into the Bay of Biscay and formed protection for the anchorage termed on the British charts the Aix Roads. As well as that it also protected from the south-west the Charente Estuary and upriver the naval port of Rochefort. There would be lookouts on the westernmost tip of the island to give advance warning to Rochefort of any approaching armada, as well as boats out fishing the offshore waters, which ensured they would be seen. Those with the wit could now see that Digby's idea to let his charges fly the tricolour at their masthead, made perfect sense; Bourbon ensigns, in this part of France, might set off all sorts of alarms.

'Mr Harbin,' he had said, as the first sign of land came into view, 'I believe you will find in Mr Pearce's quarters the French flag he took from *Apollon* off Marseilles. Be so good as to fetch it, with his permission of course, and raise it to the masthead.'

He looked out at his four charges; would they guess his game when he, himself, raised the same flag as they? There had to be warships in Rochefort of a size that he could not face; if they supposed a squadron of their own capital ships were heading north they would not stir. The real worry was the possibility of one or more frigates patrolling well offshore to give added advance warning of any threat. So far nothing had been observed.

'I would have them closer inshore, sir,' said Neame, when asked. 'Between Oléron and the Isles of Aix. With all these fishermen out in the deep waters they have plenty of eyes to see approaching trouble.'

'Then let us hope that the outlines of those seventy-fours are not too familiar to your fishermen,' Digby replied. 'I would not want them to identify vessels that were despatched to the

Mediterranean. A sharp eye on our friends yonder, for if they are going to try to break away, this is the time to do it.'

Martin Dent was in the tops again with one duty, to observe the French quarterdecks for any sign of excessive activity. Digby had executed a mighty bluff, leaving the captains in no doubt that he would treat them as hostile, and even the ordinary cannon of HMS *Faron*'s armament, in vessels so crowded, could kill and maim men in their hundreds. There was another lookout on the foremast, with his telescope trained due east; if anything was essaying out of Rochefort, Henry Digby needed to know quickly, for if something too formidable emerged he would be obliged to turn tail and run.

The twin stone towers that guarded the narrow entry to the port of La Rochelle were visible now, the pale brown weathered stone lit by the rays of a sinking sun, that same light showing the tip of the cathedral spire above the line of the fortified sea wall, and the slate roofs of warehouses cum dwellings that lined the quays. South of where the warships had anchored lay a marshy area on a promontory called *les Minimes* while another shallow bay, full of small fishing smacks, lay directly to the north of the main port, forming part of the defences of the municipality. It was obvious that they too could be seen as they prepared to drop anchor, and that must be causing no end of speculation in the town. In the bows of *Apollon* a sailor was casting a lead to check the depth of water under the keel, which was shoaling slowly but inexorably to the point where they, too, must anchor. Digby left it to Moreau to decide when that would be.

'Our flags notwithstanding, they will send a messenger to Rochefort, and the distance is not more than fifty miles. I think we can expect a reaction, so we must be away from here as quickly as we can.'

Pearce looked doubtful. 'I would rather go in at first light, sir. I want that truce flag to be in plain view.'

'I confess to being torn. I have no wish to overrule you in this, but the needs of the service must, as they always do, transcend those of any one person. I suggest you take a boat in to within hailing distance of those towers. See if you can establish anything tonight. With luck they may agree to let you land on the morrow.'

Ancient they might be, but the La Rochelle towers, as well as the sea wall that ran to the south and west of that, were still equipped with cannon, and approaching he would be the only target rowing into a narrowing arc of fire. It was a nervous Pearce who sat in the thwarts, wishing he was rowing with his back to any threat, not sitting facing it. Dysart had stepped a mast, but it was rigged with no sail. Instead, stiff on the offshore breeze, there flew a white flag. If that did not excite conjecture, nothing would; why would a vessel with a tricolour at the masthead need such a thing as a flag of truce?

There was no doubt that they had manned the defences, probably as soon as the topsails of the leading seventy-four had been sighted, and Pearce could see wisps of smoke rising from behind the walls and atop the triple tower called St Nicolas that stood, the higher of the two, on the southern edge of the port entrance. Heated shot or just warming braziers for the gunners he did not know, but he needed little of his already vivid imagination to see this flimsy cutter blown to smithereens and the men rowing so steadily crying for mercy as they drowned, given it was very likely not one of them could swim.

As soon as he decently could he raised his speaking trumpet and called out to the tower, until a voice carried on the wind insisted he identify himself. Pearce had considered lying, putting forth the tale that he too was French, and asking for permission to land the evacuees as men in need of medical care. But that would soon be exploded as a lie, the minute the first Frenchman set foot onshore, so there was no choice but to identify himself as a

British officer, making a very exaggerated gesture to indicate the white flag, and ask for permission to come closer and parley.

What followed was long-winded and difficult, with much being made of *Faron* flying false colours, which necessitated apologies and the need not to alert the town and cause panic. His interlocutor, whom he could not see, was not easily convinced that what he was being told was true, so Pearce asked only for permission to come ashore at dawn, under a *laissez passer*, when he could fully explain to whoever had power in the town what was needed. He was left drifting off the tower while messengers were despatched to whoever that might be, and it was dark by the time the answer came back; that he could come in only as far as he had this evening, when he would be asked to repeat what he had said to the head of the local Committee of Public Safety. That made him swear under his breath, before he gave orders to get back to the ship.

'That means, sir, the place is attached to Paris and the Revolution.'

'I had been hoping for another Toulon,' said Digby.

'I have alluded to this before, sir, what do we do if the leading citizens of La Rochelle refuse to accept these men?'

'Don't think I have not thought on it, Pearce. I

fear if they do that, we will have to abandon our charges and retrace our course, leaving them to decide their final destination. There is, in truth, no more that we can do. If you do not know we are engaged in a massive bluff it would disappoint me. There is no possible way I could burn or seek to sink those ships with men still aboard, nor would I leave fellow sailors, whatever their politics, to drown by being driven ashore.'

'I never thought you would, sir.'

'So, we require your very best efforts, Mr Pearce. On your shoulders, tomorrow, rests the success or failure of our intentions.'

The 'Thank you,' that received was larded with irony.

Chapter Nineteen

Pearce could not know, as he took to the cutter the next morning, what he was rowing into. News of a rising in the Vendée had filtered through to the Mediterranean, but not the extent of the rebellion against Paris; in truth there had been such a spate of uprisings against the same central authority that the one happening here in the lands bordering the Atlantic was not seen as exceptional by those outside France. Yet it was just that, a revolt led not by people seeking to temper revolutionary excess while keeping the gains of 1789 but a full-scale insurrection, an army led by real soldiers and encouraged by priests, aimed at a restoration of the Bourbon monarchy and the re-establishment of the Catholic Church. Thus it was that the strategic town and port of La Rochelle was under the jurisdiction of the most zealous kind of diehard, a representative on mission from Paris who knew that the cause they espoused could only be maintained by a reign of terror.

The guillotine had been set up in the main square before the Hotel de Ville, renamed, as every major space in France had been, Place de la Revolution, and anyone with even a hint of sympathy for the rebels called the Chouans had already been decapitated. Even before that, the cobbles of the square had been well stained by the blood of the wealthy and the aristocratic, many of whom had fled to this place hoping to take ship to safety in the Americas. The majority of the citizenry went in fear of their lives, while the dregs of local society – the ambitious demagogues, the bitter failures, and the bare-arsed discontented – had risen to prominence.

There was no shouting up to an unseen voice behind the embrasures this morning; a delegation had come down to the tiny quay that stood before the Romanesque northern tower, La Chaine. Pearce could see several blue-uniform coats, frogged with gold decoration, and a sloppy body of men behind them in National Guard clothing, bearing muskets. But the man who took his eye most was wearing the livery of those who held the power in this benighted land; a black coat with a high-backed collar and the same colour breeches inside highly polished boots. On his head he wore a tall hat with an imposing cockade, and round his waist a wide sash of red, white and blue. His face was sallow, the mouth, framed by long drooping moustaches, unsmiling. Pearce knew, even before the first exchange, that this was the man with whom he would have to deal.

'Please heave to,' a voice called. 'Do not approach any closer.'

Pearce gave the orders to his crew to bring the cutter to a gliding halt and to ship their oars. Once that had been achieved he stood, making sure of his footing in the centre of the boat before doing so; it would never do to seem unsteady in the face of this delegation.

'Please state your reasons for being here, monsieur.'

That led to a repetition of all that he had said the night before, to a stony-faced crew who seemed determined not to respond. Finally the black-coated fellow in the tall hat said, not without pomposity, 'The Revolution recognises your flag of truce. Please step ashore.'

The point at which he did so was tricky; it always was to a man's dignity when first he stepped on dry land after having been weeks at sea. Benign it might have been, but a ship was never steady and a man's legs had to adjust to constant movement to keep his balance. That removed, it was difficult to cope with terra firma, and Pearce felt instinctively he had lost a point when one of the musket-bearing soldiers had to step forward and take his arm to steady him.

Still feeling as if he was on moving ground, he introduced himself.

'Lieutenant John Pearce, of His Britannic Majesty's Royal Navy, at your service.'

'Representative on mission from the Committee of Public Safety, Henri Rafin.'

'Can I ask if I am speaking to the voice of authority in the town?'

The reply was given with a pompous air, and Pearce suspected it was aimed as his companions as much as his visitor. 'There is no other authority than the Committee of Public Safety. You will accompany us, monsieur, to the Hotel de Ville, where we will listen to what you have to say.'

Pearce spun round and looked down into the boat. 'Michael, to me with the second flag.'

O'Hagan reached down and pulled up a staff bearing another flag of truce, and without seeking permission, stepped out onto the quay, to exchange a look, first with Pearce, then a less agreeable one with the over-dressed sod he had been talking to.

'This member of my ship's company will attend on me.'

Rafin stroked his moustaches, and his expression was one of disdain, as if to say, if you are not safe on your own, what good will one sailor do?

He did not understand what Pearce said. 'Michael, anything goes wrong, you know which neck to wring first.' Pearce then smiled at Rafin, who was unaware that a sentence of death had just been passed on him. 'After you, monsieur.'

'Citizen,' said Rafin, sharply correcting him.

The route to the Hotel de Ville took them round the harbour quays, past tables piled with fish and crustaceans, crabs and langoustine, still moving, and Pearce noted that among the fishing boats there were armed vessels, which would serve as either slavers or privateers, as well as the usual knot of big fishing smacks not out that day. With an eye becoming increasingly more professional he noted the number of guns on the larger vessels and their calibre, as well as trying to appreciate their possible sailing qualities until he realised that not even the most experienced sailor could tell much regarding such things when a ship was tied up to a quay.

When they reached the busy main quay, facing the medieval towers, the power of the man leading them became all too evident, as the crowds going in both directions parted like the Red Sea before Moses, and those in his path took care not to catch his eye. In the open-fronted taverns dotted between the warehouses, the babble of noise from the customers abated for the same reason; fear of standing out in any way. Pearce had seen this before; the power of the Revolution and its activities to cow the people, a revolution that was originally intended to free them. Yet it was also true that as they marched they gathered a following, who became increasingly bellicose as their numbers swelled in another demonstration of that which Pearce had seen before: crowd courage replacing private caution.

The whole town, when they left the quay, had a medieval air; every thoroughfare busy with carts, mixed with humans and animals carrying their produce. Flagged pavements, not dirt paths, lay under arched stone canopies, which would keep the more leisurely citizens of La Rochelle out of the sun and rain, giving the place an atmosphere of long-term wealth; this had been a major French commercial port for centuries, but sugar and the slave trade had probably made it doubly prosperous, which had Pearce wondering how many of its wealthy citizens had fallen victim to the type of man he was following.

The guillotine stood in the centre of the square before the Hotel de Ville, in stark contrast to the street market that lined the edges, full of stalls selling piled vegetables and fruit, meat butchered and still living, chickens and rabbits in baskets; clearly the place did not want for plentiful food from the surrounding countryside as well as abundant fish from the sea. The engine of death, it was plain, had not been idle. There was the smell of blood as they came close, and the traces of human flesh around the place where a detached head would fall. The cobbles beneath that point were stained for yards, and Pearce knew why, because he had seen the fountain of red mist that erupted from the neck of a victim as the blade struck through. He had to close his eyes for a moment, and he staggered slightly on one of those cobbles, only to be held by Michael's strong hand.

'Steady, John-boy,' O'Hagan said. 'Do not let memory dishearten you.'

'You guessed?'

'Sure, John, and I am saying a prayer for your father's soul this very minute, though I would not want these heathens around us to o'erhear it.'

Steps led up to the raised area from which the mayors of the town had been wont to make announcements ever since it was built and Pearce had a sudden notion of the longevity of the place. La Rochelle was certain to have been a Roman settlement; perhaps there had been an Oration Platform here before, which now performed the same function for Rafin, a place from which to harangue the citizenry, as well as being the spot from which he could watch the imposition of what passed for justice. Inside the doors of the Hotel de Ville the hallway was dark in comparison to the bright exterior sunlight, but there lay yet another reminder of the fate of his own father: a large table with three long stripes of coloured cloth rising from floor to ceiling behind it, a copy of which he had seen in the Conciergerie prison in Paris.

The soldiers who had escorted them, without, it had to be said, much in the way of military bearing, dropped back and took up station as sentries. One was so much a civilian in uniform he immediately took out an onion and began to peel and eat it. The officers were different, better dressed with more of a swagger about them, which had Pearce wondering what their rank had been in Bourbon times. With Rafin, they arranged themselves along the back of the long table, this while Pearce, and Michael holding aloft the white flag behind him, heard, then saw the crowd of people who had been following come in to witness what was about to take place, their loud voices of condemnation echoing off the stone walls.

The representative himself took centre stage in front of a high-backed chair, stood for a moment and looked around him as if to underline his authority, before he sat down, the rest of the committee, who had been waiting for him to do so, following suit, the crowd immediately silenced by the simple act of him raising his right hand.

'These fellows you wish to burden us with, Lieutenant, who are they?'

For the third time Pearce rattled off his story, knowing what he was engaged in was pure theatre. Rafin wanted to be seen to be consulting the citizens of the town, by allowing them to hear what this interloper had to say. He would deliberate as if their opinion counted for something, but it was a farce; there was only one person to make a decision in La Rochelle and the cockade in his hat, his black garments and his wide tricolour sash were the badges of the authority to do that. If he ordered John Pearce and Michael O'Hagan out to face the guillotine, in total contravention of the laws of war, that too would be obeyed.

'Sailors from ports such as Lorient and Brest.' He declined to mention Rochefort, it was too close. 'Five thousand in number.'

'And why would you bring them here?'

The temptation to sigh, to let this bastard know that he had realised his game, had to be fought. The possible outcomes were too serious for him to indulge in the same measure of performance.

'The port has been taken over by the British Fleet.'

That had Rafin sitting forward, his face angry and shocked, this matched by what Pearce listened to behind him, yet they must have heard of it by now. Hood's marines had been ashore for a month.

'Traitors,' Rafin spat. 'They will pay a heavy price.'

That was another lure to be avoided, the desire to tell him not to count his chickens. 'Then you will be pleased to know these are the officers and men who refused to serve under the Bourbon flag.'

'Citizens then, not subjects!' Rafin cried, his eyes

producing a joyous look as that was taken up by his cheering audience.

'They wish to be landed on this coast. Lord Hood, who commands at Toulon—'

'For now!'

'Lord Hood agreed to release four of the major vessels to transport them to the Atlantic ports, where they could disembark and go back to their families.'

'Then why do you not take them to these ports, Lieutenant? La Rochelle is not a base for these kinds of ships.'

'You will appreciate, monsieur—'

'Citizen Rafin will do.'

'You will appreciate, citizen, that while the British government has no desire to hold in Toulon such a quantity of sailors who refuse to serve, it also has no desire to immediately return them to a position from which they could act to threaten our own ships. The vessels are sound and require only refitting with cannon, wood, water and victuals to be fully ready for service.'

'The first of which we cannot provide.' As Pearce nodded, Rafin looked over his shoulder and invited comments from the crowd. The cry of 'who is going to feed them?' was the first to emerge from the overall clamour.

'The ships are well provisioned. The men coming ashore will be given access to their stores and for the short period they are in the town I doubt they will be a burden.'

'Five thousand sailors—' a voice shouted, only to be interrupted by John Pearce shouting even louder: 'Five thousand revolutionary sailors.'

The military officer sitting next to Rafin leant forward and whispered in his ear, which had the representative nodding slowly. The crowd now observed a hushed silence, waiting for the outcome of the conversation.

'It has been put to me,' Rafin said finally, 'by General Westermann here, that a fighting sailor is only a sea-going soldier. He has suggested these men could serve to help in the trouble we have to contain the pestilence of the Vendée renegades.'

That brought forth a loud and rippling murmur, but it was hard to tell if it was positive or negative.

'What about the ships, citizen?' called another voice, posing the question Pearce dreaded.

'They will be left at anchor here, but stripped of the means to sail,' he replied.

The same voice called out. 'The anchorage is not safe.'

'You may sail them to Rochefort, which is close by, or perhaps the admiral commanding there will send a store ship and crews. Whatever, my ship will be well on its way and safe from any retaliation. I do not think my flag of truce has any validity at sea.'

'How we doin', John-boy?' asked Michael, as Rafin and his general had another whispered discussion. 'Cause I don't see how I can get to that bugger behind the table if we's in trouble.'

'I don't know, my friend. I think it is in the balance.'

Rafin stopped whispering and looked at Pearce for what seemed an age, building up the tension before he made his decision. 'General Westermann cares nothing for your charges. You cannot fight the renegades in the marshes of the Vendée with ships. You may do with them what you wish. My soldiers will escort you back to your boat and you may tell your commanding officer that the sailors can be landed from noon.'

'Thank you.'

'Common seamen first, officers last.'

Having no idea why Rafin had said that, Pearce just nodded.

A couple of scruffy and disinterested National Guardsmen escorted Pearce and Michael back to their boat. Again Pearce looked at the shipping, noticing that a pair of the best-equipped vessels were now full of men, carrying out tasks that were commensurate with getting their vessels to sea. The decks were alive with crewmen and the rigging was full of men lashing on spars and sails, in total contrast to the way they had been moribund when he had come ashore.

'Michael, you need a piss.'

'I do?'

'In the harbour and take your time.'

Without another question O'Hagan peeled off to the edge of the quay, in a way that had the most alert of their escorts twitching his musket, but seeing him undo the flap on his ducks and turning his back, the fellow just grinned, stopped and waited, indicating to his companion to do likewise. While Michael did a passable job of taking his time, Pearce was counting guns and the numbers of men, information which would be of great interest to Henry Digby.

The procession of dozens of boats, some from the ships themselves, others from the port, went back and forth all day, taking out batches of sailors, with Digby, watching from his own quarterdeck, once more blessing the weather, for though there was a swell, there were no breakers to make the task of entering the harbour difficult. With each boat went the ship's stores, some to feed the sailors, other articles demanded by the soldiers to supply an army that seemed to lack most of the necessities of campaigning, despite the profusion of food that Pearce had seen that morning.

'We shall be away from here tomorrow, Mr Pearce, with luck. Have you made the necessary preparations for the last act?

'I have, sir, though I thought it too obvious to fetch them on deck. They can be seen from the higher elevation of the larger ships.'

The incendiary devices were down below, canvas pouches filled with tow and a charge of powder, which would be soaked in turpentine then set alight, the falls from the sails laying across them. Nothing went up like dry tarred rope, and soon the rigging would be well alight. The flames would have to work harder with the wood, but the deck was dry, as were the inner bulwarks, so Digby reckoned them to be ablaze quickly, and as he pointed out to Pearce, nothing consumed a vessel like fire.

'Thank the Lord we stripped most of their powder out at Toulon. I would not want to be near four capital ships when their magazines went up.'

'The General Westermann I mentioned has demanded what remains of that be carried ashore.'

'He is welcome to it, Mr Pearce, it is little enough.'

'I spoke with some of the local boatmen, sir, when I took in the first draft. They are not all rabid Jacobins, and I have been told about this revolt these soldiers are fighting.'

'And?' asked Digby, with the clear indication that it had nothing to do with him.

'It seems a bloody affair, with no quarter being given on either side.'

'You sound as if you regret that, Mr Pearce. The French are our enemies, so let them reduce their numbers by all means possible.'

'I do believe those fighting in the marshes to the north are as one with the men of Toulon.'

'I sense sympathy, do I not?'

'I think these sailors we are putting ashore will soon be put against them.'

'It is all very well such people saying they wish to restore a King to his throne and the papist church to its stolen property, but how much nuisance have we suffered from French kings and a clergy rich enough to subsidise their warlike ambitions?'

Digby had not heard, as Pearce had, the boatmen's tales, of villages burnt, women ravished before being disembowelled, babies skewered on bayonets, men tortured over roaring fires. There was another side, of course, for those same sources had told him that no soldier of the revolution was safe from retribution. Many had been caught and treated in a like fashion, and the conflict had descended into a contest in butchery. The addition of so many men might just tip the balance against the rebellion, but when he made that point Digby dismissed it.

'Most of them will run, Mr Pearce, for a French tar is no different to his British counterpart in that article. Devious, quick to take a chance, adept at avoiding detection. I doubt your General

Westermann will still command a fifth of those he expects to have before a day or two is out.'

'*Attention, Mariette*,' called a voice from a boat, which had all aboard aware of where it came from. Not one of the men they had escorted would ever refer to the ship by anything other than its French name. Pearce went to the side, to hear an invitation from Moreau that he, Digby and Mr Lutyens should come to dine that night with the officers of the French squadron, who would be going at last light.

'Perhaps they mean to take us hostage, Mr Pearce.'

'Not with Mr Neame manning our guns. I have told you, sir, he knows very well how to employ them.'

All the French officers, to the number of a dozen, had donned their best uniforms for the occasion, and the main cabin of *Apollon*, albeit that its stern lights were boarded over, had been cleared to set up a decent table. As they ate and drank, Pearce was left to wonder how they had managed to save such provisions and wines, but it transpired they had bought most of what was being consumed from the citizens of Algeciras and it was now time to see off the last of that provender. It could not be called a jolly affair, but, if you excused the glutton Forcet, it was polite. Most of those present had been sous-officers in the old royal navy, their increase in rank coming from the decimation of that service by the flight of *émigré* senior officers. So they knew their manners, and the subject of what would happen to the ships was not discussed until Moreau was seeing them over the side, his words addressed to Pearce.

'It is not something I wish to admit, but positions reversed I would be bound to follow the same course.'

'Would it help, Captain Moreau, if I were to say there is not a man aboard HMS *Faron* who is looking forward to what must be done.'

'Surely you mean *Mariette*, my friend,' said Moreau with a grin, but it was an expression which came and went quickly as he patted his own bulwark. 'We have a sentiment about ships, do we not? Foolish. We would see them blown to pieces in battle yet to surrender them…'

'You will be ashore in an hour, monsieur,' Pearce replied, to cover Moreau's sad thoughts.

They kept to their best uniforms for the journey to the shore, with Pearce in the prow of the boat, his flag of truce prominent. Rafin was there waiting, with his military friends and his escort of musket-bearing, ill-disciplined National Guards, their bayonets glinting in the light of the sinking sun. He landed first and stood aside to let the others come ashore, introducing each one as he did so. Once they were all landed, and as Pearce moved to say a last farewell, Rafin barked out an order.

'Seize them!'

The officers were suddenly surrounded by sharp and pointed bayonets, in what must have been a prearranged instruction. Rafin's pallid face was alight with fury, and he spat saliva through those drooping moustaches as he cursed them.

'Traitors, scum, cowards, do you not think we do not know what you did? You surrendered your ships to the enemy. You have no honour and if I have my way you will soon have no heads to trouble you with notions of it.'

Pearce saw then, standing close by, a knot of French sailors, and he guessed they were the men who had tried to take the vessels off Marseilles. They had come ashore and denounced the four captains and their eight lieutenants, which in the France of the likes of Rafin was as good as a death sentence.

'Monsieur, I protest,' Pearce yelled over the cries of the same complaint from those arrested. 'These men are your supporters.'

'Citizen!' screamed Rafin, in a voice that must have been heard on the other side of the harbour.

'These men did their duty.'

'They did not. They are rats, only they stayed aboard their ship instead of deserting them. Well, they are now going to the Hotel de Ville, and tomorrow they will face me and my court of revolutionary justice. Let us hear them try and explain how they chose to surrender rather than die, chose to help you take back their ships when they should have been prepared to see them sunk.'

'Five thousand men would have drowned.'

Rafin was in a passion, spitting venom in near incoherence. 'What does the Revolution care if five thousand die, or fifty thousand? The world must be changed. Traitors like these cannot be left to think they can indulge in betrayal and live. Like the swine of Versailles and the scum who bled the poor, they will see what justice is.'

'Citizen, I am begging you.'

Rafin suddenly laughed. 'I have a notion to respect your truce flag for one more day, monsieur. Perhaps you would like to come ashore again tomorrow and witness the way Madame Guillotine deals with traitors.'

Chapter Twenty

'Mr Pearce, we cannot interfere in these matters. Much as I have sympathy for the officers we dined with this afternoon they are no longer our responsibility, and I am forced to remind you of what you told me regarding those vessels preparing for sea. We may very well out-gun them. However, they are numerous, we are not.'

Henry Digby must have been well aware he was fighting a losing battle; it was not only Pearce who profoundly disagreed with him but also Lutyens and Neame, though their protest was silent; the former said nothing, merely fixing his superior with a pained eye, and the latter was looking at the deck planking of his cabin in an attitude which indicated deep sorrow.

'Besides, I would remind you of our need to get away from this shore as soon as possible. This weather cannot last.'

'The men threatened are innocent, sir, you know that. Their death will be for the purpose of a gesture to satisfy the blood lust of that sod Rafin.'

'So?'

'So I think it behoves us to make some kind of gesture in response.'

'For instance?'

'Mr Neame,' said Pearce.

The old master lifted his head slowly and looked at his captain, the reluctance to actually speak obvious, but Digby was looking at him in a way that brooked a response, so after a long hiatus it came. 'When we first anchored, sir, them French warships each had over fifteen hundred souls aboard.'

'I am aware of that, Mr Neame.'

'Well, if'n you had placed a mark on her waterline before they was shipped ashore, you would see clear how much they has risen in the water.' The first glimmer of what was coming appeared on Digby's face, but he had the good grace to let Neame make his point. 'And since they was cleared of cannon and shot at Toulon, and the crew took ashore what stores she still carried, I reckon that her draught is nothing like as much as it would be for a normal seventy-four in full commission. I would suggest they would need ballast before setting sail, for they are as high floating as a ship laid up in ordinary off Chatham

Dockyard. If the soundings I have for the entrance to La Rochelle are accurate, then there's enough to sail them in or close to on a high tide. It be touch and go whether they'd actually make the harbour.'

There was no need to say the tide would begin to rise a couple of hours before dawn, and peak late morning, or that the rise and fall in Biscay was telling, especially at this time of year, some twenty feet, with a concomitant strong inflow towards the shore.

'Girth, Mr Neame. I doubt a seventy-four would make it through those twin towers. What beam are we looking at, fifty feet?'

'It would be a scrape and no error, but they might. See, sir, the French build their ships a might narrower than we do in England. If you have ever been aboard a capture, say like the old *Magnamine*, like I was as a lad, you will see it has had to be strengthened for the kind of service we put our vessels to, Atlantic gales, Channel storms and the like. Sure they are swift sailers, but they are not as seaworthy in a blow as our'n 'cause of that slim construction.'

'You think one might actually get through?'

'*Apollon* is the most likely, sir. I have had a look at her beam and it is of the margin of some forty-five foot, so she might just shave those towers. Worst that could happen is she would stick, which would render the port unusable.'

'This is all very well, but that still does not give us any hope of interfering in the execution of...' Digby paused then, not knowing what to call them. They were no longer their charges. It was Lutyens who filled in for him.

'Our friends, sir?'

The reply was quite brusque. 'Are they, Mr Lutyens? I cannot see that drunkard Forcet as that.'

'I can see a delicious irony in the revolution removing the head of somebody like Captain Jacquelin, given his own dogged loyalty to the cause, but several of those we dined with were men of good character.'

Pearce spoke next. 'In other circumstances, sir, I would see myself becoming close to Moreau and Garnier. I would also, even on the short acquaintance I have now, consider it a desertion to leave them to their fate.'

'You are asking me to risk men's lives, and for all I know this ship, for men who are, even if we would have it otherwise, our enemies.'

'I am.'

Pearce was tempted to relate to Digby the sight and sound of a revolutionary decapitation; the square *en fête*, as though the death of some innocent soul was a cause for celebration; flags waving, crowds cheering, the occasional sight of unbridled licentiousness. The traders seeking to profit from it selling food and trinkets, such as cockades made of dyed human hair from previous victims, model guillotines which children could take home to try out on a rat, or if they were as debased as some of the parents, on a household pet. The knock that disturbed his thoughts, as well as the entry, was peremptory, with Harbin's freckled face suddenly lit by the cabin lanterns.

'Boat coming alongside, sir, quiet like, and calling out the ship's old French name when challenged.'

John Pearce was out of the cabin and on to the deck first, to find the men on watch standing by their loaded cannon, looking towards the low glow of gas lighting from the centre of La Rochelle. On a night with a lot of cloud cover, so no moon or stars, those ashore could not be trusted to stay put and Digby had set a watch to cover all eventualities. Barring his own cabin bulkheads, the ship was cleared for action, with deadlights shipped over the stern casements, every gun on both sides of the deck loaded with canister and run out, boarding nets rigged and men in the mainmast cap bearing primed and loaded muskets.

'*Mariette*,' a voice called softly, and Pearce replied just as quietly asking them to approach into the pool of light cast by the ship's lanterns. They were not stupid these men in the boat; aware there must be a lookout ashore keeping an eye on this sloop, they rowed round to the weather side and came close, hidden by the ship's bulk. Another call from Pearce had them come alongside, with Digby issuing a sharp command to look lively in case it was some kind of trap, this while his premier carried on a conversation with someone in the boat, quiet words that to everyone else were nothing but murmurings.

'Get him aboard, Mr Pearce,' hissed Digby.

'He won't come aboard, sir, but what he has to say is interesting.'

'Interesting to you,' Digby growled, in a rare show of frustration.

Pearce let that go, instead resuming his conversation with the man bobbing up and down in the boat, which included the passing over of a piece of paper. Asked to wait, Pearce took that to Digby to show him.

'Who are they?'

'Men from *Apollon* and *Patriote*, sir, though they will give no names.'

'We have no guarantee they came here without being seen.'

'They did not come out from the port, and they have told me of a part of the town wall on the south quadrant, so much in disrepair, it has fallen down.'

'Guards?' Digby asked, before adding, 'Not that I'm taken with any notion of going near it.'

'There is a sentry detail there, but our man tells me that they are slack.' Sensing that his captain remained unconvinced, Pearce went on. 'I have seen the calibre of the local National Guard, sir, and they are slovenly in the extreme, with weapons that are so ill maintained I wonder if they could fire, let alone with any accuracy.'

'They don't have to be accurate, Mr Pearce, they merely need to make a noise to raise a screaming mob.'

'And if they are taken care of in such a way they cannot fire their weapons?'

'Is that what they are promising?'

'Only that, and I admire the honesty. They will help us to the breach in the wall and point out the guard detail, then it is up to us.'

'And what would that be?'

'They cannot do anything close to the town centre and especially the Hotel de Ville. The danger of recognition is too great and while they have a wish to see freed the men due to be condemned, they have no notion to take their place.'

'Timings?'

'We must go with them now, allow them to get us into La Rochelle, so we can be in a position to effect a rescue at around dawn. The Revolutionary Tribunal will not meet that early, very likely not till near ten of the clock, and the prisoners are incarcerated in a set of cells under the Hotel de Ville.'

'And how will you get away?'

'The harbour is full of boats.'

'And the walls are well equipped with cannon.'

'Perhaps you, sir, standing in, could distract them and Mr Neame's notion might serve as well.'

'It seems to me you are bent on this.'

That was the first crack in Digby's inclination to do nothing, and John Pearce exploited it immediately. 'I would only go ashore with men who had volunteered, and I would not dream of including anyone you deemed necessary to the safety of the ship.'

Digby began to pace, Pearce joining him with an anxious look over his shoulder lest the boatmen from La Rochelle depart. He was anxious to speak to them once more, to add to their plan an idea of his own.

'How many men?'

'Half a dozen. One of the mids if they wish, and me in command. At least if I suffer there will be no real loss to the King's Navy.'

'You seem to have a wish to continually risk your life, Mr Pearce.'

'I thought, sir, that was a prerequisite for the role of a commissioned officer.'

'Responsibility is another, sir!'

There was no doubting the tone of that; Digby was suffering a degree of pique. Not that he would necessarily go himself on such a harebrained adventure; the fact that he did not have the choice is what rankled, the needs of his command coming first.

'Make your arrangements with the fellows in the boat, then come to the cabin and see if we can concoct some plan to aid you with the help of Mr Neame and Mr Sykes.'

Michael O'Hagan volunteering, once the case was explained to him, left little room for Rufus and Charlie to decline. Martin Dent was there in a flash, and he chided Dysart into putting himself forward by alluding to their previous adventures ashore. Costello, being of dark skin and hair colour, was more of an asset, Dysart being fair. Needless to say Midshipman Harbin was all for it.

'Mr Harbin,' said Pearce, 'I appreciate your zeal, and I know that having you along would be a plus, yet I would not want to deny Mr Farmiloe the possibility of action, which I think might improve his own opinion of himself.' The tall youngster looked at him with a steady gaze, as Pearce added, 'It will not reflect badly on you, Mr Farmiloe, if you decline. There will be no record of it.'

'Except in my memory, sir.'

'Then let me once more outline the risks, for I would not want you along just for the sake of your pride. We are going ashore to a town that is in the hands of some of the bloodiest scoundrels the world has ever known. Should we fail, we might get quarter, for our captain has undertaken to bombard the port if any harm should come to us, but there is no guarantee we will not be treated as spies.'

'And if we succeed?'

'Then, Mr Farmiloe, you will be able to hold your own at any dinner you attend in your future as a naval officer, for there will be no one at that board who has partaken of an adventure to match this.'

'Then, sir, I would be grateful if you will include me in your party.'

'Then get those white breeches off,' Pearce said, as the other midshipman's face collapsed, 'and get into all dark clothes. I am sorry, Mr Harbin, I cannot take you both, but I would be obliged if you would command the boat that will take us ashore.' Seeing the gleam that appeared in the boy's eye then, he insisted – producing in doing so another gloomy look – 'And you will return to the ship as soon as you have enough light to see.'

'Sorry my old bones will be of no use to you, Mr Pearce,' said Latimer. 'Was a time I'd have been first at the gangway.'

'I don't doubt it, old friend.'

Blubber Booth cut in. 'And I won't volunteer for fear of the sight of me trying to run.'

'You'll never make a topman, Blubber, that's for certain.'

Pearce turned to the rest of the party assembled on the deck, those who had already put themselves forward. Behind him he heard Latimer whisper to Blubber.

'D'ye hear what he called me? Old friend, he said. That's the sign of a right gent.'

'Mr Sykes, wish us luck.'

'Goes without saying, sir, and I hope Mr Neame and I can do our part.'

'Just make sure, Sykes, that you do not leave yourselves exposed by delaying too long.'

'I often thought about fishing you out of the water off Deal, your honour, whether it were right or wrong.' Pearce had been swimming ashore, with the shingle of Deal beach in sight, seeking to desert, when a strong hand had grabbed him and hauled him into the boat. Sykes had been on the end of that hand, and this was the first time since it had been mentioned. 'I reckon you would have been seen by the officer of the watch.'

'As an attempt to get free, it was not the wisest. You felt it was right at the time, Mr Sykes, and that will do me.'

'You might have got clean away.'

'You didn't believe that, did you?'

'No. Even if you had not been spotted you were new pressed, with no idea of how to avoid the Deal crimps, of which there are any number, God rot them. Barclay would have had you flogged as soon as you were dragged back aboard.'

'Then I should probably thank you.'

Sykes grinned. 'That would be gilding it, Mr Pearce.'

The boat with the party of Frenchmen had stood off, sitting outside the lights of the ship, and were invisible from the deck until John Pearce and his party cast off. A voice called to them, and a single spark was struck from a set of flints to locate them, Pearce ordering his oarsmen to get them close. Once done, the Frenchmen tossed over a thin line, not to tow them in any way, but to ensure that in the pitch darkness they would stay in contact. There was the slightest trace of phosphorescence from the striking oars, but not enough to be seen from more than a few yards away.

Judging by the way the waves were hitting the bow, HMS *Faron*'s boat was being led out to sea, and at one time the bulk of one of the French warships slid by their rowlocks, clearly being used as a mark by their guides, who then turned in towards the shore. The pace was steady, designed for minimum noise not maximum speed, and with the run of the sea on the quarter the cutter was rocking back and forth until another turn had it lifting and dropping the thwarts.

'Water's shelving,' Costello called quietly from the bow, the truth of that evident as the lead rope went slack and the keel hit soft sand.

Another flint strike came through the gloom and Pearce pointed, before realising that no one could see it. 'Get ashore and gather by that spark and wait till you have your feet. Mr Harbin, stand off until first light. If we fail at the breach it is to you we will be running for succour.'

Some had to kneel in the sand for several minutes before they felt safe to stand, with Pearce demanding patience from their nervous escorts, but eventually the volunteers were steady enough to be led off the beach onto a path that took them through a forest of pines. That was narrow and ended well away from the town wall, the same battlements that had once withstood the efforts of Richelieu and his Catholic army. They had been a formidable obstacle then, but time and advancements in artillery had made them useless, so the burghers of the time saw no point in spending money on repairs.

'*Où est les sentinelles?*' asked Pearce, the reply sending him towards a windowless hut, from which came the faint glow of a smouldering fire. The next thing that came was snores, and edging close and looking through the gap that covered the place where the walls had collapsed he could just make out three recumbent bodies, one in a chair with his musket across his lap, so obviously the sentry on duty, the other two stretched out in proper sleep on a pair of cots. He crept round to the back, finding the door and establishing with the slightest of creaks that it was not locked on the inside, then he went back to where his party was waiting, near-invisible shapes silhouetted against La Rochelle.

'Mr Farmiloe, Michael, Martin, there are three

fellows in there, all asleep.' He outlined how they lay to right and left of the door, then added, 'One each, but render them captured. No killing.'

The gleam of Farmiloe's dirk also picked up a little of the gaslight from the town, and Pearce would have liked to have seen the boy's face; was it determined or fearful? It mattered not, as long as he did what was asked. As the trio went to carry out his orders, he thanked the Frenchmen who had brought them this far, and issued them an invitation to go back from whence they had come and join Mr Harbin, pointing out that they would be welcome aboard HMS *Faron*. For that he was thanked, but they declined. They had to get back to the Place de la Revolution.

The muffled grunts from the hut told him his orders in that quarter were being obeyed, and soon Michael was by his side confirming it. 'Strip them, then tie them up and I need to know when they are due to be relieved. Perhaps if Mr Farmiloe was to play with his dirk, we might find out.'

When he heard what Farmiloe had done with his weapon, Pearce laughed. There was nothing a man would not tell you if you threatened to remove from him his manhood with an instrument that was less than truly sharp. The three replacements came with the dawn, under the command of a fellow slightly more martial in his attire, probably a sergeant. Neither his rank nor his well-maintained uniform and more military bearing saved him from capture, and he too ended up in the nearby woods, lashed in his smalls to a tree, with a gag in his mouth, able to look at the half-dozen of his men in similar straits.

'Pick the uniform coat that is closest to your size, and get it on.'

'Holy Mother of Christ, are they all dwarfs in the place?' cried Michael, struggling into a coat several sizes too small. Then he picked up the musket; forty-two inches in length, he managed to make it look like a toy, while the whole ensemble, including his hat, made him look like something out of a Raree show that was designed to lampoon the French nation.

'I'll not try the boots, John-boy, for as sure as hell is hot they will cripple me.'

It was only when the light came up strong enough that the party was reminded that one of their number was still dressed in his proper uniform. Lieutenant John Pearce unwrapped from his waist the truce flag he had brought with him, and using his sword, cut off a sapling with which to carry it. He then addressed his party.

'You are my escort. I have been invited to come ashore and witness the activities of the Revolutionary Tribunal, which I fully intend to do. So, Mr Farmiloe, having taken the sergeant's coat, I ask you to form up the escort ahead of and behind me, and take me to the proposed place of execution.'

* * *

The same grey dawn saw Neame and Sykes, with a small party of sailors, aboard *Apollon,* with the master blessing the slight onshore breeze drawn in by the heat of the land. Rigging a scrap of canvas was all they could do, but if the breeze held it would serve. The problem was also compounded by that breeze, for once in motion, with so few men aboard, it would be near impossible to take the way off the ship. If forced to abort what was planned, the only option was to seek to steer her into the shallow northern bay and run it aground.

Harbin had rejoined them in the cutter, only to be told to step a mast and head out to sea to act as a guard boat for the possible sight of a French ship from Rochefort. Digby had calculated the time taken to send a horse-borne message to the admiral there, then added the time needed to act upon it – the port was miles upriver, but there would be some kind of picket boat at the mouth of the estuary, which meant that it was very possible their departure, or their course to clear Oléron, could be impeded. In fact, as he walked his deck, just as it was finished being swabbed and flogged dry, he was cursing himself for agreeing to let Pearce and his party go ashore, and wondering, if his worst fears were realised, if he might be forced to abandon them.

Chapter Twenty-One

The streets were full of the same bustle and the quay resounded with calls as the locals bargained for the first and best of the morning catch. Pearce and his untidy escort made their way by the noise of their boots, which cleared a path by the mere crack of metal studs on cobbles. Though many a glance was thrown at the British naval officer carrying that truce flag, very few of them were hateful, leading Pearce to speculate again on the difference between the mass of Frenchmen and those at the forefront of radical change.

But it was only an occasional distraction; most of his thoughts were taken up with what he had to do next, which was no easy matter since he had only a very sketchy idea of what he was about to face from the information hurriedly imparted by the men who had come out to HMS *Faron* in their boat. The National Guard was not numerous, some hundred souls of which a third would be on duty at any one time. Soldiers should not be a problem; they were encamped to the north of the town, facing any threat that might come from the Chouan rebels, which made him wonder – their commander and several of his officers seemed more content to enjoy the ease of a proper bed in La Rochelle than share the discomfort of their military encampment.

The number of carts and load-bearing peasants in the streets forced the party to use the covered walkways, which, while it scattered those wishing to share the pavements, had the benefit of severely reducing the possibility of the men with him being recognised by their French opposite numbers; after all, these were some of the same fellows who had gone aboard *Apollon* off Marseilles, and the disguise they had was far from comprehensive. A forced crossing on the main thoroughfare took them to the Place de la Revolution and to a packed square in which traders had already set out their stalls to sell their wares.

Pearce looked anxiously over their heads to what in his mind had become the oration platform, glad to see that it was empty. No sign of Rafin, who probably would not stir for a time yet. In forcing a passage to the Hotel de Ville, he noticed that most of the assembled crowd were the sailors he had helped to land the day before, and his presence set up a murmur that he could not identify; it was anger, but at whom was it directed? It seemed to him that a great deal of the looks he was getting were supplicant, not irate; they were being aimed – unfairly as it happened – at his supposed file of National Guards. It was a good thing they could not speak the Erse, a tongue in which Michael was roundly cursing those who blocked his path.

The sketch the unnamed boatman had given him told him the entrance to the prison was inside the main building, a set of steps leading up from the basement cells to the main hall and the long desk at which sat the Revolutionary Tribunal. As a point of entry, it was a choice of last resort; if possible he did not wish to go into the confines of the Hotel de Ville, because inside he would be bound to be outnumbered, and if his lot came face to face with anyone in the same uniform, it would only be a second before the fact they were impostors was announced.

There was a sunken gate on the southern side of the building in an alleyway only wide enough for one cart, down a set of steep steps. It was the way in which food, wood and water were taken in, and the waste they produced removed, while it was also no doubt the exit by which any cadaver of a prisoner who had expired would be extracted. It would be guarded on the inside and he racked his brain to find a way of getting in.

'Michael, I need to exchange hats and coats.

Stand well back at street level while I go to the bottom of the steps and knock. I want that British uniform to be visible.'

Pearce was not small, but the time it took for Michael to get into his coat was annoying, and there was no way the arms would reach his wrists nor would the lapels come close enough together to look proper, so he was ordered to hand the garments over to Farmiloe, who looked more the part of a British naval officer. His instructions were to stand sideways as Pearce went to the base of the damp steps, which smelt of the corruption caused by human beings and the wind-blown filth that filled the foot of the well. He took out, loaded and cocked his pistol, and balancing on a loose section of the lowest step, which rocked slightly, he banged loudly on the studded oak door.

The voice that replied took several seconds and was querulous, which probably meant the fellow had been snoozing. Standing well to the side as the grille-covered viewing panel was slid back, so the fellow inside could see Farmiloe surrounded by a file of National Guards, Pearce lowered his voice an octave and growled that he had been ordered to bring in the English officer. The response was a protest, but the mention of Citizen Rafin, and the information it was his personal order, proved enough to get the keys rattling and the door unlocked. As it swung open, Pearce barrelled through and had the pistol under the warder's chin in a second, grunting in French for him to back away and get down on his knees, an order the lanky fellow obeyed swiftly, with a sob that he be allowed to live.

The rest of his party were quickly through the door, only to be faced, at the end of a twenty-foot corridor, with another nail studded door, locked on the inside, which served as a doubly secure means of ensuring those taken into prison stayed there. A demand to the warder for the key brought a negative response, plus the information it could only be opened from the inside, and it was obvious the only person those on the other side of the door would respond to was now on his knees, trembling before the waving pistol of John Pearce.

'I hear noises,' said Martin Dent, who had his ear pressed to one of the points where the ancient oak door failed to meet the jamb, places at which, over the years, it had shrunk. 'Voices, keys rattling, bit o' shouting.'

Pearce edged him aside and listened himself, harbouring a deep feeling of despair as he heard what sounded like the movement of several protesting prisoners. Were they moving them earlier than he had hoped? He needed to get through the door now, but if he did he would be in the narrow confines of a prison, probably against greater odds, and while he accepted that every man with him faced the same risk as he, he felt forced to hesitate, being reluctant to commit them when he had no idea of what they faced.

'Michael, get that bastard on his feet.' The Irishman literally lifted him bodily, for although a tall fellow, there was no weight to him, and for good measure he slammed him painfully against the rough stonework of the wall, producing a cry. 'One good blow, Michael, to let him know what he faces if he does not help us.'

The prominent nose went in an instant, sending forth a fountain of blood and dropping the warder back onto his knees, his hands over his smashed snout. Pearce, leaning over him, had not enjoyed that; much as he hated prison warders and much as, in the past, he had experienced their rapacity and total lack of empathy for anyone who could not bribe them for comforts, it went against his personal grain to indulge in torture. But he suspected that if he did not, the French officers would die; in the balance of things, this fellow's pain meant little. Harsh words and threats had the man look up at him, and the pistol waving before his bleeding nose.

'You will go to the door, you will knock and use whatever password is agreed to get us through, or you will die, not by this pistol but at the hands of my friend here, who will tear you to shreds, bit by painful bit.'

Odd that Michael did not speak a word of French, yet he must have sensed what Pearce was about because he grabbed the fellow by the neck of his rough smock, rocked him back and forth against the wall, causing the warder to scream in fear and pain, which was a snuffling affair, coming as it did through the blood he was swallowing. Michael, on command, lifted him again and shoved him towards the door, one hand, when he got there, tightly gripping the fellow's gonads.

'Tell him, John-boy, that if he messes us around, I will rip off his balls.'

The knock that followed was clearly a signal, two raps at a time with a gap in between a trio of the same, but there was no response. The small panel in the top did not open, no voice answered and Pearce, with his ear to the gap at the edge, heard no sound where there had been much before. Ordered to knock again, encouraged by an extra squeeze from Michael, the warder repeated the coded request; still no response.

Pearce stood back, looking around him for something to force open the door. His eyes alighted on a set of stout fire irons by a grate, at this time of year out of use. Then he looked at the door again, with hinges and locks not visible, being on the inside, and the gap all round which might provide leverage.

'Michael, get the poker and jemmy that door open.'

Michael went to stick it into the lock side, only to be stopped by Pearce. 'The hinge side, Michael. That is the weakest point on a door.'

'And how would you know that, John Pearce?' asked Charlie Taverner.

Pearce grinned, though he was still anxious. 'If you get mixed up with the wrong people, Charlie, even if you don't want to, they tell you things like this.'

'Sounds tae me like you've seen the inside o' a place like this afore, sir,' added Dysart.

'He's one of us,' crowed Martin Dent, with a laugh. 'A felon by nature, don't you know that?'

Costello responded in a shocked voice. 'How has you missed the grating, boy, talking to an officer in that manner!'

'Too fly, Costello, that's why, ain't I, Mr Farmiloe?'

The young mid just blushed as Pearce gave an impatient signal for silence. 'Jam it in as far as you can, Michael, a foot from the top and the bottom. That is where the hinges will be, and if they are rusted, they will give.' Doing that, it was clear, even with his great weight and strength, when he bent to the task of heaving, it was not enough. 'Martin, Dysart, Costello, on one side and pull; Charlie, Rufus, push with Michael. Mr Farmiloe,' he added, pointing to the warder, now crouching against the wall, again holding his face, 'put your bayonet by that bastard's throat.'

Heave as they might, it was to little effect, and Pearce realised they needed something with which to hammer the metal point further in. 'Part of the bottom step leading to the street is loose, someone fetch it. Use the other fire irons to dislodge it. The rest, get your bayonets into the gap and see if you can enlarge it.'

'Noise, John-boy.'

'What choice, Michael?'

The Irishman shrugged; there was none. Odd then that on the fourth blow with the granite of the bottom step the sound of a key came through the wood, and in a second the door swung open. A ruddy-faced fellow came through, and, seeing a group of National Guards in various stages of dress and undress, demanded what in the name of creation was going on. So much for security, as the one in the sergeant's uniform coat put his pistol to the man's chest, and O'Hagan, in nothing more than his shirt, swung a blow that knocked the bugger right off his feet.

'You weren't hoping to talk to him, John-boy, were you?'

'If I was, there's no point now. Get the keys.'

Through the door they entered another corridor with cells off to one side. The interior of those stone-lined chambers showed evidence of recent occupation: unconsumed food and the open ditty bags and sea chests containing the possessions the French officers had brought ashore. Keys in hand, Pearce made his way to the end, ordering that the two warders should be gagged and shoved in a cell. There was yet another door, and when he put his ear to the join, Pearce could feel a slight, cold draught on his cheek. Slowly, he inserted each of a dozen keys, easing each one round till it stopped, until he found the right one, which went through the well-oiled levers. Indicating that his men should be quiet, he eased open the door to be faced with another set of stone steps leading up to a beamed ceiling.

From where he stood he could see the back of the top half of a National Guard and he could hear voices, or to be more precise one voice, that of Rafin, vilifying his prisoners, heaping every insult in the revolutionary vocabulary on their heads. He tried to imagine those being harangued, hoping most of them were looking at their accuser with defiance. Another voice protested, which Pearce recognised as that of Jacquelin, pleading he was no traitor, but a true son of the Revolution. At least Rafin stopped to listen to him, as the captain of the *Orion* cried out the tale of resistance in Toulon; how he had led his men to refuse to serve, of his reluctance to surrender to the British at any time, and of how only those cowards who could not face the ultimate sacrifice demanded by the Revolution had stopped him from running his ship into Marseilles, regardless of the consequences.

That was his undoing. Pearce had removed his hat and crawled silently up the steps to a point where, through the guard's legs, he could just see the long table at which Rafin sat. The representative on mission was sitting when Pearce first saw him, playing with his moustaches again, a look of contempt on his face as he listened to Jacquelin. 'Ultimate sacrifice' had him leaping to his feet, screaming and damning the man for the coward he had to be if he was not prepared to lead by example, the implication being that if Jacquelin had laid down his own life, others would have been inspired by his example. Not being able to see the accused was frustrating; a man who no doubt felt he had reasonable grounds to be freed. He did not know the beast with which he had been brought to grapple. Pearce could imagine him though – the crushing truth getting through: everything he had believed in was false; there was no *Libertié, Equalitié, Fraternité,* and certainly no justice.

Rafin calmed himself and began to speak in a mocking tone, detailing the misdeeds of these men who had once served King Louis. How could any decent citizen be sure of their motives? Had they not come from Toulon as agents of those traitors in that port to undermine the Revolution in another, and used the desire of the true people of France, the men they led, as an excuse to betray? He then went into a flowery peroration, detailing with little modesty his own credentials as a man who had suffered under the monarchy, though in truth it did not sound, to Pearce, like much in the way of discomfort. The audience – there must be one or no speech was necessary – listened in silence to a catalogue of self-aggrandisement.

Finally, Rafin delivered the damning words, his voice rising as he spoke. 'As a true son of the Revolution, I demand that these traitors pay the penalty of any man who holds up his hand to stop the progress of the people. I demand they face the guillotine.'

Those watching, who had not dared to utter more than a murmur during the proceedings, broke into loud cheering; they had come for blood and they were going to get it. There was then a farce while Rafin 'consulted' the other tribunal members, half a dozen army officers, General Westermann first, his inferiors in order of rank, all of whom merely said 'guilty', a verdict that had only one sentence.

'Take them to the place of execution,' Rafin shouted. 'Now!'

The sentry in front of Pearce moved, and so did he, sliding back down the stairs to join his waiting men. He and Farmiloe exchanged coats again, and Dysart, who had never left hold of the truce flag he had brought from the ship, raised it to indicate he still had it, and Pearce took it from him.

'I will go up first. If I signal with my thumb behind my back, follow me up, if I show you one pointed finger, shut and lock this door and run.'

The incongruity of having a flag of truce in one hand, a sword in the other and his pistol in his belt was not lost on Pearce, as he ascended the steps, this time going on until he could see the chamber was now empty, though he could hear the cheering from the square in front. Quickly, he indicated that his companions should join him and as soon as they did he moved past the tribunal table to a point where he could see out of the open double doors, which led to the elevated plinth. Rafin was there, facing the square, in his black coat, big hat and tricolour sash, no doubt flanked by his fellow judges, and he had his hands raised calling for silence, an instruction the crowd were unwilling to obey.

'Right, we go out through those double doors, and arrest Rafin and his companions.'

'And then?' demanded Charlie, who obviously had reservations about what would happen next.

'We collect the prisoners, march them and that bastard in the black coat down to the harbour, take a boat, and row back out to HMS *Faron*. And before you tell me it's madness, Charlie, let me say I agree with you, but I can think of no other way to save men who do not deserve to die.'

Charlie grinned, which lit up his face, and showed that look which must have been his main asset as he fleeced the unwary visitors to his part of London. It was a grin to get all your coins out of your purse. 'As long as you know it's madness, that's all right.'

'Form up, lads,' Pearce hissed, 'let's do this in regulation fashion.'

Rufus Dommet was shaking, and Pearce put a hand on his shoulder, addressing Charlie. 'Look after him, won't you?'

Charlie aimed a soft punch at the other's shoulder. 'Never fear, John. No Pelican will go down if I have a say in it.'

'I'll be sound, Pearce, I promise,' said Rufus.

'I know you will, Rufus.'

As soon as Rafin started shouting out his message to the mob, they silently approached the open doors. Not that noise mattered; the roaring voice covered their footsteps, and only those at the very far side of the square would be able to see them. Since they were in the local uniform it created no alarm, at least until Pearce raised the flag of truce, which got folk pointing. When they levelled their muskets at the backs of those lined up slightly behind Rafin, the men to either side of him turned to look, and froze.

Pearce took Michael's musket and aimed over the

shoulder of the representative on mission, who was still shouting out his slogans, though the pointing fingers and loud gestures from below should have told him there was something amiss. The crack of the musket ball whizzing by his ear did that in no uncertain terms, his body jerking in shock. That passing ball affected the crowd as well, as, aimed over their heads, it crossed the square to smack into the wall of a house, making everyone duck.

'Stay absolutely still, monsieur.' Pearce stepped forward and, pistol out once more, put it to Rafin's head, looking from the side into a face creased with shock. 'Tell your guards by the guillotine to release the prisoners at once.'

Rafin's mouth was moving but no sound emerged for several seconds; when it did come he croaked, 'You will die for this.'

'You will die too, rest assured. Now do as I ask, or are you prepared to make the ultimate sacrifice for the Revolution?'

'You hear that, Mr Sykes?' asked Neame.

'I did. A shot, faint but as clear as day.'

'Then I say it is time to let go the anchors.'

The orders were passed below, and men with mallets attacked the bitts holding the anchor cables. The stern anchor had the strain on a rising tide and as it released it started to run out through the hawse hole at such speed that those on deck could see smoke rising from the friction burn. The bower anchor went more slowly, in the process aiding Neame on the wheel to swing the bows until they were facing right towards the twin towers of La Rochelle. Creaking, *Apollon* began to drift and a few more commands had the maincourse dropped, though it had no effect until those who had let it fall could get to the deck and sheet home on both sides. That done they were ordered to the entry port to take the first of the boats back to HMS *Faron*.

'Do you think', said Lutyens, on the deck of that ship, 'that is the signal Pearce intended?'

'God only knows, Mr Lutyens, but by damn I hope so.'

Pearce, even on such a short acquaintance, had surmised Rafin was a bully and a coward, and so it proved to be. The pistol at his temple reduced him to jelly and he could hardly find the breath to issue orders to the other National Guardsmen to lay down their weapons and release the prisoners.

'Those weapons, Mr Farmiloe,' said Pearce, 'and fetch our charges up here.'

'With me, Dommet,' the boy said and the two youngest members of the party went into a crowd which parted before them to secure the muskets, carrying them back to the podium in the wake of the French officers. Moreau was not grinning, he was grim, as he asked how they were going to get from this crowded square to the port and a boat.

Pearce pushed the pistol slightly, moving Rafin's head. 'Matters are in hand, but I would hazard that it might be a bad idea to leave these military officers to lead any resistance or pursuit.'

Moreau picked up one of the weapons that Farmiloe had dropped at his feet and, walking up to General Westermann, he first threatened to bayonet him. That the man showed no fear was admirable; if he was going to die he was prepared to do so while setting an example. Moreau reversed the weapon and hit him hard on the temple, so that he collapsed like a sack of flour. With that as an example, the others arrested took on the remainder of the tribunal members, until all were comatose and bleeding, lying on the stone, with Pascal Garnier having to restrain some of the younger men, who would have beaten their victims to death.

'And now, monsieur?' asked Moreau.

'Watch, and follow me.' Pearce jabbed Rafin again. 'Look at the ground and keep your eyes there.'

Pistol at Rafin's head, Pearce moved down the steps, to a crowd that seemed too dense to negotiate. But part it did, as the sailors from the four French warships suddenly moved – they had taken up positions that morning, as a collective notion to protest at the treatment of their innocent leaders – and created a path through which Pearce,

Moreau and the rest could proceed, closing behind them to foil anyone trying to interfere, some wishing their officers *bon chance* from behind hats that hid their faces. Farmiloe brought up the rear, walking backwards, musket at the ready, as the first of the cannon spoke from the sea wall and the towers of St Nicolas and La Chaine.

Chapter Twenty-Two

Few admirals would have sent a 74-gun ship into the arc of fire presented by the cannons of La Rochelle, but if they had decided the risk to be worthwhile, the vessels would have taken on the defences on the sea wall with their own blazing broadsides. No such option existed for *Apollon* and if the French gunners knew they were firing at one of their own ships it made no difference to their intent. Blasting away, from a secure platform and at short range, the balls tore great chunks out of the warship, sending splinters flying all over the upper deck when they hit the bulwarks. Neame and Sykes ducked continually and they could hear the wounding blows being taken under their feet, as the gunports they had opened earlier, in a bid to fool the defenders into thinking the ship armed, were blown in. Worse, other shot was aimed at the waterline, with the aim of sinking her, which, given she was in the main deep water channel leading to the port, showed a want of brain on the part of whoever was in command.

'If she takes in a load of water, Mr Neame, she will settle before we get to the towers.'

The old ship's master nodded to Sykes, trying to calculate the point at which he could abandon ship, when it was clear the seventy-four was going to end up where he wanted it, blocking the harbour entrance, but it was becoming obvious that time was not a luxury the gunners on the sea wall were about to allow him. So far the quarterdeck, where he and Sykes stood, had been spared, but that could not last. The open entry port was on the maindeck below their feet, on the side of the ship pointing away from those guns.

'Best abandon now, Mr Neame,' added Sykes. 'No sense in getting cut in half for what we can't achieve.'

Neame nodded and began to lash off one side of the wheel, Sykes doing the other. They were halfway to the companionway, crouching and running, just as a ball screamed across the deck and hit the wheel square on the middle of the spokes, reducing it to matchwood, and even though they continued to run it was with the knowledge that they had just had a very lucky escape. Once on the maindeck they were far from safe; the La Rochelle defences boasted 42-pounder cannon, and at the short range at which they were firing, that was a ball that could come right through the several feet of timber that made up the *Apollon*'s scantlings.

One ball, heated shot, flaming red, flew through a gunport ahead of them and smashed into the seaward side of the ship, embedding itself and beginning to smoulder the surrounding wood. On the deck of HMS *Faron,* Digby was again producing a litany of silent curses; he found being a spectator harder than the notion of being in action, and he was praying that his master and bosun would have the sense to get off in time. The relief when he saw the jolly boat emerge from behind the bulk of the seventy-four was palpable, though short-lived, as the lookout from the masthead yelled down to him.

'Mr Harbin approaching hell for the leather in the cutter, Capt'n, and he is flying a signal at the head of his mast.'

Digby was at the shrouds and climbing before the sentence was finished; this was no time for second-hand information, he had to see for himself. Given the speed with which Harbin was heading to rendezvous, he had his signal in view from the mainmast cap and it was one of the messages which required no signal book to decipher.

'Enemy in sight,' he shouted down to the deck, then looked towards the two men straining on the oars of the jolly boat, trying to calculate how long they would take to join, before adding, 'Prepare to weigh.'

Not so long before this day Lieutenant Henry Digby had been a skylarking midshipman, so sliding down a backstay to the deck, though it might not fit with the dignity of a ship's captain, was at least speedy enough to get him onto his quarterdeck in a flash. He had a glass on the jolly boat again, which had become a target for musket fire at extreme range. *Apollon*, now within the arc of the cannon on the towers of St Nicolas and La Chaine, was taking fire on the bows, which seemed to make the vessel jerk to a halt as they struck, only for it to resume its drift between salvos. Thick smoke came from below, pouring out of the gunports, this while the whole of her upper works were being blasted with shot that hardly needed any aim to strike home. The mainmast was struck and lurched to one side, held momentarily by the rigging, until, in slow motion, it went by the board.

Switching his glass, Digby looked through the gap on those towers, hoping to see John Pearce emerge with his party. If they came with the condemned Frenchman that was good, but without would do.

The threat to kill Rafin would have been useless if the man had shown an ounce of courage. At least he did not plead, no doubt because he knew it to be useless, as he was hurried down to the quay, passing by very much the same folk who had watched Pearce and his men march by earlier. This time, when they looked, it was with jaw-dropping wonder, as the party of seeming National Guards and one British officer, with that flag of truce still held over his head, hurried by, a sight which distracted them from the sight, as they looked out to sea, of a capital warship drifting in, bits of timber flying off as it was pounded, its prow aimed straight for them. That was a sight for the rescue party as well, and one that stopped Gerard Moreau in his tracks as, with a pained expression, he recognised his own ship being torn to bits.

'Captain Moreau,' Pearce shouted, grabbing his arm, 'we must keep moving. Mr Farmiloe, we are in need of a boat that we can row. You choose.'

There was a moment, when, rushing up the side of the quay, they approached the decks of the pair of privateers Pearce had seen preparing for sea the day before, when it might have all gone wrong. Many of the crew, having seen them coming a long way off, looked to a weapon to interdict them as they passed, but the screeching orders of whoever commanded rang out telling them to concentrate on casting off and getting out of the harbour before the entrance was blocked. By the time Pearce and his prisoner stumbled by, the cables had been slipped from the bollards, and men were poling the ships away from the stone quay, this while others pushed sweeps out of the low gunports to act as oars.

'Ahead, sir,' Farmiloe shouted, 'the size of a decent cutter.'

The boy was pointing towards a large clinker-built fishing boat festooned with fenders, in which a fellow, seemingly oblivious to what else was happening in the place, was untangling his nets. His boat had a single mast and boom, as well as half a dozen rowlocks a side, indicating it was reasonably deep-water fishing smack. With so many men it would be crowded, but it would do, so Pearce gestured to Costello and Martin to get forward and see to the fisherman, who was roughly bundled out of the way as first Farmiloe, then the rest of the party, clambered down into his boat. The protests he began to make died in his throat as a musket was levelled at him.

Pearce could not believe they had got this far without having to fight, and it was only when he looked back he realised why. A solid phalanx of French sailors, twenty deep, was walking slowly along the main quay, blocking any attempt by Rafin's supporters to get by them.

'Now, monsieur, you will get down into the boat, and you will do so in the knowledge that I still have my pistol trained on you.'

That was when Pearce caught sight of the tortured face of Captain Jacquelin, clearly in an agony of indecision. He was the only one Pearce thought he had to worry about, the only one who might see his duty as an attempt to get Rafin free, and by doing so save himself from the guillotine. He had only moments, the time needed for him and Moreau's men to get the oars out and rigged for use.

'Captain Jacquelin, if you wish to stay out of the boat you are free to do so. Perhaps you have so much affection for your home soil that you would risk your neck to stay here.' The man looked at him with a hard glare, until Pearce added, 'But do not attempt anything, because if you do, not only will this bastard die but so will you. Make up your mind, go or stay.'

Jacquelin responded by sitting down amidships, between two of his own fellows who had got their oars in place.

'Slowly, Rafin. Michael, when he's down get him in the bow and standing.'

The representative on mission was handed down into the boat and so placed, Pearce joined him, spreading his own feet wide and taking his collar to keep him upright.

'*Cochon*,' Pearce said in his ear, a remark the man resented by the way he stiffened; he was not used to being called a pig. 'We have to get out between St Nicolas and La Chaine, and there are men on the ramparts who will be tempted to shoot down on us. One musket ball fired and you die, so clear your throat and get ready to call out.'

'You will kill me anyway,' Rafin replied, for the

first time showing some spunk, this as Dysart and Costello pushed off and the men on the oars began to row with more confusion than rhythm.

'No, we are not like you. Let us say we are like the majority of your countrymen. Do as I as say and we will let you live, and perhaps you will learn to grant the same gift to others.'

HMS *Faron* had sailed over her anchor, plucking it out of the soft sand that lined the sea floor as sweet as kiss my hand, and once Neame and Sykes were aboard, no more than a few minutes after, Digby gave the orders that would bring her round to close with Harbin, sailing close to the wind on the larboard tack.

'Aloft there, a sharp eye out to sea for whatever it is that has got Mr Harbin so agitated.'

'Is my presence on the deck permitted, sir?' Digby just nodded to Lutyens, and kept his telescope trained on the distant horizon, the face behind it definitely worried. 'Am I allowed to ask about Pearce and his men?'

'You are, Mr Lutyens, as long as you do not look for an answer. The safety of the ship comes first. If what is out there has to be avoided at all costs then Mr Pearce will just have to take his chances.'

Lutyens did not respond with an opinion, and in truth he had no idea if the men who had gone ashore had achieved what they set out to do or failed, but it was silent speculation that would have troubled the captain if said out loud; what would happen to them if they were taken by a group of people quite prepared to slaughter their own naval officers on a set of trumped up charges? There could only be one answer.

'He appears to have a streak of luck in such situations, Captain Digby,' Lutyens said, more to reassure himself than the man he was addressing. 'Let us hope it holds.'

'Topgallants on the horizon, Capt'n.'

'Excuse me, Mr Lutyens, I need to see this for myself.'

Digby went to the shrouds again and began to climb, Lutyens walked to the taffrail, passing Mr Neame on the way, to look back at the pillar of smoke rising from the burning *Apollon*. The master was close enough to exchange words with him, and so set in his course that he could join him in looking back to the diminishing outline of La Rochelle.

'If'n Mr Pearce ain't out of that harbour in a few minutes, he ain't never ever goin' to get out.'

Looking at the older man, and seeing that his attention had returned to a close examination of the sky and the cloud formations out to sea, he asked what they portended.

'See how the high clouds is breaking up, Mr Lutyens, into those odd oblong shapes?'

'I do.'

'Lenticular we calls it, and that is the forewarning of foul weather to come. The high winds are from the south-west, so that will be what we face, common at this time of year.'

'When?'

'Twelve hours, maybe half a dozen more if we are lucky, but in these waters, with that sky, given we can't seek shelter, we should be running for deep water as fast as we can. At the very least we need to get well clear of Oléron, which is not going to be gifted us if we have to fight another ship.'

'There must be an alternative.'

'There is. Weather the Ile de Ré, which is that long sandbar to our north, then set a course to run with the wind and hope to get so far out into blue water that, even if it lasts a week, we can weather Ushant. Trouble is, it seems there's folk out there who want to stop us doin' that.'

'Can we avoid a fight?'

'Mr Lutyens, they have the wind. The choice of fighting does not lie with us, it lies with them, and if they do choose to engage and we carry anything away aloft, even if we escape we will be in real danger. With that weather and where it is comin' from, and the strength of gale it might be, it could be us that don't get out of here.'

Obviously, Lutyens thought, the chances for John Pearce and his party had just plummeted.

*   *   *

Having pulled out towards the middle of the harbour, the men in the fishing boat were presented with the sight of *Apollon* perilously close to plugging their route of escape. Farmiloe started to chant, in order to get the oars to synchronise, and this had some effect, speeding up the boat as the oars bit the water more evenly, though they were pretty low in the water with so many souls aboard, and not in a vessel designed for speed, so they would never reach a satisfactory pace.

'Them sloops is beginning to make way,' Martin Dent said. He was in the thwarts, holding the tiller, but looking backwards, Farmiloe still chanting beside him. 'Once we is out in deep water, with them sweeps out, they's like to overhaul us.'

Silence fell as everyone aboard who could understand absorbed the information, because the time must come where the threat of a ball through Rafin's head might not work. Indeed, they were coming abreast of that now, as they approached the towers that guarded the entrance, with musketeers leaning over both ramparts, their weapons trained. Pearce pressed his pistol hard against Rafin's head and hissed, 'Time to sing, *cochon*.' The shout was as loud as that he used to harangue the crowd earlier, and it was an order not to shoot on pain of certain death. Pearce was less concerned with that than the rapidly closing gap in front of him. *Apollon,* now well alight along the length of her larboard side, was within a few dozen yards of the towers, still being hit repeatedly by gunfire, and her head was slightly down, showing him more of the deck than she should; if she came on and jammed her bulk into the gap there would be no room to escape.

The ship was drifting so slowly that, when she ran aground, it was hard to spot – a slight sway forward of the upper foremast, a dip of the smashed stump of the bowsprit – but softly aground she was, with room for Pearce and his men to row through, into the billowing pall of smoke that was being driven inland on the breeze.

'Steer us to the seaward side, Martin. Those cannon could be trained on us if we stray down the other.'

'Aye, aye, sir.'

'So you do know your manners,' gasped Costello, pulling on his oar.

Pearce glanced over his shoulder, to see that the sloop in pursuit had stopped working the sweeps and had let fly the falls on the sail it had raised. Men were jumping off the deck into a cutter, which properly manned would have little trouble in overhauling them, so they were not out of danger yet. They were in a cloud of acrid smoke, every man jack aboard coughing, which also cut off from view the tower of St Nicolas right above them and the boat in their wake. Pearce knew he was very close to the stone jetty on which he had first landed, so close that it would be possible for someone on it to attempt to bar their progress. But would they risk it? His heart was in his mouth until the smoke cleared and he could finally see where he was heading, down the flank of *Apollon*, safe for the moment from the guns of the sea wall.

'Once we see *Faron*, Martin, steer straight for her. We will have to take a chance on those cannon, for there's no way of getting out of range.'

Peering out to sea, it was only a minute more before he saw his own ship, and it was clear that she was sailing away with as much speed as she could make.

'A corvette, Mr Neame,' said Digby as he came back on deck, 'sixteen cannon on her maindeck, bow and stern chasers, and she's clearing for action.'

'How does she sail, sir?' Neame asked.

'With the wind on her beam she looks as good a sailer as any ship would, and I observed no change in her sail plan, so how she will handle in a fight I do not know.'

'Have you observed the cloud formation, Captain?'

'Your opinion would be valuable.'

That was a neat way of Digby telling Neame he was uncertain, but that was also the reason a king's ship had a sailing master, more steeped in knowledge of the sea, the weather and its vagaries than a commissioned officer, whose job it was to fight. Neame explained his thinking, downplaying the notion they might have the best part of a day to get enough of a southing to get well clear of the Ile d'Oléron. If they had more time than he thought, good, but it was not something to base sound judgement on.

As they discussed the meaning of that problem, there came the other of getting the cutter hooked on and Harbin and his men aboard, there being no way to do that without backing the sails and virtually bringing HMS *Faron* to a dead stop. The cry from the masthead, as the cutter clattered clumsily into the side, that it looked as if Mr Pearce was in a deep-laden fishing boat and had cleared both the harbour and the burning *Apollon*, was just another thing to worry about.

'Your opinion, Mr Neame?'

'If his boat is deep in the water, it argues he has the Frenchmen with him.'

Digby nodded at that, and called to his freckle-faced midshipman as he clambered aboard. 'Mr Harbin, get the animals into the cutter and have it towed astern, then report to me. I want your impressions of that ship we face.'

'I have no notion of any plan you might be thinkin' of, your honour.'

Digby's laugh was an interruption. 'I am short of a plan, Mr Neame.'

'Well, sir, that Frenchman outguns us, not by much I will say, but he has more weight of shot nevertheless.'

'But how does he handle them?'

'That's as unknown as how he sails, but I would say that standing off to fight him with cannon is not an option, quite apart from the fact we have the means to give him a shock if we range up close.'

'Mr Pearce's love of a carronade may pay a dividend.'

'But to truly beat the fellow, if he's any good, we may need to board, and that requires numbers.'

Digby nodded slowly, then said in a dispassionate tone that must be at odds with his feelings, 'Bring us about, Mr Neame, let us close with Pearce's boat and get our men aboard.'

'And the changing weather, sir?'

'One risk at a time, Mr Neame.'

Pearce had been watching HMS *Faron* with a sinking feeling that got worse the greater the gap between them. They were out past the three anchored seventy-fours now, and he had Rafin on his knees, the motion of the boat on the swell too pronounced to remain standing. Behind him the cutter from the privateer rowed steadily along, keeping a distance but with the means to close at any time, armed men aboard ready to fight them if the occasion arose. Could he trade Rafin for safety? Or would such a policy result in certain capture, for he could see no way how any arrangement he could make, some kind of parole, could be trusted to hold with such a murderous radical. Rafin could say he would exchange his freedom for theirs, but renege as soon as he had the advantage.

'Only way tae do it, your honour,' said Dysart, when he opened up the problem to them all, 'is to take half their sticks off them as well. Then they'll no' be able to keep up with us.'

'For how long?' Costello responded. 'The oars will float, they will get them back on board, and with *Faron* sailing away they will have all the time in the world to close with us.'

Dysart reluctantly acknowledged the truth of that, and a deep gloom descended over men who had no doubt what they faced if taken. It was Farmiloe, who had never taken his eyes of their ship, who cried out that she was coming about, and looking forward they could all see that she was halfway round, presenting her side instead of her stern. The cheer was not just from English throats; most of the French sailors cheered too, and Moreau had that grin on his face again, which cheered Pearce up immensely.

'Perhaps now, Dysart, your notion has merit.'

Pearce, slowing, called out to the pursuit,

offering the exchange if they ditched four of their eight oars, which led to a long discussion, which could only have come about because their mother ship was a privateer and thus a decision had to be collective. All the time Pearce was glancing over his shoulder, to see HMS *Faron* coming on hand over fist, trying, and he thought failing, to work out the time needed for them to be close enough to threaten that cutter and the contentious souls manning her. Eventually the exchange was agreed, and half the oars were slipped out of their rowlocks to float inshore on the still rising tide. They would have to come about to retrieve them and that would take time, but there was one other way to slow them down.

'Monsieur, stand up and let your rescuers see you. Costello, throw off those fenders.'

Having listened to the exchange, Rafin knew what was about to happen, and he looked to the men rowing the boat he was in to raise their oars. He waited in vain.

'Can you swim?' As Rafin shook his head, Pearce said *je suis désolé*, and, taking him by the collar and tail of his black coat, he threw him into the water, as close to those fenders as he could.

Chapter Twenty-Three

'The only thing that floated at first was his hat,
though the sod did come up for air twice before
they got to him, and he had all the appearance of a
drowned rat as they hauled him in.'

Digby was only half listening to Pearce; they had
come about again and were once more closing with
the enemy, now hull up, identified by the
Frenchman, Forcet, as *Pandarus*, who, with the
weather gage, had gone down to topsails very
quickly, a luxury denied to his opponent, still forced
to beat up into the wind in order to gain the kind of
sea room both captains would see as necessary for
the forthcoming fight. The route north-west was
closed to them by the Ile de Ré, to head due south
was to take them closer to the anchorage of the Aix
Roads, not a pleasant prospect, which would make
even harder the task of weathering the Ile d'Oléron.

'I think, Mr Pearce, had you known we faced an

enemy at sea, you might have rather seen the fellow drown.'

Pearce could not believe that Digby had any anticipation of being beaten – it went against the grain of the man and the service of which he was part – yet it was obvious from his tone that he had calculated the prospect of such an outcome and the obvious corollary of what might follow should they be taken into La Rochelle anchorage as a captured enemy vessel. For Moreau et al it would be the guillotine for certain and he, following on from the treatment he had meted out to Rafin, could not feel safe from a similar fate.

'As it is, I look to you to ensure that our French friends understand that they too must be prepared to fight.'

'I would say they are too aware of the alternative not to.'

'I would be obliged if you would confirm it.'

The French officers were gathered in a knot in the fo'c's'le, watching the approach of what should have been a friend. Pearce had the distinct impression the subject he was about to broach had already been discussed, but it was on quite another matter that Moreau engaged him; the approaching change in the weather, plus the fact that being from the Breton port of Concarneau he knew only too well what those elongated cloud formations portended.

'The captain is aware of that, but you will see our way is barred.'

'Might I suggest that he attempts to get to windward of *Pandarus* and then tries to outrun her.'

Without a fight in which you might be compromised, Pearce thought, but he said: 'I will pass on your comments, but you know that is not why I have come to speak with you.'

Moreau nodded. 'A dilemma, I think.'

'If you are prepared to fight, Captain Digby is prepared to give you the means. If not, we must find somewhere below to keep you secure.'

'Our own countrymen, and where will we go even if your captain wins?'

'We – that corvette and the weather permitting – will make all sail for the Straits of Gibraltar and Toulon.'

'Do you still have your flag of truce?' Pearce nodded. 'Then I would like the use of it, to speak to the captain of *Pandarus* and see if we can find an alternative to a battle in which I must fight men who should be my comrades.'

Digby's refusal to consider the request was so empathic as to make any discussion pointless, and Pearce, who would have said the same, was treated to a sharp and near-public reminder that his duty lay to the flag at the masthead, not the Frenchmen he had fetched aboard. It was really the first time he had seen his captain angry, and the words he used, though they contained certain truths, were not easy to swallow without the temptation to deliver an equally sharp response.

'Just because you have no care for your own commission, Mr Pearce, does not mean that you can play ducks and drakes with the prospects of others. I have set my course for a life in His Majesty's service, and I have spent eight years working to get to my present rank. I do not believe for a moment, as matters presently stand, I shall survive as a Master and Commander on my return to Toulon, so I will revert to being just another lieutenant on a very crowded list. And it may have escaped your attention, but it has not mine, that we have abandoned three capital ships I would hazard are, at this very moment, being re-manned to sail them away from a lee shore on which they must face certain destruction, something unlikely to raise my profile with Lord Hood or the Admiralty.'

'Yet if you best that corvette...?' There was no need either to finish the sentence or for Digby to answer; if he won a single-ship action against what was a superior force, he would be made. It might not gain him post rank and a rated ship, but no admiral would shift him from his present situation with such a victory under his belt. Pearce, stung by Digby's rebuke, added: 'I daresay you are comfortable risking the lives of everyone aboard to enhance your own prospects of advancement.'

Digby flushed angrily, and, in truth, Pearce regretted the words as soon as he spoke them, for had he not just risked a half-dozen lives to rescue Moreau and his associates? It was that old devil in him; he would not be talked down to by anyone, even a man he quite admired.

'Mr Pearce...'

A second interruption was very necessary, to stop Digby before he made this spat so serious that neither would be able to step back. 'Forgive me, sir. What I just said was unwarranted and I would like to withdraw the insinuation.'

'Sir,' said Neame, 'if I could draw your attention to the enemy. The point is coming where you need to tell us what we are to do.'

The old man's intervention was, in terms of discipline, worse than the words Pearce had used, and in reality, given the rates of sailing, and the fact that his opponent was drawing him out into deeper water, action could not be joined before the glass had run through at least twice. An argument between commissioned officers was one thing; a barbed comment from a warranted ship's master, however old and able, was enough to cause real friction. Yet Digby did nothing for a moment, possibly seeing it for what it was, a way to stop his superiors continuing the argument.

'I thank you for reminding me, Mr Neame. Mr

Pearce, you will oblige me by asking Captain Moreau what he intends. If he will not fight he and his men must be confined; there is no alternative. Mr Neame, your opinion on what our opponent will do.'

Pearce only realised halfway to the fo'c's'le that he had been the subject of a snub; Digby should have asked him first and he had not. Yet he could not continue to be angry with a man who had shown him much kindness, had never once publicly alluded to his lack of knowledge, who had indeed gone out of his way to help him absorb the duties which went with his rank both on deck and over books in his cabin. So he would attend his guns and fight as best he could, because the responsibility of success or failure did not lie with him, and it was, no doubt, a burden felt keenly by the man who had it.

Moreau made it a matter of individual conscience, so that half the French officers went below to be confined, while the other half, with the captain of *Apollon* at the head, were issued with cutlasses. Looking back along the deck as he made his way to his station he was impressed by the calm demeanour of the gunners, the midshipmen and the two men in close discussion on the quarterdeck. Was it Neame who hinted that Digby had gone too far, or was it the captain himself? Whatever, he was summoned for an opinion, and with the yards braced right round, the sight from the wheel – a clear view of the enemy – was not encouraging.

'I doubt I can add much.'

'Nonsense, Mr Pearce, you have seen action, I have not.'

'Does not our friend yonder have all the choices?'

'Not all. He has the advantage, certainly, but how will he use it?'

'He should try to keep the wind,' said Pearce, 'even I know that, so I suspect he will seek to cross our bow and rake us when we are struggling to reply in the hope of hitting something vital.'

'Then?'

'If he fails in that he should put up his helm and invite us to attack.'

'At which point,' Digby continued, 'he will let fly his sheets, come about and fetch us another broadside, with enough time and way on his ship to resume his course and stay clear until he had wounded us enough to surrender the weather gage and seek to get across our stern. It is Mr Neame's opinion that *Pandarus* will be a ship set to guard the Rochefort approaches, and therefore near continuously at sea, so the crew will be efficient on the sails, yet possibly less so on their armaments.'

'At this stage, sir,' Neame added, 'a guess more than an opinion, and I would point out once more that neither we nor the enemy commander have much time for anything with the promise of a south-westerly gale in the offing. These waters are his and he must know what that cloud formation means. So for him too, if the business is to be done, it must be done with alacrity.'

'We must get close, sir.'

Digby's smile was grim. 'I fear he will not let us, Mr Pearce.'

'Can we not fool him?'

Pearce suddenly remembered, and made mention of the incendiary devices they had made up to burn the French seventy-fours. The appearance of *Pandarus* had made any attempt to use them impossible, but they were still available.

'Fire is a hazardous thing aboard ship,' Neame insisted.

'Yet smoke and seeming panic on our deck may make *Pandarus* act precipitately.' Seeing the uncertainty, Pearce pressed home his point to Digby. 'I think we can assume he knows, as we do, that time is pressing. He will want to take us whole as much as you would want to take him as a prize, so let us show him he is in danger of total loss.'

'You think he will seek to save the ship rather than see it burnt to the waterline?'

'Flames and smoke could be accompanied by the useless discharge of cannon, as though the powder in the touch-holes has been set alight by a blaze. If he thinks we are on fire, and that we cannot use our guns, he will be bound to range alongside to try and board, with the aim of putting out the conflagration and taking the ship as a prize. If he comes that close he will be at our mercy, ready to board instead of sitting off with his guns manned.'

'If it is to be done,' said Neame, 'it must be done now, or their lookouts will see everything.'

Digby never got the chance to finish his nod. Pearce called for Harbin and Farmiloe, as well as the men he had led ashore, with instructions to one mid to get all the cook's coppers and the other to take from him every ounce of slush he had, and damn the fact that he would lose by not being able to sell it. The copper cauldrons were rigged by lines across the fo'c's'le so they did not touch the deck, a square of canvas laid underneath as a precaution.

'Dysart, Costello, get the fire engine up here into the bows. I want it played on the base of that canvas, and if it shows any sign of spreading to the timbers, douse the coppers with water.'

He had the Pelicans, Latimer and Blubber fetch up the incendiaries, used turpentine to soak the sacking and tow, to be carried on pieces of damp canvas into the bows so the smoke they created would blow back over the deck.

'The captain of *Pandarus* will be wondering what we are about, will he not?' Pearce pointed to Moreau and his fellows, watching what was happening with bemused expression. 'The captain of *Apollon* is no wiser, I hope.'

Digby was looking back to the near-invisible shore, to the pall of smoke that rose higher and higher in the sky, yet it was clear at the base, broken from the land, so he had to assume the fire had been contained. Right now they would be trying to refloat the ship and tow her clear to free the shipping in the harbour, another reason to avoid being tardy. The tide had not finished rising when she went aground; plug the holes, pump hard and she might lift from the sea bed. A couple of cutters could then tow her far enough off to open the entrance so bigger vessels than a cutter could exit. A couple of well-armed and handled privateers, added to *Pandarus*, and HMS *Faron* would be done for.

'Mr Neame, I know the masthead is a perilous position in a fight, but I need someone aloft to keep an eye on the prospect of those privateers Mr Pearce mentioned emerging from La Rochelle.'

'Martin Dent, get aloft. Keep an eye out dead astern for any sign of a sail.'

If the boy knew that it was a point of danger, given the French generally tried to dismast an enemy, it made no difference to him; he went aloft with his usual cat-like speed. Pearce was still working in the bows, rigging a run of canvas to screen the cook's deep copper pots. He also had a tub of slowmatch fetched forward, his aim to light the incendiary devices as soon as their ship was in receipt of a broadside. Meanwhile Harbin and Farmiloe were going around the deck with his instructions to the crew to pretend to panic as soon as the smoke became thick enough to make them cough.

Down below, Lutyens, his instruments laid out in readiness, wondered at the amount of running feet he could hear through the planking. An enquiry to a sailor gave him the information that while the enemy was closing, it would be half a glass of sand before they engaged, so he went up to the quarterdeck. Once explained, he gave the opinion that the men on deck should place something damp over their mouths to keep the smoke out, which led to a severe diminution in his stock of bandage. Digby, sensing the time had come, had a tot of rum served to each man, to get some fire in their bellies.

'Range is closing, sir,' called Neame. 'I would say he'll be putting up his helm in no more'n five minutes.'

A final check was made: the carpenter was ready with well-tarred canvas, plugs and mates to fix any hole in the hull; Sykes had men standing by for a fast repair of any vital rope or sail, and axes to cut away anything that, damaged, might imperil the ship; while the gunner, having filled all the cartridges he had available, and being a religious man of the Methodist persuasion, was praying to Almighty God to be spared. Digby had gone into his cabin and put in a weighted sack the ship's books and the list of recognition signals used by British warships to identify each other, and then he came back on deck, to look at the half-dozen gloomy, cutlass-bearing Frenchmen in the waist.

'Lads,' he shouted, 'he can hit us and all we can reply with are our bow chasers. So when I shout to get down I do not want you looking to see if I am serious. Get flat on the deck immediately. If you do not know what Mr Pearce is about, we are trying to fool the enemy, and I have to tell you, given that he has seen action and survived, we must assume that what he lacks in experience he makes up for in luck. So do as he orders, and we will win the day.'

They cheered, but Digby was left to wonder if it was brought about by enthusiasm or rum, though when he gave the orders that took them down to topsails, it was done with a normal level of efficiency. As an act, it was like a signal of intent to their opponent. The first ball from the bow chasers of *Pandarus* sent out a thick cloud of black smoke, which, billowing forward with the onshore breeze, had Pearce asking for any rubbish powder or bottom of the barrel grains the gunner might have to be brought up. It also reassured him; when the corvette fired a broadside, the smoke from their own cannon would obscure what was happening on his deck. The balls only fell short by half a cable, and the way the range was closing it could only be minutes until the expected salvo came from his main battery.

'An eye on his deck,' Digby called to the men in the mainmast cap with muskets. 'Let me know as soon as they move to let fly the sheets.'

Silence fell, with only the slight whistle of the wind in the rigging still audible, and even on open water, everything came down to the closing gap between the two warships. When a voice from the masthead gave the alert, Digby shouted, and every man not an officer or midshipman dropped to their knees on the deck, Neame and the quartermaster on the wheel being the exception. The mighty crash of the guns was carried on the wind and it had passed them by when the balls struck, high in the rigging, parting ropes and dislodging blocks which were caught in the rigged overhead nets. Sykes and his men were quickly into action, to splice a break or run a replacement line and were still at that task when the second salvo came. A ball took one of Sykes's mates and plucked him off the rigging like a shot bird, carrying him screaming into the water, where he was certain to die.

'Belay that, Mr Sykes,' Digby called. 'Get your men to a place of safety until something vital is wounded.'

Smoke reached HMS *Faron* in a dispersing cloud, to mix with thicker stuff from the back blast of her own bow chasers. Pearce put the slowmatch to the incendiaries, and as they flared up he ladled slush onto the flames, which produced a cloud of pungent smoke that had him spinning away to get his breath.

'Water that deck,' he croaked, as he nearly retched over the side. He made his way to the bowsprit side of his brew and added more slush till the whole deck seemed to be in the grip of the smoke it created. Mentally he was counting; how long to discharge a gun and send a ball uselessly into the sea off the ship's side, that followed by a couple more? Would the captain of *Pandarus* be fooled? Would he close to try to take possession of the ship?

Digby, before the smoke obscured his enemy, had seen the corvette come about and head away, slow enough to tease him to try and close, though it was obvious he could tighten his falls and increase his speed at will. Yet he also saw him check as the smoke rose from the bows, and if he could see the rising and flickering flames then he had to assume his opposite number would too. Digby jerked involuntarily as first one, then a second cannon went off, arcing a pair of nine-pounder balls into the sea off the larboard beam, sending up telling water spouts, this accompanied by frenzied shouting and a scene of apparent panic as men rushed around the deck.

That must have decided him; the captain of the

Pandarus let fly his sheets, hauled hard on his rudder and started to come round on the wind in short order.

'Mr Harbin,' Digby said, in a calm voice, 'please be so good as to inform Mr Pearce that his ruse has worked. Get those guns run in and reloaded.'

'Topsails astern, sir,' shouted Martin Dent, 'something's coming out of the port and I reckon it's one o' them privateers.'

'If there is one, boy,' Digby said to himself, 'there will be two.'

In terms of his present situation it made no odds; he still had to engage the closest enemy vessel, but it did have an effect on the whole; he could not linger for fear of what was coming and he dare not risk a gunnery duel in which he might have his ability to sail impeded by the loss of a mast.

'Mr Harbin, ask Mr Pearce to join me.'

That took less than a minute, with Michael O'Hagan now fanning away at the flames and Rufus and Charlie ladling the slush, this while the rest of the crew kept rushing about.

'Sir?'

'Mr Pearce,' Digby said, then stopped to cough as a cloud of smoke enveloped him. 'Earlier this day you alluded to my willingness to sacrifice the crew for my own advancement.'

Pearce had to take his wetted handkerchief from his mouth to reply. 'A remark I withdrew, sir.'

'Indeed you did, yet the stigma mentioned prays upon me. Our masthead, as I am sure you have heard, tells me that more vessels are coming out from La Rochelle, so if I stay and fight *Pandarus*, I suspect I am taking an unwarranted risk. Do you agree?'

'*Pandarus* round and closing, sir,' called Neame, seemingly unaffected by the smoke.

'I am happy to abide with whatever decision you make, Captain.'

'That will not do, Mr Pearce,' Digby barked. 'I want your opinion.'

Pearce's blood was up; his ruse had produced the desired result and he felt in his bones they could take the slightly better-armed vessel. Yet he was aware of his excitement, aware he was thinking along the same lines which he had accused Digby of earlier, thinking of himself and not the needs of the ship and the men she carried.

'We cannot face three opponents.'

'Obviously, Mr Pearce, only I doubt they can close with us in anything less than a hour.'

'Yet can we face two if we sustain damage?' Digby shook his head, and it was with some effort that he responded. 'Then I think, sir, that discretion is the better part of valour.'

A fit of coughing meant he had to wait for Digby's conclusion. 'Thank you, Mr Pearce. Now go back to your station on the larboard battery, and stand by to give our friend yonder a surprise.'

There was a wait, to get to the point where the Frenchman was committed, the point where he could not change his mind. As soon as Digby reckoned that to be the case he yelled out for everyone to get back to their stations.

'Forward there, get those coppers emptied over the side.'

Hands wrapped in thick canvas, the Pelicans obliged, though Charlie, ever fly, was wise enough to hide the remaining slush, which would come in handy to ease down his throat the hard ship's biscuit. As the flaming sacks hit the water they fizzled and died, and they took with them most of the smoke. Digby could see his opposite number gesturing and pointing, he was so close, and the agitated way he was acting was evidence he had been severely discomfited by the sight before him; a disciplined deck with manned guns waiting to rake him. He screamed an order that, though it could not be heard, had his crew, lined up with pikes, axes and swords to board, running for their cannon.

Had he held his course, he would have endured only an exchange of broadsides; that he put up his helm and tried to turn into the wind was not only stupid, it was dangerous, because he diminished the arc of fire available to his own guns and created a corresponding increase in the target left to the cannon of HMS *Faron*. Added to that, he had brought himself into range of one of Pearce's carronades, and though the nine-pounders did damage, sending great chunks of wood and splinters flying, it was that stubby weapon that did the real injury. Pearce waited until the stern of *Pandarus* came abreast and then sent the huge ball through the deadlights. Those were smashed to pulp, as were the casements they protected, and the ball carried on along the maindeck, the screams that came across the water evidence of the death and destruction being inflicted.

'Mr Neame, take me alongside the enemy if you please. Mr Pearce, when you are reloaded I want elevation on your cannon. Let us see if we can ensure we stop any chance of a pursuit.'

Pandarus was wounded, but she was not out of commission, and Digby was being obliged to sail past her undamaged side to get clear, and that had loaded and unfired cannon. His opponent had the same notion as he; Digby wanted a mast brought down to cripple the corvette, the Frenchman wanted the same for HMS *Faron*. The only difference was in the discipline of the firing; *Faron*'s crew were steady on a ship that had suffered little damage, the French on a deck that had taken casualties. Added to that, Digby had his first broadside fired early, which further disrupted the enemy gunners as they were assailed by falling ropes and tackle, but most telling was the speed with which *Faron*'s gunner reloaded, the same advantage Britannia usually enjoyed against Gaul: the number of broadsides they could get off in a short time.

Pandarus's fire was slow and well aimed, though not well enough to wound a mast, albeit the amount of debris that came through the nets had Neame and Digby looking aloft with alarm. Yet as the French were reloading they took another broadside, and this time, without instruction, Pearce had ordered the wedges driven out to lower the aim. Half of the Frenchman's bulwark disappeared, while the clanging sounds of struck guns was clearly audible, and such was the effect on those conning the ship that the corvette fell away as the rudder was put down, either deliberately or in panic, it made no odds.

HMS *Faron* was clear and even before Henry Digby called for a report on damage and casualties, he gave loud orders to set all possible sail and set a course to clear the tip of the Ile d'Oléron.

Chapter Twenty-Four

The screaming south-westerly came upon them later than Neame had anticipated, a full eighteen hours from the point at which he had raised the matter of those lenticular clouds with his captain, and it came with a force that precluded any form of advance. Huge waves, with crests hundreds of yards apart, rolled in from the deep waters of the Atlantic, as high as the caps on the masts, forced forward by a wind that had only one virtue; it was steady, while above their heads dark grey clouds scudded along, blocking out the sun and creating a false twilight in the early morning sky. Having cleared the Ile d'Oléron before the tempest struck they had made good progress and they were now, Neame informed Digby, abreast of the Gironde Estuary, though well out to sea, with only a scrap of canvas aloft to try and maintain steerage way.

'I suggest, sir,' he yelled, 'that we up our helm

and make for shelter. This will get worse before it gets better and we are already close to being driven north and west. If it continues for any length of time all our efforts to clear the lee shore will be wasted.'

'Do we not risk the same on the northern shore at Royan?'

'The Gironde is thirteen miles wide at the estuary, and wider yet past the Pointe de la Chambrette, and this wind will carry us in at speed if we run before it. I am sure we can weather the Pointe de Grave and drop anchor in the Verdon Bay, which is sheltered from the south-west.'

In Digby's cabin it was less noisy, but the bucking motion of the ship as it rode those great rollers, and the water running off their oilskins, made examining a chart difficult. To leave the deck at such a juncture made little difference; the four men on the wheel, who included for his muscle, Michael O'Hagan, had no other task than to keep HMS *Faron*'s head into the wind, with young Harbin in command. As for the rest, double stays had been rigged on the masts before the storm developed, the hatches, bar one, were battened down, there were relays of men manning the pumps and bosun Robert Sykes had everything in hand to repair any unforeseen damage. The crew snatched what sleep they could and right now, having been on deck and working for twelve hours as they prepared the ship for the coming storm, John Pearce and Farmiloe were having four hours' well-earned rest.

The spread chart showed the north-west-facing estuary, with the great hook of the Pointe de Grave poking up like a claw that protected the river behind it from the blow they were facing, but Digby was quick to point out the one obvious flaw in Neame's suggestion, when he placed a finger on the chart that showed a French fort commanding the very bay Neame was suggesting as an anchorage.

'Quite apart from that, Mr Neame, we will be in enemy waters, and while I accept that Bordeaux is not a naval station, it is a commercial port and must of necessity have warships to guard it and some kind of military garrison.'

'I would suggest, sir, that they cannot be out to sea for the same reason as us, it being too dangerous, and if I had the choice in such weather I would retire well upriver, in fact all the way to the Bordeaux docks, rather than stay in deeper water when no enemy could possibly approach in strength.'

'The fortress?'

'We still have a tricolour, do we not, and we are in a captured French vessel.'

Digby smiled. 'I see Mr Pearce and his methods have affected you, Mr Neame.'

The older man responded with some pride. 'I take that as a compliment, sir.'

'It was meant as one, Mr Neame, rest assured, but I am not sure that even that will serve. We cannot anchor for an indeterminate time without paying compliments to the fort and whoever commands it. Failure to do that will make them curious and I cannot see how, if they come out to investigate, we can keep them convinced we are French. We can get out of range of their cannon, but we could not stop them sending word upriver.'

'You said, sir, kindly, that I was thinking like Mr Pearce.'

'I did.'

'Then I would like to rouse him out and put to both him and you this proposition. That we ask Captain Moreau and his party to cooperate. If they cannot convince a party of Frogs that they are of the same nation who can?'

'Why would they do that?'

'For the offer to put them ashore, sir, at a point of their own choosing, and one in which they will be in no danger of retribution.'

'In which case we need Mr Pearce to make the suggestion.'

It was a groggy John Pearce who entered the cabin, clutching the bulkheads to keep himself on his feet until he made a chair that had been secured to the deck. He listened as Neame outlined his proposal, nodding slowly, his eyes red-rimmed with tiredness.

'I cannot see how a decision can be made without first consulting Moreau.'

'Very true,' Digby replied.

'Then someone must go and fetch him.'

One of the things Pearce had noticed about Gerard Moreau was his swift intelligence; he could grasp a problem quickly and act upon it, which no doubt made him a good ship's officer. Another was his honesty, and while he accepted that the proposed ruse was tempting, he did point out that once committed, there would be no guarantee that one of his comrades, Jacquelin for example, might not renege.

'I think I have a solution to that, Captain Moreau. Tell him that all the time he converses with his fellow countrymen, there will be a musket a few feet from his back.'

'A dozen men?'

'We have a dozen muskets, and I will be on deck and understanding every word, as well as examining every gesture. In return we will put you ashore anywhere you like between here and the Spanish border, which will allow you to go where you please, as long as you evade people like Rafin.'

'I agree to put it to my officers,' Moreau replied. 'After all, anything must be better than a return to Toulon.'

*   *   *

Coming about on such a wind was a risky manoeuvre. It had to be timed perfectly and the sails needed to get steerage way with a gale on their quarter had to be sheeted home and drawing before a wave threatened to broach them to. It was so dangerous that having been informed of the intention, all the French officers were on deck, a willing addition to the crew, prepared to render any assistance required, which had more to do with self-preservation than the prospect of the pretence that would follow if they made the Gironde.

They had accepted the proposal to a man, and when questioned Moreau had told Pearce why. Bordeaux might be a worse place to land than La Rochelle; they had no idea who controlled the town, but as one of the country's major commercial ports the odds were on men having been sent from Paris. Having had one brush with such a creature there was no appetite to face another, and if they were landed in some spot away from any towns, they would have a chance to make their way, individually or collectively, to a place where the danger of decapitation would be nil.

Digby was on one side of the quarterdeck, Pearce on the other, both with arms hooked through the rigging to stay upright. The topmen were ranged along the upper yards, soaked to the skin, their bare feet on the slippery foot ropes, bent over the timber, ready to release the ties on the mainsail, which would need to be quickly reefed if it was not to blow out of its bolt holes. Others were forward on the falls that controlled the jib, which would have to be got up fast to force round the ship's head.

Neame was on the wheel with three others, peering forward into the gloomy, spume-filled daylight, watching the waves as they rolled towards the ship, trying to time his turn away from the biggest, that measured by the lift of the bows to a point where he could not see anything but scud soaked planking. There was no guarantee that a big wave would not be followed by another, just the odds that the next roller would be diminished in size by its predecessor.

He stepped back from the wheel, to be replaced by Michael O'Hagan, and taking hold of a man rope with one hand, he raised his speaking trumpet to his mouth. The bows reared up until he was pressed back hard into the bulkhead and he waited till the ship hit the crest before shouting. The task of getting round had to be completed in the following trough, for if a big wave hit them beam on with no sail set they would roll sideways and over, with buoyancy the only hope of survival. His orders were yelled out as the wave came amidships, so that HMS *Faron* was perched atop the crest, like a toy on a fire mantle.

The wheel swung and a rudder that was practically clear of water moved easily, then bit hard as the ship began to drop into the trough, beginning to turn the bowsprit. Neame yelled again as they drove down towards the base, and up went the jib, what wind hit that in the vale of water acting on it to turn the sloop's bows. They were three quarters round and lifting on the next wave when Neame ordered the mainsail dropped, and as they rose to the next crest it was sheeted home, the ship driven by the strength of the gale that hit them to stay on that crest for what seemed an age as HMS *Faron* took off like a greyhound. There was joy on the deck, but in the minds of those who knew, it was tempered by the thought that what happened next depended on Neame's navigational skills. If they were out of the position he supposed, and set a course based on wrong assumptions, they would be driven ashore by this very sea and probably drown.

'Thank God for the lighthouse,' said Digby, as the glim from the burning wood showed once more on the spinning bowl. 'Mind, we will have to shave the point damn close to have any chance of coming round into shelter. Time to rouse out Mr Neame.'

Pearce went to get the exhausted master, and it took a lot of shaking to wake him from a deep slumber, but he was on deck before he was truly needed, taking the con and steering the ship to shave the point, which had deep water to within a quarter mile of the shore. The tricolour was already aloft, so that those on watch in the estuary would see a French vessel making for a home port, and it was no more than two hours before Neame could put up his helm and adjust his sail plan to take them into the shelter of the landmass, the lighthouse now well astern.

The wind was still strong; apart from the point itself, the land was too low-lying to impede it much, but without that running sea they could manoeuvre easily and within another hour, as darkness fell, they had dropped anchor out in the Baie de Verdon, choosing to do so well away from the fort at the western end. Digby set an anchor watch, with Farmiloe in command, who had strict orders to keep a sharp eye out for anyone coming out from the shore, and sent everyone else to get some well-earned rest. It was Pearce who made sure his Pelicans were armed with pistols and in a position to keep an eye on the French officers.

A boat came out from the shore at dawn, to be greeted by Moreau acting as captain, Jacquelin as his mate to assuage his pride, and the rest, Garnier and Forcet included, in the guise of ordinary seamen. Everyone else, apart from those set to kill anyone who betrayed them, stayed on the opposite side of the deck, ostensibly carrying out repairs. The officer from the fort seemed ready to accept the explanation offered; that the ship was carrying

despatches for Brest, and would get back to sea as
soon as the weather moderated, adding, in a nice
touch, that there were certain deficiencies in stores
which needed to be made up, if the fort and the
traders, most especially the local wine growers,
would not mind accepting the English gold they had
captured from a merchant vessel in the
Mediterranean.

Thus, in a cabin so crowded that backs were
pressed to the bulkheads, French and British
officers, midshipmen and the master, had an
excellent dinner, with fresh fish, newly plucked
chickens, what an Englishman would have called a
baron of beef, all washed down with outstanding
Medoc clarets from further down the coast, of the
kind and quality that, in normal times, only the rich
could afford. That they got them for so little was
evidence of the lack of rich men left in France, plus
the fact that the better claret market, Britain and
Ireland, was now, without smuggling, barred to the
growers.

'It falls to me,' said Gerard Moreau, in his toast,
which Pearce translated, 'to thank you for saving
our lives. It also falls to me to tell you that we are
true Frenchman and sailors and warriors, and
though it would give us no joy, should we meet in
future, we will do our very best to take whichever
vessel you are on, and should it be unfortunately
necessary, to kill you in the process.'

Pearce tempered it slightly, because he knew that, for the likes of Moreau, pride had been wounded. Digby then toasted the sea and all who sailed on her, which was a sentiment with which they could all agree.

It took six days for the wind to abate sufficiently to make sail, and that could not be achieved until they had taken the French officers to a point between the fishing villages of Talmont and Mortagne of the northern Gironde shore, and said farewell.

'Who knows what will become of us, monsieur,' said Moreau. 'We will perhaps pretend to be ordinary sailors, we will certainly stay out of any town that seems to be in the hands of a Rafin, and we will make our way back to our homes and wait to see what transpires.'

'Just keep your head, my friend,' said Pearce.

Moreau nodded and grinned, as Pearce had the cutter pushed off the beach and out into deep water. He did not look back as they rowed back to HMS *Faron*; it was those rowing who saw that the Frenchmen lined the beach and stayed there, ever smaller figures, until the cutter was out of sight.

It took a week to beat all the way to the Straits and with the favourable in-going current there was no need to stop at the Rock. Once through, that same wind, which had made hard their passage south, sped them towards Toulon, and it was with mixed feeling that Pearce, standing in the bows, saw once more the tip of Mont Faron emerge from the clouds which covered its summit. As soon as they came into view, HMS *Victory* made their number and signalled for the captain to come aboard. Pearce had permission to also take a boat, and after dropping off Lutyens at the hospital, he went aboard HMS *Britannia,* to seek the date for the day he would see Ralph Barclay at his court martial.

No vessel could approach the anchorage of Toulon without engendering a degree of curiosity, and HMS *Faron* was no exception. At first, in the distance, with just her topgallants showing, she had raised speculations regarding reinforcements, but it was soon realised as her topsails came into view that she was too small to offer anyone ashore that comfort. Closer and hull up, she was recognised for what and who she was; no ship was quite like another, and sailors took pride in recognition. By the time she gained the Grand Rade, there was scarce an English-speaking soul ashore or afloat who did not know her identity.

Even Ralph Barclay, on duty at Fort Mulgrave, knew of her return, and while the information was not received with anything passing for delight, he knew in his heart that matters had been taken care of which left him free from any threat from John

Pearce. Toby Burns, off duty, sat in a dark and empty midshipman's berth, shuddered when he heard the news being passed by shouts through the lower deck. The thought of John Pearce back in Toulon, when he was bound to hear of the evidence given at the court martial, did nothing to ease his fear that one day the man would get him alone and exact vengeance. He wanted to go to Ralph Barclay and ask to be sent home – the captain ignored him, and his aunt now barely exchanged a civil word – but shied away from the consequences; what would the people who had so praised him at home say if their boy hero came home to skulk in the country?

The news came to Emily Barclay through Shenton, sent by Mr Glaister, who in obedience to her husband's orders kept lookouts at the masthead of HMS *Brilliant*, even though she was tied up to the quay. Shenton had taken the occasion to once more glower at her, then at Cornelius Gherson, sat yet again on the casement lockers with the ship's logs and ledgers. Emily wondered at the thickness of the man's skin, given she felt she had made it plain that his constant occupancy of her husband's cabin, when he was absent, was unwelcome.

'I daresay you will be happy to see so many of your husband's crew once more, Mrs Barclay,' said Gherson.

Was that a smirk on his face? Emily was unsure, for he seemed to have an almost permanent sneer on the rare occasions when he actually spoke, instead of sneaking surreptitious looks at her from under those long, blond eyelashes, which clearly he suspected she could not see. And was there a double meaning in those words?

'Mr Gherson—'

His interruption was swift, and delivered with what he thought was a winning smile. 'Could I not persuade you, Mrs Barclay, to call me Cornelius?'

The sharp reply wiped away the smile. 'No, Mr Gherson, you cannot! You are my husband's clerk and it would be unfitting to be so familiar given our respective positions. And might I add that I find your continual presence in this part of the ship, which is supposed to be the preserve of the ship's captain, equally inappropriate.'

'My dear Mrs Barclay—'

Emily cut across him, unfazed by his expression of hurt. 'You do not dare ask for the use of it when he is aboard, do you?'

The reply that Cornelius Gherson wanted to give was not one that would be possible. An open declaration of his attraction would be fatal, though he was forced to admit that, even after many hours spent in this very cabin, he had not advanced one iota in his aim of seduction. Emily Barclay was a hard nut to crack, but such was his assurance in his own capabilities that he took her rebuffs as proof that the notion of dalliance was both acknowledged and discomforting. Yet he could not resist an attempt to puncture her conceit, just to let her know, in no uncertain terms, that if her husband refused to accept the world as it was, he did.

'I wonder what John Pearce will make of the outcome of your husband's court martial?'

The implied meaning was made plain by the arch look Gherson used to accompany the words, for a man would have to be blind, deaf and dumb not to realise how strained the atmosphere was between Captain Barclay and his wife, the reason for that strain no secret either.

'Mr Gherson, please take your ledgers and return to that place which you have been allotted in which to work.'

'If I have offended you, Mrs Barclay—' he protested.

'I would not wish to have to ask my husband to issue the same request.'

Gherson did not move immediately, instead he was staring at her with what looked like increasing comprehension. Then the look changed to a pout of displeasure, a petulant expression which was near-feminine. Emily thought it was because he was being chucked out of the cabin, but she was wrong. Gherson was pouting because of a sudden notion: could it be that Emily Barclay had not taken John Pearce's side against her own husband through a desire to maintain the truth; could it be there was another even more telling reason? The thought made him so angry he had to turn away, and he used the excuse of gathering up his books to keep his face and expression hidden.

'I am sorry to have offended you, madam.' It was said in such a way as to make Emily feel a pang of guilt. 'I assure you I will not trouble you again.' As he left, Cornelius Gherson was thinking that was all she was ever going to get from him from now on; more trouble than she could ever hope to cope with.

'Shenton,' she called, looking at him hard and wiping a half-smirk off his face. Clearly, given his love of eavesdropping, he had heard the recent exchange. 'Request a boat from Mr Glaister. I wish to see Mr Lutyens now that he is returned.'

The boat was ready quickly, and she was handed down to sit in the thwarts. The sailor in charge did not bat an eyelid as she said, as soon as they were out of earshot of HMS *Brilliant,* 'Take me to HMS *Faron.'*

'Aye, aye, mam.'

'I demand to see the admiral,' John Pearce growled, trying to lean over the desk and by his height and weight threaten Hotham's secretary.

'You cannot.'

'I must. I demand also an explanation.'

The secretary, knowing that he had marines within earshot, was not to be cowed. 'You can demand away, sir. The day a lieutenant can demand anything of a Vice Admiral is not yet come. If you wish to see him put it in writing, and wait.'

Pearce wanted to take out his sword and cleave the man in two, but he knew it would achieve nothing. He had been lied to and humbugged, and what was worse he did not know what had happened, so he forced himself into a more calm mode of address.

'It makes no odds what the verdict of the court was. It was a travesty and based on a lie. I shall demand that Captain Barclay face trial again.'

The smirk that he got from the secretary made his blood boil even more. 'I have heard you are much taken up with spouting the law, Lieutenant Pearce, so it surprises me to find you so ignorant. Do you not know there is such a thing as double jeopardy?'

'What?'

'Precisely,' the secretary hissed. 'A man tried and acquitted cannot be tried again for the same offence. Captain Barclay was reprimanded but that is all, and there is nothing you, or anyone else, can do about it.'

'I shall go and see Lord Hood!'

'Do so,' was the reply, and it was given in the confidence that he would be wasting his time there too.

* * *

'I had his word, Heinrich. That swine Hotham told me to my face that there could be no trial without my presence and that of Michael, Charlie and Rufus. His secretary was taking notes and he was writing the words down as they were spoken.'

'And?'

'I asked to see those, and I knew when he was so willing to show me that I was about to be humbugged. There was no record of that part of the conversation, so I asked for the depositions I and the others made. The sod looked as me as though I had just come out of the gates of Bedlam.'

The words rang in his ears yet, 'What depositions?'

'Am I disturbing anything?'

Both men turned to the doorway to see Emily Barclay standing there. Pearce had a flash of anger, quite prepared to put the blame for what had happened on her shoulders; after all she was married to the brute who had escaped justice. Yet her words totally deflated that sentiment.

'Lieutenant Pearce, I was told that you might be here. It is you I have come to see.'

'Why, madam?'

'To apologise for my husband.'

'Emily,' said Lutyens quickly, with a look that was telling her to be guarded.

'I know it could be seen as a betrayal, but I attended the court martial, even though he did not want me there, and when I did I could see why. Everyone who gave witness did so with a pack of lies. My nephew, the new clerk Gherson...'

'Gherson!' Pearce snapped. 'Clerk?'

'...Coyle, the master at arms, did not so much lie as protect himself, but Kemp was vicious.'

'Why are you doing this, my dear?' Lutyens asked softly.

'From shame, Heinrich. My husband not only committed perjury, he induced others to do so on his behalf and with the assistance of authority got out of the way those who could attest he was telling untruths. And in the process he has lied to me more than once, and on other occasions withheld things he should have shared. I wish you, Lieutenant Pearce, to know that I was not party to this deception.'

'I never thought you were,' Pearce said, unsure if that was the truth. They looked at each other for several seconds, her eyes moist with sorrow at the revelations she had made, his still hard from the same, yet there was admiration for her beauty, as well as sympathy for what it must have taken to come here and confess what she knew. Then he had an idea.

'You said, madam, that Captain Barclay perjured himself.'

'He was not alone in that, sir, they all did.'

'Then the case is altered. A man cannot, under

the law of double jeopardy, be tried for the same offence twice. But perjury, I happen to know, is a separate offence, and a far more damning one. If I have my way, I will have your husband and his witnesses tried for that offence and locked up in a King's Bench prison or transported to Van Deiman's land for the rest of their lives.'

'And what of your friends?' she asked. 'The ones for whom you have gone to so much trouble?'

The excited look immediately died in John Pearce's eyes, to be replaced with one of deep wretchedness. 'I must go now, Mrs Barclay, and tell them that I have once more completely failed them.'

'They will forgive you, I am sure.'

'They may well that. The real question is: can I forgive myself?'

Standing outside the hospital later, once Emily Barclay had departed, he looked at HMS *Faron*, riding on her anchor in the Grand Rade. He knew that the telling of what had happened would be hard, but not as hard as the remedy. Talk of getting Ralph Barclay into court on a charge of perjury was easy to say, but it would damned difficult to accomplish. With a heavy heart and deep foreboding, he went to his own boat, and gave orders to head back to the ship.

Author's Note

The story in *A Flag of Truce* has some basis in fact. There was a problem in Toulon with radical sailors from the Atlantic ports who had no desire to support the administration which had taken over the town and port.

Lord Hood, for the sake of security, was obliged to ask Rear Admiral Trogoff for four seaworthy 74-gun ships, which, stripped of their guns, would be used to transport the seamen to their home ports of Brest, Lorient and Rochefort – not a policy that proved popular when it became known in London what he had been obliged to do. The act may well have led to hints that he should retire, thus proving how difficult it was, in the days of long time-lag communication, for a commanding admiral to know what course to adopt on a foreign station.

Sad to relate that many of the officers who refused to serve Trogoff fell victim to the

Revolution they had attempted to support. Some were accused of treason and executed in the port of their arrival, while others were transported to Paris to be tried by a Revolutionary Tribunal, then guillotined in one of the great public squares in front of the usual howling mob.

The Revolution, by the time they made their landfall, was already eating its own.